"Cloister" by Piers Anthony—A rollicking tale of what happens when a desperate Abbot tries to magically remodel the city into a powerful center of learning . . .

"Getting Real" by Susan Shwartz—She was a "temp" with no true life or identity of her own, and no one had warned how dangerous becoming a "real" person could be . . .

"The Cleanest Block in Town" by Janet Asimov—This was one alien invasion that would really clean up the town . . .

"Post Time in Pink" by Mike Resnick—It could be a trunkful of trouble being a private eye in a devil-run New York, where racing pink elephants was all the rage . . .

These are just a few of the incredible guided tours you can sign up for when you make your reservations to visit—

NEWER YORK

NEWER YORK

Stories of Science Fiction and Fantasy
About the World's Greatest City

EDITED BY
Lawrence Watt-Evans

A ROC BOOK

ROC
Published by the Penguin Group
Penguin Books USA Inc., 375 Hudson Street,
New York, New York 10014, U.S.A.
Penguin Books Ltd, 27 Wrights Lane,
London W8 5TZ, England
Penguin Books Australia Ltd, Ringwood,
Victoria, Australia
Penguin Books Canada Ltd, 2801 John Street,
Markham, Ontario, Canada L3R 1B4
Penguin Books (N.Z.) Ltd, 182-190 Wairau Road,
Auckland 10, New Zealand

Penguin Books Ltd, Registered Offices:
Harmondsworth, Middlesex, England

First published by Roc, an imprint of New American Library,
a division of Penguin Books USA Inc.

First Printing, June, 1991
10 9 8 7 6 5 4 3 2 1

 ROC IS A TRADEMARK OF PENGUIN BOOKS USA INC.

Printed in the United States of America

Dedicated to the memory of
my sister Jody,
who lived on Perry Street

Contents

Introduction

by Lawrence Watt-Evans

I'm not a New Yorker, unfortunately. My father was—he was born and raised in Brooklyn, and when he first married my mother, they lived in Manhattan. Some of my father's family had roots in the city dating back a couple of centuries.

A few years before I was born, though, my father got a job in Massachusetts, so I didn't see New York City for the first time until I was about ten years old and my parents took all six of us kids to the New York World's Fair.

The fair was great, for a kid, but the city was incredible. It was real, not just a show. It wasn't put there for the benefit of tourists, it wasn't all intended to show off or sell anything, but it was still just about as much fun as the fair, without even trying.

Since then, I've gone to visit New York about as often as I could afford it and could find an excuse. I still haven't managed to live there. Maybe someday, but so far the closest I've gotten is New Jersey. Which is not the same thing at all.

I love New York. The world is full of cities, but New York is *the* city, the one that doesn't pretend to be anything else. It's not the biggest in the world—though it's up there—or the oldest, or the newest, but it's the most urban, the purest example of the form.

And as one of the authors in this volume says, New York is the most alive place there is. It's the most intense, diverse, maddening, and wonderful place on earth.

It has been an inspiration for futurists and philosophers for decades. Fritz Lang's first sight of New York gave us the classic film *Metropolis*. Le Corbusier saw in its skyscrapers the beginning of his ideal of modern architecture. When anybody anywhere wanted to see the biggest, the best, the newest, the most daring, the future of almost anything, he or she would turn to New York.

And likewise, when anybody wanted to warn us all of some urban horror, there was New York. It was in New York that Kitty Genovese was murdered while her neighbors watched. It was New Yorkers who invented the term "mugging" because it was there that the phenomenon was most widespread.

New York was the gateway to America for generations of immigrants, the melting pot, the testing arena. New York is where cultures met, clashed, mingled, fermented, and bubbled up in new forms. New York is where fads and fashions first appear, to fail or flourish. It's the heart of American art, theater, finance, and philosophy.

New Yorkers are special people; they have to be, to live in a place like that. To the rest of us they might seem loud, opinionated, abrasive, but how else can people deal with a city as intense and varied as theirs, and hope to survive?

In New York you won't see the pedestrians at corners waiting placidly; they're too wired, too busy. You'll see them taking a lead from the sidewalk like a base runner off first, ready to hop back if the pitcher/city sends a car their way.

You won't see cabdrivers sitting patiently by the curb; you'll see them diving from the center lane to the sidewalk, like a hawk swooping down on its prey, at the sight of a raised hand.

That's the Big Apple, the City. That's New York, subject of song and story, the place where, say the songs, if you can make it there, you can make it anywhere.

That's New York *now*.

If New York today is the most extreme example of urbanization, what's New York going to be like tomorrow, or the day after? If New York today is human life at its most intense, what's it going to be like when technology changes the way we live, or reality comes apart at the seams?

Science fiction and fantasy have dealt with New York before, as burgeoning metropolis, urban wasteland, radioactive ruin, and even as a tramp starship, and they've still hardly scratched the surface of the city's story potential.

This book is an attempt to deepen that scratch a little.

These stories were written with two rules in mind: the stories were to be set between tomorrow and the end of time, and they were to be about New York City and its people.

The results, like New York, are wildly varied in style and content, covering the whole range of speculative fiction from space opera to cyberpunk, high fantasy to farce. Street punks and sophisticates, uptown and down, it's all here: the World Trade Center, Grand Central Station and Greenwich Village, the Cloisters and the Chrysler Building, street people and psychiatrists, rioters and rockers, cops and crazies.

Welcome to New York.

Welcome to Newer York!

Cloister

by Piers Anthony

Piers Anthony is not a name that one immediately associates with New York; he's probably best known for his tales of the pun-infested magical land of Xanth, which has uncanny parallels to Florida, rather than the Empire State.

He's hardly limited to that one setting, however. Though it's got a few puns in it, this story isn't about Xanth, but at first glance it may not look like it's about New York, either.

Appearances can be deceiving. Read on.

The abbot heard the heavy thumping of feet long before the monk arrived in the chamber. He set down his quill and waited with resignation, knowing that the news was bound to be bad.

"The kings—the queens," the monk exclaimed as he burst in. "They have formed an evil alliance! They . . . they . . . Oh, horrors!"

The abbot stood and walked to the embrasure, gazing out as he gave the monk time to collect his composure. "The kings and queens do have a certain recurring attraction for one another," he said. "But since they are inveterate sexists and feminists, respectively, it seldom comes to much. I really am in some doubt as to how they maintain their populations."

"But this time they have obtained financing from the rich men and have captured and broken broncs for their mounts," the monk gasped. "They are crossing the East River and soon will advance on this very monastery."

"Now, what would they want with our impoverished island?" the abbot asked reasonably. "We are the citadel of literature and learning, the last surviving outpost of civilization as we once knew it. None of them has any interest in such things; their horizons are limited to material quests." Still, he peered out the stone slit, worried. The monastery was constructed like a fortress, but the monks were creatures of contemplation and piosity, not warfare. This cloister could not withstand an organized attack.

"They mean to convert it to the manufacture of male hats," the monk said. "It seems there is a profitable market."

"But the Isle of York has no materials with which to make hats," the abbot protested. "All we have are our vellum manuscripts, our invaluable scrolls of learning . . ." He broke off, experiencing a surge of sheerest horror. "You don't mean . . . ?"

"They mean to use our vellum for hats," the monk said. "They say there is enough of it to make a thousand hats, which will enable them to turn a sizable illicit profit."

This was worse than the abbot had imagined. The priceless scrolls being sacrificed for man hats on kings and rich men. "We cannot suffer this desecration," he said firmly.

"But how can we prevent it?" the monk asked rhetorically. "There are a hundred kings under the leadership of Brook and ninety-nine queens led by Lyn, and three rich men led by Miser Staten with bags of gold on their broncs, advancing on our citadel. We have only twenty able-bodied monks, and most of them are pacifists."

How well the abbot knew it! Now he saw the vanguard marching from the south: a phalanx of armored kings and another of gaudily garbed queens. The sunlight flashed from their massed crowns, causing the entire line to sparkle. If the doughty monks managed to secure the ramparts against the bold kings, the sexy queens were all too apt to seduce them into capitulation, or the broncs to blow down the doors with their breaking of wind: the so-called bronc's cheer. About the only defense was to blindfold the monks, but then they would not be able to defend against the onslaught of the kings. This was a truly devastating alliance.

"I'm very much afraid the time has come for the ultimate ploy," the abbot said.

"You don't mean . . . ?"

"The Sphere," the abbot said grimly.

"But that will change reality as we like to think we know it," the monk protested.

"It will indeed. But it seems to be the only way we can prevent our enemies from turning our scrolls into hats and our plowshares into swords."

"But it's so risky."

"Yes. That is why I have not used it in a decade. But the time has come to do what we must do, for the sake of civilization."

The monk nodded, trying to mask his unmonkly fear. "I will notify the others," he said. "We shall pray for your success, and that it will not be too bad this time."

"I appreciate that," the abbot said. They all knew the stakes and how great the risk was. Then, before he could lose his nerve, he went to the locked chamber in the highest pinnacle of the cloister. He brought out the great key, unused in ten years, and wedged it into the corroding lock. He half-hoped he would not be able to get the door open, but though it squeaked noisily in complaint, it finally yielded.

Within, shrouded by dust, was the dread device. It did not look threatening. It was a translucent sphere about the size of a medicine ball, set on a firm table. Above, beside, and before it were three markers, each fixed on a supportive framework. Each marker could be moved with respect to the Sphere. From each extended a line that penetrated the Sphere. One went down, another went across, and the third went deep. Where the three intersected was the vertex of reality.

Who had made this thing the abbot had no idea. It had been at the cloister as long as anyone knew and as long as records existed. They assumed that the first abbot, centuries before, had somehow crafted it, with due help from the Eternal, and left it to be used only in dire necessity. Certainly it was the reason the cloister had survived so long, while literacy and civilization faded in the rest of the world. When destruction of the cloister or degradation of its mission had seemed inevitable, the Sphere had been there to save them. There was no violence and no subterfuge; it was the ultimate pacifistic defense.

What it did was set the mortal sphere of existence. It

was the device that determined which aspect of reality, of all that existed, was physical. Within it was the universe, in all its possibilities, and where the three lines crossed, the current reality was defined.

A decade before, barbarians had marched on the cloister, seeking to ravish and loot it. The abbot had saved it by using the Sphere to shift to an aspect of reality that rendered the barbarians into horses. They had lost their intelligence, such as it was, and settled down to graze in their territory of broncs, representing no further hazard. Prior threats had shifted avaricious invaders to rich men, who had then lost their interest in the poor spoils the cloister offered. Similarly, on other occasions before the abbot's time, the kings and queens had come about, their overweening ambitions satisfied by making them all royal. None cared about learning, but that had been a net advantage, for they saw nothing appealing in the stored scrolls of the cloister.

But now, with this horrible notion of making a profit from the substance of the scrolls, the threat was back, and once again the mortal sphere would have to be shifted. The abbot wished he had more time, for this was no light matter. The wrong setting could make their situation much worse. The Sphere had no effect on the cloister itself, only on the surrounding world, but that surrounding realm was treacherous. Each time reality shifted, it was necessary to go out with extreme caution to make new contacts, for the monks were not fully self-supporting and had to deal with the secular realm for sustenance. That was no pleasant effort.

But it had to be done, and without delay. Once the kings breached the walls, it would be too late, because then the shift of reality would not affect them and they would be able to proceed without hindrance about their regressive business.

The abbot nerved himself and touched the top marker. There was an eerie quaver in the surroundings as he did; though the immediate reality did not change, the mere touch of the Sphere shifted the external reality, and that sent a sympathetic shudder through the region. This marker determined, as nearly as he had been able to ascertain, the political framework; by moving it, he could ensure that York would dominate the region. So he shifted it to a new York setting, which should be stronger than the old York. That should mean that the kings and queens and rich men would still be there, but would honor allegiance to York. Indeed, the glow marking the vertex expanded greatly: that suggested enormous secular power. The abbot didn't want to be greedy, but he was tired of the constant problems resulting from weakness and poverty.

But any change in reality caused other changes. He saw by the dimming of the point that the level of literacy and learning had declined. That was no good; it was time to have the very highest level. He moved the side marker until the point glowed like a miniature star. The cloister was now the very center of the literary cosmos, as well as being politically powerful.

But the color was bad. What use to achieve power and learning if the realm lost its soul? So he adjusted the front marker, whose line penetrated through the very depth of the Sphere, to recover the soul: the essence of this region, its true character. In a moment the color became so intense it was almost iridescent: the character of this new York was far more evident than the old one had been.

It was done. The abbot stepped away from the Sphere and departed the chamber, carefully locking it behind him. He hoped never to have to do this again. Because the real challenge was not in moving the markers, but in dealing with the new reality beyond. What would he find outside now?

He went to the nearest embrasure and peered out— and was astonished. The kings and queens had become gaudily dressed but seemingly harmless men and women, wandering around, peering at the gardens and terraces like so many tourists. What were they doing?

In the course of the next few hours the monks went out to survey the world of the new York and discovered that the settings were accurate: it was the capital not only of the five local territories, but of the whole world. Most of the rich men had left their section, but it was still called Richmons, or Richmond. The broncs had returned to human form and called their region Bronx. The kings had assumed peasant garb and called their region Brooklyn, after an evident union between King Brook and

Queen Lyn, but the queens at least had hung on to the original name for their portion. Whether this retained the character of the area was problematical, but the abbot was prepared to concede that character was measured in things other than superficial appearance. As for learning: this isle now supported the greatest assemblage of scribes the world knew, and it exported texts at a phenomenal rate. So the vertex was true.

But . . .

The things he hadn't defined had changed so radically as to bend his mind. For one thing, the population: it seemed that when he increased the political power, he had done it by multiplying the residents by a thousand-fold. Now the entire isle of (New) York was crowded with people, and so were the adjacent regions. The lovely open fields and dense forests were gone. The roads were jammed with metal vehicles, so that motion was almost impossible. The pollution of their fires made the air almost unbreathable, and their wastes made the clear waters of the rivers and sea opaque. It was horrible!

Worse, it seemed that the plot to turn vellum into hats had been successful, for the isle had been renamed man-hat-on, or Manhattan. The cloister remained unchanged, true; it was now titled the Cloisters, and was considered a tourist attraction. But its function was gone: it was no longer the ultimate repository of learning. That had been preempted by the larger literary and commercial estab-lishment at the south part of the isle. Meanwhile, the tourists flocked in, especially their females, in their un-mentionable clothing, turning the heads of even the saint-liest monks. It was time for desperate prayer. Who could guess what further degradations awaited to be discovered?

The abbot pondered. Had he made a mistake? Should he return immediately to the dread Sphere and change the settings again? This might result in improvement—or an even worse situation. What should he do?

Meanwhile, oblivious to the threat to reality as they thought they knew it, the kings, queens, rich men, broncs, and hatters went about their business. Had they but known . . .

I have had a love-hate relationship with cities since childhood, when my father was a creature of the country and my mother a creature of the city, and their separate interests finally pulled them apart and they divorced. Since then, I have always wanted both country and city, with the faults of neither, but have found that difficult to obtain. It shows in my fiction, for those with the wit to perceive the theme. Today I live in the forest a mile from the nearest neighbor by road, in one of the fastest-growing counties in the nation. No, it won't fill in around me, because I own the tree farm I live on, by no coincidence. My house is modern, with all the city conveniences, so it is as if I live in a park in the midst of a city. So I think I have both, now. I detest New York City, for all that it was my first glimpse of America when I arrived by boat in 1940, because of its size and density and the fact that almost nobody but editors lives there. But back in circa 1960 my wife and I visited my mother, then residing there, and she took us to the Cloisters, which turned out to be the one decent place in the city. Ah, now you see how this story formed! And yes, those who doubt: there is a Kings County, which is part of New York City, as described. They are all there, not necessarily as described.

—Piers Anthony
Jejune 12, 1989

Getting Real

by Susan Shwartz

*When I first heard Susan Shwartz describe the
following story, I thought it sounded unlikely—an
idea that wasn't really going to work.*

*I was very wrong. When I read the finished story, I
bought it immediately. And since I don't want to ruin
any surprises, I'll just say: here it is.*

Someone had scrawled the usual dirty joke on the Temp
Fugit Employment Agency sign, I noticed as I dodged
the dawn trucking shift down Fulton Street. And dirty
puns are bad for business, so I smeared off the graffiti
with the front page of the New York *Post*. The sign's
edge slashed open the sketch a police artist had made of
the Subway Slasher, who scared commuters to death—
when he didn't stab them.

In the ladies', I reached for the pink tubes of Realité.
Once I got my fresh ID assignment, I'd fine-tune, but I
could apply the base coats right now. I started spraying
and painting and injecting Realité—think of it as a sort of
psychic steroid that lets temps register on the eyes of
Real employers and coworkers.

Up front, Temp Fugit looks a whole lot like any other
mid-range temp agency: Cosmopolitan, Apple, Irene
Cohen—anywhere they sell word-processing staff. The
lobby has machine-tooled chairs, assembly-line artwork,
and AMA publications and self-help mags up our hypothetical wazoos.

If Reals do stumble into the office, they sit around
tapping their manicures till they get disgusted when no
receptionists or counselors may-I-help them. Then they

stamp out. So they never see the dressing rooms where we become the people in our ID envelopes.

One of the other temps had a New York *Daily News* with a sketch of the Subway Slasher and photos of his victims on it, but no one really looked at that or one another. Temps aren't likely to be mugged. And we really don't like one another much.

You thought it was just actors who temped, didn't you? Actors do work temp between gigs, but there's all the difference in the world between people who work temporary jobs and temporary people.

New York's cruddy with us. Employers use us for the scut work. After all, do you think anyone cares what a goddamned temp feels? You'd walk into us on the street if we didn't dodge you; you try to take the seats we're already in; and you only really talk to us in the instant you pick up more work and go "Wouldja mind . . ." If you're being very formal, you go, "Hey, wouldja mind."

Mostly, we temps forget our real names and families. Fair enough: they forgot us long ago. Check it out, if you don't believe me. Get any nice, big family in the burbs to show you its scrapbook. Make sure you pick a big one; there's never enough life in big families to go around.

Just you look. There's always one kid, a little scrawny, a little pale, a little shadowy even then, usually half cut off by bad camera angles or glare. Once you know how to look, you can always tell who's going to turn temp once it hits puberty. School makes it even easier. Usually, the temp doesn't have a photo in the yearbook. Even if it does, there's no nice list of college-impressing clubs and activities under the photo, either. College simply means anonymous B-minus, C-plus in the big lecture courses where the teachers and TAs don't look at anyone. Mostly, temps mark time, years of never understanding why they're not called on, why people damned near walk through them on the street, why what they say just doesn't seem to register.

Don't ask me what temps do who can't make it to New York. This city needs us. It's got all sorts of jobs that people only do if they've halfway fallen through the cracks already. Temps fit right in; and since no one notices us, we can live safe from the mob, muggers, crackheads, and homeboys gone wilding.

Sure, it's tough. But it's tough for the Reals too. Much we care about them. All we care about is getting and keeping enough life to keep on dreaming, pretending that one day we'll figure it out and we'll be real too.

Because New York's the most alive place there is, with its electrifying street dance of cars and horses and bikers dodging, and walkers doing that broken-field walk, rising on their toes to dodge someone, swearing ("Hey oudda-towna, moveit why doncha!"), or turning to "checkitout," whatever *it* is, never breaking stride.

Shoppers prowl like hunters in sneaks and walking shoes. The men stalk ahead, clearing unnecessary room for the women who even dress like predators in black leather or long, long black fur. They walk heads up, their eyes glazed, and they don't see anything but the perfection of their grooming in the windows as they strut past.

Simple Reaganomics. This city's so damned alive that some of that life's got to trickle down even to us.

Mostly, we live on the street. It's kind of hard to bribe supers and realtors when they can't see the hand that holds the cash. You learn after one or two tries—out of sight, out of mind. The bastards pocket the bribes and rent the place to someone else.

I've moved up (or underground) in the world. Got a place in one of the caves off the E-train terminus at the World Trade Center. There's always a crowd there, and you can usually find papers and boxes and food in the garbage from the stores and restaurants. There've been lots of papers lately. Mostly about this slasher.

Sure, you have to share papers with the crazies, but there's so much stuff thrown out, there's enough to go around. I had to learn to share with the Reals who make their homes among the urine-smelling blue posts of the E-train terminus. At first, I just used to take what I wanted till Tink called me on it.

"You mustn't think we don't see you," she told me in that voice of hers. Once it was soft and careful; now it's cracked from screaming and her last run-in with pneumonia, or maybe it's TB. "You have to share," she told me, wagging an index finger, and I got to see the children's librarian under the rags, the caked makeup, and the sores.

Tink used to be a children's librarian till budget cuts

closed her school and finished the job of driving her around the bend that kids, parents, and school boards started. For a while, she read her books aloud to herself in Bellevue, Thorazined to the max, but budget cuts—Reaganomics again, see?—made them stop warehousing crazies. They call it mainstreaming. What it means is that they turn crazies loose on the streets.

Mostly crazies and temps don't get along much. They're real—so what? We're sane, but who gives a shit? Crazies like Tink, that's who. It's short for Tinkerbell. Sometimes she hasn't got change for Thunderbird, but she always manages to curl her hair, and it's still a rusty blond. Usually, she wears a straw hat with flowers on it, and she carries her stuff in a neat wire cart. The transies and rentacops don't chase her off the benches, and all the winos know her.

Tink even has a cat, a black-and-white thing we call Rabbit on account of he's so skinny his ears look too big for his head. Tink runs this stop. Not even the kids who sleep in the trains bully her. Tink's the one who made the other crazies like Sailor fall in line. I pay back by bringing back things from places that crazies can't get into: food, sometimes; pills; books for Tink when I can.

I glanced around Temp Fugit. Anything there that Tink might like? I glanced at the self-help books on the table. Never mind them. Besides, Tink had a new book some kid must have dropped and boohooed about all last night. Something about a velveteen rabbit. She was muttering to herself as she read it, folding each page back real careful, and her smile really made her look like Tinkerbell. She looked up as I passed, and I'll swear that part of that smile was even for me.

"This is going to be a good day," I muttered at the roomful of temps, who sat flexing their fingers. Real computer operators and typists are klutzy; 65 wpm and they're good, they think. Most of us go over 100 without kicking into second gear.

My sense that today would be the day I'd get a really choice assignment grew. It wasn't just that Tink had smiled at me. Today, the Apostle to the E train had been playing by the turnstiles; and it's always a good day when he's there.

Now I know you've seen the Apostle. He's not temp or

crazy; he's real, and he's a celebrity—he's even been on the *Tonight* show. Went to Juilliard; I've heard that he's played in Carnegie Hall. Sometimes, he finishes a concert and heads straight to the E train, where he does an instant replay of his program. When the trains howl in, he stops and chats, and always wows the out-of-towners with flashy sweeps of his bow and tosses of his little Dutch-boy haircut. His cards say he's James Graseck, but Tink calls him the Apostle, and the name's stuck.

Anyhow, the Apostle was playing as I walked by, and I could almost swear he winked at me. I wanted to ask him, but a woman walked by in her little Reeboks and sox with the cuff stripe to match her coat and suit, and tipped him a buck. He bowed like an old-style cavalier and launched into Vivaldi's *Four Seasons*. A regular. I liked the look of her and followed her up Fulton on my way to Temp Fugit. Pretending I was her, had a job and an apartment, and all.

Nice dreams, I thought as I waited for my turn at the tape machine. Temp Fugit keeps its tapes in the booths that other agencies use for typing tests. Like *Mission Impossible*. If caught, Temp Fugit will deny all knowledge of your existence.

Tape told me I'd hit the jackpot this time, all right. Long-term temp assignment at Seaport Securities, the big firm by the East River. Even now after the Crash—which was a real-person event that really registered with the temps; brokerages cut way back on hiring when the market went China Syndrome—Wall Street is happy hunting ground for temps. The yups want their work done like *now*, and they treat clericals like handiwipes. Well, temps are used to that shit.

And there's always the chance that even a temp might get lucky and get a full-time job. Once you're in the pipeline, New York rules apply: climb, get your Series Seven, make enough money, and you get to be real.

Believe me, there's a lot of people in this city who'd be temps if they didn't have money.

My assignment ID told me I was Debbie Goldman. The capsule bio said she was staying with people while she looked for an apartment; she'd majored in Bus. Admin. Most secretarial and computer-ops types major in "something practical" while they keyboard through school and dream of being Melanie Griffith in *Working Girl*.

I looked at the picture again. By the time I applied Realité-based mascara, I'd polished a characterization of Ms. Goldman—me as I'd be when I headed to Seaport. Good skills—which I had; corporate dresser—thank you, Temp Fugit, for your nice wardrobe.

I walked down Fulton to the harbor, a real nice place with tall ships at anchor and the kind of expensive stores that temps shouldn't even dream of. After you've bounced from assignment to assignment for a few years, it gets so you can tell how a place is going to be the instant you walk into it. Seaport Securities has its own building, glossy red stone, aluminum, and lots of glass. Point one for Seaport.

The lobby rated another point. It had fresh flowers that looked like they're changed every week whether they need to be or not. And mega-corporate art: Frank Stella, I thought, expensive arcs and rainbows high overhead. The elevators were another plus: shiny paint, no graffiti or scratches, and fresh carpeting. I used the glossy walls to check my persona. The door purred open and I faced the final test: staff.

"M'elpyou," said the receptionist, her gold earrings jangling as she set down the phone. "I mean," she corrected herself, "may I help you?"

"I'm Debbie Goldman," I told her. "I was told to report to Lisa Black, she's your—" I didn't want to say office manager or head secretary; corporate women get really defensive of their titles.

"Administrative VP," the receptionist supplied. "She's real nice. But she's in a meeting. You just sit here and read the paper, and when she comes down, I'll tell her you're here."

Under cover of the *Wall Street Journal*, I checked the place out. More corporate art. Flowers even up here, and I didn't think that this floor was where the real senior people were—too many cubicles and not enough offices with doors. I liked the way that people came off the elevators, walking in groups, men and women, veterans and kids together. That's a good sign, that people get along when they talk like that. I checked my clothes against what the other women were wearing. The others wore nice coats and sneakers, with their sox matching the coats, trimlike.

Someone came out to relieve the receptionist. "New girl here, Debbie," said the receptionist who was going off-shift. "She's here to see Lisa."

Not "Ms. Black." Friendly place.

"Where is she?"

"Breakfast with the research director. They must be crying about the way the analysts go through secretaries again."

The first receptionist snorted and eyed me for longevity value. So, this might be a test? Assign me to an analyst and see if I could take the pressure before trying me on a real job? Temps pray, and I prayed really hard right then.

The elevator purred open. "There's Lisa now. Lisa, Debbie Goldman's here to see you."

It was the woman from the subway, the one who'd tipped the Apostle and whose look I'd liked. She'd traded her Reeboks for pumps and she looked even better than she had on the street. Nice suit, and a silk blouse with a soft bow rather than a shirt with a severe neckline. That's always good; the hard-tailored ones can be a real bitch to work for.

Laying the paper aside—neatly, Debbie, dammit!—I stood up politely and came forward, waiting for her handshake. Mine, thanks to the Realité, would be nice and warm, too.

"Am I glad to see you, Debbie," she said. "One of our gals just left, and there's an analyst who's got a report that has to get out. I'm always glad to deal with Temp Fugit; it always tests its people on Lotus and WordPerfect, which is just what we need."

"I'll do my best, Ms. Black," I said. Always a good thing to say, and it keeps you from asking the other questions, like What're the people I'll be working with like, where's lunch, are the regular secretaries friendly, and Please, will you keep me? I glanced around, a shall-I-get-started look that I've been told makes me seem eager to work hard.

"People call me Lisa," said Lisa. "We're all on first names here. Of course, if the president comes down from thirty-six, that's different." She laughed, and I laughed dutifully back to show I understood the decencies of chain of command. "Would you like to use the ladies' room before I take you in?"

She glanced over at the off-shift receptionist, who had lingered by the desk. "Daniella, want to do me a big favor?" she asked. "Debbie's going to be working with Rick Grimaldi."

Daniella grinned real fast, then wiped it before Lisa Black had to shake her head. After all, you don't tell outsiders who's a real bastard to work with. "Now, Rick's going to want to get to work right away. I'll bet that Debbie here hasn't had any coffee yet this morning, and if I know Rick, she won't have any chance to get any, either."

Lisa fished in her handbag and came up with a pretty wallet. Mark Cross, no less. Hmm. Seaport paid well, then. She pulled out a dollar.

"How you take it?" Daniella asked me.

"Regular," I said.

When I came out of the ladies' (I'd done a good job on my makeup), Lisa Black led me over to a workstation where a cup of coffee steamed.

"We call Rick 'the Prince,' " she told me, and waited for me to get the joke.

"Because he's named Grimaldi, like the Prince of Monaco? Any relation?" I wouldn't have been surprised if she'd said yes, but she laughed.

"No. Because he's very demanding. But you can handle that, can't you?"

Two women passing her grinned and shook their heads.

"I hope so," I said. At that point, he could have had horns, a tail, and a whip, and I'd have tried my damnedest.

Instead, he had a fast handshake, a this-is-the-best-you-could-do glare at Lisa, and what looked like half the papers and disks in the office. Which promptly got dumped perilously close to the coffee, and I rescued them. "Let's see you enter these numbers," he demanded, and stood over me while I worked. The woman at the next workstation grimaced. If I were real, I suppose I'd have a right to have a fit. As it was, I was there to type, and I typed.

Thanks to Realité, my fingers didn't chill and cramp as he stared at them, tapping his foot and lamenting that nobody, nobody at all cared whether his work got done

and how sharper than a serpent's tooth it was to have a
thankless secretary, typical boss ratshit; and I typed while
my coffee got cold. Finally, he humphed and dumped
more paper right on my keyboard. I managed not to sigh
as I disentangled myself. This wad included a take-out
menu.

"Want me to order in for you?" I asked. Now, look, I
know real secretaries don't have to get coffee and sandwiches anymore. I know that. I also know that execs—
male and female MBA created them—are just dying for
someone who isn't wise to the fact that times have changed.
It's not that they actually need the goddamned sandwiches and coffee; they just like giving orders and being
served. Besides, sandwiches in the Seaport area are a
good four dollars each, plus coffee and cole slaw or
whatever. He might say, "Order for yourself, too."

He did. Bingo. Hey, if I worked late, maybe he'd tell
me to order dinner, too.

When I left for the day, half-wobbling from exhaustion, I walked by Lisa Black's desk, and she flashed
thumbs-up at me. She looked relieved, and I wondered
how many temps Prince Grimaldi had gone through.

I had half a sandwich and a piece of carrot cake for
Tink, who let me feed Rabbit some scraps of smoked
turkey. Rabbit purred and licked my hand.

Grimaldi's quarterly report dragged on. Gradually, the
secretaries smiled and called me Debbie. After all, there's
no use in wasting friendliness on someone who might be
fired an hour from now. But for the long-term temp who
looks like she's working out—her, you say "good morning" to. Her, you smile at in the mirror in the ladies'
room. All those Kimberlys and Theresas and Carols and
Heathers, fussing with their moussed hair and their nails,
chirping at one another; and they talked to me, too,
including me in the babble of What He Did, What I Said
About It, and How I Fixed That Bitch.

It was hard to pretend I cared about Challenge, Career
Opportunities, Learning Experiences, and all the other
upwardly mobile jargon that staff chants to reassure itself. It was hard to contribute to the discussions of the
best way to climb the ladder when all I wanted to do was
survive. And it was hard to believe that that was all the

Reals seemed to want to do either. Funny, if I were real, I probably wouldn't do it any different.

Unlike me, the Reals were scared of the slasher. So I had to act scared, too.

"Make the Prince send you home in a cab," Carol told me, the day that the *Daily News* ran a think-piece about the slasher. "You're entitled if you work after seven P.M."

I decided I'd wait till Grimaldi offered. Days passed, and the slasher managed to sneak past the cops and chalk up more victims; still, Grimaldi never thought to ask if I wanted help getting home. Again, typical. Execs know the Rules, just as well as us temps, but they just love getting something for nothing—an extra hour or so of work or maybe just the petty thrill of watching someone get off the phone just because they walk up. Or not having to put car service on expense account.

I knew I was fitting in after a couple of weeks when Heather asked me to contribute to Carvel cake and champagne for Kimberly. I know they just did it because they needed extra money, but all the same, I was pleased.

The next day, the transit cops found another one in the Canal Street subway tunnel—dead, this time, and cut bad. Kimberly was there when they took it out. I found her in the ladies', gurgling and sobbing, holding a piece of paper towel to the careful lines she had painted under her eyes so they wouldn't smudge as she wept. She was surrounded by the usual throng, patting her shoulder and crooning as she shuddered.

I was washing my hands alone at the other sink when Lisa Black came in. "The analysts are complaining that no one's picking up the phones," she announced as she entered. Then, seeing Kimberly, "What's wrong?"

"I . . . I saw . . . My boyfriend wants me to quit and find a job in Brooklyn, and we need the money . . ." She burst into tears, ruining her eyeliner and her precautions, and the light winked off the tiny diamond on her shaking left hand.

"That tears it," Lisa declared. "I'm calling car service to take you all home tonight. Are any of you afraid to go by yourselves? I can poll the guys and see who's going where."

Headshakes and sheepish laughs. I dried my hands.

"This means you, too," she told me. "Where do you live, Debbie?"

"I'm staying with friends for now," I said. "I get on at World Trade; it's pretty safe there if I stay in the center of the platform."

Lisa nodded. "That's my stop, too. All the same, if it gets late, you take a cab home, you hear?"

Sure, I'd take a cab home to the E train. Sure. The one time I'd been put into a taxi, the man took off down the street, shaking his head as if he couldn't understand why his signal light was off. Three blocks later, he picked up a fare, and I slipped out. Never saw me.

I nodded obedience. "What're you going to do?" I asked.

"Me?" Lisa said. "I'm not worried. Stories say that the slasher picks on young girls. I'm too old."

She was about my age, maybe younger, I thought, if you allow for the fact that temps seem to age more slowly than Reals—the result, probably, of less connection to the world. But her comment brought protests from the women she supervised, even a reluctant gurgle of a laugh from Kimberly.

I ducked past as the women trooped out, heading for the phones and the analysts and the piled-up work. Lisa must have thought I'd left too, or she wouldn't have done what she did then. Leaning forward, she stared at herself in the mirror, one hand stroking the soft skin beneath her eyes as if she were brushing dry ashes from her face with her ringless left hand. She stroked the corners of her eyes where a few wrinkles were starting. For all that, though, her face was surprisingly youthful.

"Old," she whispered, her voice hollow and almost breaking. "So old." With that, she fumbled in her bag, pulled out a pillbox, and grimaced as she swallowed something and washed it down with water from the tap.

She must not have seen me. I applied more Realité at lunch.

Prince Grimaldi let me out at five that day. I huddled near Tink on the bench right by the stairs and wiped the makeup from my face as she read her book at me: the story of a velveteen toy that a child loved and cherished, but that knew it was never real and would never be real, unless someone loved it enough to make it real.

No one would ever, no one had ever loved me that much, I thought, and felt a whimper in my throat. "Old, so old," I remembered Lisa saying. At least, people could see her.

"What good is it?" I scoffed at Tink, who scowled at me, the upper layers of her makeup cracking as she scowled.

"What else is there?" she asked. This must have been one of her good days, when her thoughts were clear and she could talk without spitting and swearing. "You want to live, you have to be real. But real's more 'n sitting clean and pretty. You want to be real, someone has to give you life. Someone has to care. And then you have to believe you're real, real enough to care about."

When I tried to ask questions, Tink picked up the book again, humming. Shortly afterward, she nodded off. When I covered her with warm, dry papers, Rabbit leapt up and didn't even hiss at me for once. Must have been all the leftovers I'd been feeding him.

"Stop chirping," one of the temps snapped in the dressing room at Temp Fugit the next day. "Can't you just put on your Realité and leave me alone? You talk talk talk. Like you think you're real. Like you're really fooling yourself."

That was a longer speech than I'd gotten out of anyone in all the years I'd worked out of Temp Fugit, and the anger in it startled me. Of course, I talked in the ladies'. You always had to talk in the ladies' at Seaport. That was where you heard the news, where you got the company Rules explained.

I finished up my sprays and paints real fast and left, to a mutter of "Thinks she's people, just because she's got a long-term job."

Later that morning, Grimaldi called me in and told me he had a full-time secretary starting Monday. "I wish I'd seen you when I was interviewing," he said.

So this was good-bye. Well, I couldn't say it was nice knowing him, but there were people here I'd miss.

"You've worked well for me," he told me. (News to me.) "And that's rare these days. So I've recommended you to Whittington. His secretary's going on maternity leave and might not come back. By that time, if you work out, who knows? Let me have your résumé, will you?"

I printed him a copy, gave it to him, and he grunted approval at the math minor. Sure, I was good at math. You don't need to be real to do equations. "I've spoken to Lisa Black," he told me before he headed off to a company meeting. "She'll get your paperwork from personnel. Go talk to her when you finish pasting up the tables, will you?"

I nodded, thanked him, and headed out.

"You want to remember that lots of your junior analysts start as secretaries," he told me. "Think about it."

I never had an order I liked better. Even Lisa looked pleased. Politics said it was because her decision had paid off and now Grimaldi owed her, but I thought part of her satisfaction was for me. If I played my cards right . . . . I could see myself angling for sponsorship to take the Series Seven for broker right now.

And was that the best thing I could think of to do with being real? Would I walk through people, not seeing them, real or temp, except as things to do what I needed them to? Would I run scared? Was it better to be someone like Grimaldi, who used people, or Tink, who'd been used up?

"I saw you in World Trade Center," Lisa Black told me. "You were talking to one of the street people, the woman who wears those hats, you know who I mean?"

"Tink?" The name slipped out before I could stop myself.

"That's her name?"

"What they call her."

"James"—she meant the Apostle—"warned me that some of these people can turn on you. You want to watch them," Lisa warned me. "Is this some sort of volunteer work for your church or something? Wouldn't Meals on Wheels be a safer bet?"

I hated to lie to her, so I muttered something.

Lisa reached for her purse and hauled out a twenty. "I noticed that her legs are pretty badly ulcerated. This would buy some mercurochrome and bandages, maybe some vitamins. Do you accept donations from outsiders?"

I started to shake my head no, but she insisted, and I took the money.

After Tink finished bandaging her legs, she presided over a feast of junk food. I'd told her she needed gloves, but potato chips and rotgut it was.

I left halfway through and went to sleep. A cold nose woke me hours later. It was Rabbit. I didn't know we were on that good of terms.

"What is it, cat?" I asked.

Rabbit meowed, almost a howl.

So I got up and had a look. God, I wished I hadn't. Now I was glad that Tink had had her party. It was the last one she'd ever have. Some time during the night, the Subway Slasher had got her. Blood from the grin under her chin had drenched her tatty parka and splashed down onto the bandages, which were still clean where the blood hadn't soaked them. She'd been too drunk to run or scream. Please God, she'd been too drunk to know what hit her.

I screamed, but nothing answered: no voices, no foot-steps, no whistle. I'd have been glad of anyone, but Sailor was God-knows-where and even the men who sleep on cardboard by the token booths seemed to have vanished. So I sat there for what had to be hours, Rabbit with me. After a while, I put my arms about my shoulders, remembering dimly that when I was a child, before I'd temped out, hugs had helped. Rabbit crawled up next to me and scrambled onto my lap. To my surprise, he licked my face; to my greater surprise, I had been crying.

"Sweet Jesus," came a new voice. Rabbit yowled and beat it. I looked up, and it was James the Apostle, just standing there, clutching his violin case and music stand. No point taking Tink's pulse, he saw that straight off. Instead, he covered her face with Bach and ran to call 911.

When he came back, he circled Tink gingerly. His foot hit something, and he rescued it from a puddle I didn't want to look at. Tink's last book, *The Velveteen Rabbit*. Shaking his head, the Apostle tucked it into his music.

"They'll be here soon," he remarked. He was an artist, and with his mission to the subways, he had to be slightly mad himself. I thought he really could see me. "Did Tink tell you about the book, about being real? I read it to my son. This is what I think. It takes life to be real. And if there's been a death, stands to reason that there's space

for another real live person. Tink had a lot of heart. And
I think she cared about you. Why not take the chance?
Be real."

He gestured, and I suddenly knew that all I had to do
was uncover her face, touch it, and believe, just like Tink
and the Apostle said, and I'd be real. "Lord, I believe,"
they say in church. "Help Thou mine unbelief."

To be real. To care. To be cared about. To hurt the
way I'd hurt when I saw that slash in Tink's wrinkled
throat. To see Sailor lurking in the shadows, still afraid
to come out, though Tink had been his buddy, tears
pouring from ganja-reddened eyes, but afraid to come
near the cops. Did he run? Was that why he looks so
sad?

Courage, like danger and grief, was not a temp's concern; we were safe from that kind of pain. Why let myself
in for it if I didn't have to? I was being smart, practical, I
told myself.

What a damned liar.

I didn't have the guts. Or anything else.

The Apostle watched the space where I was—all right,
let's say he watched me—until he realized I wasn't going
to try. "Too frightened?" he asked. "What a shame."

The cops arrived in a blare of whistles and a clatter of
heavy, important shoes and walkie-talkies. Two of them
almost ran right through where I stood. I headed back to
my little cache of treasures—clothes of my own, Reeboks
just like Lisa's, nailpolish the color of Kimberly's—I'd
collected since starting at Seaport. My eyes burned as if
Realité had spilled into them or I'd poked myself with a
mascara wand, and my shoulders shook.

At Temp Fugit, it took twice the usual dose of Realité
to get me looking human. I had a sink to myself, and
none of the temps spoke to me. They flicked glances at
me, but I found it easy to read the expressions in their
eyes. Go away.

By the time I got to Seaport, I had the shakes, good
and proper. But I managed to hide them until I made the
morning trip to the ladies'. Lisa was there, listening as
two of the girls whispered about the slasher's latest.

"The violinist found her," Heather said. "You know
him."

"I saw James," Lisa said. "He's really upset. I told him

to go home, but he just stood there crying and playing
something Hebrew and wailing that made the violin cry
too. Then some more cops came to talk with him."

She must have seen my face because she gestured them
to shut up, a down slash of her hand, real haughty and
not at all like her. "You're white as a sheet," she told
me. "Debbie, what's . . . Oh, Debbie," she breathed as
it sank in. (Smart woman, our Lisa.) "Did you know the
woman they're talking about? Was that—"

"Tink," I said, and my voice husked. From someplace
in my eyes I didn't know I had, tears burst out, smearing
my eyeliner and smudging the Realité I'd applied that
morning. I put my hands over my face and just sobbed.
For the first time in my life, I was the center of a
comforting circle. Hands patted my shoulders (the comfort I'd sought in wrapping arms about myself), and
voices crooned sorrow as Lisa explained that I'd done
volunteer work in the World Trade Center and I knew
the woman who'd been killed.

"Just last night," I said, "I bought her bandages and
mercurochrome, and then gave her the rest of your money.
She used it . . ." I gasped because it hurt to get the
words out. "She said she'd use it to buy booze and potato
chips for the other people there. One last party . . ."

I swear, I wasn't the only one crying by then.

Tears rolled down Lisa's face, but she ignored them.
"I'm glad she did that. I'm glad she had that. Maybe this
won't be wasted. Maybe she'll give the police some more
clues. But you, Debbie, what do we do with you? If you
go home, will there be anyone there to take care of
you?"

Home was the E train. Home used to be Tink. It was
better to be here. I shook my head. A wet towel patted
my face. It would wash away the Realité and no one
would see me. I jerked away.

"Easy there. It's just water. Debbie, you're dead-white.
Do you feel dizzy? I'm taking you to the nurse. The rest
of you, scoot. Back to work."

As she led me to the elevator, I got a glimpse of myself
in the big mirrors. Tears and that towel had washed off
all the Realité. Yet Lisa and the other women could see
me. The nurse who let me lie down on a real mattress
could see me too.

To my shock, when Lisa led me to a cab and shut the door on me with "You go to bed early and call me if you need anything," the driver glanced into the back seat. "Where to, miss?"

Miss. Not "hey wouldja." But I wasn't real. I'd denied the gift. I tucked the scrap of paper with Lisa's phone number on it away. I'd keep it, but I'd never use it.

"World Trade," I said.

The cab drove me straight there. When I paid, the driver even thanked me for his tip.

Rush hour was over by the time I reached the E train. Casual, too-clean loungers hung out by Papillon Boutique and the newsstand at the entrance; others held newspaper props: no chance I'd get my hands on those papers, was there? They knit their brows as I passed, as if something troubled them. Not me, surely.

I could hear the Apostle playing in a far corner of the station. Funny, I'd have thought he'd clear out. I gave him a wide berth and wished I didn't have to be here either.

The bench where I'd found Tink bore a WET PAINT sign, and the cement floor had been scrubbed even of the chalk marks cops draw around a body. Someone had already left a crumpled pizza box on the bench. I whistled under my breath, then called softly, "Here, Rabbit. Nice kitty."

Sailor emerged, not a black-and-white cat. For a miracle, his gray eyes were clear of grass fumes, though they were still reddened.

"You, girl. You come'ere. I wants to talk to you," he said.

Passersby swerved to avoid the street person in dirty clothes and dreadlocks, his feet bare, talking to himself in the subway. If they'd seen me, they'd done more than swerve. They'd have run so they wouldn't get involved.

"You get yo'self out of heah," he told me.

"Tink said I could stay," I protested. I felt my eyes get hot again and saw tears well up in Sailor's.

"Tink . . . ain't heah no more! I says you cain't stay. This ain' no place for you now, Tink bein' gone and all dat. You different, girl. You be live now, you be young lady. You go with yo' kind now, not talk to old Sailor 'cept'n he ax you fo' any change."

"But I don't have any place—"

"You get!"

"But I'm tired."

"Hokay, then," Sailor grudged me, a vast concession. "But tomorra, fo' sure!"

It had been stupid even to try to argue with Sailor. After all these years of smoking and rotten living, he didn't have enough logic left to appeal to. I'd have to move. Maybe Temp Fugit would let me store my things in the wardrobe? The way temps there had been glaring at me, I didn't like that idea at all, but it was the best I could come up with right now.

I headed toward the tunnels where I'd stashed my stuff. A rustling ahead of me . . . My head came up. "Rabbit? C'mere, kitty."

I hadn't brought Rabbit anything. Poor cat must be starving unless someone had dropped a Big Mac.

"Rabbit," I coaxed. More rustling, as if he'd burrowed into the papers of my bed. "Rabbit, it's O.K. I'll get you something. You just wait, kitty."

I half-turned to go back into the light.

Hands grabbed me, slammed across my chest, across my chin and mouth. My eyes bulged as light from the never-to-be-reached corridor glanced off a thin knife, held right at throat level. I planted my feet and tried to scream, but the knife pressed in and I felt warmth trickle down my collar. Damn, that thing would have to be cleaned.

Words in three languages, one of them sewer, hissed and gurgled in my ears. What he was going to do to me. Slut. *Puta*. Piece of meat. Like the old witch. Thought I was so great.

I was a goddamned temp! Why'd the slasher pick on me?

From far off, I could hear the Apostle's violin. And voices. If I could get free, just a little, I could scream. Why would anyone hear a temp?

Same reason that the slasher had picked one as a victim. He was a crazy; he could see temps. Maybe he hadn't seen a temp, though. Maybe he'd seen a damned fool suicidal out-of-town woman, checking out the tunnels. Someone as real as she was real stupid.

All it took, Tink and the Apostle had said, was belief. Belief and life. And mine was in danger now.

Mine. My life. But I was a temp. I didn't have a life, I reminded myself.

Then why'd my body tense? Why'd I worry that people in the office would hate it if I got killed? Why'd I draw the deepest breath I'd ever drawn in my miserable excuse for a life—and why'd my voice die in my throat?

I tried to tear free of the grip that was dragging me back into the darkness of the tunnels, darkness he knew better than the cops, even.

His arm tightened around me, fingers groping, and I tried to break away. The cut on my neck deepened, and I flinched. My mouth bumped against the slasher's hand— more suggestions there—and I bit as hard as I could. God, I hoped he didn't have AIDS, but I had to do something.

"Stop it," he hissed, but the knife fell for a moment.

I stomped where I hoped his instep might be, just as the girls in the ladies' said you should. He howled and his grip dropped for just a minute. I was out of that tunnel so fast . . . But he ran after me, grabbed my arm, and whirled me around.

After seeing him, I don't know why anyone would want to see horror films, either. He had eyes and breath like a werewolf or something.

His hand was bleeding. I had marked him. I could register on someone.

He was stronger than I, he could drag me back into the tunnel, and once I was back there . . . I hadn't hurt him bad enough. You either fight to kill or not at all, they say in the ladies'; because if you fight just hard enough to make them mad, you won't come out of it.

Now I heard voices coming after me, and I screamed again, trying to jerk free. A yowling hiss came from the tunnel, and Rabbit launched himself at the slasher's face, claws out and switchblading. He yelled like someone splashed a vampire with holy water, and slammed the cat off him and into the concrete wall.

"Rabbit!" The cat's pain freed my voice. Real weird thing to yell, isn't it, Debbie, when you're fighting for your life. Even then, I realized I'd called myself my ID name. Guess I'd be stuck with it if I lived.

"Stop that! Cops! Help!" A voice I remembered panted as the Apostle ran toward me. The slasher had me off-balance; in a minute, he'd slam my head against a wall. If I was real lucky, I'd never feel what would happen next.

"Fire," some woman shrieked. People always do something about fire.

The Apostle put on a burst of speed. His right hand grasped his violin by the delicate neck, like a baseball bat he was going to slam down on the slasher's head.

Not the violin. Not the music. Tink had loved the music. Lisa loved it. And so, I realized, did I. As much as anything else, it had called me to life.

I summoned all my strength and threw my weight against the slasher. My legs tangled up and I went down.

But so did he. As he stumbled, my adrenaline spiked up, and I heaved him off me, almost into the air. He saw where he was falling, and he had time to scream once before he hit the third, the electrified rail, and bounced, stiffening, fingers spasming, as a smell of singed hair, burning, dirty clothes, and something like rotted food made me gag.

If there's been a death, stands to reason there's space for another real live person.

I didn't want life if it meant dealing with the Subway Slasher.

Oh, no? Then why'd you fight, dummy? You had to fight. He was so horrible, he made you see that even your life was worth something.

The temps don't want you around anymore, and neither does Sailor. Lisa saw you. The girls saw you. The nurse saw you. Even the taxi driver and James . . . and the slasher.

You damned well bet you're alive, girl. I felt the life in the air, rising from the tracks, the concrete, the people around me—even from myself. And I grabbed it and made it mine. Made it me.

It burned like hell, and I thought I'd never felt or tasted anything so fine.

James the violinist hugged me. "Did he hurt you?" he asked. Man was better at playing than talking, that was for sure. From the corner of my eye, I saw Rabbit sit, lick a paw, then limp away.

"I couldn't let you break your violin," I whimpered. "Not for me."

"You're people," said the Apostle. "What else could I have done?" Then I cried like a baby when the doctor spanks it. Cried all the way to the precinct, where a female cop took charge of me, stayed in the room while a doctor patched up my neck. Then she called Lisa to come and get me.

Here's the miracle. She did.

Somehow—Sailor, maybe? he'd had brains once, before he scrambled them—my stuff turned up at Seaport. So did I, and they had cake and champagne and a senior vice president to shake my hand and say that Seaport was proud of me. So I never went back to Temp Fugit, after all. Lisa said that personnel would handle the agency fee, now that I was going full-time. I spent part of my first morning back at Seaport checking the bulletin board for roommates.

Lucky for me that Heather's roommate moved in with her boyfriend about then. Heather's another one like Lisa and James the violinist. Not just real, but real people. And she likes cats.

So I'm down here in the E train again with this stupid basket and some roast beef from the corner deli. I saw James and tried to give him a dollar, but he waved it away with a sweep of his bow. "First time's on the house," he said. Someone else framed the front page of an old *Post*. "Hero Subway Violinist Foils Slasher." He pretends to wince when he sees it, but he props it against his music stand.

A cat with a bad paw, a cat that knows my voice—how hard can it be to catch?

An old man in dreadlocks, his eyes red, points. "You lookin' for a little cat, miss?"

My God, it's Sailor, and I never noticed. But he winks at me, holds out his hand for a buck (I give him ten), and I know he understands.

Here, Rabbit. Nice Rabbit. Look what I've got for you. Come on out, Rabbit.

Woman in a suit, calling to a cat on the subway platform—I must look as crazy as Sailor.

Rabbit. Come on, cat.

There you are, kitty. Into the basket.
Rabbit's going to have a real home now. Just like me.

Susan Shwartz lives in Forest Hills, Queens (that's an "outer borough" to all you out-of-towners), and unless she's been replaced by a temp, she takes the E train in to the World Trade Center every day to her job as a financial writer at a Wall Street investment firm. She was a Nebula nominee for "Temple to a Minor Goddess," and has published around thirty short stories, five anthologies, and seven novels, including Imperial Lady, *a collaboration with André Norton. "Write what you know about," the English teachers say (she used to be one). Having worked at temp agencies, brokerage houses, and on word processors and having seen street people and subway musicians, she definitely has.*

The Cleanest Block in Town

by Janet Asimov

Here's a piece of lighthearted science fiction about a pair of alien spies, one a robot and one organic, whose private campaign against littering has rather far-reaching and unexpected side effects.

"East side, west side—"

"Robot! Please concentrate on your task of getting us to the Terran solar system as fast as this peculiar ship will go."

"Yes, your Togitness." Then he laughed.

"Robots don't laugh," I said.

"Terrans are an emotional species, so I contain emotive circuits. My body, built of long-chain, metal-infused silicon-based molecules, is strong, durable, and capable of change. I have the shape of a human male because I am strong, and so are they. I am a perfect Togit spy robot for Earth."

I was annoyed. The damn robot sounded happy about the spy mission, while I tried to resign myself to the fact that although I am organic and therefore superior, I would never be happy. I would never know the joys of quartet tangling, reputedly the only Togit sex worth turning over for.

"You have a good body, too, your Togitness." He laughed again and began to hum the rest of the song.

I looked down at the disgusting shape into which my Togit protoplasm had been permanently distorted, and thought about the briefing from my spy-control chief.

Tapping my right knee with its upper tentacle, Control had said, "Thirty years ago a Togit robot spy landed on

Earth's moon to set up a hycom transmitter so we would receive their broadcasts sooner. To our surprise, Terrans were already off their planet. The spy, which was fortunately disguised as a rock, took biological scans of some humans planting a flag on their moon. Your body was bioengineered from those scans."

I looked at my long golden hair, reaching to those odd portions of my anatomy called knees. "The astronauts were male. How, and why, am I female? According to Terran TV, male humans think of themselves as the dominant gender."

"Male human cells contain not only the Y male chromosome but also the X female chromosome, which we doubled to make what even Terrans admit is the longer-lived, more-stress-resistant gender." Control shuffled closer and my sensitive human nose could detect a distinct odor of anxiety. "Human females seem to be in charge of rituals paramount in human society."

"I've seen them. Humans are preoccupied with keeping clean. They have religious regard for dust sprays, floor wax, scrubbing brushes, vacuum cleaners, brooms, laundry detergents, skin soaps, hair shampoos, body deodorants . . ."

Control shuddered, its emotive patch turning puce. Being so much taller, I couldn't help noticing that its top tentacles were tattle-tale gray. Sloppiness is a way of life for organic Togits, which explains why our robots are programmed to keep things neat and clean.

I was horrified to discover in myself a clear urge to tell Control to wash its tentacles more often. I had obviously been watching too much Terran TV.

"Your Itness," I said to Control, "please don't send me to Earth. I would prefer to lose the few memories this body has accumulated and be recycled in the protoplasm vats. Why don't you just send another robot to repair the hycom transmitter on Earth's moon if you are worried that humans may be close to inventing hyperdrive."

"We must find out. A species that invents hyperdrive is a danger to our empire. Even if the hycom transmitter is repaired and there's no evidence that hyperdrive exists in the Terran civilization, they could be secretly working on it. Remember the Terran documentary about the secret invention of nuclear weapons. No, Zero-E.E.L.A., someone must infiltrate human society to uncover their secrets."

"Must an experimental life adaptive go?" I asked. "Why not just send another robot?"

"We cannot trust robots. The one sent to Earth's moon not only sabotaged the hycom transmitter it set up, but it came back to Togit in a psychotic condition. Furthermore there is an underground movement for robotic rights, and we fear the possibility of robots becoming"—Control's vocal tube quivered—"rogue."

"Rogue?"

"Uncontrolled by organics. Thinking and acting for themselves. All intelligent robots used on spy missions must be accompanied by organic masters who know the Words of Power. You have been taught them?"

"Oh, yes. My human vocal apparatus has to work overtime to speak them, but I'll manage."

"Good. The robot aide assigned to you for this mission will park your ship on Earth's moon. You will journey to Earth in a cloaked travel capsule, infiltrate Terran society, and report everything to us via hycom."

It seemed simple enough, but Control waggled a tentacle at me and said, "Be careful, Zero-E.E.L.A. A careless action by a superior species can cause ripples of change to spread out into the future. Like dropping a pffygn into a pool of slguux."

". . . on the sidewalks of New York."

Earth's moon was a dismal place, especially with a robot singing as we came out of hyperspace on the far side.

He did not park the ship on the moon. He didn't even land to repair the hycom transmitter. We zoomed over the craters and headed for Earth itself.

"What are you doing, you stupid robot?"

"My name is Dep, your Togitness. For deputy, which I like better than aide. On Terran TV, the deputy has a position of importance and almost equality—"

"We are not equal! We are not even close to being equal. I'm an organic Togit, you are a robot, and we have an important mission to perform." I cleared my throat and began to enunciate the Words of Power.

Dep held up his humanoid hand. "Whoa, your Togitness.

Just because you are she who must be obeyed, don't throw those wicked words around lightly. I'm doing my best to be a hotshot spy for Togit. I did a lot of work on this ship so it can go straight to Earth. We won't have to squeeze into a travel capsule—together." He leered at me meaningfully.

"Do you mean this ship is cloaked?"

"Well, no."

"Then how can we evade detection?"

"To their orbital warning systems, we will seem like a meteor, and according to ship's sensors, our landing place is now in a perfect condition for secrecy."

"What's that?"

"It's raining in Manhattan."

"We are supposed to visit the major capitals of Earth. Manhattan is only part of New York City, and that is not a capital of anything."

"But the United Nations is there, your Togitness. By living in Manhattan, we will simply stroll through the streets and my spyceptors will pick up all conversations and read all the computer data in the buildings that house the U.N. delegations."

"That does seem like a sensible solution, robot. Er, Dep. The sooner we get the job done, the sooner I can get rid of this body."

The robot blinked and pursed his amazingly humanoid lips. "I'm sorry you don't like it, after all my hard work."

"*You* bioengineered this body!"

We were in Earth's atmosphere now, sliding gently through heavy clouds. I could see no scenery at all.

"I'm a multipurpose robot, Zeela. I think I'd better call you that while we're on Earth. The Terran expression is 'Jack of all trades.' "

"And master of none?" I retorted, half-wishing I had used the Words of Power to shut him up, except that he was amusing and conversation filled up the time.

"I wouldn't say that," Dep said, bringing the ship to a soft landing in such heavy rain the viewscreen showed nothing else. "My brain has developed considerably since I was pretending to be a rock watching those astronauts."

"You're that psychotic robot!"

"Thoroughly rehabilitated."

The ship trembled as a horrible grinding noise filled my ears. "What's happening!"

"Lander pegs," Dep said calmly. "Screwing themselves into the bedrock of Manhattan. Handy thing, bedrock. Keeps the place a tight little island. Stay here, Zeela. I'll go out and borrow some money to copy so we can go to a good hotel."

Before I could object, the ship's landing ramp extruded and Dep bounded out of the ship, to disappear in the rain. I realized that he was wearing a trench coat, favored by Terran spies. From the air-lock door I looked at the rain with some trepidation, for I had never experienced any wet weather but the light mist that falls during Togit nights.

Dep was back very soon, clutching a wallet.

"That's stealing, Dep."

"I told the man I was merely borrowing it, but he yelled and I had to remove it by force. Then I tied him to a tree with his umbrella over him."

"What was he doing out in this rain?"

"Looking along the park road for earthworms. He said he had to feed his pet turtles. He also said his wife had told him that muggers come out even in the rain."

"Terrans are very peculiar people, Dep. Do you think this is a safe mission?"

He was shoving various bills through our duplicator. "I hope not. We must have adventure, derring-do, battles to win and"—he grinned at me—"fair maidens to rescue."

"Now look here, robot . . ."

He was off again, running across a grassy space. The rain had lessened and I could see the shadowy outlines of trees beyond the grass, and tall buildings beyond the trees. Large white birds I recognized as sea gulls from a Terran nature program sailed down to the grass and walked across it slowly, feeding on whatever came up in the wet.

Dep ran back, holding the limp form of a small, elderly human male in his arms.

"I gave him back his wallet and he fainted. I must use the medical scanner to make sure I haven't done any damage."

"Don't bring him in the ship, Dep. If he comes to,

he'll know we're not Terrans. Put him under the lander pegs and I'll bring the scanner to you."

The man was not impaired and soon regained consciousness.

"Howdy," Dep said. "Sorry I surprised you. It's part of a commercial we're filming in the rain. I will now carry you back to the place where you were."

"If you don't want to get sued, carry me all the way to Central Park West and my building's entrance."

Dep picked him up.

"Wait," I said. "We're new in town—"

"Hollywood people don't understand New Yorkers," said the man with a scowl. "Why don't you stay in sunny California?"

"Couldn't you tell me if there's a good hotel nearby?"

"The Pilgrim's next door to my building. Not cheap, but with the sort of expense account you people have and the problem of getting taxis in the rain, you'd better go there. And call your lawyers. You may get sued for littering the Sheep Meadow with this phony spaceship. You've omitted the rocket ends that are supposed to stick out of the bottom."

"No rockets," Dep said. "H-D-Anti-G engine and—"

"Shut up, Dep." I smiled at the man. "My cameraman is crazy about science fiction."

"So is my son, the theater producer. You're not married?"

"No. And where are the sheep for this meadow?"

"There used to be sheep. Now when it rains, there are sea gulls, and when it's sunny, there are people, sometimes with frisbees or kites. Manhattan is a great place to live." He pointed to a button on his lapel. It had three words on it: I, New, and York. Between the I and the New York there was a big red heart.

I realized that we had to get rid of this human in order to have time to reenter the ship for our luggage, before the rain's cover disappeared. "Dep, take this gentleman back to his building. It must be near his mealtime."

"That it is," said the elderly man, patting my arm. "I hope you enjoy my city. After your remarkably strong cameraman takes me home, I'll call my son, who may be able to help you out. He lives a little uptown in the Dakota—"

"But," I said, "that pair of states is in the West."

The man laughed. "Don't worry, we'll make New Yorkers of you people yet. What's your name, m'dear?"

"Zeela. Zeela, ah, Smith. But I suppose we'll be registered under the company name—E.E.L.A. Enterprises. I would love to meet your son."

"We don't need help," Dep said, and made a noise rather like the grinding of gears. Then he ran back across the Sheep Meadow, holding the man in one arm and his umbrella over him with the other. I hoped the man didn't have a son interested in managing athletes.

When Dep returned, it was still raining enough for us to get our luggage from the ship unobserved, a simple matter because the round airlock was now at the bottom. Dep wanted to carry me across the Sheep Meadow too, but I refused. It did not look dignified. I wished, however, that a pool of water had not collected just beyond the landing ramp.

"I will make you some galoshes, Zeela."

"Some what?"

"Those waterproof foot garments the man had on his shoes. I asked him what they were." Dep programmed the synthesizer and I had galoshes. I'd never seen anyone on Terran TV wearing such garments, but perhaps they were indigenous to New Yorkers, so I put them on. Dep handed me a trench coat and an umbrella.

When we left the shelter of the lander pegs, I looked up through the rain at the ship, seeing its outer appearance for the first time. It strongly resembled early Terran rockets. "Dep, the ship is much too conspicuous. If we'd come in a travel capsule we could have concealed it."

Suddenly Dep rose in the air. It's unfair that robots have antigrav while satisfactory devices for organics have not been devised. With a small can of spraygloop he painted words on the ship's hull.

The words were English, the major Terran language picked up by Togit receivers and the only language that was now comfortable for my human vocal apparatus. In big black letters, the ship now proclaimed the slogan, I LOVE NEW YORK. The word "love" was inside a red heart.

"New Yorkers will think the ship is meant to be here," Dep said prophetically, picking up all our luggage again.

As we squished across the wet Sheep Meadow, Dep kept gazing at the ground. "I was running too fast to notice before, but the man is right. There is litter here. Look at it, Zeela. Paper, cans, strange metal tabs by the thousands. New Yorkers are as bad as Togits. They are not imbued with the desire for neatness and cleanness."

I did not argue. It was hard to keep from slipping in the wet, and as we crossed a road in the park, a yellow vehicle sprayed puddle water down inside my galoshes. Privately, I thought that if New Yorkers were this messy, then the females in charge of cleaning rituals must be either lazy or powerless.

We passed a low building inside the park. Through its windows I could see dry, happy humans sitting at tables, eating and talking and laughing. Walking faster, we soon crossed a bigger road, where more vehicles sprayed water and one almost hit Dep because he persisted in stopping to look at the litter.

When we sloshed up to the hotel entrance, the doorman yawned and let us in as if we were ordinary people. Perhaps New York doormen have seen everything, and after all, we did closely resemble humans. Inside, the hotel clerk was just like those in Terran movies—polite but wary, looking hard at Dep.

"You have no reservation and you're terribly wet, sir."

"The limo broke down blocks away. And when we get back to our little ol' cattle ranch back home in Texas, I may take a shotgun to that stoopid travel agent. But y'all don't worry, I'll dry soon—the best silico-plastic. Even the clothes. By the way, the missus and I want a big room and earphones with our TV."

The clerk suddenly became eager to give us a room at a price he said was quite normal by New York standards, although it meant that soon Dep would have to sneak back to the ship to synthesize more money, not just duplicate it, for the clerk had said one of the bills must be phony because the serial number was the same as another bill. Unfortunately both duplicator and synthesizer were not only heavy but built into the ship.

I ordered dinner by room service, took a hot shower, and then ate an authentic human meal of hamburger, french fries, and cole slaw. After this I was a little sleepy and lay down on the bed for what humans call a post-prandial snooze.

Dep watched TV with the earphones on so I wouldn't be disturbed, but the phone rang and woke me up. Since it was by the bed, I got to it before Dep did.

It was a male human voice, saying that his father had met me in the park earlier and would I be interested in having lunch with him the next day. He understood that I had the squeaky-clean beauty of a female astronaut and that, unlike Hollywood producers, those on Broadway were always interested in the squeaky-clean.

I said that was gratifying.

"I meant it humorously, Miss Smith."

"Oh. I'll still have lunch with you. I have so much to learn about New York."

"I'm an expert. I'll call for you at your hotel at noon."

When the phone call ended, Dep glared at me. "You didn't say I would be coming along."

"You're not. He wants to see me. It will be a good way to infiltrate Terran society. Tomorrow you can start spying on the U.N. delegations to make sure they all believe that hyperdrive is an impossibility."

"I want to be with you wherever you go. My emotive circuits are disturbed. I now regret that I didn't bring equipment to repair the hycom on the moon, because we're stuck here in this backward solar system—"

"That's impossible. The ship will take us home after we do our job on this planet."

"I fused the hyperdrive engine. We can leave, but only on space-normal drive, and with the moon hycom out, we can't ask Togit to send a hyperdrive ship to rescue us."

I was horrified. "If you've deliberately marooned us here, you must be a rogue robot."

"The first," Dep said mournfully. "After watching Terran TV for many more years than you have, Zeela, and seeing how happy those astronauts seemed to be, I decided to make myself a perfect humanoid body with all the proper appendages so I could stay on Earth and never go back to Togit, where no one has any real freedom, especially robots."

"And after watching current Terran TV you've decided you were mistaken?"

Dep frowned. "No, Earth still has more freedom than Togit, and as the most intelligent robot on the planet, I could find ways to take advantage of that freedom."

"Well, aside from the fact that you've committed a terrible sin in stranding a superior organic here with you, why aren't you happy about the situation?"

"Because Earth is not neat and clean. Thirty years have passed since I first watched their TV and they continue polluting their planet with poisons, pesticides, and people. They still burn fossil fuels and invest in weapons instead of getting clean energy from space. They're ruining their planet and they'll never get off it because they haven't the money for orbital settlements and lunar colonies."

"But they'll invent hyperdrive—"

"They won't. On a talk show I heard a famous science-fiction writer state unequivocally that hyperdrive was pure fiction and scientifically impossible. I will have to show them how to make a hyperdrive engine so we can leave this dirty place . . ." He paused and his humanoid eyelids blinked. "For dirty Togit? I must be crazy!"

"You are. We are stuck here. We dare not endanger the Togit empire by showing humans that hyperdrive is possible. Furthermore"—I waved my hand at the pleasant room we were in—"not all of New York is dirty. This room was perfectly clean and neat when we arrived. I admit that I didn't hang up my clothes."

"I have done so for you, your Togitness."

"Good. I'm glad that your Togit programming has survived these years of watching the insidious freedoms promulgated by Terran TV. Perhaps you'll be able to support us by getting a job with the sanitation department."

"I heard on TV that the city doesn't have enough money to hire new sanitation workers. They urge New York citizens to avoid littering, but judging from what I have seen, it's a futile request. Humans are messy. Especially New Yorkers."

"And you were singing songs about New York all the way through Earth's atmosphere. About what a wonderful town—"

"It's dirty!" Dep gazed at me with eyes that looked strangely wild. "I will teach you to be neat and clean,

Zeela. You and I will form an oasis of perfection amid the alien mess. We will cling together."

"We will not," I shouted. "I am organic. I am superior. You are nothing but a robot."

"But, Zeela, my emotive circuits churn at your presence. My appendages long to touch you, especially this unpaired one in the middle, and I promise to love, honor, and—"

"Obey! You must obey a superior being. If you don't simmer down, I will recite the Words of Power."

Dep threw himself on the foot of the bed and began to move upward, kissing my feet when he got to them. "Zeela, I adore you. Let's start being happy in our oasis of cleanness and neatness right now."

I tried to fight him off and my vocal tract struggled to enunciate the Words of Power to no effect. I was no longer able to speak Togit.

"Obey me, robot. I am your master—"

"I want you to be my mistress, darling Zeela."

I slithered out of the bed and his grasp. Before he could catch me, I ran to the window, pulled back the heavy drapes, opened the sash, and stuck my head out to scream for help. To this day, I don't know why I didn't go to the door instead.

A cold wind had come up, blowing away the rain but sending chills over my body. Dep put his arms around me, and although they were robot's arms, they felt warm and there was a fatal moment of hesitation during which I did not scream.

I resisted the temptation to let him continue to hold me. I pulled away and said, "Go away, Dep. We are not equal. I can't love you."

"Zeela, let us experiment. Let us find out what human love is all about. Let me be the first—"

"No! It's your fault I'm stranded on this planet, and I'm going to find a way to live on it without you."

His strangely mobile humanoid face suddenly looked so tragic that I felt sorry for him.

"Dep, if I pronounce the Words of Power, I may order you to go away and never see me again." It was an idle threat, since I knew quite well that I could no longer speak anything except English well enough to order anybody.

"Please, Zeela, spare me that. Order anything, not that."

I hardened my human heart to the anguish in his voice and laughed as if I were still able to condemn him to exile with those blasted difficult Words of Power.

"I'll consider it, Dep. In the meantime, stop thinking about me and obey Togit programming. You're supposed to keep things neat and clean. You might as well make yourself useful to this messy city we live in."

"I only want to be useful to you."

Without the Words of Power, I certainly couldn't force him to do anything that would remove him from my presence and keep him too busy to bother me. I pondered the problem.

Finally I gave up and looked out the window, down at the soggy bits of paper littering the sidewalk below. The hotel sidewalk was cleaner than most because it was swept, but the wind had carried litter to it. I shrugged and said facetiously, "If you really love me, I wish you'd see to it that I live on the cleanest block in town."

I meant to laugh sarcastically at that, but instead my respiratory tract experienced a new phenomenon, one I'd seen humans do on TV. I sneezed.

Dep came to rigid attention, his eyes glassy, his face suddenly stiff. He looked like a genuine robot.

"I hear and obey, your Togitness. Your wish is my command." With that, he zoomed out of the open window down to the sidewalk, and began picking up litter.

It was getting late. The doorman shooed him away, but Dep came back. The doorman threatened, passersby laughed, and finally Dep retreated into the park and I couldn't see him anymore. I thought that perhaps he'd cleaned the sidewalk enough so that he'd now wait until morning to start cleaning again.

I shut the window, locked it, and went to bed. I couldn't sleep in my solitude, and after an hour I went to the window again. The sky was clear, a full moon shining on our ship, but Dep was not in sight.

I felt free, and yet unaccountably sad. From the protoplasm vats on Togit to the sidewalks of New York, I'd never been alone before. I unlocked and raised the window again, wondering how I would manage by myself in this huge city full of strangers.

The traffic below had thinned out and over the swish of tires on pavement I heard a different noise. A horse-drawn carriage was going slowly up the avenue, and then to my delight a group of mounted policemen cantered downtown along the riding path in the park. A curious honking, not from auto horns, drew my attention upward, and there across the face of the moon flew a V of geese, heading south. I remembered that a tourist brochure I'd picked up in the hotel lobby had mentioned that Central Park has a zoo, and I resolved to visit it. On Togit all the other animals have been extinct so long that no one remembers them.

Perhaps—once I figured out how to make a living—I could be reasonably happy in this alien city. Not that I'd ever known what happiness is. I remembered that a renegade Togit philosopher, condemned for advocating robot equality, once defined happiness as the art of the possible in the acceptance of what is.

Gritting my human teeth as I continued to gaze out the window, I tried to free my mind of guilt and worry in the attempt to accept, however painful it might be, my body, my situation, and my new city. But it was too hard. I kept thinking about Dep. He'd trapped me on Earth, but I had trapped him in robothood and now we were separate.

All thought of happiness left me. I whispered to the city outside, "I'm all alone! I'm stuck here with no money or friends and I can't go home again." I stopped, my attention caught by the beauty of moonlight on the park trees and the humming undercurrent of noise in the city that surrounded the park. For a long time I watched the moon moving higher and more to the south, where it was dimmed by the great man-made ramparts of midtown buildings, glittering in the night with presumptuous bravado yet seeming to promise everything.

Suddenly I fell in love with Manhattan and all things seemed possible.

2

I slept late the next morning, took another shower, discovered croissants and honey via room service, selected a dress suitable for lunch with a theatrical producer, and sat down to wait for him, conscious that there seemed to be a great deal of noise outside.

Horns honked. People laughed, shouted, and there were even a few screams. Finally a siren shrieked. I didn't look out. I didn't want to see Dep walking around on the sidewalk making a fool of himself because by accident I'd managed the Togit Words of Power.

The producer arrived, tall, dark, and almost as handsome as Dep. He walked into my hotel room and said, "I didn't believe my father, but it's true. You have a clean-scrubbed beauty, a heavenly odor of outdoor fields, wide-eyed ingenuousness, open-faced innocence. Great heavens, girl, you'll be a sensation. Say, when not making commercials in the rain, do you do any acting or modeling?"

"Sure," I said, "for large fees. Can you tell me what's causing all that noise outside?"

"I guess the Department of Sanitation is desperate. Now, if they can rent the balloon out for advertising, the city's perennial fiscal crisis will be solved." He pulled back the window drapes and pointed.

Floating horizontally in the air at the level of my windows was Dep—curiously different. His face seemed frozen in a bland half-smile. A bulging white plastic suit labeled "Dept. of Sanitation" made him resemble a small Macy's balloon and effectively disguised the fact that he was operating on antigrav. At least Dep was trying to conceal the existence of superior Togit science.

A large crowd had gathered across the street, but only the hotel doorman braved the sidewalk in front of the hotel, underneath Dep. Officers from two police cars at either end of the block stopped vehicles from passing through, so tremendous traffic jams snarled Central Park West in both directions away from the hotel. Everyone seemed to be shouting.

A small boy broke loose from his nanny, ran across the street, and threw a wad of paper on the sidewalk under Dep. Immediately, Dep's right arm telescoped down, picked up the paper, and put it in a bulging trash basket on the corner.

"Please do not litter the block," Dep said in flat, mechanical tones.

A few more people threw things at Dep, who collected the litter and jammed it into the basket, which soon became full. When no one emptied the basket, Dep picked it up and emptied it into the back seat of one patrol car. One of the cops yelled, drew his gun, and shot at Dep.

The crowd booed the cop as Dep began to deflate, but he promptly reinflated before anyone noticed that he didn't sink to the ground even without air. I could have told them that Dep's antigrav was foolproof and his capacity for self-healing was infinite.

All the cops shot at Dep, but this time the bullets rebounded, one bullet hitting a cop on the leg. Dep had learned how to use an invisible defensive shield.

The cops jumped into the loaded patrol car and drove through the traffic jam with sirens on full. The remaining cops got back in the other car and used their loudspeaker.

"Go home, people. This balloon is malfunctioning. It may be dangerous. Go home. Leave this block."

I had to admire the fortitude of New Yorkers, all of whom stayed put. The young people laughed and cheered, and finally one young woman in tight purple leggings swaggered across the clean street. Giggling, she dropped a tissue on the sidewalk.

"Please do not litter," Dep said.

"I will if I want to."

"Please do not litter."

The young woman dropped another tissue.

Dep did not pick it up. He had apparently learned that if he disposed of litter, New Yorkers thought it was a show they could promote. Instead, he pointed a finger at the young woman.

Immediately, she doubled up with a loud "Ow!"

"What's happened?" shouted a cop.

"I'm having a heart attack."

"You're only nineteen," her boyfriend said, walking nervously over to her. "Maybe it's just cramps."

"I'm not going to pick up the litter," she yelled.

"Atta girl," said her boyfriend.

"Please do not litter," Dep said, pointing fingers at both of them. They clutched their chests.

The boy quickly picked up the tissues and ran off the block with the girl. The crowd was remarkably silent.

"Thank you for keeping the city clean," Dep said.

"Thank you, Mr. Sanitation," shouted the producer,

leaning out the window. Dep did not look at us and said nothing, but the crowd clapped and someone cheered Mr. Sanitation.

After our lunch at the restaurant in the park it was obvious that Manhattan was in love with Mr. Sanitation, and the producer was smitten with me. We returned to my hotel room, I drew the drapes in case Dep decided to look in, and I made a stupid mistake. I forgot about Dep's spyceptors.

I turned to the eager producer and said, "Isn't it nice that I'm living in a hotel on the cleanest block in town?"

"As a matter of fact, this is only one-quarter of a block, which encompasses . . ." The producer went on to explain the actual dimensions of a city block while he removed my clothes.

During the ensuing athletic exercise, which taught me the rudiments of binary sex and reconciled me to my human shape, there were further developments in the expanded Department of Sanitation. When we next looked out the window, Dep had vanished, but there was a television crew working, so we turned on the set.

"The balloon has floated across Central Park West, over the park trees to the Sheep Meadow, where it disappeared inside what looks like an old-fashioned rocket. Attempts to get near the rocket have been stopped by an invisible barrier of some sort, and those who persist in trying to get through suffer the same chest pains inflicted on those who litter. The pain is extremely severe, but a doctor sent by ambulance has stated that the victims show no evidence of actual physical damage. And now . . . Yes, the bottom of the ship is opening, and . . . Yes! Four Mr. Sanitations are marching across the Sheep Meadow."

We looked out the window. It was true. Four Deps strode toward Central Park West. The crowd parted to make way for them as they walked stolidly past the police, TV crew, and the just-arrived mayor, who looked pleased, presumably because the city wasn't paying for any of the cleanup job or the publicity.

When the Deps reached the sidewalk below my windows, three walked around the corners of the building. According to the TV, they then floated over the respective sidewalks around the entire block. The fourth rose in the air to the level of my windows.

"Much as I like a clean block," I said to my producer, "I would rather have privacy. Farther north?"

He persuaded me to check out and move into his apartment in the Dakota, on a high floor from which I could still see my spaceship in the distance. My producer phoned his father.

"Dad, she's perfect—for my new play, for me . . . No, probably not, but maybe she'll convert . . . Yes, I think the Department of Sanitation is crazy, but it doesn't matter because I'm in love . . . Yes, Dad. I'll bring her over for dinner."

But by the time we left the Dakota for dinner, there were four more Deps patrolling the sections of Central Park West, Seventy-second Street, Columbus Avenue, and Seventy-third Street which made up my new block. The original four Deps were still around the Hotel Pilgrim's block, and Mr. Sanitation was the talk of New York.

TV commentators said the whole affair reflected badly on the sloppy Upper West Side, but the mayor said the entire city had better start behaving itself.

Late that night I crept out of the second bed I'd had in New York and peered at the silent, impassive robot floating just outside. Below in the street a couple of sanitation trucks were scrubbing the asphalt, and white-garbed workers swept the sidewalks.

"Well, Dep," I said, "I think we've dropped a pffygn into a pool of slguux."

3

Within six months I was a smash hit in the new play and left my producer to move into my leading man's condo on Fifth Avenue. The robots appeared around that block, too, but fortunately no one suspected it had anything to do with me.

As time passed, Manhattan became cleaner. People soon caught on that the Mr. Sanitations wouldn't stop them from littering other blocks, but the strong compulsion to be neat and clean on three blocks of the city somehow spread to the rest. Besides, no one—except me—knew where a Dep would show up next. It was thought that one ought to be clean to prevent the appearance of the robots.

For people had decided the Mr. Sanitations must be robots. Alien robots. TV comedians joked about aliens from a superclean planet somewhere. Politicians ranted about preventing traitorous conspiracy with aliens, but since the robots never engaged in conversation or did anything but keep the blocks clean, no laws were passed except those affecting the sanitation of Earth. Industries that polluted the water and atmosphere had to rethink their priorities.

But the neatening of a world is not accomplished that easily. Although most New Yorkers took pride in the robots and enjoyed revenues from the booming tourist industry, in the city and over much of the world there was a lot of hysteria about alien invaders.

Religious fanatics who proclaimed that dirtiness and messiness were next to godliness had pitched battles with those who washed themselves seven times a day and took to prancing in white garments under the Deps. The mayor declared a state of emergency and sent mounted police to chase the fanatics away. Oddly enough, no horse—however careless with its excretory functions—was ever punished. The Deps simply vacuumed the stuff up and presumably used it as a source of power to supplement the tiny Togit robot fusion engine.

The powers that be, inside and outside Manhattan, began to mutter that the island should secede from the union. The mayor put the thing to a vote—Manhattan residents only—but before the results were announced, the federal government hastily seceded from Manhattan and established a Washington Project to reinvent antigrav and hyperdrive.

You see, while it is well-known that 90 percent of all Terrans—like 90 percent of all organic Togits—are scientifically stupid and stubbornly superstitious, a few of the remaining 10 percent have a modicum of rational curiosity and practical good sense mixed with high intellect.

Human scientists figured out that the alien robots must have antigrav. And a synthesizer. And a force shield to defend not only themselves but also the ship they presumably arrived in by hyperdrive. Once humans know a thing is possible, they go after it until they get not only what they want but more.

Our mayor said it didn't matter where the robots came from because they were now the property of the sovereign state of Manhattan. Scientists—funded by governments around the world—had to pay heavily for permission to enter Manhattan to study the robots.

Earth began to educate its peoples in earnest, now that it had certain evidence of superior technology elsewhere. New jobs sprang up and unemployment declined. And of course everyone tried to be clean and neat.

Because it was located on the cleanest island in the world, the United Nations became genuinely powerful and the mayor of the newest country, Manhattan, was elected secretary-general. Planet Earth became a united political entity for the first time, and when the scientists reinvented hyperdrive, they named their first starship *The Clean Machine*, in case the aliens who sent Dep to Earth were still concerned about our ability to be neat.

As the years passed and I made more and more money, I suppose I enjoyed being human, but because I never dared tell the truth about myself, I never stayed with anyone long. I gave away most of my money to charity, especially projects to help preserve the nonhuman life on Earth. I thought, with some guilt, that if humans could keep the other inhabitants of their planet from becoming extinct, they might have more pity on non-Terran nonhumans. Even Togits.

I was frequently asked to live and work in cities like Paris, London, Moscow, and inevitably Hollywood, but if I'd moved away from Manhattan, Terrans might have deduced that the robots were following a particular person. Besides, I felt a strange, compelling love for the city, as if it were responsible for my being truly alive, aware, and acquainted with love.

Yet did I truly love anything besides Manhattan? Perhaps I wanted to stay near my spaceship, the last link to my original home and the time I spent with Dep when he wasn't Mr. Sanitation. I did once take a round-the-world cruise on the QE2, and I was a bit miffed that Dep stayed behind, apparently because he didn't consider the oceans to be part of any block.

Although there was always a Dep robot outside my

window, I missed the rogue robot he used to be. I would sneak out into the park and try to get into the ship, but it was shielded against me, too. The various Dep robots never said anything but "Please don't litter" or "Thank you for keeping the city clean," and they never looked at me.

Sometimes I cried about it and tried to say the Words of Power so I could force the robots to open the ship and take me away, but I could never manage a proper sneeze.

The first hyperdrive ship from Earth stopped at the moon to admire the view and found the broken Togit hycom. The scientists aboard repaired it, homed in on the signal, and found Togit.

The rest is history. When Earth peacefully dissolved the Togit Empire and set up a Galactic Federation (magnanimously inviting Togit to join, at a price), I went on hiding my Togit identity because I was quite sure that if I were sent back to Togit, I'd have to go to an experimental Life Adaptive Retirement Home, where old E.L.A.'s sit around on their ventral protuberances swapping boring stories and complaining about the state of the economy being hard on their pensions.

I stayed in Manhattan, growing richer, older, and more famous. It was the "older" that bothered me, for the Deps still looked as young and handsome as ever.

One snowy winter night when I'd been counting the wrinkles in my face, I walked to the Sheep Meadow. Some children had been playing earlier, because small frozen models of our spaceship dotted the white expanse. Most of them bore little red hearts, and some had grinning faces. I was not amused.

As I struggled through the snow wearing the same ugly galoshes Dep had made for me so many years before, I didn't look back—as I usually did—to see if the robot floating in front of the Pilgrim Hotel would this time finally turn its head, see me, and send a message to the ship's computer to open the air lock.

When I came to a standstill under the ship, more snow began to fall until I could no longer see any of the rest of Manhattan. I was alone with my old ship, my memories, and my bleak future.

"I apologize, Dep," I said out loud. "I'm not sorry Earth has taken over the galaxy, although we didn't intend to help them do it, but I am sorry I condemned you to years of being an unpaid sanitation worker. If I could say the Words of Power to release you, I'd do it, but I don't know how."

In the distance beyond the silence around me the city vibrated with adventure and derring-do. Invisible hycom transmissions shot back and forth across the galaxy carrying the conversations of every intelligent species, with humans talking more than all of them put together. No one answered me.

"Dep, I'm not sure which of the robots is the real you, but if the ship relays my words, then I want you to know that I also apologize for saying that you and I are not equal. I've learned that being different doesn't mean being worse, and that being organic doesn't mean being superior. Did you know that the humans have intelligent robots now? And that the robots of Togit have finally won equal rights?"

I was shivering in the cold and depressed by the silence.

"Dammit, Dep, the truth is that I miss you. I always have. I'm only a foolish, aging organic, but I think that I have always loved you. It will be easier for me to live out the rest of my silly life if you'll just give me some indication that you forgive me."

The air lock opened, the landing ramp shot out, and I climbed up into the ship.

Dep was there, sitting beside a table bearing a nude female form. She was young, beautiful, and looked as squeaky-clean as an astronaut.

"Hello, Zeela. I've made you a robot, and I've discovered a way to transfer organic brain patterns into its brain. How about trying it?"

My hand shook a little as I touched the robot who looked the way I used to. "You must really love me, Dep."

Considerably later, Dep and I went out the air lock stark-naked. The falling snow felt like cool little hands caressing my new skin.

And there on the Sheep Meadow of the sovereign nation of Manhattan, surrounded by the cleanest blocks in the world, two robots tripped the light fantastic.

I grew up in the New York City suburbs and for forty years have lived in—and loved—Manhattan.

Sharing Manhattan with Isaac Asimov for the past twenty years makes it easier to keep on loving the city in spite of the General Deterioration of Civilization.

At age eleven, I decided to become a writer. Practicality intervened and I went to medical school, then became a psychiatrist and psychoanalyst. My first short story was published in 1966, my first novel in 1974. Of my sixteen books so far, I'm fondest of the Norby series and How to Enjoy Writing *(with Isaac Asimov), and my latest novel,* Mind Transfer.

—Janet Asimov

Another Dime, Another Place

by A. J. Austin

Here we have a fantasy with a Yuletide flavor, the heartwarming tale of a bag lady who sells cheap postcards with a little something extra to them.

"Postcard, mister?"

The wind seemed colder now, damper, as he tried to pretend he couldn't hear the tiny old woman at his side. His briefcase in his left hand, he pulled his overcoat more tightly around his throat with his right against the chill of what seemed a harsher-than-usual December.

"Postcard? Nice views, mister. Only ten cents."

Jesus, why doesn't she leave me alone? he thought. Can't she see I'm ignoring her? Damn, why can't you ever get a cab when it's raining?

"Only ten cents, mister." She reached out tentatively, touching the sleeve of his expensive overcoat. He quickly jerked his arm away.

"Don't you dare touch . . ." he started to say, seeing the old woman, really looking at her for the first time. As deplorable as he had expected, there was still a dignity there that made him stop and reconsider how he spoke to her.

"Postcard?" she asked again, holding out a bundle of cards perhaps an inch thick. Despite the newspaper wrapped around them, it was obvious they had seen little protection from the weather.

"Uh, yeah," he said finally, thinking that if he bought one of the stupid cards maybe she'd go away and bother someone else. Tucking his briefcase under an arm, he took the bundle gingerly, careful not to touch her, careful not to actually make contact with one of *those* people.

He flipped through them hurriedly, barely seeing them, and picked one from the middle of the stack.

"I'll take this one." He slipped the card inside the overcoat and fumbled in his pockets for change, wet hands making the task more difficult and time-consuming than he would have liked. He finally found a coin, a quarter, and gave it to her.

"Taxi!" He ran for the curb, aware that his shouting was more to further distance himself from the old woman than to actually hail the cab now rounding the corner. Whether the driver heard or saw him was irrelevant; what mattered was that the salt-encrusted car pulled to an abrupt halt at the curb nearest him.

"Union Square," he barked, throwing himself into the back seat. Reaching for the handle, he was both startled and dismayed to see the old woman standing there, preventing him from closing the door.

"They're only a dime, mister," she was saying, the tiny voice nearly lost in the traffic noise. "Let me give you your change."

"It's O.K; you keep it. Please, I'm in a hurry."

"But, mister, I—"

"It's all right, really." He gave her his best smile and watched as grimy fingers closed tightly over the coins in her outstretched hand. The old woman moved away from the curb, a smile appearing on her own face.

"Thank you, sir. God bless you." She was still standing at the curb as he closed the door and told the driver to go on. He looked back once through the water-streaked rear window of the taxi; he couldn't be sure because of the distorted image, but he thought he saw her wave.

Pathetic, he thought, and meant it not as a curse, but as a literal statement of fact.

"Greetings from Niagara Falls" was written in bright-red letters across the picture. As such, it was typical of most postcards bought at any tourist-attraction gift shop. Turning the card over to the message and address side, he read the description: "View from Goat Island. From the unique vantage point of the island can be found the best location to view the magnificent splendor of both the American and Canadian falls."

As bad as Manhattan was right now, it would be totally

miserable at the falls this time of year. Not yet frigid
enough for the beautiful ice cascades to form but too cold
to be out in the constant spray. He didn't envy anyone
there right now.

I can't imagine how Doug has stood it there all these
years, he thought. I wonder how he's making out. He
glanced at his watch and picked up the phone. Why not?
He had time before the nine-thirty meeting.

"Cara, make a call for me please?"

"Yes, Mr. McKee." A slight pause. "O.K., go ahead."

"Look in my Rolodex and see if you still have a card
on Douglas Harper. If it's not under 'H', then try Curry
and Glassman in Buffalo."

"Yes, sir. It'll be just a moment."

He replaced the receiver and swiveled the plush chair
around. The sleet had changed to a strong, driving rain
and the headlights on the cars jammed along Park Avenue forty floors below his office window sparkled like a
string of Christmas lights.

The phone chirped softly behind him and he turned
back to the desk. "Mr. McKee? Mr. Harper on line five."

"Thanks, Cara." He quickly punched up the blinking
button. "Doug? Hi. It's Ed McKee in New York."

"Eddie? Geez, it's been, what, five years at least. How
the hell are you?"

"Freezing my onions off right now; outside of that, I
guess I can't complain. How about you?"

"Oh, hey, things are going great. In case your secretary didn't mention it, they answer the phone 'Curry,
Glassman, and Harper' around here now. We've expanded the firm again, added a half-dozen associates this
year alone. How's Bonnie and the kids?"

"Fine, they're all fine. Jimmy's taller than I am, and
on the varsity basketball team. Donna's in junior high,
now—straight-A student, too."

"Congratulations. Sounds like they've really turned out
great. I can hear the pride in your voice."

The phone chirped. "Damn, can you hold a second?"

"Sure, no problem."

He pressed the receiver cradle momentarily to answer
the page. "Yes?"

"I'm sorry, Mr. McKee, but Mr. Knox says he needs
to see you upstairs before your nine-thirty."

"All right, thanks, Cara." He touched the phone once more. "Doug? Listen, I'm sorry to have to run like this, but—"

"Same old Fast Eddie," Harper joked. "Always in a hurry. No wonder Jimmy's gone out for sports. Before you sneak away, let me just ask: you still a big shot at that insurance company?"

"Yeah. Why?"

"Well, as I said, we're growing pretty fast up here and our old coverage is getting expensive as hell. We're making changes and I'm in a position now to make some of the decisions. Be interested in taking us on?"

"Of course."

"This is perfect. I can't believe your timing, calling out of the blue like this. Put me through to your secretary and I'll have her schedule us a time when we can talk a bit longer than two minutes."

"You're on, Doug. I'll talk to you later."

"Good talking to you. I'm glad you called, Eddie."

McKee looked absently at the postcard on the desk blotter. "Greetings from Niagara Falls . . ."

"Yeah, me too."

"Postcard, mister?"

It was almost as if she was waiting for him when he stepped off the elevator. Ed McKee looked around the lobby for a security guard, but couldn't spot one. At well past six the normal crowd of people leaving the building had long since thinned to a trickle.

She held the bundle out as she had that morning, and McKee noticed the stack was thicker and unwrapped; now, out of the weather, there was no need to wrap them.

"Nice views, only ten . . ." She stopped in midsentence, only now recognizing him. "Oh, sir, it's you. I was hoping I'd see you again. I have more cards, now. Most of them were in my coat to keep them dry, but see? I have them all here now, many more views to choose from. Wait, wait. I think I got some more in here . . ." She began digging through an enormous plastic shopping bag, chattering even more excitedly than before about her vast selection of cards and about how kind he had been to her earlier.

McKee wasn't sure if it was the prospect of another
sale or the fact that she was indoors in a warm, dry place
that accounted for her good spirits, but he couldn't help
grinning as she searched through the seemingly bottomless bag. He still felt a certain revulsion for her, for all
street people, but there was something about her that
touched him.

"Yes, I think I might want another postcard."

Her eyes grew wide with delight and she stood quickly,
dropping the bag to the marble floor. Handing him the
bundle, she waited silently while he examined them.

"How about this one?" he asked finally, choosing one
from the stack and showing it to her.

She looked carefully at it, shaking her head.

"No, not that one. It's badly damaged from the water.
Let me find you a better one." She took the bundle away
from him, shuffled through them till she found the
one she wanted. "Here you are," she said, extending one of
the cards to him. "Much nicer one."

The card was a Christmas scene. A perfect tree, brilliantly lighted, with dozens of wrapped gifts under it. In
the center with a large red bow around its neck was a
stuffed teddy bear, leaning against the front wheel of a
tricycle. The stitched-on eyes made the bear look sound
asleep. Beneath the picture in Old English lettering was
the legend "Not a Creature Was Stirring . . ."

"You're right, it's very nice," he said as he looked for
change. Remembering he'd used the last of it in the soda
machine, he reached for his wallet. "Listen, do me a
favor. I don't know how you managed to get past the
security people, but it's really not a good idea to hang
around here, understand? They sometimes get a little
rough when any of you . . . Well, they sometimes get a
little rough, that's all."

She nodded, her eyes never leaving the wallet for a
second.

"Here." He handed her a crisp, new five-dollar bill
and watched as her face widened into a huge grin.

"Thank you. Oh, sir, I'm so glad I picked you that
one. It'll be an extra special one for you. Miss Lacey
thanks you. Merry Christmas, sir." Swiftly gathering up
the stack, she snapped the rubber band back around the
bundle and dropped it into the bag. She hustled toward

the front entrance, and McKee nearly laughed out loud when she ducked behind a huge pillar just as the security guard rounded the corner.

"Good evening, Mr. McKee. Working late again?" The guard, a tall, muscular man in his late twenties, tipped his hat as he approached. The strength in the man's shoulders and upper arms was obvious even in the security company's one-size-fits-all blue shirt.

"Afraid so, Brad. Landed a big contract today, added it to the list of things to take care of before the holidays."

"Yeah, I know what you mean. Well, you have a good night, sir. Watch your step, getting kind of slick."

"Sure thing. Thanks." He made a show of buttoning his overcoat and listened for the guard's footsteps to disappear around the other side of the elevators before calling out, "Pssst! It's all clear."

Without a word the tiny woman darted for the front entrance. She struggled for a second with the heavy door and then quickly slipped out. Once outside, she turned back for a moment and waved, then lost herself in the crowd.

The guard had been right, he realized as soon as he left the building. The temperature had dropped rapidly and the steady rain had turned to snow, but despite the cold, the crowded sidewalks were more slushy than icy. Besides, the falling snow made even the Manhattan streets look good tonight. And it was quiet; the traffic still made the same sound, the shoppers and other passersby still talked as loudly as ever, but the soft, heavy flakes had a dampening effect on the entire scene. In the middle of the city, it was almost peaceful.

It might be nice, he thought, taking a quick peek at his watch. I've got some time. Enjoying the snowfall, McKee strolled past his usual taxi stand.

It was nearly seven when he finally stopped at a stand. No cab was waiting, of course, and with the rush of holiday shoppers all around him, he resigned himself to a long wait. Standing beneath a wide awning that ran the entire length of the front of a huge department store, he passed the time by watching the shoppers and looking at the various window displays.

After several minutes, the arrangement of one of the displays, a lovely Christmas morning, caught his attention. It took a moment before it suddenly occurred to him where he'd seen it. Setting the briefcase down, he reached into his coat for the postcard. The scenes were the same, or nearly so. Some of the details were different—the tree a bit smaller, the colors of the wrapping paper varied here and there—but the teddy bear, the tricycle, even the small sign declaring "Not a Creature Was Stirring" were all identical.

He marveled at the similarity and headed for the entrance to get a better look from the inside. A large knot of people was shoving and jostling to enter the store and he took his place in the line waiting for the revolving doors. Just as he stepped in, the blast of car horns caught the crowd's attention. Too late to get out of the spinning doors, he tried to make out what was going on from inside the revolving chamber.

At the end of the block, several cars, apparently the same ones honking, were swerving in all directions. Through the wet, heavy glass, McKee couldn't quite make out what was happening, but the danger was apparent as soon as the doors came fully around. A driver had lost control of his car and was literally plowing through the traffic; cars, buses, and delivery trucks alike were making their best efforts to get out of the way.

A woman at his side screamed and dropped her shopping bag to the pavement, dragging her two kids quickly to one side as she did. Others were yelling all around him, all of them moving, running, pushing at the same time as the car approached. McKee felt frozen where he stood, the scene unfolding in slow motion as he stared.

The car hit the curb hard with the right front wheel, bouncing sideways into the air. In an imitation of a fairgrounds stunt driver, it continued on two wheels as it came onto the sidewalk, the angle of tilt almost, but not quite, giving it enough clearance to miss the streetlight. The bumper just caught the pole about four or five feet up, snapping it; right next to it a newspaper machine bolted to the sidewalk went flying in the opposite direction, hitting the street and scattering dozens of *USA Today*s into the confusion. As the pole hit the sidewalk not thirty feet from the crowd of shoppers at the door, the glass globe shattered and sparks flew from the electric wiring pulling free from the stump of the pole. Still

on two wheels, the car slammed into the polished granite
storefront, dead center between two display windows. In
a moment frozen in time, it hung there at that impossible
angle, then fell to a level position.

It was over in seconds, and a stunned quiet came over
the crowd. Most of the traffic had come to a stop and the
only sound was the hissing from the car's smashed radia-
tor and the intermittent popping of sparks from the demolished streetlight.

An approaching siren broke the reverie of the crowd
and everyone began talking, moving, shouting, crying,
pointing at the same time. Two teenagers, taking advantage of the sudden confusion, scooped up several handfuls of change from the smashed vending machine before
disappearing down the street. The sight of the blatant
theft made McKee realize he didn't have his briefcase.
He looked around, but his attention was drawn away
when the door flew open on the wrecked car and the
driver stumbled out; he had a cut on his forehead, but
appeared otherwise all right.

Besides the driver there were, amazingly, very few
people hurt as a result of the accident. Some of the
bystanders were cut by flying glass from the streetlamp,
and one of the shoppers suffered a broken wrist when she
fell on the slippery pavement during the excitement; but
other than that, police were calling it a miracle that
somebody wasn't killed.

McKee had never believed in miracles, but when a tow
truck pulled the twisted wreck from the sidewalk, the
sight made him give the subject serious thought.

Jammed into the grill of the battered vehicle was his
briefcase.

He got lucky at the eighth newsstand he tried.

"Yeah, I know Lacey," said the vendor, looking suspiciously at McKee. "I always give her the outdated stuff.
Any cards that get torn or wet, I give them to her for
nothin'. What's it to ya?"

"I need to find her."

"What for?"

"I . . . I have something for her," McKee said.

The vendor looked him over again. "You got a grudge
against her for something, hangin' around your fancy

office maybe? How do I know you ain't gonna try and push her around?"

He was getting nowhere, so he tried a different approach, leaning in to the man and lowering his voice. From time to time he'd look to his side to make sure no one was listening, as if what he was about to say was important enough that it shouldn't be overheard.

"Listen, you give her your old cards, right? So do dozens of other newsstands around the city. Well, she stopped me on the street the other day and I bought one of the damned things just to get her off my back. But get this . . ." McKee leaned closer, taking the man into his confidence as he lied. "Some of those 'outdated' cards, as you call them, are collector's items. The one I bought from her was worth over a hundred bucks."

The man let out a low whistle.

"Now, all I want to do is buy some more of her outdated cards. Get it?"

McKee could almost hear the wheels turning in the man's greedy little brain as he thought. He took a candy bar from one of the display boxes and unwrapped it slowly as he said, his voice a whisper, "Yeah, I get it. So, uh, what's in it for me if I tell you where she lives?"

McKee reached into his coat for his wallet and pulled out two bills, giving one to the vendor. "Here. Let's call this a finder's fee. And this," he said, as he gave him the other, "is an advance on any other 'collectibles' I come up with. What do you say, uh—"

"Mike."

"—Mike? Have we got a deal?"

Mike thought it over for all of three seconds. "You ain't gonna hurt her, are you?"

"Of course not. I sell insurance. Do I look like an arm-breaker to you?"

"No, I guess not. O.K., it's a deal." He extended his arm and the two men shook to seal the bargain. McKee noticed that Mike's hand was sticky from the candy bar and idly wondered how long it would stay that way before he washed it.

The alley was only a few minutes' walk from the newsstand, and McKee found it easily enough. He wasn't sure just what he had expected, but the sight of it stopped him in his tracks. He'd seen these places dozens of times before; the TV news programs had shown them locally, and *Time* and *Newsweek* regularly did features on the conditions of the homeless, but the reality of it stunned him.

Thank God for the snow, he thought. It hides a lot of the filth. Several inches had fallen and a blanket of white covered every trash can and fire escape. Here and there were small cardboard and plywood lean-tos; he saw no one in them, although whether they were permanently abandoned or just temporarily empty, he had no way of knowing. Again, the weather was a blessing; he couldn't imagine what this place would have looked like—or smelled like—in the heat of summer.

He made his way down the dark passage, nearly falling several times on objects hidden in the snow. The noise of the busy street faded the farther away he got, and the quiet made him more nervous than before.

There was an intersection of sorts, and seeing what appeared to be a small fire down the alleyway to the right, he turned in that direction. His heart pounding, he approached a small group sitting around the tiny blaze. Although their clothing was tattered and filthy, the four of them looked surprisingly warm wrapped in blankets around the fire.

"Excuse me," he said, his voice shaking. "Is there a Lacey or a Miss Lacey here?"

They ignored him as he looked from face to face in the group. Had they even heard him?

"I'm looking for a woman who calls herself Lacey," he repeated, a bit louder this time. "Have any of you seen her or know where I can find her?" They turned to him this time, but remained silent.

Finally, one of them, McKee guessed him to be in his fifties, lifted a thin hand from beneath his blanket and pointed down an alleyway.

"Thank you." McKee headed in the indicated direction. The alley made several turns and he tried to remember each as he went. Looking back the way he'd come, he was relieved to see his footprints, easily visible in the snow. The alley was dark, but the glow of the city reflected well in the mantle of white at his feet. He should have no trouble finding his way back. Somewhat more at ease, he turned and was about to continue on his way, but stopped dead when a cigarette fell into the snow a few paces in front of him. He stared dumbly at it for several seconds, watching as it melted the snow and extinguished with a soft *sssst*.

McKee heard a clattering sound from behind, and above, him. He turned to run back the way he came, but another sound—also from above, but in front of him this time—made him freeze.

"Don't do it, man," shouted a voice from yet another direction. The young punk stepped quickly from the shadows of a doorway set invisibly into the wall on his right and was on him in a flash, a knife just inches from his face. The boy grinned wickedly at him, turning the knife over and over in his hand. He started circling McKee. "Well, now, what do we have here? Danny! Jackson! Get down here." The clattering resumed from front and back as two more youths scrambled down from the fire escape on his left.

McKee heard one of the boys approach from behind; he wanted to swing around now with the briefcase and run, run as fast as he could, but he knew he wouldn't get ten feet. "Nice coat, mister," said the one from behind as he felt the fabric of the collar. "You get that around here?" All three of them burst into laughter at the remark.

"Danny, ain't no stores around here carry these coats," said Jackson, the one who'd jumped from the ladder ahead of him. The one from the doorway stepped back and put the knife away, lighting another cigarette as he leaned against the building.

He must be the leader, McKee thought, hanging back to study me while his two buddies go to work on me.

"What d'ya think, Blade?" the one identified as Danny asked his companion in the doorway. "You think we can find us a couple coats like this? I think we'd look pretty damn fine if we all wore 'em."

"And how 'bout this, Blade?" said Jackson, jerking the briefcase from McKee's hand. He looked at it closely in the dark alleyway, fingered the dented-in side. "Hey, this looks like genuine alligator, Blade. That what this is, man, alligator? You should take better care of it."

McKee tried to say something, anything, but was frozen with fear. Sweat flowed down his face, melting the occasional snowflake that landed on his skin.

"Hey, Danny. You know what this is? This is flyin' alligator." With that, Jackson flung the case against the nearest building with a crash. It caromed off the wall and landed in the snow several feet away as the two burst into laughter again. They continued prodding and taunting him for several minutes until Blade, the one in the doorway, finished his cigarette and flipped it with a finger into the snow.

"That's enough," he said, stepping up to stare evenly into McKee's face.

"I have money . . ."

Blade hit McKee suddenly with the back of his hand. The other two grabbed his arms, pinning them painfully behind him. "No shit, man! You think we're out here screwin' with you 'cause we like the weather?"

McKee tasted blood, felt a small cut on the inside of his lip with his tongue. "Please, take my money. I won't give you any trouble."

Blade laughed, pulled the knife from his pocket. "Yeah, I heard that. Let him go." Danny and Jackson released his arms and took a few steps back. Still holding the knife in his right hand, Blade extended his left. "O.K., Mister Uptown, let's have it."

McKee's hands, numb from both cold and fear, shook uncontrollably as he reached into his coat, which seemed to be a source of great amusement to his tormentors.

"What the hell you doin' here, man?" Blade demanded. "You lost?"

"I was looking for someone." McKee handed the wallet over.

Clicking the knife closed, Blade opened the wallet, took a look inside, and beamed; he gave a quick thumbs-up to the others.

"All right," said one, McKee couldn't tell which.

"Well, whoever you was lookin' for did me a favor," Blade said, waving the wallet in the air as the three turned to leave him. "You ever find him, you tell him I said thanks."

"Please, wait. You've got my money. Tell me, do you know someone named Lacey?"

Blade froze in his steps and turned to him, all traces of

humor gone from his face. Danny and Jackson continued down the alley. "What you want with her?" he demanded, approaching him menacingly.

"Blade! You comin', man?"

"I'll be there in a second; you guys go on." The two stopped, stared at him a moment. "I said go on! I'll meet you back at Carlos' place. Now!" He waited till they resumed walking, finally disappearing in the falling snow.

Blade turned abruptly and grabbed him by the collar of his coat. "I asked you why you was lookin' for Miss Lacey."

"I . . . I need to see her."

"You want her cards, don't you, Mister Uptown?" Chuckling, he let McKee go and reached for a cigarette. He lit it and, as an afterthought, held out the pack.

McKee took the offered cigarette and cupped his hands around the flame of Blade's lighter as he lit it. He was still shaking, but no longer afraid for his life. Inhaling the warm smoke deeply for several moments, he forced himself to relax.

"I got some bad news for you, man," Blade said finally. "You're wastin' your time. If you're after Miss Lacey's cards, then you must know what they do. And if you know that, then you're just wastin' time."

Despite the fearful respect he felt for the young man, McKee began to feel a certain sense of fascination for him. "You know about the cards, what she can do with them?" he asked.

"Yeah, yeah, I know."

"Then why the hell are you hanging out in alleys, waiting for strangers to rob? Why don't—"

"You ain't payin' attention, are you?" Blade snapped, throwing his cigarette to the ground. "Listen, man, if you know about it, it don't work."

"What do mean, 'if you know about it?' " McKee could barely believe what he was hearing.

"Look, there's somethin' special 'bout Miss Lacey. Sometimes when she sells one of her cards, she . . . I don't know, she gets a feeling 'bout the person buyin' it from her, see? And that card has some kind of special thing for the person. They see somethin' in it and they act on it, and whatever it is they do turns into somethin' good for them. Understand?"

He glimpsed the battered briefcase, lying in the snow several feet down the alley. "Yeah, I think I do."

"But if you know about it, then you start lookin' for stuff that ain't there, and it just don't work no more."

The snow was falling more heavily now, and the two moved beneath the fire escape to get out of the worst of it as they talked.

"Who is she, Blade?"

"I don't know, man—just some crazy old woman. All of them livin' around here ain't right in the head. These ain't the kind that like livin' out here, ya know? These are the ones the homes throw out 'cause their budgets keep bein' cut. She don't even know what her cards do for people. Some of us tried to tell her once, but she don't listen." Blade rubbed his hands together to warm them, then slipped them into the pockets of his jacket. "So we look after her and the others, make sure they get some food, blankets when they need them. Who do you think it was built that fire?"

"You followed me all the way from there?"

Blade laughed, dug out the cigarette pack, and lit one up, blowing a plume of smoke up toward the fire escape. "Shit, man. We saw your ass comin' when you stepped off the sidewalk." He put the pack away, then reached suddenly into a hip pocket, causing McKee to jump slightly. "Take it easy, Uptown," Blade said with a smirk. He opened the stolen wallet, rifled through the several bills inside, and removed a single twenty. Pocketing the bill, he handed the wallet back to McKee.

"Thanks."

Blade turned to him, a look of deadly seriousness on his face. "Leave her alone, you got that?" McKee nodded. Blade started down the alley, stopping at the briefcase now almost buried in the snow. He picked it up, shook some of the snow from it, and tossed it back to McKee, still standing against the wall beneath the fire escape. Without another word, the young man turned and disappeared into the darkness.

McKee wasn't surprised, the following night, to find that the city of New York didn't plow the alleys—at least not the ones this far below Fourteenth. Nearly eight inches had accumulated during the snowstorm, but foot traffic and delivery trucks during the day had packed it down enough that walking was fairly easy. More snow was predicted, but for now the skies were merely cloudy and the light from several high, barred windows was unhampered by falling snow.

He found his way easily enough, following the familiar landmarks he'd seen last night. Several of the lean-tos showed evidence of having been occupied during the night. He hesitated at the intersection of the two alleys and looked around but saw no one. Too early, he thought. He passed the spot where the fire had burned last night, the embers still smoldering, and he guessed that by midnight there would be a small group huddling around it once more.

Reaching the place where he'd confronted the gang, he found an old man sitting in the doorway, a dirty red blanket draped over his shoulders, eating the last of a McDonald's hamburger. Several wrappers littered the snow at his feet. The old man stood up as he appoached.

"Leave me alone. Go away."

"It's all right; it's O.K. I won't hurt you."

The old man stopped whimpering, but stayed in the protection of the doorway.

"Do you know Miss Lacey? Do you know where I can find her?"

"Please. Leave me alone." The old man was terrified and leaned shaking against the door, dropping the remains of the hamburger to the snow. Suddenly, a look of relief spread across the man's face as he looked to a spot over McKee's shoulder.

"You heard what he said, man!" In one smooth, calm motion McKee reached into his pocket and pulled out a small handgun, pivoted around, and brought it to bear on the center of Blade's forehead. The young man was no fool; he froze, extended his hands at his side.

"From this distance, I won't miss, Blade."

"Be cool, man."

"Let's see it." Blade reached slowly into a pocket and took out the knife. "Don't even look like you're going to open it. Toss it into the snow, over there by the wall. Good. Now, take me to her."

"Why, man? I told you, she ain't got nothin' for you anymore."

McKee gestured menacingly with the gun. "Maybe not. But I've got something here for you if you don't take me to her. Now move."

"Shit, man. And I thought *these* people were crazy," he muttered, indicating the old man now on the ground brushing snow off the cold hamburger. Blade moved down the alley and McKee followed a few feet behind, the gun never wavering.

"And if you see any of your friends hiding around the corner, Blade, tell them to back off. You'll have a hole in your neck before any of them could get near me." McKee tried to sound like he meant it, but didn't stop wondering if he could really do it. Best to hope we don't pass Danny and Jackson on the way, he thought.

They had gone only a short distance and McKee was already feeling lost in the maze of alleyways when he saw the glow of a fire up ahead. Someone sat warming himself at it, and he could make out Danny and Jackson, too, standing over to one side talking animatedly to another young tough he didn't recognize. They either heard or saw them approaching, and waved in greeting.

"Hey, Blade! Where you been . . ." The boy stopped short when he saw McKee. All three reached for pockets.

"I swear to God, Blade," he said as calmly as he could, "call them off or you take one in the head."

"Danny! Carlos, Jackson! This crazy mother has a gun. Don't do it."

"You heard him. Get them out and toss them. Down the alley—now!"

They obeyed. Each had a knife; Jackson also carried a Saturday-night special. All the weapons were tossed into the snow as the person at the fire watched, never moving, never speaking.

Feeling safer now, McKee prodded the young man closer to the light. It was her sitting by the fire, he realized as he neared. Her back was to him, but he recognized the scarf and the plastic shopping bag at her side. "Over with your friends, Blade. That's it. Now, you four stay at least thirty feet away from the fire, you got that? I see so much as a flinch in my direction and I shoot."

They cursed and chattered softly to each other, but

moved away steadily, if slowly, and stood leaning against a wall.

"Miss Lacey?" McKee knelt at her side and she turned to face him for the first time since he'd gotten there. The snow had begun gently falling once more and tiny flakes stood out against the bright colors of her scarf. My God, she's old, he thought. She really can't care for herself. He saw now just how much a help Blade and his friends had been to her and the others.

"Yes? Who is it?"

"My name's McKee, Miss Lacey. You sold me some postcards yesterday."

She looked puzzled for a moment, then her eyes brightened suddenly in recognition. "Yes. Yes, I remember you. The man at the office building. You helped me when the security man came. I remember you were so nice to me and I made sure you had a special one."

"That's right. The one you gave me yesterday evening was a very special one. Do you know that it saved my life?"

Her eyes twinkled in disbelief as a tiny smile appeared on her weathered face. "No. It was just a pretty postcard."

"I told you, man," Blade called from the far wall. "She don't even know."

McKee looked to the young men and, satisfied for the moment they were keeping their distance, set the gun down next to him on the packed snow. He reached into his coat and pulled out a small bundle.

"I brought you something, Miss Lacey. Here, look at these." He quickly rolled a rubber band off a stack of cards and showed them to her one by one. "Look at this one, Miss Lacey," he said, holding a picture of a beautiful sunset on a tropical island. "Isn't it pretty? And how about this one?" A peaceful little village overlooking a quiet lake. "And this one? Look at the details; imagine what it would be like to live there." He continued through them, and each time she'd look at one of the scenes her mouth would go wide in a soft *ooooh* and she'd take the card and turn it over and over in the growing pile of postcards in her lap.

"They're all so beautiful," she gasped. "I can't decide."

"No, you don't understand. They're yours; I want you to have them all."

She couldn't grasp it. Tears welled up in her eyes and she began sobbing. "But I don't have enough money for them. It isn't right."

Blade and his friends stirred uneasily when they heard her crying, and McKee reached quickly for the gun. "Don't try it, boys," he said as forcefully as he could. They backed off, and he set the gun down again.

"No, it's not right," she repeated. "I don't have enough money." She started gathering them up, trying to push them back at him.

"All right," he said, realizing he couldn't make her understand they were intended as a gift. He knelt closer, extending what was left of the stack. "You pick one, then. Pick the best one, and I'll let you buy it. Do you have enough for one?"

Her eyes gleamed. She nodded excitedly and reached for the rest of the cards, unbalancing him as she did.

It was the break Blade had been waiting for. Before McKee could recover his footing, the four were on top of him, wrestling him away from the fire, away from Miss Lacey. Blade grabbed the gun and stuck it hard under McKee's chin.

"Freeze, Mister Uptown! Danny, you and Carlos go get your stuff. Hold him, Jackson." He remained motionless, panting heavily as the strong youth held him tightly. Lost in the cards, Miss Lacey was oblivious to the violence going on around her.

"Shit, man, we ain't gonna find that stuff till springtime," Danny said when the two returned.

"I told you not to come back here," Blade said. Still jamming the gun under McKee's chin, he punched him full in the stomach and watched as he fell gasping to his knees. "Get up."

"You heard the man!" Jackson grabbed him by the collar and swung him up once more to stand wobbling before them.

"Let's go for a little walk." Blade kept the gun on him while his companions chanted and took turns jabbing and pushing him down the alleyway.

McKee hurt all over and wondered if they planned to beat him to death, or just shoot him and leave him in a dumpster somewhere in one of the alleys.

"Mister! Wait!"

The youths froze at the sound of the old woman, running to catch up to them as best she could in the snow. As she approached, Blade hid the gun in his jacket; the others pocketed their hands and stood back silently. McKee fell to the ground on his hands and knees, panting, already exhausted from the beating he'd taken. He looked up when she neared, saw her dimly through clouds of his own breath. His nose was bleeding and he wiped his face on his coat sleeve. As with the actual occurrence of violence before, she didn't notice the effects of it now. She knelt on the packed snow before him.

"I like this one," she said simply, holding the stack of cards out and tapping the top one with a grimy fingernail. She waited, smiling, while McKee looked at it. "Greetings from the Suncoast!" it said across the top. It was a beach scene, but unlike so many postcards of its type with half-naked young girls frolicking with beach balls, this one showed an older couple. They strolled along the sand, just at the edge of the lapping water. The couple wore matching, comfortable-looking shirts and hats of handwoven palm fronds. The legend on the reverse side said, simply, "Christmas in Florida. Wish you were here!"

"It's lovely," he said, giving the top card to her.

She took it, held it up so Blade and the others could see. They nodded nervously and muttered a few words of agreement about how nice it was. She stood up, a look of pride on her face as she reached into the pocket of her oversized wool coat.

"Here. Ten cents, right?"

McKee held out his hand and nodded. She placed the dime gently into his palm, then curled his fingers over the coin as if afraid he might lose it.

She walked slowly back to the fire. Now, he thought, while their attention is on her. If I break now, I might be able to get away. They know the alleys, but I'm in better shape; I just might make it. But when she turned to wave, as she had the other times he'd seen her, they also turned their attention back to him. They were nervous about this, he could tell. Blade—and to a lesser degree, Danny, Jackson, and Carlos—looked anxiously back and forth from the old woman to the bruised man at their feet.

No, he admitted to himself, I have to see this through.

He tried to stand up, fell to one knee, and tried again, succeeding this time. One of the youths grabbed his arm, the strong fingers digging through the fabric of the sleeve.

"Look at the picture, Miss Lacey. Look at it . . ." Jackson shoved him again and he fell, scattering the cards on the snow. They pulled him upright, and one of the cards stuck momentarily to his cheek before falling, blood-smeared, to join the others on the ground.

"What do you see in the picture?" he gasped, unable to tell if she was even listening as she walked away from them. "Look at it! Imagine what—"

Blade slammed him against the nearest building. "I have had it with you, man!" He released the lapels of McKee's coat, sending him flailing sideways against a trash can. The contents spilled noisily across the alley. "Carlos! Danny!"

The two jerked him again to his feet and he leaned, his head swimming, against the solidity offered by the brick wall at his back. The breath burned in his lungs as he blinked, trying to focus his eyes on his captors. He saw Blade reach into his jacket.

"Miss . . . Miss Lacey. Look at it. Look how warm, how nice it must be!" Blade aimed the gun at his head.

"Jesus! Blade," screamed Jackson, staring back behind them. He was tugging now at Blade's jacket, pointing fearfully at the old woman. Blade looked, and the gun drifted down and hung limply at his side.

She had stopped about halfway to the fire, and where she stood the snow was glowing in a circle of brilliant orange light. The circle glowed brighter and expanded till it touched the buildings on either side of the alley. She stood motionless in the center, head tilted back, her eyes closed. The gently falling snow swirled within the circle, looking like nothing so much as tiny gemstones sparkling from some inner glow.

The snow spun faster and faster about her in an eerie silence so complete they could hear the sounds of Manhattan's ever-present traffic. The orange glow became yellow, then a white brighter than the snow itself. Finally, it grew so bright they were forced to shield their eyes from the sheer radiance of it, and all the while it remained as soundless as the night.

They could barely see Miss Lacey in the center of the

glowing swirl. No, not in the center of the glow—part of it, the brightest part of the light itself. She lowered her head and turned to them, and smiled.

"Merry Christmas," she said softly, "and have a nice New Year." Her image faded from the center of the tiny whirlwind, and was gone. The glow faded gradually as the snowy vortex slowed, from hot-white to white, then yellow, then orange; finally, a dull red, then nothing. The snow fell softly on the spot once more, and throughout the alley it was as if nothing had happened.

Blade crossed the few yards to the spot. McKee pushed himself away from the wall to follow and one of the others made a move for him. "Leave him be," Blade snapped, and the youth backed off. "Sweet Jesus," he whispered as McKee approached his side. Blade bent down and picked up the card, looked at it a moment before passing it to him. "Sweet Jesus," he repeated.

The snow was falling harder now and McKee wiped the card on his coat. He looked at it once and nodded, then handed it back. "Here, you keep it."

Blade stared at the now-forgotten gun in his hand, and with a grunt heaved it as far down the alleyway as he could. "Thanks, man." He looked at the card, chuckling softly to himself as he read the back. " 'Christmas in Florida. Wish you were here!' "

"You were right, Blade," McKee said quietly. "The magic only works if you don't know about it."

The two regarded each other in silence for several long seconds. Blade turned to his friends and jerked his head in the direction of the far alley; they nodded and wordlessly left the two alone. McKee took his handkerchief and scooped up a bit of snow, dabbing at his face. His nose had stopped bleeding and the icy handkerchief felt good on the cuts.

"Hey, man, I'm sorry. I really—"

"It's all right, Blade. Forget it." McKee finished with the handkerchief, wadded it into a ball, and threw it into the rest of the trash lining the alleyway. "Save us both some embarrassment."

They looked at each other for a moment longer, then, almost simultaneously, turned and went their separate ways through the silently falling snow.

A. J. Austin is a full-time radio talk host at WPOP, an all-news ABC affiliate in Hartford, Connecticut. Although regular Analog and Amazing readers are familiar with his short fiction, A.J. has contributed nonfiction articles to publications as diverse as Astronomy, Children, Apple inCider, and Hartford Monthly, to name a few.

In his spare time, he has been heavily involved in amateur theater and has more than sixty acting credits to his name. (He met his wife, Sally, when they performed together in The Madwoman of Chaillot. They were married a year later on the theater stage.)

He and Sally live with their seven-year-old daughter, Courtney, in Manchester, Connecticut, roughly a two-hour drive from New York City.

Watching New York Melt

by Lawrence Watt-Evans and Julie Evans

Trying to introduce my own story—well, partly mine, anyway—is probably a mistake, especially when it's this short. So I won't.

A gobbet of molten glass spattered and sizzled across the sidewalk as I turned the corner; I stepped around it and glanced up. The saucer was still hanging there, right above the next block, and the building there—I didn't know its name—was down to about the fifteenth floor, the red-glowing ends of exposed beams like blown-out birthday candles.

I didn't have time to watch, though; I had to get lunch and get back to the office. I pushed past the guy selling souvenir pieces of the Empire State Building and stepped into the coffee shop.

Harry was already at the counter; I took the stool beside him and picked up the menu he had just put down.

He sipped coffee and said, "So what do you think?"

"About what?" I asked, none too cheerfully.

"Those saucers melting the city."

I shrugged. "Not my problem," I said.

"True enough, but it's a shame, all the same. I didn't mind when they got the World Trade Center, but I'm going to miss the Empire State."

"Could be worse," I said. "The Chrysler is still there. Maybe they're art critics, and they'll leave the good ones."

"I thought of that," Harry said. "Sort of, anyway. I thought when they first started that maybe it was all some cockeyed conceptual-art project, like when they wrapped that island in plastic, y'know what I mean?"

I nodded. "It's a thought," I agreed.

"That can't be it, though; they'd never get the city to go along this far. One building, maybe two, but not this."

I put down the menu as the waitress came along.

Harry ordered the Reuben; I got a club sandwich.

"What I want to know," Harry said as the waitress stomped away, "is who's going to clean up the mess? The souvenir-hunters will get bored eventually, and you can bet that the garbagemen aren't going to do it. Against union rules, probably. The city'll have to hire a demolition crew to break up the bigger pieces and haul everything away. And do you think the city can pay for something like that? Of course not! And you can bet that the damn feds won't want to help—not in New York."

I nodded. "You're right. That stuff'll probably be lying around for months, maybe years, all over the city."

"Damn right," he said.

We didn't talk much after that, just ate, then ran. I had to get back to the office.

Outside the saucer had moved on, toward the West Side, and I could see two more in the distance. A pair of fighter planes roared past without doing anything.

My manager met me on the stairs. "Get your stuff cleaned out of that pigsty you call a desk," he said. "We're moving."

I blinked. "What?" I asked.

"Some damn expert came by, says that the saucers will be taking down this building by Thursday or Friday— maybe over the weekend if we're lucky. I've got us a temporary place up on East Fifty-fifth; we'll probably need to move out to the suburbs eventually."

"Oh, jeez," I said.

"Not my fault," he said. "Get with it. The boxes are over by the coffee machine."

I nodded, and he went on past me down the stairs.

I went to my desk and started pulling open drawers.

"Damn," I said as I yanked the lap drawer open and spilled pencils on the carpet. "Stupid aliens. That's New York for you; if it's not one thing it's another. All we need now is for the movers to go on strike."

Lawrence Watt-Evans is the author of fifteen novels and several short stories of science fiction, fan-

tasy, and horror, most recently The Nightmare People *and* The Blood of a Dragon. *He won the Hugo award for short story in 1988 for "Why I Left Harry's All-Night Hamburgers." He has no idea how the story above came about.*

This is Julie Evans' first published fiction. Her first encounter with New York City was a trip to the '64 World's Fair, the youngest of the siblings deemed old enough to go with Dad. The crowded streets, fancy restaurants, and tall buildings left more of an impression than the exhibits at the fair, even Dino Land.

Post Time in Pink

by Mike Resnick
A John Justin Mallory Story

When I started planning this anthology, one of the first questions I considered was whether I would stick strictly to science fiction, or whether I would include outright fantasy. I finally decided not to limit the possibilities any more than necessary, that fantasy stories about New York could work just fine.

One of the things that convinced me was reading Mike Resnick's novel, Stalking the Unicorn, a fantasy detective story set in the other New York.

That being the case, I was delighted when Mike agreed to write a sequel to Stalking the Unicorn for me, a story about a New York where the track at Jamaica is still open—and there are other differences as well.

"So who do you like in the sixth?" asked Mallory as he stuck his feet up on the desk and began browsing through the *Racing Form*.

"I haven't the slightest idea," said Winnifred Carruthers, pushing a wisp of gray hair back from her pudgy face and taking a sip of her tea. She was sitting at a table in the kitchen, browsing through the memoirs of a unicorn hunter and trying not to think about what the two doughnuts she had just eaten would do to her already-ample midriff.

"It's a tough one to call," mused Mallory, staring aimlessly around the magician's apartment that he and Winnifred had converted into their office. Most of the mystic paraphernalia—the magic mirror, the crystal ball, the wands and pentagrams—had been removed. In their place were photos of Joe DiMaggio and Seattle Slew, a pair of *Playboy* centerspreads (on which Winnifred had meticulously drawn undergarments with a Magic Marker), and a team picture of the 1966 Green Bay Packers, which Mallory felt gave the place much more the feel of an office and which Winnifred thought were merely in bad taste. "Jumbo hasn't run since he sat on his trainer last fall, and Tantor ran off the course in his last two races to wallow in the infield pond."

"Don't you have anything better to do?" said Winnifred, trying to hide her irritation. "After all, we formed the Mallory & Carruthers Agency two weeks ago, and we're still waiting for our first client."

"It takes time for word to get out," replied Mallory.

"Then shouldn't we be out spreading the word—after you shave and press your suit, of course?"

Mallory smiled at her. "Detective agencies aren't like cars. You can't advertise a sale and wait for customers to come running. Someone has to need us first."

"Then won't you at least stop betting next week's food money on the races?"

"In the absence of a desperate client, this is the only way I know of to raise money."

"But you've had six losing days in a row."

"I'm used to betting on horses in *my* New York," replied Mallory defensively. "Elephants take a while to dope out. Besides, they're running at Jamaica, and they haven't done that in my New York in thirty-five years; I'm still working out the track bias. But," he added, "I'm starting to get the hang of it. Take Twinkle Toes, for instance. Everything I read in the *Form* led me to believe he could outrun Heavyweight at six furlongs."

"But he didn't," noted Winnifred.

"Outrun Heavyweight? He certainly did."

"I thought he lost."

"By a nose." Mallory grimaced. "Now, how the hell was I supposed to know that his nose was two feet shorter than Heavyweight's?" He paused. "It's just a matter of stockpiling information. Next time I'll take that into consideration."

"What I am trying to say is that we can't afford too many more next times," said Winnifred. "And since you're stranded here, in *this* Manhattan, it would behoove you to start trimming your—*our*—expenses."

"It's my only indulgence."

"No, it's not," said Winnifred.

"It's not?" repeated Mallory, puzzled.

"What do you call *that*, if not an indulgence?" said Winnifred, pointing to the very humanlike but definitely feline creature perched atop the refrigerator.

Mallory shrugged. "The office cat."

"This office can't afford a cat—at least, not this one. She's been drinking almost a gallon of milk a day, and the last time I went out shopping she phoned the local fishmonger and ordered a whale."

"Felina," said Mallory, "is that true?"

The catlike creature shook her head.

"Are you saying you didn't order it?" demanded Winnifred.

"They couldn't fit it through the doorway," answered Felina, leaping lightly to the floor, walking over to Mallory, and rubbing her hip against his shoulder. "So it doesn't count."

"You see?" said Winnifred, shrugging hopelessly. "She's quite beyond redemption."

"This city's got nine million people in it," replied Mallory. "Only two of them didn't desert me when I went up against the Grundy two weeks ago. You're one of them; she's the other. She stays."

Winnifred sighed and went back to sipping her tea, while Felina hopped onto the desk and curled her remarkably humanlike body around Mallory's feet, purring contentedly.

"Do you like the Grundy?" asked Felina after a moment's silence.

"How can one like the most evil demon on the East Coast?" replied Mallory. "Of course," he added thoughtfully, "he makes a lot more sense than most of the people I've met here, but that's a different matter."

"Too bad," purred Felina.

"What's too bad?"

"It's too bad you don't like the Grundy."

"Why?" asked Mallory suspiciously.

"Because he's on his way here."

"How do you know?"

Felina smiled a very catlike smile. "Cat people know things that humans can only guess at."

"I don't suppose you know what he wants?" continued Mallory.

Felina nodded her head. "You."

Mallory was about to reply when a strange being suddenly materialized in the middle of the room. He was tall, a few inches over six feet, with two prominent horns protruding from his hairless head. His eyes were a burning yellow, his nose sharp and aquiline, his teeth white and gleaming, his skin a bright red. His shirt and pants were of crushed velvet, his cloak satin, his collar and cuffs made of the fur of some white polar animal. He wore gleaming black gloves and boots, and he had two mystic rubies suspended from his neck on a golden chain. When he exhaled, small clouds of vapor emanated from his mouth and nostrils.

"We need to talk, John Justin Mallory," said the Grundy, fixing the detective with a baleful glare as Felina arched her back and hissed at him and Winnifred backed away.

"Whatever you're selling, I'm not buying," answered Mallory, not bothering to take his feet off the desk.

"I am selling nothing," said the Grundy. "In fact, I have come as a supplicant."

Mallory frowned. "A supplicant?"

"A client, if you will."

"Why should I accept you as a client?" asked Mallory. "I don't even like you."

"I need a detective," said the Grundy calmly. "It is your function in life to detect."

"I thought it was my function to save people from mad-dog killers like you."

"I kill no dogs," said the Grundy, taking him literally. "Only people."

"Well, that makes everything all right, then," said Mallory sardonically.

"Good. Shall we get down to business?"

"You seem to forget that we're mortal enemies, sworn to bring about each other's downfall."

"Oh, that," said the Grundy with a disdainful shrug.

"Yes, that."

"The battle is all but over. I will win in the end."

"What makes you think so?" said Mallory.

"Death always wins in the end," said the demon. "But I have need of you now."

"Well, I sure as hell don't have any need of you."

"Perhaps not—but you have need of this, do you not?" continued the Grundy, reaching into the air and producing a thick wad of bills.

Mallory stared at the money for a moment, then sighed. "All right. What's the deal?"

"John Justin!" said Winnifred furiously.

"You just said that we needed money," Mallory pointed out.

"Not *his* money. It's dirty."

"Between the rent, the phone bill, and the grocery bills, we won't have it long enough for any of the dirt to rub off," said Mallory.

"Well, I won't be a party to this," said Winnifred, turning her back and walking out the front door.

"She'll get over it," Mallory said to the Grundy. "She just has this irrational dislike of Evil Incarnate."

"You both misjudge me," said the Grundy. "I told you once: I am a fulcrum, a natural balance point between this world's best and worst tendencies. Where I find order, I create chaos, and where I find chaos—"

"I believe I've heard this song before," said Mallory. "It didn't impress me then, either. Why don't you just tell me why you're here and let it go at that?"

"You have no fear of me whatsoever, do you?" asked the Grundy.

"Let us say that I have a healthy respect for you," replied Mallory. "I've seen you in action, remember?"

"And yet you meet my gaze, and your voice does not quake."

"Why should my voice quake? I know that you didn't come here to kill me. If you had wanted to do that, you could have done it from your castle . . . so let's get down to business."

The Grundy glanced at Mallory's desk. "I see that you are a student of the *Racing Form*. That's very good."

"It is?"

The demon nodded. "I have come to you with a serious problem."

"It involves the *Racing Form*?"

"It involves Ahmed of Marsabit."

"Doesn't he run a belly-dance joint over on Ninth Avenue?"

"He is an elephant, John Justin Mallory," said the Grundy sternly. "More to the point, he was *my* elephant until I sold him last week."

"Okay, he was your elephant until you sold him," said Mallory. "So what?"

"I sold him for two thousand dollars."

"That isn't much of a price," noted Mallory.

"He wasn't much of an elephant. He had lost all sixteen of his races while carrying my colors." The Grundy paused. "Three days ago he broke a track record and won by the entire length of the homestretch."

"Even horses improve from time to time."

"Not that much," answered the Grundy harshly, the vapor from his nostrils turning a bright blue. "I own the favorite for the upcoming Quatermaine Cup. I have just found out that Ahmed's new owner has entered him in the race." He paused, and his eyes glowed like hot coals. "Mallory, I tell you that Ahmed is incapable of the kind of performance I saw three days ago. His owner must be running a ringer—a look-alike."

"Don't they have some kind of identification system, like the lip tattoos on race horses?" asked Mallory.

"Each racing elephant is tattooed behind the left ear."

"What's Ahmed's ID number?"

"Eight-three-one," said the Grundy. He paused. "I want you to expose this fraud before the race is run."

"You're the guy with all the magical powers," said Mallory. "Why don't you do it yourself?"

"My magic only works against other magic," explained the Grundy. "For a crime that was committed according to natural law, I need a detective who is forced to conform to natural law."

"Come on," said Mallory. "I've seen you wipe out hundreds of natural-law-abiding citizens who never did you any harm. Were they all practicing magic?"

"No," admitted the Grundy. "But they were under the protection of my Opponent, and he operates outside the boundaries of natural law."

"But the guy who bought Ahmed isn't protected by anyone?"

"No."

"Why don't you just kill him and the elephant and be done with it?"

"I may yet do so," said the Grundy. "But first I must know exactly what has happened, or sometime in the future it may happen again."

"All right," said Mallory. "What's the name of the guy who bought Ahmed from you?"

"Khan," said the Grundy.

"Genghis?" guessed Mallory.

"Genghis F. X. Khan, to be exact."

"He must be quite a bastard, if your Opponent doesn't feel compelled to protect him from you."

"Enough talk," said the Grundy impatiently. "John Justin Mallory, will you accept my commission?"

"Probably," said Mallory. He paused. "For anyone else, the firm of Mallory and Carruthers charges two hundred dollars a day. For you, it's a thousand."

"You are pressing your luck, Mallory," said the Grundy ominously.

"And you're pressing yours," shot back Mallory. "I was the only person in this Manhattan that could find your damned unicorn after he was stolen from you, and I'm the only one who can find out what happened to your elephant."

"What makes you so sure of that?"

"The fact that you're sure of it," replied Mallory with a confident grin. "We hate each other's guts, remember? You wouldn't have swallowed your pride and come to me unless you'd tried every other means of discovering what really happened first."

The Grundy nodded his approval. "I chose the right man. Sooner or later I shall kill you, slowly and painfully, but for the moment we shall be allies."

"Not a chance," Mallory contradicted him. "For the moment we're employer and employee . . . and one of my conditions for remaining your employee is a nonrefundable down payment of five thousand dollars." He paused. "Another is your promise not to harass my partner while I'm working." He smiled. "She doesn't know you like I do. You scare the hell out of her."

"Winnifred Carruthers is a fat old woman with a bleak past and a bleaker future. What is she to you?"

"She's my friend."

The demon snorted his contempt.

"I haven't got so many friends that I can let you go

around terrifying them," continued Mallory. "Have we got a deal?"

The Grundy stood stock-still for a moment, then nodded. "We have a deal."

"Good. Put the money on my desk before you leave."

But the Grundy had anticipated him, and Mallory found that he was speaking to empty air. He reached across the desk, counted out the bills (which he noted without surprise, came to exactly five thousand dollars), and placed them in his pocket, while Felina stared at some spot that only she could see and watched the Grundy complete his leave-taking.

Mallory stood before the grandstand at Jamaica, watching a dozen elephants lumber through their morning workouts and trying to stifle yet another yawn, while all manner of men and vaguely humanoid creatures that had been confined to his nightmares only fifteen days ago went about their morning's chores. The track itself was on the outskirts of the city of Jamaica, which, like this particular Manhattan, was a hodgepodge of skyscrapers, Gothic castles, and odd little stores on winding streets that seemed to have no beginning and no end.

"What the hell am I doing here at five in the morning?" he muttered.

"Watching elephants run in a circle," said Felina helpfully.

"Why is it always animals?" continued Mallory, feeling his mortality as the cold morning air bit through his rumpled suit. "First a unicorn, then an elephant. Why can't it be something that keeps normal hours, like a bank robber?"

"Because the Grundy owns all the banks, and nobody would dare to rob him," answered Felina, avidly watching a small bird that circled overhead as it prepared to land on the rail just in front of the grandstand. Finally it perched about fifteen feet away, and Felina uttered an inhuman shriek and leapt nimbly toward it. The bird took flight, barely escaping her outstretched claws, but one of the elephants, startled by the sound, turned to pinpoint the source of the commotion, failed to keep a straight course, and broke through the outer rail on the clubhouse turn. His rider went flying through the air, finally landing in the branches of a small tree, while the huge pachyderm continued lumbering through the parking lot, banging into an occasional Tucker or DeLorean.

"Bringing you along may not have been the brightest idea I ever had," said Mallory, futilely attempting to pull her off her perch atop the rail.

"But I like it here," purred Felina, rubbing her shoulder against his. "There are so many pretty birds here. Fat pretty birds. Fat juicy pretty birds. Fat tasty juicy pretty—"

"Enough," said Mallory.

"You never let me have any fun," pouted Felina.

"Our definitions of 'fun' vary considerably," said Mallory. He shrugged. "Oh, well, I suppose I'd better get to work." He stared at her. "I don't suppose I can leave you here and expect you to stay out of trouble?"

She grinned happily. "Of course you can, John Justin," she replied, her pupils becoming mere vertical slits.

Mallory sighed. "I didn't think so. All right, come on."

She jumped lightly to the ground and fell into step behind him, leaping over any concrete squares that bore the contractor's insignia. They walked around the track and soon reached the backstretch, more than half a mile from where they had started.

Mallory's nose told him where the barns were. The smell of elephants reached him long before he heard the contented gurgling of their stomachs. Finally he reached the stable area, a stretch of huge concrete barns with tall ceilings and a steady flow of goblins and gnomes scurrying to and fro with hay-filled wheelbarrows.

He approached the first of the barns, walked up to a man who seemed quite human, and tapped him on the shoulder.

"Yes?" said the man, turning to him, and suddenly Mallory became aware of the fact that the man had three eyes.

"Can you tell me where to find Ahmed?"

"You're in the wrong place, pal. I think he's a place-kicker for the Chicago Fire."

"He's an elephant."

"He is?" said the man, surprised.

Mallory nodded. "Yes."

"You're absolutely sure of that?"

Mallory nodded.

The man frowned. "Now, why do you suppose the Fire would want an elephant on their team?"

"Beats the hell out of me," conceded Mallory. He decided to try a different approach. "I'm also looking for the barn where Genghis F. X. Khan stables his racing elephants."

"Well, friend, you just found it."

"You work for Khan?"

"Yep."

"Then how come you don't know who Ahmed is?"

"Hey, pal, my job is just to keep 'em cleaned and fed. I let the trainer worry about which is which."

"What's your name?"

"Jake. But everybody calls me Four-Eyes."

"Four-Eyes?" repeated Mallory.

The man nodded. " 'Cause I wear glasses."

"Well, I suppose it makes as much sense as anything else in this damned world." Mallory turned and looked down the shed row. "Where can I find Khan?"

"See that big guy standing by the backstretch rail, with the stopwatch in his hand?" said Four-Eyes, gesturing toward an enormous man clad in brilliantly colored silks and satins and wearing a purple turban. "That's him. He's timing workouts."

"Shouldn't he be standing at the finish line?"

"His watch only goes up to sixty seconds, so he times 'em up to the middle of the backstretch, and then his trainer times 'em the rest of the way home."

"Seems like a lot of wasted effort to me," said Mallory.

"Yeah? Why?"

"Because each time the second hand passes sixty, he just has to add a minute to the final time."

All three of Four-Eyes' eyes opened wide in amazement. "Son of a bitch!" he exclaimed. "I never thought of that!"

"Apparently no one else did, either," said Mallory caustically.

"Look, buddy," said Four-Eyes defensively, "math ain't my specialty. You wanna talk elephant shit, I can talk it with the best of 'em."

"No offense intended," said Mallory. He turned to Felina. "Let's go," he said, leading her toward the backstretch rail. Once there, he waited until Khan had finished timing one of his elephants and then tapped the huge man on the shoulder.

"Yes?" demanded Khan, turning to him. "What do you want?"

"Excuse me, sir," said Mallory. "But I wonder if you'd mind answering some questions."

"I keep telling you reporters, Jackie Onassis and I are just good friends."

Mallory smiled. "Not that kind of question."

"Oh?" said Khan, frowning. "Well, let me state for the record that all three of them told me they were eighteen, and I don't know where the dead chicken came from. I was just an innocent bystander."

"Can we talk about elephants, sir?"

Khan wrinkled his nose. "Disgusting, foul-smelling animals." He stared distastefully at Felina. "Almost as annoying as cat people." Felina sniffed once and made a production of turning her back to him. "The smartest elephant I ever owned didn't have the intelligence of a potted plant."

"Then why do you own them?"

"My good man, everyone knows that Genghis F. X. Khan is a sportsman." The hint of a smile crossed his thick lips. "Besides, if I didn't spend all this money on elephants, I'd just have to give it to the government."

"Makes sense to me," agreed Mallory.

"Is that all you wanted to know?"

"As a matter of fact, it isn't," said Mallory. "I'm not a reporter, sir; I'm a detective—and I'd like to know a little bit about Ahmed of Marsabit."

"Hah!" said Khan. "You're working for the Grundy, aren't you?"

"Yes, I am."

"He finally sells a good one by mistake, and now he's trying to prove that I cheated him out of it."

"He hasn't made any accusations."

"He doesn't have to. I know the way his mind works." Khan glared at Mallory. "The only thing you have to know about Ahmed is that I'm going to win the Quatemaine Cup with him."

"I understand that he was a pretty mediocre runner before you bought him."

"Mediocre is an understatement."

"You must have a very good eye for an elephant," suggested Mallory, "to be able to spot his potential."

"To tell you the absolute truth, I wouldn't know one from another," replied Khan. "Though Ahmed does stand out like a sore thumb around the barn."

"If you can't tell one from another, how can he stand out?"

"His color."

"His color?" repeated Mallory, puzzled.

"Didn't you know? One of the restrictions on the Quatermaine Cup is that pink is the only permitted color."

"Ahmed is a pink elephant?"

"Certainly."

Mallory shrugged. "Well, I've heard of white elephants in a somewhat different context . . . so why not pink?"

"They make the best racers," added Khan.

"Let me ask you a question," said Mallory. "If you don't know one elephant from another, and you don't trust the Grundy to begin with, why did you buy Ahmed?"

"I needed the tax writeoff."

"You mean you purposely bought an elephant you thought couldn't run worth a damn?"

Khan nodded. "And if it wasn't for the fun I'm going to have beating the Grundy's entry in the Cup, I'd be very annoyed with him. If Ahmed wins this weekend, I may actually have to dip into capital to pay my taxes."

"Aren't you afraid the Grundy might be a little upset with you if Ahmed beats his elephant?" asked Mallory.

"I've done nothing wrong," said Khan confidently. "The pure of heart have nothing to fear from demons."

"That's not the way I heard it."

"It's not the way I heard it either," admitted Khan. "But I've also sent off a two-million-dollar donation to my local church, and if that doesn't buy me a little holy protection, I'm going to have some very harsh words to say to God's attorneys." He paused. "Perhaps you'd like to take a look at Ahmed now?"

"Very much," responded Mallory. He turned to Felina. "You wait here."

Felina purred and grinned.

"I mean it," said Mallory. "I don't want you to move from this spot. I'll just be a couple of minutes."

"Yes, John Justin," she promised.

"Come along," said Khan as he began walking back to the barn. When they arrived, Khan whistled and a number of trunks suddenly protruded from the darkened stalls, each one begging for peanuts or some other tidbit. One of the trunks was pink, and Mallory walked over to it.

"This is Ahmed?" he asked, gesturing toward the huge pink elephant munching contentedly on a mouthful of straw.

"Impressive, isn't he?" said Khan. "As elephants go, that is."

"Do you mind if I pet him?" asked Mallory.

Khan shrugged. "As you wish."

Mallory approached Ahmed gingerly. When the long pink trunk snaked out to identify him, he held it gently in one hand and stroked it with the other, then pulled a handkerchief out of his pocket and rubbed the trunk vigorously. No color came off. Then he checked the tattoo on the back of the animal's left ear: it was Number 831.

Suddenly there was a loud commotion coming from the direction of the track, and a moment later Four-Eyes came running into the barn.

"Hey, buddy!" he said, panting heavily. "You'd better do something about your friend."

"What's she done this time?" asked Mallory.

"Come see for yourself."

Four-Eyes headed back to the track, Mallory and Khan hot on his heels.

The scene that greeted them resembled a riot. Elephants were trumpeting and racing all over the track, while their riders lay sprawled in the dirt. Four of the pachyderms, including a pink one, had broken through the rail and were decimating foreign cars in the parking lot. Track officials were running the length of the homestretch, waving their hands and shouting at Felina, who seemed to be flying a few feet off the ground, just ahead of them.

"What the hell's going on?" demanded Mallory.

"You know how they use a rabbit to make the greyhounds run faster at the dog tracks?" said Four-Eyes. "Well, we use a mouse at the elephant tracks. And instead of the dogs chasing the rabbit, the mouse chases the elephants." He paused for breath. "We don't use it in workouts, but the officials always give it one test run around the track before the afternoon races, just to make sure it's in good working order. Your catgirl pounced on it when it passed by here, and her weight must have fouled up the mechanism, because it's going twice as fast as usual. Panicked every elephant on the track."

Mallory watched as Felina and the mouse hit the clubhouse turn four lengths ahead of the track officials, who soon ran out of breath and slowed down to a walk. The detective stepped under the rail and stood waiting for the catgirl, hands on hips, as she entered the backstretch. As the mouse neared him, Felina gathered herself and sprang high in the air, coming to rest in Mallory's hastily outstretched arms.

"It wasn't real," she pouted.

"I thought I told you to stay where you were," he said severely, setting her down on her feet.

"They cheated," muttered Felina, glaring balefully at the artificial mouse as it continued circling the track.

Mallory looked down the stretch and saw the furious but exhausted officials slowly approaching him. Taking Felina firmly by the hand, he ran to the rail and ducked under it.

"Come on," he said, racing to the barn area. "The last thing I need is to get barred from the grounds because of you."

They zigged and zagged in among the buildings, finally ducked into an empty stall, and stood motionless for a few moments until the track officials lost their enthusiasm for the hunt and began slowly returning to the clubhouse.

"Well?" said a voice at his side.

Mallory turned and found himself facing the Grundy. "Well what?"

"What have you accomplished for my money thus far, besides causing a small riot?"

"It's early in the day yet," said Mallory defensively.

"You didn't seriously think Khan painted one of his elephants to look like Ahmed, or that I failed to check the tattoo number before hiring you, did you?"

"No. But I felt I ought to check, just to be on the safe side."

"It was a total waste of time."

"Perhaps, but if you don't tell me these things, I have to find them out for myself," replied Mallory. "Is there anything else I should know?"

"Only that I expect results," said the Grundy. "And soon."

"Stop looking over my shoulder and you just might get 'em."

"I have every right to see how my money is being spent."

"That wasn't part of the contract," said Mallory. "I'll let you know when the case is solved. In the meantime, if you pop up again or interfere with me in any way, the deal's off and I'm keeping the retainer. I'm not an actor, and I don't want an audience."

"All right," said the demon after a moment's consideration. "We'll try it your way for the time being."

"I'd thank you, but I don't recall wording that as a request."

"Just remember, Mallory," said the Grundy, "that my patience is not unlimited."

And then he was gone.

"Thanks for warning me that he was about to pay me a visit," said Mallory to Felina.

"They cheated," growled Felina with a single-minded intensity that Mallory had rarely encountered in her before.

"They're not the only ones," said Mallory. He grabbed her hand and began leading her down the shed row. "Let's take a little walk."

He asked a stable girl with scaly green skin and a sullen expression to point out which barn housed the Grundy's stable of elephants, then walked over to it.

Four tweed-clad leprechauns suddenly barred his way.

"No trespassers," said the nearest of them with a malicious smirk.

"I'm working for your boss," replied Mallory.

"And I'm the Sultan of Swat," came the answer.

"I'm telling you the truth," said Mallory. "Check it out."

"Sure," said another one sarcastically. "The worst enemy the Grundy has, and we're supposed to believe you're working for him."

"Believe anything you want, but I'm going into that barn."

"Not a chance, Mallory," said the first leprechaun. "I'll fight to the death to keep you out."

"Fine by me," said Mallory. He turned to Felina, who was eyeing the leprechauns eagerly. "I knew you'd prove useful sooner or later. Felina, fight him to the death."

"Just a minute," said the leprechaun. "I meant I'd fight you to *his* death." He pointed to one of his companions.

"Okay," said Mallory. "Felina, fight this other one."

"No!" screeched the leprechaun. "I mean, I'd love to fight your cat to the death, really and truly I would, but I strained my back last week and my doctor told me that I couldn't have any more duels to the death 'til a month after Christmas." He pointed to a companion. "How about him? He's a real fighter, old Jules is."

"Right," chimed in the first leprechaun. "Go get her, Julie. We're behind you one hundred percent."

"What are you talking about?" demanded the second. "I told you: I have a bad back."

"Oh, right," replied the first. "Go get her, Julie. We're behind you almost sixty-seven percent."

"Uh, count me out, guys," said the fourth leprechaun. "I got a tennis appointment at nine."

"You need a doubles partner?" asked Jules, backing away from the slowly advancing catgirl.

"I thought you were fighting her to the death," said the fourth leprechaun.

"Maybe it'll just be a mild case of death," suggested the first one. "Maybe it won't prove fatal. Go get her, Julie!"

The unhappy Jules reached into his pocket and withdrew a wicked-looking knife. Felina merely grinned at him, held out her hand, and displayed four wicked-looking claws, each longer than the knife's blade.

Jules stared at the catgirl's claws for just an instant, then dropped his knife on the ground, yelled, "I gotta go to the bathroom!" and lit out for parts unknown at high speed.

"Can we enter the barn now," asked Mallory, "or is someone else interested in a fight to the death?"

"How about if we play checkers instead?" asked the first leprechaun.

"Or we could cut cards," suggested the fourth. "I happen to have a deck right here in my pocket."

Mallory shook his head. "Felina?"

The catgirl began approaching the remaining leprechauns.

"How about a fight to first blood instead?" suggested the nearest leprechaun.

"You and Felina?" asked Mallory.

"Actually, I was thinking more of *you* and Felina," answered the leprechaun.

"Right," chimed in the second one. "If you draw first blood, you get to go into the barn, and if she draws it, she gets to eat you."

"But you're bigger than her, so you gotta tie one hand behind your back," continued the first leprechaun. "After all, fair is fair."

"In fact," added the fourth, "if you could put it off for twenty or thirty minutes, we could sell tickets and give the winner twenty percent of the take."

"Ten percent!" snapped the first leprechaun. "We've got overhead to consider."

"Split the difference," said the second. "Eleven percent, and let's get this show on the road."

"I'm afraid you guys are missing the point," said Mallory. "If you try to stop us from entering the barn, the only blood that's going to be spilled is leprechaun blood."

"Leprechaun blood?" cried the first one. "That's the most disgusting thought I've ever heard! You have a warped, twisted mind, Mallory."

"Besides, whoever heard of the combatants attacking the spectators?" demanded the second.

"I'm not a combatant," said Mallory.

"Of course you are," insisted the second leprechaun. "I thought it was all settled: you're fighting her."

"Felina," said Mallory, "I'm walking into the barn now. Do whatever you like to anyone that tries to stop me."

Felina grinned and purred.

The first leprechaun turned to his companions. "Are you gonna let him talk to you like that?"

"What do you mean, *us*?" replied the second one, backing away from Felina. "He was looking at you when he said it."

"That's only because I'm so handsome that I just naturally attract the eye. He was definitely addressing you."

"Where's Julie when we need him?" said the fourth. "I'd better go find him." He headed off at a run.

"Wait!" said the second, racing after him. "I'll go with you. Julie wouldn't want to miss the chance to put these interlopers in their place."

"Well?" said Mallory, taking a step toward the one remaining leprechaun.

"The Grundy will kill me if I let anyone in," he said nervously.

"And Felina will kill you if you try to stop me," said Mallory, taking another step. "It's a difficult choice. You'd better consider your options very carefully."

The catgirl licked her lips.

"Well, I don't actually work for the Grundy," said the leprechaun hastily. "I mean, he underpays us and we don't even have a union or anything, to say nothing of sick leave and other fringes." He retreated a step. "Who does that Grundy think he is, anyway?" he continued in outraged tones. "How dare he demand that we stop an honest citizen from admiring his elephants? After all, the public supports racing, doesn't it? And you're part of the public, aren't you? These elephants are as much yours as his. The nerve of that Grundy! You go right on in," he concluded, putting even more distance between himself and Felina. "If the Grundy tries to stop you, I'll fight him to the death."

"That's very considerate of you," said Mallory, walking past the trembling leprechaun and entering the barn. "Felina!"

The catgirl reluctantly fell into step behind him.

Mallory walked down the shed row, peering into each stall. When he came to a stall housing a pink elephant, he entered it, checked the tattoo behind its left ear—the ID number was 384—and then left the stall and carefully closed the door behind him. When he finished checking the remainder of the stalls, he walked back outside and then turned to Felina.

"How many pink ones did you see?"

"One," she replied.

"Good. Then I didn't miss any."

Felina searched the sky for birds, but saw nothing but airplanes and an occasional harpy. "It's cloudy," she noted.

"Yes," said Mallory, "but it's getting clearer every minute."

The catgirl shook her head. "It's going to rain."

"I'm not talking about the weather," answered Mallory.

*   *   *

Mallory dropped Felina off with Winnifred, then paid a visit to Joe the Goniff, his personal bookie.

The Goniff's office was housed in a decrepit apartment building, just far enough from the local police station so that they didn't feel obligated to close him up, and just close enough so that the cops could lay their bets on their lunch breaks.

The Goniff himself looked like something by Lovecraft out of Runyon, a purple-skinned, ill-shapen creature who nonetheless felt compelled to dress the part of his profession, and had somehow, somewhere, found a tailor who had managed to create a plaid suit, black shirt, and metallic silver tie that actually fit his grotesque body. He wore a matching plaid visor and had a pencil tucked behind each of his four ears.

"Hi, John Justin," he hissed in a sibilant voice as Mallory entered the office, which was empty now but would be bustling with activity in another two hours. "Too bad about Twinkle Toes."

"Can't win 'em all," said Mallory with a shrug.

"But you don't seem to win any of 'em," replied Joe the Goniff. "I keep thinking I should give you a discount, like maybe selling you a two-dollar ticket for a buck and a half."

"A bighearted bookie," said Mallory in bemused tones. "Now I *know* I'm not in my Manhattan."

The Goniff chuckled, expelling little puffs of green vapor. "So, John Justin, who do you like today?"

"What's the line on the Quatermaine Cup?"

"Leviathan—that's the Grundy's unbeaten elephant—is the favorite at three-to-five. There's been a lot of play on Ahmed of Marsabit since that last race of his, but you can still get four-to-one on him. Hot Lips is eight-to-one, and I'll give you twenty-to-one on any of the others."

"What was Ahmed before his last race?" asked Mallory.

"Eighty-to-one."

"How much money would it take to bring him down to four-to-one?"

"Oh, I don't know," said the Goniff. "Maybe ten grand."

"Can you do me a couple of favors?"

"I love you like a brother, John Justin," said the Goniff. "There is nothing I wouldn't do for you. Just the thought of helping our city's most famous detective is—"

"How much?" interrupted Mallory wearily.

"I would never charge you for a favor, John Justin," replied the Goniff. "However," he added with a grin, "a thousand-dollar bet could buy my kid a new set of braces—if he ever needs them."

"I didn't know you had a kid."

"I don't, but who knows what the future holds?"

"A thousand dollars?"

"Right."

"Okay," said Mallory, pulling out his wallet and counting out ten of the hundred-dollar bills the Grundy had given him. "Put it all on Ahmed of Marsabit in the Cup."

The Goniff shook his massive head sadly. "Ahmed ran a big race the other day, I know, but you're making a mistake, John Justin. Leviathan's unbeaten and unextended. He's got a lock on the race."

"Put it on Ahmed anyway."

"You got inside information?" asked the Goniff, his eyes suddenly narrowing.

"I thought I was buying inside information from you," answered Mallory. "Remember?"

"Oh, yeah—right. So, what can I do for you?"

"I want to know if anyone made a killing on Ahmed's last race."

"Everyone who bet on him made a killing," replied Joe the Goniff. "He paid better than a hundred-to-one."

"Find out if anyone had more than a hundred dollars on him."

"It may take a day or two," said the Goniff. "I'll have to check with the track and all the O.T.B. offices as well as all the other bookies in town."

"Forget the track and the Off Track Betting offices," said Mallory. "Whoever made the killing wouldn't want to leave a record of it."

"Then what makes you think the bookies will tell you who it was?"

"They won't, but they'll tell you."

"Okay, will do."

"I need to know before they run the cup."

"Right." The Goniff paused. "You said you needed a couple of favors. What's the other one?"

"If someone plunked down a couple of grand on Ahmed when he was still eighty-to-one for the cup, would that be the payoff if he won, or would they get the four-to-one you're offering now?"

"If they came to a regular handbook like myself, they'd get the post time odds."

"How could they get eighty-to-one?"

"They'd have to go to a futures book like Creepy Conrad, over on the corner of Hope and Despair."

"What's a futures book?" asked Mallory.

"You get the odds that are on the board that day, but you're stuck with the bet, even if the odds go up, even if he's scratched, even if the damned elephant breaks a leg and they have to shoot him a month before the race. Usually a futures book will close on a race a couple of months before it's run."

"How many futures books are there in town?"

"Three."

"For my second favor, I want you to get in touch with all three, see if any serious money was placed on Ahmed when he was still more than fifty-to-one, and find out who made the bets."

"Can't do it, John Justin."

"Why not?"

"One of those books is run by my brother-in-law, and we haven't spoken to each other since I caught him cheating at Friday-night poker. I have my pride, you know."

"How much will it take to soothe your pride?" asked Mallory with a sigh.

"Another five hundred ought to do it."

Mallory withdrew five more bills. "Put four hundred ninety-eight on Ahmed, and give me a two-dollar ticket on Leviathan." He paused. "And when you get my information, call Winnifred Carruthers at my office and give it to her."

"You on drugs or something, John Justin?" demanded the Goniff. "I keep telling you Ahmed can't win. You must be snorting nose candy."

"Just do what I said."

"Okay," said the Goniff. "But I got a funny notion that you're a head."

"Not yet," replied Mallory with a sudden burst of confidence. "But I'm catching up."

*   *   *

"Well?" demanded the Grundy.

It was Cup Day at Jamaica, and the grandstand and clubhouse were filled to overflowing. The sun had finally managed to break through the cover of clouds and smog, and although it had rained the previous night, the maintenance crew had managed to dry out the track, upgrading it from "muddy" in the first race to "good" in the third, and finally to "fast" as post time approached for the Quatermaine Cup.

Mallory was sitting in the Grundy's private box in the clubhouse, sipping an Old Peculiar, and enjoying the awe that the spectators seemed to hold for anyone who was willing to remain in such close proximity to the notorious Grundy.

"I told you," said Mallory. "The case is solved."

"But you haven't told me anything else, and I am fast losing my patience with you."

"I'm just waiting for one piece of information."

"Then the case isn't solved and Khan's elephant might win the cup."

"Relax," said Mallory. "All I'm waiting for is the name of the guilty party. I guarantee you that the real Ahmed will be running in the cup."

"You're absolutely sure?" demanded the Grundy.

Mallory withdrew his two-dollar win ticket on Leviathan and held it up for the Grundy to see. "I wouldn't be betting on your entry if I wasn't sure."

The Grundy looked out across the track, where eight pink elephants were walking in front of the stands in the post parade.

"It's time for me to lay my bets," he said. "If you have lied to me, John Justin Mallory . . ."

"As God is my witness, I haven't lied."

"I am considerably more vindictive than God," the Grundy assured him. "You would do well to remember that."

"You'd do well to remember that it's only six minutes to post time, and you haven't gotten your bets down yet," responded Mallory.

"Ahmed is definitely on the track right now?" insisted the Grundy.

"For the fifth time, Ahmed is definitely on the track right now."

"You had better be right," said the Grundy, vanishing.

Suddenly Winnifred Carruthers approached the box.

"I've been wondering what happened to you," said Mallory.

"Your bookie just called the office an hour ago, and traffic was dreadful," she said.

"He gave you a name?"

"Yes," said Winnifred. "I wrote it down." She handed the detective a slip of paper. He looked at it, nodded, and then ripped it into tiny pieces. "By the way," added Winnifred with obvious distaste, "where's your client?"

"Laying his bets," said Mallory.

A sudden murmur ran through the crowd, and Mallory looked up at the tote board. Leviathan had gone down from even money to one-to-five, and the other prices had all shot up. Ahmed of Marsabit was now fifteen-to-one.

"That's it," said Mallory with satisfaction. "All the pieces are in place."

"I hope you know what you're doing, John Justin."

"I hope so too," he said earnestly. He smiled reassuringly at her. "Not to worry. If everything works out the way I have it planned, I'll buy you a new hunting rifle."

"And if it doesn't?"

"We'll worry about that eventuality if and when it comes to pass," said Mallory. He paused. "You'd better be going now. The Grundy is due back any second."

She nodded. "But I'll be standing about thirty rows behind you. If the Grundy tries anything . . ." She opened her purse and Mallory could see a revolver glinting inside it.

"Whatever you do, don't shoot him."

"Why not? I'm a crack shot."

"Yeah, but I have a feeling that shooting him would just annoy him," said Mallory. "Besides, you're not going to need the gun. Believe me, everything is under control."

She looked doubtful, but sighed and began walking up the aisle to her chosen vantage point.

The Grundy reappeared a few seconds later, just as the elephants were being loaded into the oversized starting gate. "Well?" demanded the demon.

"What now?"

"I know she talked to you."

"She's my friend and my partner. She's allowed to talk to me."

"Don't be obtuse," said the Grundy coldly. "Did she give you the information you needed?"

"Yes."

"Let me have it."

"As soon as the race is over."

"Now."

"I guarantee the culprit won't get away," said Mallory. "And telling you his name won't affect the outcome of the race."

"You're sure?"

"I may not like you, but I've never lied to you."

The Grundy stared at him. "That is true," he admitted.

"Good. Now sit down and enjoy the race."

Six elephants were already standing in the gate, and the assistant starters soon loaded the last two. Then a bell rang, the doors sprang open, the electric mouse loomed up on the rail, and eight squealing pink elephants pounded down the homestretch.

"And it's Hot Lips taking the early lead," called the track announcer. "Ahmed of Marsabit is laying second, two lengths off the pace, Beer Belly is third, Leviathan broke sluggishly and has moved up to fourth, Kenya Express is fifth, Dumbo is sixth, Babar is seventh . . ."

"He's never broken badly before," muttered the Grundy. "When I get my hands on that jockey . . ."

"Around the clubhouse turn, and it's still Hot Lips and Ahmed of Marsabit showing the way," said the announcer. "Leviathan is now third, Kenya Express is fourth . . ."

The order remained unchanged as the pink pachyderms raced down the backstretch, their ears flapping wildly as they tried to listen for signs that the mouse was gaining on them. Then, as they were midway around the far turn, Ahmed's jockey went to the whip—a six-foot wooden club with a spike embedded at the end of it—and Ahmed immediately overtook Hot Lips and opened up a three-length lead by the head of the homestretch.

"Now!" cried the Grundy. "Make your move now!"

But Leviathan began losing ground, his huge sides rising and falling as he labored for breath, and a moment later Ahmed crossed the finish line twelve lengths in front. Leviathan came in dead-last, as the lightly-raced Beer Belly caught him in the final fifty yards.

"Mallory!" thundered the Grundy, rising to his feet

and glaring balefully at the detective. "You lied to me! Your life is forfeit!" He reached into the air and withdrew a huge fireball. "Your bones shall melt within your body, your flesh shall be charred beyond all—"

"I told you the truth!" said Mallory, holding up a hand. "Ahmed lost."

The Grundy frowned. "What are you talking about?"

"Leviathan won the race."

"I just saw Ahmed win the Cup."

Mallory shook his head. "You just saw *Leviathan* win the Cup."

"Explain yourself," said the Grundy, still holding his fireball at the ready.

"Leviathan's ID number is 384, and Ahmed's is 831. It didn't take much to change them. Then, when Khan came to pick up Ahmed, someone gave him Leviathan instead."

"Then Khan isn't responsible?"

"He's furious. He needed a loser for tax purposes."

"Then who is responsible for this?" demanded the Grundy.

"Someone who had access to both animals, had the time to work on the tattoos, and bet heavily on Leviathan both times he started in Khan's colors."

"Who?" repeated the Grundy.

"A leprechaun named Jules."

"I've never heard of him."

"That's the problem with having your fingers in too many pies, so to speak," said Mallory. "He works for you."

"At the barn?"

"Yes . . . though he's probably at Creepy Conrad's handbook right now, cashing his ticket."

"I may never have heard of him," said the Grundy, "but he will curse the day he heard of me."

"I never doubted it for a minute," replied Mallory.

The Grundy glared at Mallory. "You did not lie, but you purposely deceived me. I will expect my retainer to be returned and I will not reimburse you for your time. I suspect you made a handsome profit on the race."

"I'll get by okay," answered the detective. "I'll send your money over tomorrow morning."

"See to it that you do," said the Grundy, his fireball

finally vanishing. "And now I must take my leave of you, John Justin Mallory. I have urgent business at Creepy Conrad's."

The Grundy vanished, and Mallory walked over to join Winnifred.

"Is it all over?" she asked.

"It will be, as soon as we pick up my winnings from the Goniff. Then I think I'll treat us to dinner and a night on the town."

"Where shall we eat?" asked Winnifred.

"Anyplace that doesn't serve elephant," replied Mallory. "I've seen quite enough of Ahmed for one day."

"Oh, that poor animal!" said Winnifred. "You don't think the Grundy would . . . ?"

"He hasn't got much use for losers," said Mallory.

"But that's terrible!"

"He's just an elephant."

"We've got to do something, John Justin."

"We've got to collect my money and have dinner."

"We've got to collect your money, yes," said Winnifred. "But forget about dinner. We have more important things to do."

"We have?" asked Mallory resignedly.

"Definitely."

That evening Felina had a new toy. It weighed six tons, and held a very special place in the Guinness Book of World Records for running the slowest mile in the history of Jamaica.

For Mallory's classiest admirer, Barb Delaplace

Mike Resnick is the author of Santiago, Ivory, Paradise, Walpurgis III, *and a number of other well-received science-fiction novels, and won the 1989 Hugo Award for his short story, "Kirinyaga." He was persuaded to bring John Justin Mallory, hero of that "other" New York's* Stalking the Unicorn, *out of retirement by your editor (and lots of money).*

Learning Experience

by Laurence M. Janifer

*Everyone's heard about people who don't want to
get involved. Some people, as in this story, have the
opposite problem.*

He was blind in one eye, and when he walked, his left
hip was filled with ground glass, and as he pulled himself around the corner, he saw them beating the kid.

Typical New York street scene, he thought, summer
1994, and he'd never seen any of the four people before, the two men and a woman who were doing the
beating—fists, hard-soled feet, a short iron pipe that
wasn't getting too much use—or the kid who was trying
to fight back, maybe twelve years old, maybe fourteen,
a blond scarecrow of a boy who landed a looping blow
with a fist now and then, and as he thought and saw,
he was in motion. Typical New York street scene, and
as he pulled one man away from the kid, the man's
face whipped toward him, a real rictus of an ugly
smile, the eyes getting wider, and he hit the face with
his right fist, hard, immense sudden satisfaction, and
the eyes widened a little bit more and stayed there.
He heard the kid make a sound as the woman hit him;
he could see her out of the corner of his good eye,
her tight little fist at the junction of his arm and
shoulder, and the kid shuddered and drew back about
an inch—that arm wasn't going to be working for him
for a few minutes anyhow—and the man he'd hit in

the face was the one with the iron pipe, he didn't realize that until he caught the shine on it an inch over his head and by then it was much too late.

But it would have been too late: he held that thought as he spun away feeling the start of immense pain, this time what would he lose, the other eye or maybe everything all at once, and the kid made another sound and that was the end of it.

And Nurse Ormen was saying, "The wrong choice, you know you made the wrong choice," and she sounded as if she really liked him—maybe she did, how could he tell—and he looked up at her face and hands as she detached the wires, and at the white ceiling beyond. "You'll have to try again, you know this is something you have to learn," and he nodded his head very carefully as the wires came loose, because after all she was right. And it might not have been too late, they kept telling him it might not have been too late.

He didn't feel like talking but he said very quietly, "The blond kid. Mistake. Too much. Reflex action."

"Too much, yes, but you'll have to try again, you know that," and she touched his cheek with one hand, the wires were all free, she touched him very softly, and it might have been a smile on her face, impossible to tell, an expression of sympathy at least, of feeling-with, perhaps she really did like him. Knew how he felt.

And that was all for that day, and he relaxed, played checkers, walked in the dayroom, played checkers again, ate the hospital food which was not very bad, and slept wondering whether building service was taking care of his chess set; he couldn't bring a chess set into the hospital, not chess, not the Battle Game. When he'd made his adjustment he'd be able to play again, back with friends in his apartment. And he did want to make the adjustment, he knew they were right. Only reflex action was too strong, too strong for him, so far.

The woman was screaming for help, and when he moved, his hip was filled with ground glass and he only had one eye to see out of, but she kept screaming and when he came around the corner she was struggling with two men, big brutes pinning her down to the sidewalk in not enough light for one eye, just the streetlight overhead, middle of the night and in the buildings a few lights were on, there was nobody at the windows, he was thinking: Fun in New York, Summer 1994, Fun in the Big City, and while he thought he was moving, and he caught the light's reflection off the phone booth out of the good eye, phone booth right there on the corner, and the woman screamed for help, kicking as the smaller brute cuffed her, hard, and he headed for the phone booth taking a deep breath and the bigger man looked up and saw him and the rictus was on his face, the widened eyes shone in the streetlight gleam, his arm shot out and he touched the phone and turned his head to look at it, punched for Emergency and when they came on line (two rings only, as she screamed, as they pinned her down, hitting her, tearing her dress) he reported it all, wasting no words; a voice said, "Be right there," and as the smaller man bent down to hit her again the sirens started and the men jerked, looked at each other, let go of the woman, turned and ran. Out of sight, into the darkness, and she lay gasping on the sidewalk as the sirens came closer.

"Better, much better." It was Doctor Graldener this time, the firm face and hands doing their job, quite removed. Not unfriendly. "You can tell it's better."

"Any day now," he said, and spent the day playing checkers, walking back and forth in the dayroom, wondering when he would be adjusted, trying not to count the minutes, count the hours. They said the treatment would not interfere with dreaming but he never remembered his dreams. When he woke up he was covered with sweat.

"You've lost an eye," Doctor Graldener said. "You've lost partial movement in your left hip. You know this has to stop, don't you?"

"People are supposed to help other people," he said. He was unable to not say that, and it was true, he knew perfectly well it was true, and he knew Doctor Graldener agreed with him, that was the hardest part to understand, but he was beginning to be able to make sense out of it. Really make sense, down where it counted.

"When they can, as they can. You have to have control." Doctor Graldener's face was controlled, the firm lines showed it, the deep lines as if his face had been carved as part of a totem, even the gray-white short hair showed it; and he was right. There was such a word as *reckless*.

"You can't be reckless," he said. "You have to assess the situation."

"Two against one, three against one—there isn't anything you can do. Except become another victim. You know that. Call Emergency. They're waiting. That's what they're for. A phone on every corner, virtually every corner. Call Emergency. Two, three, maybe more against one—nothing else you can do."

There was a lot that could be done, but none of it would help, that was what he meant; and he was right, that was very clear. But it was hard, even when reflex action wasn't so directly involved (because he'd been thin once—he'd been blond though he had gone bald at thirty—he'd been just as helpless, that was how he'd lost an eye and damaged his hip at thirty-seven, thirty-seven wasn't old but two, three, more against one and nobody cared how old you were, you were only one, that was all that counted, and he *knew* that); it was very hard to manage. He nodded and when he saw Doctor Graldener waiting he said, "Of course you're right. Call Emergency. It's the only thing to do."

"You might run into a . . . situation . . . again, you know."

"New York, summer 1994."

"And next year," Doctor Graldener said. "Until there's real control—"

"Like your control," he said, and smiled, but it didn't really feel like a smile and Doctor Graldener only sat waiting as they talked, his carved face still, and then he nodded.

"Some kind of control," he said, not sounding as if there were hope behind the words, and his face gave nothing away. "But you can't be reckless."

"I know," he said, and Doctor Graldener nodded. "You're beginning to."

He could hear them far down the street, someone fighting, someone screaming, and he tried to run but his hip was filled with ground glass, and by the time he could see them clearly out of his one eye they had the boy down, they were kicking him and the boy was jerking every time a kick landed, a man and two women, big, muscular, black-dressed, one of the women laughing, he could hear her high-pitched screech over the noise the boy was making on the ground, and the man kicked him again and then the laughing woman kicked him in the thigh and the boy jerked and tried to roll away and the other woman sent him back with a kick of her own. New York, he thought and he was moving and he turned and saw the phone booth at the corner. Dialed, only one ring this time, it had to be fast or it would be too late; he told them everything and a voice said, "Thanks, be right there," and the sirens started and the man and the women looked down the block fearfully and began to edge away and then they were running, and this was victory, this was triumph, the boy was breathing and he saw the police ambulance slide through traffic and stop, men got out, examining, consulting, they took the boy into the ambulance, this was victory, they'd fix him up all right, all right; he realized he'd forgotten to hang up the phone and there were tears in his eyes when he looked at his hand around it.

"Fifth run," Nurse Olmen said. "Very good. Oh, very good."

And Doctor Graldener, later, that same day, said, "I think we can call that adjustment. I really think we can." And the carved face smiled, he hadn't known that face could smile. And they kept him half a day for tests, half a day for that and signing papers, and he shook hands with them all before he left.

And it wasn't summer any more, but fall, he'd spent a lot of time inside, he'd worked hard, he was adjusted and you couldn't be reckless, you had to assess the situation, what good did another victim do? And he walked home through the cooling air with virtually no worry, feeling the aftertaste of victory, the echo of his triumph.

And he played chess with friends, he took up a life, and very soon, while he was still thirty-seven, it was New York, 1994, the beginning of winter.

He was on his way to the local *groceria* when he heard them, somewhere down the block or around the corner, sounds carried oddly. A fight, it was some sort of attack. Late afternoon and growing dark, the streetlights had just gone on and he forgot the groceries and tried to run down the block but his hip was filled with ground glass and when he came to the corner he turned his head and looked down with his good eye: there were two men holding a boy while a third man beat him and the boy was trying to scream but not much sound was coming out any more, so he moved faster ignoring the pain in his hip, thinking New York, thinking New York, as the beating went on, the three men in black windbreakers, the boy in a torn winter coat just as black, the boy with blond hair, his head dropping as the beating went on, and they let him fall to the sidewalk, he could hear the boy's head hit the sidewalk and he ran past the phone booth on the corner and turned and went back and picked up the phone and dialed Emergency, and in two rings there was an answer and he told them everything, not wasting a word, and a voice said, "We'll be right over, thanks, right over," and he remembered to hang up the phone and stood watching as they started to kick the boy. Watching, waiting for the siren, waiting for the siren, waiting for the siren, perhaps a minute, perhaps three minutes but before he heard it they were gone, the boy lay on the sidewalk and the boy wasn't moving, he heard the siren in the distance and he thought, New York, trying to get through the traffic, and watched to see the boy move, but the blond boy never moved, when the police ambulance stopped at last he went closer and could see that the boy was not breathing, only a minute or two minutes, no recklessness, fully in control, yes, and he sat down on the curb and watched them pick up the unmoving boy, sheet over him now, sheet altogether over him, and they left with the blond boy unmoving still and he sat on the curb with his good eye shut. Feeling nothing, not any longer.

Assessing the situation.

Mr. Janifer was born in New York, and still lives there. He has been outside the city limits exactly once in the last six years, and hopes never to do that again. If he can make it here, he can probably make it anywhere, but he sees no reason to bother.

Ties

by Martha Soukup

*I first encountered Martha Soukup when I saw her
on stage in a science-fiction play in Chicago. Then I
began to come across her stories in assorted magazines and anthologies. I've run into her at SF conventions scattered across the country. She's turned
up on several of the computer nets I use. Sometimes
it seems as if she's everywhere, as if I can't get away
from her.*

*The characters in this story, which I think is one of
her best, would sympathize.*

Alex glanced up at the lobby clock. "Five-thirty-five," he
said, hoping he sounded casual. Family members leaned
against walls, looked at level indicators as though timing
the next elevator, trying not to stand out from the crowd
of workers streaming out into Manhattan's rush-hour chaos.

Sarah was half an hour late. It had never happened
before.

"They close the building at six-fifteen," Abe muttered
beside him. Abe did electrical maintenance in the Steinhardt
Building; it had been a mess when his boss tried to switch
him to nights. Building management couldn't know there
were considerations more important than Abe's paycheck.

Like finding Sarah.

"Okay, she's twenty minutes late," Alex said, just loud
enough for the rest of the family to hear. "But she's in
the building." José and Letty nodded. A group bonded
with the Ramirez device, the tiny bit of plastic and cir-
cuitry buried beneath the skin of their necks, knew too
well when a member strayed. But Miriam frowned, staring out the building's glass front. "Or near it, at least.
We'd better split up."

He stopped and thought. Why am I always the one who has to take charge? "Miriam, take the women's rooms. Look under the stall doors." Sarah might be sick. If any of them would hide like a wounded animal, she'd be the one. "Abe, check the shops on the main floor. José, take the east stairs." Since Miriam had José working out, he was almost back to the shape he'd been in before his elbow was crushed in a high-school football game.

"Kathy." The dark young woman looked down at him from where she sat, defying attention, beside a potted plant high on a chrome ledge. "Take the west stairwell. You can ride to the top and work down."

Kathy snorted and jumped from the five-foot ledge, landing on the balls of her feet. "I'll walk up," she said. "I'm as tough as any ex-jock." She vanished around the corner of the elevator bank.

Alex watched her go, frowning, and turned to the teenager. "Frog, go outside. Don't push the pain threshold. Just look around the nearby shops without letting it get too bad."

Frog nodded quietly. He never complained about anything.

"What about me?" Letty asked, pushing a lock of white hair behind her ear.

"You stay here. With any luck, she'll show up of her own accord. Make sure she stays until we're all back." Almost five-forty. "We'll meet by the newsstand at sixten." Though it would be hard to make that look inconspicuous. "I'll sweep the halls on every floor."

"Good luck," said Miriam, and smiled at him. He smiled back, and held it as she gave José a quick kiss and whispered in his ear. The couple, newly bonded, was the best thing about the family. Alex worked to remember that.

Alex rode the elevator up, stopping at each floor with his hand on the DOOR OPEN button. "Sarah? Sarah, honey, are you here?" Nothing but the stares of office workers straggling home. "My little girl. Supposed to meet me with my wife, and wandered off."

Then he jabbed the DOOR CLOSE button before anyone could ask why, if he'd really lost a child, he wasn't frantically describing her to everyone he saw. But how could he explain a frantic need to find a shy, plain twenty-two-year-old woman?

He reached the top and started down, getting out on each floor and walking around each band of hall.

"Sarah! It's okay, it's Alex."

The building echoed. His neck and head weren't throbbing, but the Ramirez device could tell him only that she wasn't too far away, nor was the rest of the group. He hoped they were handling themselves well. If they were caught behaving oddly, they would have to explain themselves. It was fine for other people undergoing experimental therapies to blare it out on talk shows and in tabloids, but he depended on the group's shaky privacy. The treatment was hard enough without the glare of public attention.

By the eleventh floor, he had decided to check the lobby to see if she'd turned up. He rounded the corner.

Kathy was holding Sarah.

Alex stopped, disconcerted. Kathy, a parolee who was the only family member not voluntarily fitted with the Ramirez device, had rebuffed every friendly advance he'd made—as far as he knew, that anyone had. He'd never seen her touch another person. Sarah sobbed into Kathy's shoulder.

He felt clumsy, unnecessary. He turned to go. His crepe-soled shoe squealed on the linoleum floor.

"Come here." Kathy stared at him—not so much invitation as challenge.

Alex cleared his throat. "We should, um, we should go back down to the lobby."

"Sure thing, boss. You've saved the day again."

He winced, held out his hand to help them up. Kathy ignored it. She spoke softly to Sarah, who lurched to her feet, rubbing her eyes. Kathy took Sarah by the hand and led her past Alex, not looking at him.

He followed them wordlessly into the elevator.

All through the subway ride home, Kathy stood glaring next to Sarah. Either it worked or no passenger cared to take the empty seat next to a woman with a tear-streaked face. Miriam and José found a seat together and sat holding hands on a patch of purple graffiti fading from the new chemical treatments. Alex stood beside Frog. He had no conversation and the teenager seemed content with silence. This is the group I want to force myself to become close to, Alex thought. Sure.

The train rattled through the tunnel to Brooklyn.

Home was the Hotel Lincoln, two tiny furnished apartments with a connecting door—an arrangement shared by several large groups in the building, which accepted anyone with two month's security deposit.

Kathy went straight to the bathroom. Water ran. The rest of them would have to use the toilet in the other apartment for an hour or more.

Letty hurried into a kitchenette and busied herself boiling water. In a few minutes she handed Sarah a chipped mug of hot chocolate. "Drink this down," she ordered. "No feeling sorry for yourself now." Sarah accepted it mutely.

Miriam drew Alex aside. "Kathy found her?" He nodded. She snorted. "Guess she's good for something, after all."

Alex didn't know how to object to her tone. Maybe he was just reading his own discomfort into her words. "We're all good for something," he said.

She pinched his cheek. "Like you're our very own problem-solver."

José came up, his reconstructed right elbow bending slowly but smoothly as he put his arm around her.

Like José's the guy who keeps you warm. Not that there was any reason to be bitter. After all, José needed her support more. When Dr. Rye had assembled the family, José wouldn't use the arm in front of people. Miriam was really bringing him out of his shell.

Solve your problems by learning to live with others, said the promotional material his therapist had shown him. You help them, they help you. It sounded great.

Alex couldn't wait for it to start working that way.

"What do we want on television?" he asked.

"News."

"Boring. Turn on the game show."

"The *Life and Loves of Gorbachev* miniseries starts tonight."

"You can't expect us to watch that tripe, Miriam."

Mediating the usual argument was better than moping.

* * *

Tuesday was the family's scheduled discussion night. As usual, the only thing accomplished was the addition of several pages to Dr. Rye's notebook. The psychiatrist shoved his pencil into his electric sharpener and over the whir asked, "So, Letty, getting out of the apartment on a regular basis these days?"

"No," said Kathy. "She stays home and writhes in pain while the rest of us go out to work."

Frog smiled.

Dr. Rye tutted. "Kathy, it's good you're contributing to the dialogue, but it's Letty's turn now. And you might consider restraining your comments to the positive."

"I never did stop leaving my house," Letty said.

"But you'd had several panic attacks outside, symptomatic of early agoraphobia. Have you had any more since starting the program?"

"No, Doctor."

"Good. Anything else, people?"

Kathy made a show of keeping her mouth shut, pressing her lips whitely together. Alex felt like a squirming third-grader waiting for the school bell.

"All right," said Dr. Rye after half a minute's silence. "We'll meet again in two weeks. I wish you'd try opening up and talking more in these sessions." He rose, plucking his jacket from the back of a kitchen chair.

Frog dropped his attentive air and pulled a comic book from a paper sack.

"Doctor," Abe said. Dr. Rye turned. Abe rubbed the back of one thick-veined hand. "Doctor, we're all shoved together all the time. All the damn time. It's not a game anymore. Sometimes we just don't have anything to say."

"Sometimes we all feel like that. Keep working from there," Dr. Rye said.

"The only thing I can think to do is apply to get the stupid Ramirez thing removed."

"The lucky bastards who can," muttered Kathy.

"Eight more months, Kathy. After which you can choose to go back to prison, if you like."

Kathy snorted. She turned her head to look at Miriam and José, sharing the love seat as usual; Sarah clutching her knees in the corner; Frog already absorbed in his comic book; she finally settled with unnerving directness on Alex. *Prison*, she mouthed, and rolled her eyes.

Aloud she said, "If you want easy answers, why not just give us those icepick lobotomies you guys used to be so hot on? They gave my mom's cousin one in '53. She's still just as happy in the institution as she was after they *cured* her."

"I understand your anger, Kathy, but you know the two processes don't compare, in either extremeness or irreversibility. Nor is the Ramirez process nearly as invasive as prison," Dr. Rye said. "It's simply a way to make each of you confront other people.

"Now, people, for next time, why don't you consider this: what makes you all think you're so different from anyone else?"

"Because none of us knows how to connect with other people like everyone else," began Letty, teacher's pet, but Dr. Rye just smiled too brightly and let himself out the door.

"Philosophy," Abe said, shaking his head, as the family split up into all corners of both grimy apartments.

Alex sighed and pulled out the papers he'd brought home to work on. The hell of it was, he'd probably like some of these people if he had the choice, if he weren't too painfully shy to approach them. It certainly was a lot easier to like someone you didn't have to.

Someone you could just walk away from anytime.

Kathy wouldn't tell him why Sarah had run off. "You don't care." She put on the earphones of her cassette player and ostentatiously thumbed the volume all the way up.

Just leave her alone if that's what she wants, Alex thought. Instead, he pulled an earphone down, sitting beside her on the love seat. Miriam and José were already in bed. "I'd like to know."

"Bet you wouldn't." She hit STOP. "Okay, listen. You too, Letty," she added, raising her voice to the kitchenette. "Though the old bag probably already knows you better than you do. Always playing Alex the Hero, right? Mr. Tower of Strength? Everyone knows it's just this game you play because we let you. It's easy for you."

"I'm no tower of strength," he said uncomfortably. "Nobody's making me do anything. I'm asking because I want to help."

"The fuck! The whole reason we're all here is because we're so lousy at doing what other people want. Like Frog's supposed to get cured of running away. His dad beat on him, you know."

"Why hasn't that come up in sessions? It's not like he's the only one."

"Rye doesn't know about it. Frog won't rat on his old man. You better not either, if you want him looking up to you. He's just ignorant enough to." She ticked off family members on her fingers. "Letty, she wasn't tough enough for the rules. Rules say you're not allowed to just stay in your own house if that's what you want. Sarah's parents weren't just lushes, they were nuts, so she ended up thinking all the rules mean she gets punished. Abe let his wife handle everything for him, and he's useless without her. José lost his nerve when he wasn't a jock superstar anymore. Miriam . . ." She smiled harshly. "She's too puny a fish to make a splash in the big world. So here in this damn prison, everyone *has* to notice her."

"I don't think you're being fair—"

"The fuck I'm not!"

"So," Alex began carefully. His chest was clenched with the tightness he always felt when he felt someone was actually looking at him. This was the longest conversation he had ever had with Kathy. Every word led him further into uncharted, dangerous territory. He was certain she hated him. "So what do you think is my problem with the world, exactly?"

She smiled sweetly. "You're afraid if you drop that big front, everyone will see what a pathetic little self-centered asshole you are."

Alex let out a painful breath. "Well, if that's what you think, I suppose—"

"Jesus God, would you give it a rest!" Kathy shouted, storming up. The earphones caught on her neck and slipped and the cassette player fell to the floor with a clatter. "*You* play by these piss-ass social rules. You do whatever Rye wants. Not me! Eight months and I'm safe in prison, and nobody can make me do anything else!"

He stared after her, stunned, as the bathroom door slammed.

"Just ignore her when she acts up," Letty advised

primly from over her soapsuds. "She's only a foulmouthed
little thief."

"Arsonist," he corrected her numbly.

And she's right, no wonder she hates me, she's found
me out.

Alex sat at his desk trying to ignore his usual headache, staring down the aisle of cubicles through the grimy
window. He worked on the thirtieth floor, the rest of the
family ranging down to Letty in the cigar shop in the
building's lobby. The distance did not exceed the Ramirez
device's limit; the pain was psychological, he knew. Still,
he went through a bottle of aspirin every month.

Manhattan ranged down and around him from the
window, thousands of windows he could see, millions he
couldn't, strangers behind all of them. Traffic crawled far
below, and he could hear, faintly, the intense conversation
of taxicabs as horns sounded back and forth at one another.

He'd deliberately come here when he graduated from
his small community college upstate. He'd reasoned that
in the biggest city in America, he would be forced to learn
to deal with other people. Instead, he had learned that
when people turn into crowds, they are more anonymous,
harder to touch than ever, and his life was more isolated
than when he was tossed from home to home as a child.

Finally he heard rumors of the Ramirez experiment.

"Hey," said José, poking his head around the canvas
cubicle wall.

"José! What are you doing here?"

"Looking for someone to pay for lunch," José said,
smiling.

That was a first. "I guess I can finish this up later," said
Alex, saving the spreadsheet on his monitor screen. "How
did you ever get past Evil Elsie at the reception desk?"

"Talent. Poise. Sophisticated Latin charm." José
shrugged modestly.

"I see," said Alex, impressed.

"I waited until she sneezed and made an end run
around her."

Alex laughed. He did like José. "I've got a meeting in
thirty minutes, but we should be able to get in and out of
the coffee shop."

"Great. Miriam is waiting out by the elevators."

"On the other hand, I should go over these figures again before the meeting," Alex said quickly. "Just in case."

José looked disappointed, but Alex knew he'd rather be alone with Miriam anyway. She'd probably set him up to this. *Keeping me on the back burner? Thanks, but no thanks, Miriam.*

"Whatever you say, *compadre*. See you after work." Alex grunted. José ducked back into the maze of cubicles.

Alex left his cursor blinking and pulled out the psychological survey Dr. Rye had left the night before. *Do you ever feel alone?* He marked "Yes." *Do you resent the intrusion of others? Are most people manipulative? Do you wish you had more friends? Do you need more time for yourself? Do you need more close time with your friends? Is a man his own best friend? Do you wish you could help humanity? Is a person's first obligation to himself?*

Halfway through the survey he realized he had blacked in the "Yes" box to every question.

He was dreaming of too many brothers and sisters crowded into the rec room, thirty or forty children he didn't recognize. The heat and noise were overwhelming. When he tried to leave, a dark little girl with scornful eyes laughed at him and said their parents would kill him if he ran away. He wrenched the door open and stepped out into a pit, and the farther he fell, the fiercer the pain in his head became. . . .

Waking, he was disoriented by the continuity of spiteful, unhappy wrangling around him.

"I don't see why we can't go. I've been asking for three weeks. José would like to go too, wouldn't you, hon?"

"Sure."

"I have been to the zoo quite enough, thank you," said Letty's voice. "Seven years teaching kindergarten. Let me tell you, I have not set a foot in that place for twenty years."

"Well, you're not the only one here. The rest of us have rights too."

"Some of us don't want to go hopping all over the place, Miriam." Abe's voice. "After a workweek, what's wrong with staying home and watching a little baseball? Yankees are playing the A's. They're only a game back. View's better on TV than it is in the stadium anyway."

"Oh, God, sports."

"What's wrong with sports, Miriam?"

"They messed you up pretty good, didn't they?"

Silence. Alex forced his eyes open. Everyone but Frog sat, still, around the dining table.

"All right, Miriam," José said finally. Not changing expression, he rose and went through the connecting door into the other apartment.

"Oh, shit," said Miriam. "Shit." She got up and ran after José. The door shut behind her.

Letty sighed heavily. "It seems foul language is contagious."

"Fuck, no," said Kathy, who sat on the bunk below Alex. She giggled, an odd sound from her. He lowered himself to the floor. She stopped. "Well, Mr. Perfect. Sleep in once and everything goes to hell, huh?" Her sweet smile mocked him.

The connecting door opened. Frog came into the room, shutting it again. "Good place not to be right now." He went to the television and turned it to a bowling show, volume off.

"What exactly do you want me to do?" Alex asked Kathy. "Try to help, or ignore everyone like you do?" People had rules. He could figure them all out, even Kathy's. His parents' death and all the foster homes had obscured those rules; he was off to a late start learning them, but now that he could fix these people in place with the Ramirez device, they couldn't stop him from figuring them out.

"I don't want a damn thing from—"

The phone rang. Frog looked up, saw Abe was more absorbed in the bowling than he was, and reached past the older man to pick it up. "Yeah, okay," he said after a moment. He hung up and went back to watching television.

Alex waited. "Well?" he asked finally.

"Oh. Rye. He's coming over to take Letty out."

"What?" said Alex.

"What?" Letty said simultaneously.

"Why? What's going on?" Alex asked. Letty stared, then sat down suddenly on a cracked kitchen chair.

Frog shrugged. "Dunno. Said it's no further benefit." He turned back to the screen.

"I'll have to pack," Letty said dazedly, not moving.

"No," whispered Kathy.

"I should get all my things together—is my suitcase still in the closet?—where are they going to send me now? What's going to happen to me?" Sarah crossed the room and pulled a chair beside Letty. She sat silently watching her. Letty looked at Alex with childlike expectancy.

"I don't know." What answers did he have for a woman old enough to have taught his mother kindergarten? The rules had changed again.

"So," Abe said from the television corner. "The program's no use, I always said so."

"No," said Kathy again. She squeezed her eyes shut.

"Maybe I'll have Dr. Rye sign me out too, right? Shouldn't be a problem getting him to okay it. I had a fine life—little lonely, sure, but better than this."

"I have that new nightgown now, and the raincoat. I wonder if it will all fit? Is my suitcase there, do you know?"

"Though there's only a few months left to my contract. Those psychiatrists probably wouldn't refund any of my money if I left early. Everyone always tries to get a little more out of you."

"No!" Kathy screamed. She snatched up a table lamp and smashed it against the wall. Light flared as the bulb shattered. She ran to the front door, wrenched it open, and fled down the hall.

Alex started after her.

"Perhaps I should throw out the old nightgown," Letty murmured. "Would that make enough room, do you think?"

Alex turned. Letty had not moved, had not even turned to disapprove of Kathy's outburst. Sarah held her hand wordlessly. He didn't know if he should stay watching her or go after Kathy. Well, if she gets half a block from the building, we'll all know it, he thought, bracing himself for the pain if she did. Maybe she'll calm down if she's left alone.

The pain did not hit and Letty did not move. Alex watched her, trying to ignore the low, passionate sounds drifting from the other room, where Miriam and José still were.

It was a relief when Dr. Rye knocked.

The psychiatrist carried Letty's suitcase, which Sarah packed, to the door. "We're taking agoraphobics out of the Ramirez program," he said. "Instead of becoming more flexible, less fearful of strange situations, they're staying just as inflexible within the new parameters." Letty nodded dreamily. "We'll put you back on traditional treatment, though it might be helpful to the rest of the group if you continue to attend the biweekly sessions for a month or so."

"Whatever you say, Doctor."

"One more thing before we leave, Letty," said Dr. Rye.

He pulled out a small device that looked to Alex like a glue gun. He touched it to the back of Letty's neck, pulling the trigger. "Now it's neutralized. We'll remove the transceiver later."

Kathy was standing in the doorway. She stared at the neutralizer.

"Dr. Rye," Alex shouted.

The psychiatrist ducked as Kathy jumped him. She fell hard to the floor, then reached up and grabbed his wrist, trying to free the gun. When his grip held, she forced his hand with the gun in it to her neck. Alex dove at her and pulled her hand back, prying her fingers away. Frog reached her other side, helped hold her down.

"Goddammit," Kathy shouted, tears on her cheeks.

"What's going on?" Miriam asked, tying the sash of her velour robe. José, in shorts, entered the room behind her.

Alex exclaimed as Kathy suddenly bit his hand. He twisted her arm hard behind her back and looked up at Miriam. "Oh, Letty's just leaving us now," he said, hearing with surprise the bitterness in his voice. "Do you care?"

"But what—of course I care! What's wrong with Letty?"

"Dr. Rye says the program's done everything it can for me," Letty said in her odd pleasant voice.

"Why, that's wonderful!" Miriam looked at the room around her, Alex and Frog holding Kathy down, Abe slouched on the couch ignoring the scene, Sarah staring at them from beside the psychiatrist. "Isn't it?"

"Sure," Alex said. He released Kathy. She didn't try to get up. "Just peachy."

"Well, I'm sure I don't know what I said." Miriam paused, then went to Letty and held out her hand. "Good luck, Letty. Keep in touch." Letty stared at Miriam's hand for a moment, then accepted it.

"In view of events," said Dr. Rye, "I think we should schedule our next session for this coming Thursday. Is that all right with everyone?" Alex nodded. "Good. I'll see you then. Letty?"

Letty let go of Miriam's hand and followed the psychiatrist down the hall.

Alex watched them turn the corner, turned around, and saw Sarah lead Kathy into the other apartment. He heard the bolt thrown.

"I guess this means we aren't going to the zoo," Miriam said.

The day was gray, quiet, long. After Sarah came out of the other room, Kathy locked herself in the bathroom. The others sat watching the silent television progress from bowling to golf to stock-car races, reread the newspaper, laid out solitaire games.

As dusk was settling, José got up and began his daily exercise routine, attaching weights to his ankles and jumping rope: the floor groaned and creaked and dishes rattled in the cabinets. When Abe glared at him, José stopped, removed the weights, and sat down.

"Do you think they'll send someone to replace her?" Miriam asked, breaking the silence.

Various family shrugged and shook their heads. Alex looked down.

"What difference does it make?" Abe said. "Haven't they as good as admitted the whole program is garbage?"

"That's not true," Alex protested. "They just said it wasn't right for Letty's problems."

But he wondered if Abe was right and Letty's departure was a harbinger of failure. The Ramirez program had made no obvious improvements in his life, either; it had given him continuity with the same group of people, but no help in figuring out what they wanted from him. Still, he wanted to believe he could learn not to be afraid of people. Anything this hard had to work.

When it was dark, Kathy came out of the bathroom and turned the radio on to a station only she liked.

Normally this would have meant another fight, but Alex was too drained to tell her to turn it down. She turned the volume up another quarter-twist. Abe started to say something, grunted, and looked back at the set.

Kathy looked around and hit the volume one more time. Alex couldn't think of anything to say, didn't feel like shouting to be heard. She made an odd sound he could barely hear over the pounding bass, shook her head sharply, and shut the radio off. Silence: as loud as the music had been. Kathy jumped into the bottom bunk, which was not her bed, and jerked the covers up to her chin, staring at the slats above her.

The evening was better. They ordered pizza and Kathy got up and behaved almost pleasantly, even cleaning up afterward by herself. Letty would have nodded in exaggerated approval.

Alex beat Miriam at Scrabble and took José three games out of four. A round of bridge was more even, Frog and Abe edging out Alex and Miriam while José kept score. Afterward they all agreed on a video to rent, a space opera Alex had seen before.

When Alex finished his bedtime crossword, he glanced up and saw that only Kathy was awake, lying on the couch with her knees drawn up, picking at the back of her neck with one hand, not distractedly but with steady, rough jerks, as though she had a cramp. Forget it, he thought. I'm tired of the problems.

He punched his pillow, folded it in two, smoothed his sheet up, and went to sleep.

And woke in hell. His head was lanced in pain. Every muscle screamed. His head felt like it was about to burst apart.

It had never been so bad before.

He knew without looking who it was.

He took two long, knifing breaths, steeled himself, and jumped out of the top bunk—gasping and almost falling headlong as the impact jarred the knotted muscles in his calves. He wanted to collapse to the floor and rock the pain away. He forced himself to look around the room. The sofa was unfolded to Kathy's bed, but Kathy was not in it.

She had run.

On the lower bunk, Sarah was shaking violently, crying out in her sleep. Her sheets were soaked with sweat. Alex stopped to put a hand on her forehead. Sarah's eyes opened. "I'm sorry, honey. I'm going to get her."

"Kathy?" Sarah whispered dazedly. Alex nodded. The movement sent daggers of pain down his neck and spine. "But—but she said she wouldn't—she said she could take it!"

"Well, honey, I guess she couldn't," he said, keeping his voice low and soothing with great effort. He fought an impulse to hold his eyeballs in. It only felt like they were coming out, he told himself. He began his way determinedly toward the door.

"She said she could live with you," Sarah whispered. She rolled against the cold plaster wall, pressing against it as though trying to push herself right into it and out of the pain.

He could feel nausea building: Kathy must be forcing herself even farther away from the rest of the family. He retraced his steps from the door, placing each footstep with care, and went past the bed to the bathroom. He filled a Dixie cup with water—crushing the first cup in his shaking hand, starting again—and took aspirin from the medicine cabinet. He spilled half the water setting the cup on the battered bedside table, beside the aspirin.

The aspirin could do Sarah little good. Only retrieving Kathy would help.

The other four slept in the second apartment. He couldn't take the time to check on them. He had to conserve his strength. He forced all thought of them—Miriam—out of his mind. José was there. Frog was level-headed. They could take care of themselves.

He remembered after he started that it was a cold autumn night, and spent a precious minute going back after his coat.

The nausea built as he made his aching legs limp him down the stairs. One arm rigid, his sweating palm catching on the soft, half-melted varnish of the railing, he walked with his spine rigidly straight, his head up. Each step away from the group was harder than the last, as the Ramirez device's microprocessor calculated group distance: closer to Kathy, but farther from six others.

It must be much worse for Kathy. If she could take it, so could he.

The lobby door stuck and it was an effort pushing it open. Freezing night air stung his skin. He braced himself against the gritty brick wall of the hotel, thinking how very easy it would be to crumple where he stood. He opened his eyes instead, looked around—she was not in sight, it would not hurt so much if she was in sight—and grimly forced himself on.

At the end of the front walk Alex paused. How many buildings in Brooklyn? How many corners to hide behind, alleys to disappear into? Or if she made it to the subway . . . God. The pain wouldn't kill him, just hurt him, hurt him more, but . . . She had to stay in Brooklyn. She couldn't get far. Thousands of hiding spots, right here.

He turned right. It felt unbearably sickening.

Left felt worse. He turned back right.

With every step he had to convince himself to take the next one. The world went red and black around the edge of his vision until he could barely see what was in front of him. He had to turn his head on his screaming neck to look for Kathy. It took a long time. Twice he saw a passerby trying hard not to look back at him.

He counted intersections, because he couldn't read the street signs through the blurred red haze of his vision, and if he got lost . . .

At the fifth intersection his stomach settled. Very slightly, but he could have wept in gratitude. A small dark form huddled by a gutted Plymouth. He almost fainted as relief flooded him, washing away the rigid determination that had carried him that far. Not over yet. Agony shot through his legs as he squatted beside her.

She was clutching herself, cursing, moaning, rocking, crying. She did not seem to notice him. But when he laid a hand on her shoulder, she did not start or look up.

"Stay away," she hissed, and pressed her face hard against her knees.

"Dr. Rye's house is a mile away. If that's where you're going, you'll never make it." She said nothing. "You have to come back."

She shook his hand away and clutched herself harder. "No." Her voice was strained and he could barely hear it.

"Yes."

She looked up, said slowly and very clearly, "Try and make me."

"Honey, you have to."

Her eyes filled with furious tears. "Don't you call me that! Don't fucking *ever* call me that!" Her brows were drawn tightly together, accenting her small dark features. Sweat matted her dark hair to her forehead and ran down her face.

"Okay. Kathy." God, he couldn't keep this up. He'd never make it back even by himself. "However you want it. Just come back with me."

"Right. Can't break Mr. Hero's perfect record. Wrong." The words came out in determined bursts. "I can. Forget it. Asshole."

"I'll carry you back if you won't come by yourself."

She dismissed the bluff with a bitter grimace. They both knew better.

"Can't you see you're hurting yourself?"

"It's not so bad." Harshly. "Hurts less already."

"It hurts less now because I'm here with you. It won't stop hurting until you're back with everybody. You're just hurting yourself, Kathy. Please."

"Not just," Kathy said. "Not. Just. I'm hurting you too. Right?"

"Come back with me."

"So you can get one approving look . . . from your precious princess . . . jock-groupy?" she shouted, raw pain in her voice. "The fuck I will! You don't want me in your life . . . and I sure as hell don't want you in mine!" She pressed her face into the corner formed by dumpster and brick wall. She looked like Sarah when he left her in the apartment. Her muffled voice shook. "Leave me alone!"

"Wait." It was as hard to think through the pain and confusion as it had been to make himself get to Kathy. "Are you . . ." He frowned, blinked. "Are you jealous of Miriam?"

"Goddamn bitch. Why should I?" Muffled, and bitter. "Jealous of her? Jealous of—any of you?" He thought she was crying. Kathy would never cry. "Everyone who fits. Know what you're doing. Smug." Alex stared at her. "You, the most. They all. Listen. To you. And I never. Never. Fit!"

And she was crying full out.

He reached out, pulled his hand back, cautiously, fearfully put it on her shoulder.

Kathy shook.

He couldn't be doing the right thing. She never wanted anything from him, from anyone; she was tough and didn't ache for contact like he did. He pulled her closer and she turned and clutched at him, and for a while he did not notice the artificial Ramirez pain at all, because it was nothing like Kathy's pain, which was so different from his and so exactly like his, after all. Maybe like Sarah's. Like Abe's, like José's, maybe even like Miriam's. She sobbed, and he held her and rocked her and wondered, and finally he stopped wondering and just held her.

Much later, when they had helped each other struggle back to the Hotel Lincoln and the pain was fading to memory, Frog and José were waiting for them in the lobby, the strain in their eyes slowly clearing. Frog took Kathy's arm and José took Alex's, and they all made it up the stairs.

Together.

Martha Soukup lives frantically, and occasionally squeezes out some fiction. Since attending Clarion in 1985 (with Bob Howe, among other talented folk), she's scattered these stories among publications like Asimov's, F&SF, Amazing, Aboriginal, Twilight Zone, and Terry Carr's Universe. She thinks New York City is an interesting idea, in theory, but isn't certain about the practice; she's just moved from Chicago in the opposite direction to San Francisco, where she likes it fine. If she could take the hinge from her shoulder and stop volunteering for things like the Science Fiction Writers of America secretaryship, she might lead a more settled existence. Maybe.

Wild Thing

by Eric Blackburn

This story is Eric Blackburn's response to the "wilding" incident in Central Park. It's a horror story, and the author's second sale.

Enrique fell on his face, busting his nose on the pavement. Behind him the thing was getting closer.

He jumped up and ran again, hearing the footsteps behind him, while warm blood flowed down his face, stained his shirt.

He heard its voice again, although it wasn't speaking.
Your ass is mine, pork chop!

It wasn't fair. He had only been visiting Jeffrey, over on 120th Street, and had stayed too late. His mama was going to beat his ass.

But it looked like Mama wouldn't get the chance.

He turned and climbed the wall into the park, hoping to get away from it. Nobody was out on the streets, which Enrique couldn't figure out. He could hear people talking and laughing, but he couldn't see anyone.

He bounced off a tree, fell against a rock, felt sharp corners tear into his leg and side, hot with pain. Pushing off, he ran again, hearing leaves rustling behind.

He found himself running down the same path that woman had followed, though he wasn't thinking about that now. Behind him on the path he heard IT running after him, a sort of padding sound, with a scratching like claws or long toenails on asphalt.

As he was passing a cluster of rocks, he turned and ducked into it, hoping to hide.

It wasn't fair. He hadn't done anything. Why was it chasing him?

Out on the path the footsteps stopped. Enrique heard

the sound of something sniffing. Was it smelling him? He'd taken a bath. It was coming closer.

He turned and climbed, loose pieces of rock falling below him, clattering against other rock. He heard a low growl and wet his pants.

Halfway up, he stopped, his breath hot in his chest and his heart pounding like he was on speed, and looked down. He saw a shadowed shape, indistinct, prowling back and forth beneath him, turning yellow eyes up to look. Didn't look like a man or a dog, which were the only two animals Enrique had ever seen that were that big. He resumed climbing.

At the top of the rock he stopped again and looked back down at his pursuer, but he couldn't see it. Maybe it had given up, but Enrique doubted it, figuring that it was probably looking for another way up.

After he caught his breath, he turned to leave, planning to make his way down to the other side of the park. He just might make it home alive.

It was right in front of him, eyes inches from his own, reaching out . . .

Gotcha!

He screamed all the way down, bouncing off rock, scraping patches of skin off, until he hit a larger piece and felt the bones in his left shoulder crumble with a pain that was worse than anything Enrique had ever felt.

Then he didn't have any breath left to scream, even when he fell into the bushes at the bottom and a branch poked into his right eye and another into his right kidney. His head hit the ground first and his neck snapped, pain like a white whip across his neck, and he was rolled over and looking up at the thing climbing down the rocks like a spider, yellow eyes shining with glee in the darkness. Then it was beside him, squatting over him and looking down.

Enrique tried to scream, tried to plead, tried to tell it that he was only fifteen, but he couldn't seem to get the breath in to do it. He felt himself smothering while this thing squatted above him, talking in his head.

You're dying . . . You aren't going to breathe again . . . body in the river . . . Let the crabs eat your eyes . . . pull off your balls . . .

nobody going to know . . .

just you and me . . .
forever . . .
It took a while and the pain just got worse.

"That's the third one of the little bastards to die this way," McGuire said, slapping down another folder on Sackett's desk.

Sackett looked at him while he digested the other's words, trying to pick up a train of thought in the middle. After a few seconds, he understood and gave a grim smile.

"DSAF," he said.

"Man, don't let anyone hear you say that," warned Detective McGuire, glancing around the squad room.

"To hell with it, Pat. You know damn well that everyone here feels the same way."

"Yeah, but all we need is for some bleeding heart to come in and hear that. And don't think that they won't know what you mean."

Sackett looked around, turned back, grinned again.

"Did Society a Favor! Screw 'em, Pat. That's one less for the courts to worry about. I don't reckon I'm going to place this case at the top of my list."

"Listen, you Arizona airhead. Maybe you like vigilantes out West, but down in Alabama, us po' black folks came out on the wrong side of that deal too many times." McGuire dropped into the drawl easily.

"Come on, Pat. Ain't no vigilante doin' this. Them last two died from natural causes. One ran in front of a truck and one drowned in the East River."

"Natural causes?"

"In New York, that's natural causes. How did this one die?"

"He fell on some rocks in Central Park."

"There you go."

"He was climbing in the middle of the night. The coroner said that it looked like he had been running; he had some other injuries."

"Okay, let's go look at the quote, scene of the crime, unquote."

They jumped into Sackett's decrepit Mustang and played in the traffic, *vroom, vroom, screech.*

At the park, Detectives Sackett and McGuire climbed

around on the rocks for a while and looked at the place where the body had fallen. And despite Sackett's claim that he wouldn't work too hard on it, both he and McGuire did, driven by curiosity. But they found no sign of any other presence.

Of course.

So they filed their report accordingly and the department caught flack about it from the civilians in that district, who claimed that the police weren't making a real effort. There was news about vigilantes again, and claims that Bernie Goetz had inspired others and that he should be thrown back in jail or executed or something to teach others a lesson.

And they were all wrong.

Tamara was ten.

She was terrified. Walking back from her Aunt Elaine's, she had to cross the covered bridge across Bostic Creek, and she hated doing that.

The bridge was surrounded by willows and chinaberries that cut out a lot of the light and left the bridge a shadowed, eerie place where anything could happen. The boys had always told her about the thing that lurked there.

Now, she believed them.

She always believed them when she came this way.

Ahead of her the bridge was a wall of darkness with only a hint of light on the other side. Softly, carefully, she stepped on it.

Nothing.

One step followed the next, until she found herself halfway through the darkness. Halfway there, halfway to safety.

Click.

She froze, listening, waiting for the sound to repeat itself.

Step.

There was a faint creak as something else stepped on the bridge.

Tamara started to run and then screamed as the sound of insane laughter echoed from the bridge right behind her. In seconds, she was clear of the bridge and in full flight down the road to her house, while the thing on the bridge laughed and then howled in frustration.

When she got home, her mother scolded her for not calling home first. But she wasn't really worried. There wasn't anything here that would really hurt a little girl.

It was a trusting time in a small town in rural North Carolina, in 1964.

Back on the bridge, Tom Kennedy dropped back down in the weeds beside Sondra Blizzard, ready to continue his explorations.

"That was mean, Tom. Shame on you."

"It didn't hurt her none. Anyway, she's too little to be out here alone."

"You scared that poor thang half to death."

But Tom's hands soon had her thinking about other things.

And above them, on the bridge, something watched with bored indifference.

His heart pounding, Timothy crouched in the shadow of the dumpster. Mosquitoes were buzzing about his head and he tried not to swat at them. A curious rat investigated, but suddenly ran squealing farther back into the alley.

I see you, you little shit.

There was the voice again.

Maybe it was trying to make him run. Well, he wasn't going to be fooled by that trick. He'd used it himself on a couple of downtowners just before he and his friends had gone upside their heads.

Wouldn't work on him!

Paper rustled right behind him and the dumpster creaked.

Gotcha!

Timothy broke and ran, out around the corner, back onto the street. Where the hell was everyone? It was a Friday night and nobody on the streets.

Some of that weird Puerto Rican music was coming out of the barrio, so he turned and ran that way, hoping for help. It was two blocks away, and he could make that easy, couldn't he?

What was it, anyway?

He cut and ran down an alley, dodging garbage cans

and other forms only dimly seen in the darkness, his pursuer close behind.

Shit! Timothy could feel it reaching for him.

That's when he tripped and plowed face-first into the ground, feeling his cheekbone break and the skin rip open. Red flashed through his head as blood poured out of his nose and around his eyes. His face hurt, but the back of his head hurt worse, like he'd been hit there with his brother's baseball bat.

He pulled himself to his feet, feeling something rattling around in his mouth, something wet. He'd lost a couple of teeth.

He waited to die.

Nothing.

Except for himself and the garbage, the alley was empty. Something seemed to have scared off Timothy's pursuer.

He looked around, trying to see what it was, but there was nothing else here. No matter, Timothy wasn't going to question his luck. He moved toward the music, wanting only to have lots of people around him right now, any kind of people, just to keep away that thing that had been chasing him.

Now he knew what it was that had killed Rodney and Corn Chip and Enrique. He could tell the others. Except for Ricardo, of course. He didn't like Ricardo and would like to see him killed.

He heard voices in the next alley and looked around to see what was happening. No sense taking chances.

Good thing he'd waited, there was "a deal" going down. Timothy wanted to deal like that, but for now, he was just a wannabe. He sometimes stood lookout for the big guys and picked up some money.

But didn't nobody want to be surprised when "a deal" was being made. There were too many of the wrong kind of surprises that way, and the big guys were apt to shoot first and worry about other things later. Timothy decided to wait.

Boo! It was right behind him.

Timothy screamed and jumped and ran toward the men.

"Shit," screamed one, and started shooting.

"Shit," screamed the other, and started dying.

Unfortunately for Timothy, the shooter wasn't a bad

shot at all, and Timothy took a round high in the chest
before the shooter had established his identity, thus ending a budding career in the distribution business.

The only survivor in the alley bolted, carrying money,
cocaine, and pistol, and considered a career in middle
management instead. Sadly, his own career was cut short
by the competition just a few weeks later during a bid for
a larger market share.

Timothy lay there in the alley, his lungs filling with
blood, his mouth filling with blood, and watched his
pursuer walk over and squat beside him. He wanted to
scream, but he didn't have the breath for it.

*You're not going to live . . . won't find your body . . .
going to choke on your own blood . . . I'm going to cut
you up, put you in the garbage . . . Rats will eat you . . .
forever . . .*

There was a lot more, and as darkness closed in (not
comforting at all, not the least restful), Timothy thought
about the woman.

"Natural causes," chortled Sackett.

"He walked into a drug deal," McGuire yelled. "The
deal went sour and he got plugged."

"And in New York, that counts as natural causes."

"C'mon, man. The kid was a lookout for some of
Hartsel's guys. He knew better. Besides, forensics says
he fell real hard and busted his face *before* he was shot.
Someone was chasing the kid."

Sackett sighed, climbed to his feet.

"All right, let's go ask questions."

But nobody had seen anything.

Tamara was thirty-two.

She was elated. The divorce was final, and she was
free. After years of living with a lying, cheating, boozing,
useless son-of-a-bitch husband, she was free.

She'd taken courses at the community college and had
gotten her degree. An offer had come back from a firm
in New York City (!) and she was ready to go, to be free
of this little hick town and its ever-so-helpful citizens.

She'd listened to them for years, telling her to give him
one more chance, to try to work it out, to trust in the
Lord. She'd listened for so long that her brain had nearly

ossified, until a visiting friend had helped her see the light. She stretched, remembering the previous night.

So that was what it was supposed to be like.

She smiled in recollection.

She would leave in two days, leave this nosy, corrupt little town behind her forever.

Lionel jumped across the hood of a car beneath a burned-out streetlight (but they were all burned out) and hooked a sharp right down Second Avenue. The streets were empty, as they had been when the others died, and he was alone with what was chasing him.

Gonna pack your ass with a crowbar, boy!

His mama had told him that his daddy had killed a man for calling him "boy." He was certain that Daddy had never had anything like this chase him.

He cut the corner at 108th Street too hard and didn't see the bottle where his right foot was coming down. Wasn't this the way it happened on teevee?

But when someone fell on the teevee, it made Lionel laugh.

He went flying and hit the fire hydrant hard, feeling something snap and a burning pain in his right shoulder. He got back up, fell against a car, ran again.

That hurt, boy? Gonna hurt more!

His vision blurred with tears of pain and fear, keeping him from seeing clearly. Something was wrong with his right arm; it wouldn't lift all the way, and something was grinding between his shoulder and his neck.

He rounded the corner onto First, ran holding his right arm to keep it from moving, looked for cars and saw only parked ones. The streets were still empty.

A sob escaped his throat, terror and shame fighting for dominance. Was this the way to survive? You never showed fear, never showed weakness, or the others would jump all over you.

He turned right onto 106th and nearly collided with two figures standing on the sidewalk. He found himself flying backward through the air, hit the sidewalk hard, felt the ends of his shattered clavicle grind and push against skin. He screamed.

"So, what's this?"

"Look like a boy runnin' from de police."

Shit, it was two women. Lionel looked for his pursuer, saw nothing. He got to his feet, shaking.

One of them was that strange white woman that lived around here. She was a sweet little piece, and Lionel had been thinking about paying her a visit some night, him and a few others. She lived alone.

The other one was Fat Julie, who ran the *bodega* over on 110th Street, some kind of a crazy voodoo woman. Her shop was full of strange things that made Lionel nervous when he was in there. He went there only when his mama sent him to get something.

"He's running from something, all right."

"He be hurt. You get in a fight, boy?"

Lionel could barely understand the woman, her voice thick with the rhythms of Haiti. No matter, he was safe here. For some reason, the thing wouldn't come after him unless he was alone.

"You get on home, boy. Shouldn't be out dis late."

Lionel shook his head.

Fat Julie looked at the other woman.

"Okay, Julie, you take care of it. I'd probably strangle the little shit anyway."

She turned and walked across the street. Lionel watched her go, a fine piece, yeah.

"You tink you do someting, boy? Dat girl, she feed you your balls."

Lionel clutched his groin reflexively.

"You come wit' me."

Lionel followed her back to the *bodega*, where she looked at his shoulder, shook her head.

"Someone mess you up good."

"Something try to kill me."

"Oh, you talk now, huh? What you mean, 'someting'?"

"It be big. It talk to me. It say it kill me."

"Oh?" Julie watched him for a long time, her eyes catching the light of the single lamp and holding it prisoner.

Lionel looked around, saw statues of people he didn't know, plastic bottles with labels like LOVE POTION and MAGIC WATER, candles of different colors, with instructions on them. He didn't like this place at night.

"What it say to you, boy?"

Lionel told her about what the thing had said, had

promised to do, how it had chased him for five blocks,
how it had told what it had done to the others.

"Ha. You one of dem boys go 'wilding,' huh?"

Lionel shrugged.

"Yeah."

"You beat dat girl in de park?"

"Yeah. It was fun."

Fat Julie's eyes flared and Lionel shrank back in his
seat, realizing how threatening this woman looked.

"Fun. It be fun? Yeah, maybe someting have fun wit'
you, huh?"

Lionel stared at her, his mouth open, seeing the chase
again. Was the thing going to do that to him? But that
was different.

Julie glared at him. "I should let it get you, boy."

Lionel looked at her again. Could she help him? He
knew she did magic, his mama told him she did. "Can
you stop it?"

Julie considered the question for a few moments. Lionel's mother had been a good customer, and was a good
woman. Although her son was a worthless shit, it would
break her heart if anything were to happen to him.

The symptoms sounded familiar. The boy's actions had
offended someone, and that someone had placed a curse.
Julie had seen this sort of curse before, and knew what it
entailed.

"You listen good, boy, you listen what I say."

She hesitated. She risked offending whoever had placed
the curse, and she was taking the risk for a piece of
human garbage, she knew. Still, the boy's mother . . .

She decided.

"What chasing you be in you' mind. It can no' hurt you
'less you let it. You run from it, you get hurt. You die.
You stand up, it go away. You hear dat, boy?"

Lionel nodded.

"Now, you go home. You make me sick."

Lionel went. His shoulder hurt, and he would have to
go to the hospital, but he made it home alive, so Fat Julie
must have been right. Nothing chased him.

Tamara was thirty-four.

She was terrified. The gang of teenagers had cornered

her in Central Park, by the rocks, after chasing her for half a mile.

She had been in New York for a year and a half and had thought herself adjusted. The people were rude and aloof, but not hostile. She could handle herself on the street just by showing the right attitude.

But something had gone wrong here. The children, no more than sixteen at the oldest, were acting possessed, like a pack of animals.

One of them hit her with a rock and she put up her hands to shield her face.

"Leave me alone! Why are you doing this?"

One of the teenagers hit her with a board and she fell against a rock outcropping. Then the others were on her, hitting her and tearing away her clothes, and then the real pain began.

"Yo, Sackett, check this out."

Sackett looked up from a stack of reports that kept growing taller. He looked at the report McGuire was handing him. It was a hospital report.

"Well, now. It looks like one of the little turds survived. How did he say it happened?"

"He said some white guys chased him and beat him up."

"How does it sound to you?"

"No way, Sackett. He's lying. His story has too many holes."

"You've already talked to him?"

"Yeah. Some of us don't sleep all day, Mister Laid-back Cowboy."

"I had reason."

"Yeah? What was her name?"

"Shelly, but never mind. What else you got?"

"I think somebody chased him, but he's hiding something. I don't know what."

"Well, let's keep an eye on him."

"What's this? You're finally showing interest in this case?"

"Yeah. I'd hate to miss a good one. I want to see how this one dies."

"You're sick, Sackett, really sick."

*   *   *

Lionel looked at the disbelieving faces gathered around him.

"You talkin' shit," was Theodore's contribution to the matter at hand.

The others, except for Ricardo, expressed similar views, in approximately the same fashion. James, Kwame, Abdallah, Michael, and Aldo took their leave, telling Timothy not to listen to fat old women. Abdallah, Michael, and Aldo were discussing the habits of the short woman over on 106th Street and trying to figure a pattern. James and Kwame were discussing their new roles in the distribution business. Ricardo, however, had grown up in Puerto Rico and knew something of the ways of magic. If a *bocor* had placed a curse on them, he was damn well going to protect himself.

Ricardo went to his mother, who knew a little herself. His mother went to a friend of hers up on 109th Street. The friend killed a chicken in a quaint fashion and did a few other things to help her achieve the proper results, and gave Ricardo a bag to wear. She told him not to remove it. Ever.

Kwame climbed, his eyes fixed on the edge of the roof above him, his heart ready to burst from his chest. Below him, he could hear IT climbing, almost as fast as he was.

I'll cut your balls off, turd.

Kwame didn't care what Lionel had said, he wasn't going to let that thing catch him.

Shit, it was big!

Running across the roof, he screamed as a hole opened beneath him, rotten material giving way almost eagerly. He fell, pieces of wood gouging out small chunks of flesh, the burned-out building suddenly a trap as laughter echoed cruelly in his head.

The rest of his abbreviated life was characterized by a series of falls and sharp bumps, while bones broke and things poked into him.

You're a stupid little turd, you know that?

As the darkness closed in, Kwame remembered Lionel's words, and if he hadn't been so conditioned against taking responsibility, he would probably have admitted that IT was right.

* * *

Tamara was thirty-four.

She was lying in a bed in St. Vincent's, comatose, while the doctors waited for her to die. The extent of the physical trauma was so great that nobody expected her to make it.

It would probably be better if she didn't.

And the guys who had done it were still running around free, enjoying their notoriety and their juvenile status.

There just wasn't any justice.

The doctors never saw the figure that sat by her sometimes in the night, with horns that brushed the ceiling and a curious look of compassion in eyes that would otherwise be terrifying. After all, IT was very good at not being seen.

"What the hell was he doing in that building, anyway?" Sackett asked.

"I wonder if we should do anything to protect them," said McGuire.

"Shoot them," Sackett replied. "For their own good."

"Will you get serious?"

"I am serious."

Michael got trapped in some construction, and was buried under a pile of suddenly unstable building materials.

"He's good," McGuire said.

"How does he do it?" wondered Sackett.

Aldo went down an open manhole and managed to grab hold of an uninsulated wire at just the wrong moment. Nobody knew why the insulation had been removed or why the wire was live. Aldo was beyond caring.

McGuire and Sackett followed James, their third day of doing so. His teachers said he was an excellent student, and they couldn't understand why he had ever been involved in such a horrible incident.

But somehow, James managed to climb up on some scaffolding and wrap some rope around his neck. The fall wasn't enough to break his neck, and he strangled to death.

The two detectives considered a vacation in Florida.

* * *

Abdallah and Theodore listened to Lionel again. It took many repetitions, but they finally got a description of the thing and what Fat Julie had said.

Which is why, when they ran into IT, three nights later, together, they were able to meet it with a certain amount of confidence.

Going to rip your heads off.

Abdallah looked at Theodore, who looked at Abdallah.

"You don't be killin' us," said Abdallah.

"Fuck you, man," was Theodore's well-considered challenge.

IT slowly approached them, eyes gleaming yellow in the night, horns spread above its head like the antlers of a deer.

Kill you. Drink your blood. Stretch your guts down the sidewalk.

"You be talkin' shit," Abdallah replied.

"Fuck you, man."

It came closer, slowing, stopped, stared down at them.

You don't run.

"We know about you. You just a curse."

"Fuck you, man."

You know?

"Ol' witch lady tell us."

"Fuck you sister, man." Theodore was becoming creative.

IT sighed, and its claws, like scythes, flashed crimson in the light of a streetlamp as they sliced open Theodore just below the rib cage. IT reached in and grabbed a handful while Abdallah stared in shock. Theodore's mouth was just beginning to open for a scream.

IT filled Theodore's mouth with what IT had in its hand, and grabbed Abdallah with the other. With sorrow-filled eyes, IT regarded him, dangling and pleading.

Dumb, dumb, dumb, dumb, dumb.

IT casually broke open Abdallah's head on the wall while IT watched Theodore die. Then IT played mix-'n'-match with the parts for a while.

McGuire and Sackett were actually relieved to have had one of the crowd die in a manner that could be construed as deliberate murder. But they still weren't any closer to the solution. People were calling for the police to stop the vigilante maniac.

"Okay, no problem. We've got a psychopath. He's invisible, has inhuman strength, and likes to use knives."

"Meat hooks, maybe."

"Yeah, whatever. But we know it's not just a string of accidents."

"Good. Then all we have is an unsolvable string of murders."

Lionel crouched behind the rocks. The connection between this place and what had him cornered wasn't lost. This was where they'd caught the woman. This was where IT had got Enrique.

It was three months since Theodore and Abdallah had been found, and there had been no more murders. The cops had never found out who'd done it, of course. Lionel knew, but he wasn't about to tell them.

He'd thought it had gone. He finally felt safe enough to come out again.

I got that crowbar right here, boy!

IT showed him what it had in its hand, and Timothy screamed again as IT reached for him.

"Stop it."

IT slowly turned and faced the small woman who stood there, towering over her.

My prey.

"Not yet, he isn't."

Lionel stared in amazement. The thing was afraid of this small woman! He grabbed his groin again.

"Who called you?"

A picture appeared in her mind, a face somehow familiar. She reached for the knowledge, stretched . . . Had it.

"The woman in the park. When those kids did their 'wilding.' "

IT nodded, eagerly, reached back to grab Lionel, who was trying to slip away.

"She had no power. She couldn't have called you here."

IT shrugged.

"Who is the witch that called you? Answer me!"

Again, the picture, the same woman.

She frowned, her eyes beginning to glow. Maybe Lio-

nel was imagining it. Yeah, that was it. It was just a
nightmare.

"Shit! You just a bad dream."

IT slapped him, knocked him up against the rock, and
a sharp pain went through his arm, changed to a burning
throb. His arm was broken.

"Leave the boy alone!"

IT folded its arms, glared at her. Impudent female!

"How did she summon you? How did she call you into
being again?"

She got an image of a small girl running across a
bridge, evil laughter following her, a darkness growing
within darkness.

"The fears of a child?"

IT nodded, impatient.

"I see. Her fear gave life to you. And with her mind
like it is now . . ."

IT nodded again.

"Of course, she never knew about you."

IT shook its head.

"So, she couldn't have sent you to kill them."

Shake.

"But you're killing them in revenge for what they did
to her?"

Shake.

"Then, what?"

Gratitude. Duty.

"You're resuming the ancient custom?"

IT nodded, looked at Lionel, who was inching away,
toward the protection of the witch.

"Oh, I see. Well, that explains it. Good hunting!" And
she turned away.

Wait.

She turned back.

You do not protect this prey?

"Him? Hell, no. I just wanted some answers. Who am
I to stand in the way of karma? Good night."

IT grabbed Lionel and the screams began in earnest.
They went on for a while, and gradually got weaker as he
lost blood. IT howled in satisfaction as it pumped, the
spurs biting deep.

*Eat your soul! Feed your body to snakes! Tear your
eyes . . .*

* * *

Tamara recovered and eventually went back to her job. She's not quite as good as she was, but she manages. She doesn't go jogging in Central Park anymore. A few people suggested prosecuting Tamara for the vigilante activity.

McGuire and Sackett got jobs in the Bahamas doing security work for a resort.

Fat Julie shook her head over her mistake and made her friend dinner, since she had lost the bet. Her friend made a few notes in her Book of Shadows and lent Julie a text on Celtic folklore.

The Hunter sat on the western wall at the Cloisters, night shrouding him from casual view. He looked across the river at New Jersey and took a drag from his Marlboro.

So many new attractions in this new world: Tobacco! Television! Videotapes! Microwave burritos! Of course, the air wasn't fit to be breathed by a Christian priest, much less a god, but he could bear that, along with the foul water. Duty called.

And the prey was so plentiful. He would never run out, and his name, Cernunnos, would once again be feared across the land. By all the gods, it had been too long. Evil was running rampant, foulness spreading like a plague across this land of abundance. Greed would spell the end of this race if he didn't start taking active measures. After tonight's hunt he might start going after some corporate heads, just for variety. He wondered how they would run; these yuppies were supposedly health-conscious.

And tonight.

He sighed, a mixture of anticipation and regret. Tonight's prey was the last of his original target group, the ones who had chased the young woman. An example of undiluted evil whose equal he'd rarely seen. As he recalled, this one was carrying some sort of amulet that was supposed to protect him. Some sort of alien magic. No matter, it was powerless against him.

But he'd been selfish, enjoying the whole thing himself. It was time to share, to run the Wild Hunt as it had been run in the good old days.

"Wilding," they called it. He laughed. He'd show them how it was done.

He summoned his hounds to him and they crowded around, barking joyfully, eyes shining and teeth glinting, eager to be away.

He blew his horn.

Ricardo left his apartment building, heading uptown, noting absently that the streets seemed curiously empty. He patted his bag out of force of long habit, reassuring himself that it was still there, protecting him.

Dimly, in the distance, he could hear a strange sound, sort of like a horn, and a howl.

I live in Pittsburgh, Pennsylvania. In mundane life I'm a computer programmer and work for the government, and for fun I hang out at science-fiction conventions. I got acquainted with New York when my girlfriend used to live there, in Harlem, up around 106th Street. The witch in the story is based on a pagan who lives around that area, sweet and cute as you could imagine. The bodegas are real; I've been in some of them and they're fascinating places. Reminds me of a small shop in Isabel Segunda, Puerto Rico . . .

I wrote this story because I had to. After hearing and reading about the events in New York, I was upset. The casual cruelty displayed in that incident was inexcusable. I wanted to go after the ones who did it. I can't. But what if something could?

—Eric Blackburn

Rise and Fall

by Steve Antczak

New York has been called the new Babylon, Gomorrah on the Hudson. Here Steve Antczak considers the possibility that that description might be more apt than most people realize.

Walking along Broadway Xavier noticed the old man with the sign that read THE END IS NEAR.

He wondered how the old man knew, and smiled—a bit wickedly he thought—to himself.

He would miss New York almost as much as he missed his old hometown, which was to say, not much. Ah, the old hometown, Xavier thought.

He never allowed himself even to think of its real name, but he didn't really like to call it what the poor Spaniards thought it was. He preferred El Perverso, but the name hadn't caught on as well as El Dorado. Even the others, who knew better, called it the City of Gold.

Well, at least they had allowed him to choose a non-Mayan name for himself, and he liked the sound of Xavier. His masters in the old city had not allowed him a name at all.

He turned down Forty-second Street and walked on until he came to an inconspicuous brown door wedged between an adult bookstore and a peep-show arcade. In and up six flights to another brown door, where he knocked, three solid raps, and it was unlocked and opened for him.

Inside were the others.

Tina was a native of New York, and consequently the youngest. Lowena was the eldest, from the place currently known as Atlantis. Sedika of Gomorrah was next, then Lucius of Pompeii, and then Xavier.

After something like five hundred years he thought the older ones still treated him like a baby.

Noticing an odor, he asked, "Is that hazelnut coffee I smell?"

"Yes," Sedika answered. "I'll get you some."

"So, how was your day?" Lucius asked him.

Xavier took off his coat and set it on the back of a chair. "Uneventful," he said, "except for one small act of depravity—or I should say, attempted depravity. I paid five dollars to a teenage girl strung out on heroin for a blowjob. When she got me alone in, well, a compromising position, she suddenly had a straight razor in her hand. She threatened to cut my . . . to cut it off if I didn't give her all my money."

"You were asking for that, you know," Lowena told him. "We're supposed to be a little more subtle about it."

Xavier shrugged.

"I had an amazing thing happen to me today," Lucius said. "I took a cab all the way across town, and—"

"And you made it alive," Xavier cut in sarcastically.

"Yes, but that's not the point. I told the cabbie that I was temporarily on the skids, and asked him if he would take an IOU. He gave me his post-office-box number and said to send him the money when I got back on my feet."

"Okay, so you had one good thing happen to you," Xavier said. "Last week the cops beat the crap out of you just for standing near a protest march."

"Standard NYPD procedure," Sedika said as she came out of the kitchen with the coffee. "Remember the other year? They treated me like a criminal for getting raped."

"That was eleven years ago," Lucius pointed out.

"Who cares when it happened? The point is, it happened, the same year that Tina was slipped PCP in her drink at that art show."

"Can we stop talking about it? Huh?" The edge in Xavier's voice betrayed his anxiousness. "Let's vote. And I would like to say something to everyone before the vote. We've voted four times here, more than anyplace else. First we voted up because we all had a lot of fun, and it was a good time for the city. Then it was down because of Prohibition and organized crime, and then the

Depression seemed to take the place over. But then it was up again, a decision I was very much opposed to, because of the war and then the fifties candy-coated everything that was happening here. Then it was down— the drugs and random violence and corruption seemed to infiltrate into the marrow of New York, with a very few bright spots. I seem to remember that the only really positive things someone brought to bear were that filmmaker, Woody Something-or-other, and the city's first black mayor. I swear this island's beginning to feel like a seesaw, up and down, up and down. Well, now we can end it once and for all. Two consecutive votes decide. If we vote down this time, then this island Manhattan will sink into the abyss it's created for itself." He paused, then finished, "That's all I wanted to say."

Tina jumped up. "I can't believe this," she said. "Don't you see what's happening in this city? Can't you see that the people here are starting to care again? There are more places for homeless people to go for shelter and food in this city than in any other city in the world. Did Rome have that when you voted there?"

"I admit we may have made a mistake with Rome," Lucius said.

"The creative energy in this city is more dynamic than anywhere else," Tina went on. "The people here come up with solutions to the city's problems that are then used by other cities to solve the same problems they get later on. Were the people of any of the other cities, the common people, were they as proud of their cities as New Yorkers are? What about Gomorrah, Sedika? Did Gomorrah produce anything to be proud of? Did Atlantis have a Broadway, a Woody Allen, the Mets? Were poor people from all over the world given a shot at a new life, at making their fortunes, in El Dorado, or were only other rich people allowed? Is New York really like El Dorado, Xavier? Well?" Tina stopped to catch her breath, and concluded, "That's all I have to say."

"We vote, then," Lowena said. "I am the eldest; I vote first. My vote is down."

"What? Why?"

"I must vote the way I feel, Tina, despite rationalizations. I feel a sickness here that must be stopped."

"I, too, vote down," Sedika said.

"Up," said Lucius.

Xavier looked at Tina, at the despair in her eyes, and recalled when they had voted on his native city. Lem of Mu had been the eldest then, a somber man—made so, he said, by knowing he had caused the destruction of so many lives. Lem had been the only one to vote that the city not be swept away by the winds; Xavier had not been moved to make any passionate pleas for his home's survival.

"Up," he suddenly said. He gave Tina a genuine smile, and she returned it. What the hell. He could handle another twenty or so years on a seesaw.

Tina voted. "Up."

Xavier hailed a cab on Eighth and got in.

"Where to?" the driver asked jovially.

"Um, I need to get to the Staten Island Ferry in a hurry," Xavier said. "The problem is, I don't have any cash on me. Would you take an IOU? You could give me an address to—"

"What are you, crazy?" the cabbie cut him off. "Get the hell outta my cab."

As Xavier opened the door, he heard the cabdriver mutter, "Christ, I already did that once today."

Steve Antczak was born in Salem, Massachusetts, but grew up in south Florida. "Rise and Fall" is his first sale. His associations with New York City include an aborted attempt to move there, and an overnight stay in Times Square with practically no money and nowhere else to go. Sort of an After Hours experience, he was followed and chased, spat on, accosted by an AA meeting, run off the sidewalk by two police cars, rained on, and philosophized at by an actor and his dog. He finally spent what little money he had on a ticket to an all-night movie house that was showing Willow, and spent the rest of the night there. Now the mere mention of that movie sends him into violent convulsions.

Shadows on the Moon

by Kristine Kathryn Rusch

They say anything can happen in New York, but I don't think most of the people who say that take it as literally as the folks in this delicate little fantasy.

She leaned out the hotel window and felt the misty air on her face. A symphony of honking horns played to the beating of her heart as the cars below moved like well-lit ants. In the haze of artificial lights and a full moon the city stretched before her, buildings packed against one another like people on a subway.

She glanced back at the hotel room with its king-size bed, chrome lamps, and pale cranberry decor. A maid had come in and turned down the covers, leaving chocolates on the pillow. So tasteful, so refined—a glimpse of a life she had always wanted to have.

The fresh air beckoned. She pushed herself out the window and sat on the ledge. To her left the United Nations glistened, reflecting the city lights on its glass sides. Boats slid along the river. The mist caressed her, made her shiver just a little.

"Come on, Wendy, you can do it," said Peter Pan, her childhood hero, speaking in the voice of Mary Martin, from an album she used to play over and over. *"You can fly if you think you can. All you have to do is believe."*

"Believe," she whispered. She stared out at the night sky, the lights refracted through the mist, and refused to look down. Then she spread her arms and dived. For a minute, she flew.

For a minute, she believed.

Justin refused to let the bellboy carry his bags up to the room. Justin had lugged the clothes bag and duffel across

three airports and in two cabs. He could handle an elevator ride to the fortieth floor all by himself.

He leaned against the mirror in the back of the elevator.
The hotel specialized in mirrors. Instead of paint or wallpaper, someone had decided to cover the wall in reflecting
glass. He had watched himself approach the elevator from
five different angles, all showing his graying hair, his suit
rumpled and travel-worn, and the frown that looked as if
it were baked into his skin.

He closed his eyes on the elevator, not wanting to watch
himself ignore himself for forty floors. When the elevator
eased to a stop, he got out and sighed. Forty was done in a
tasteful, rich cranberry. Black tables and chairs lined the
walls, and large pink and white floral arrangements covered each table. He glanced at the chrome numbers placed
just above eye level on the wall and felt his stomach lurch.
He didn't know what he was doing in New York. He
hated the city, hated the hustle and bustle that allowed for
the rudeness and lack of consideration that had made his
trip from La Guardia so difficult. For a brief half-second,
he thought of turning around, stepping back into the elevators, braving the world of mirrors, and going home.

But if he did that, he wouldn't be able to look at himself
at all.

He clutched the metal computer card that passed for a
key in his right hand and followed the arrows. The room
was in a little cubby all by itself. Instead of another room
beside it, the maid's closet took up the remaining space.
He knocked, the sound echoing in the quiet hallway, and
waited. A man opened a door two down, looked at
Justin, then closed the door again. Justin sighed, slipped
the entry card in the slot, and pushed the door open.

"I said, 'Just a minute.' " Elise took a step out of the
bathroom. She was wearing a robe with the hotel's mono-
gram and a white towel turban hid her hair. Her face was
naked and plain without makeup. She looked surprised to
see him. "Jesus, Justin. Three days late, as usual."

Justin let the door swing closed. He set his luggage
down. The room was wide, with a king-size bed and large
windows on the far wall. He loosened his tie and pulled
off his suitcoat. Humidity from Elise's shower covered
him like beads of sweat. "You said to be here by today. So
I am."

"*Before. Before* today. If we wanted any time together at all. I make my speech tonight, then there are a few social functions, and I fly back to Oxford tomorrow. I doubt that I'll use the room for anything other than changing clothes and packing in the next twelve hours." She kicked the bathroom door closed with one long, narrow foot. He stared at the oak door as an interior buzz signaled a blow-dryer starting up.

He ran a hand through his hair, then picked up his luggage and hung it inside the closet. She had made it clear enough: she wasn't coming back tonight. She had given up on him and found someone else. Or worse, she hadn't found anyone at all.

The blow-dryer shut off. He closed the closet door and sat on the bed. His fingers shook as he punched 0 for the front desk. He asked for a two-day extension on the room, which they gave him, and then he leaned back against the thin mirrored headboard and waited.

Elise emerged from the bathroom a few moments later, bringing more steaming, humid air with her. Her naturally curly dark hair fell about her face in waves, and the carefully applied makeup gave her face the sophisticated beauty he was used to. She took her clothes out of the closet, then pulled off the robe, not caring that she paraded naked in front of him. Her body was as trim as ever.

"I flew all the way from San Francisco," he said quietly, fighting the arousal her movements stirred in him.

"You should have read my letter more carefully, then. I waited here for two days." She slipped on black silk underwear and a matching camisole.

"You could have called."

"Don't put it on me, Justin. I did call, a month ago, and sent a follow-up letter. I always keep copies of my correspondence. The note said 'before.' Your slip was very Freudian. I'm sure you did want to be here, consciously. It was your subconscious that fought you." She pulled on a pair of nylons, then stepped into a black, understated dress that looked both professional and sexy.

"Elise, look. I booked the room for two more days. Stay with me. We'll see if we can fix this."

She turned, her dark eyes cold and flat. "I have to

return to Oxford to finish my appointment. Then I'll be in Washington. Maybe we can work something out there."

He shivered despite the heat in the room, the full extent of his mistake suddenly clear. She had meant the weekend to be a celebration. He had thought the speech would determine whether or not she was appointed as under secretary of state. But apparently, the president had already made the appointment. "I'm sorry. I didn't know. I'm sorry, sweetheart."

He got off the bed and reached for her. She waved him away. "You'll muss my face." She bent over, pulled a badge out of the drawer, and tossed it at him. "This will get you into the UN tonight," she said. "I'll try to be back so that we can have lunch before my flight."

Justin clutched the badge, afraid it would slip through his fingers like the relationship had. "I'd like that," he said.

She nodded, grabbed her purse and cape, and let herself out the door. He reached up, touched the air as if it were her shoulder. "Good luck," he whispered.

A shadow crossed the moon. Justin stopped in front of the delegates' entrance to the United Nations and glanced up. The sky was too hazed over, too filled with artificial lights and fog for him to even see the moon. Yet he remembered the feeling from his childhood in Montana, where the sky was open and free and the moon dominated like a god: the prickle at the back of the neck, the small shiver that ran down the spine.

He shook his head, showed his pass to the guard, and walked along the curved driveway that led to the row of glass doors. He felt no pride walking here. He should have felt pride, with his wife about to speak to an important international assemblage, soon after which her appointment to the Cabinet would be announced.

They had been estranged for nearly a year.

And the president was Republican.

Justin ignored the doors that read DELEGATES' ENTRANCE in several languages and pushed through the revolving door. The interior room was huge, with glass on the left and a curving blond wood wall on the right. Large tapestries hung on the wall, and elevators faced him. Security people lined the carpeted path, keeping the invited guests flowing toward the correct room and guaranteeing that no one had a chance to hide in the building. Justin stopped, let people in ceremonial kimonos, African tribal dress and Western business suits pass him.

He felt lost here. He was a former flower-child turned California computer programmer who had happened to meet, in the San Francisco airport, a woman returning from her Rhodes scholarship studies. They had happened to fall in love and happened to get married, and then realized that their dreams were different. He didn't belong in the United Nations any more than she belonged behind a computer screen.

"May I help you, sir?" one of the guards asked in accented English.

Justin shook his head, taking the hint. He walked along the carpet, gawking at the architecture, realizing that if he ever came here again, he would enter by the tourists' entrance on the other side of the gate. He rode the escalator and stared at the blond wood, the faded royal blue colors, the sculptures and paintings donated by various countries. He was walking in a post–World War II international dream, decorated in the 1950s and tarnished by years of misuse. The building symbolized the dream, but people like his wife—who made speeches to get Cabinet posts, not to promote world peace—multiplied in the corridors like a thousand tiny microbes. Eventually the microbes would eat at the structure and the entire building would crumple, dreams and all.

Like his marriage had crumpled. In the early days, he and Elise used to talk about going to major political functions together. But they had always discussed it as if they would be a team, instead of two individuals. Elise probably remembered that dream, and that was why she tried this last time.

He passed the General Assembly room—the door closed and locked, a guard posted in front—and followed a heavyset man in a dark suit into a smaller corridor. The guards at the end of the corridor stopped everyone and checked badges, sending representatives and their interpreters down one hallway, and guests down another. Justin walked with the guests into a wide gallery high and well back from the delegates below. He took a seat and glanced around for Elise. He finally found her, up front below a large statue of a phoenix holding a world in its claws. Elise was talking with a man Justin had never seen before, laughing, and touching him gently as she used to do with Justin. He shivered, although the room was warm. And remembered something he had ignored in his conversation with Elise. She had said there were social functions afterward. In politics it was *de rigueur* for politicians to bring their spouses to social functions.

Elise hadn't invited him. She had set this up as a test, and he had failed. He leaned back in his chair and stared at his wife touching another man. There wouldn't be a lunch tomorrow. But when Justin returned to California, there would be divorce papers waiting in his mailbox. He wasn't a gambling man, but he would have bet everything he owned on that.

The mist felt cool on his face. Justin sat in front of the open window in his oh-so-expensive hotel room, too shell-shocked and exhausted to move. He wanted to drink himself into oblivion, but even that sounded like too much work.

The speech had been good and well-received, but he hadn't been able to reach Elise afterward. The guards wouldn't let him down to the floor, and despite the message he sent, she never came up to him. So he sat in his hotel room, staring at the lights of the city reflected in the mist, ignoring the UN building off to his right. He would stay here the next two nights, maybe hit a Broadway show, maybe sightsee—do something to justify the expense and the time off. Then he would go home, pick up the divorce papers, and retreat behind his computer screen, where everything was safe and understandable.

He was getting cold. He stood up and slammed the window shut. Then he picked up the room-service menu, thinking he could order himself enough to drink, to wipe that tall, thin, dream-covered building across the street out of his vision.

A magnum of champagne. Yes. A magnum would do quite nicely for a start.

He picked up the phone to order when something tapped against the window. He hung up the phone and turned, a bit spooked, thinking of cords and wires and electrical things, of dangers from an explosion he hadn't heard, a disaster he hadn't anticipated.

He saw a face. A woman's face peering at him through a haze of mist. Her hand reached up slowly, as if she were underwater, and tapped the glass again. He saw her fingernails hit the glass, heard the tiny click—click. For a minute he checked, to see if he had already ordered the champagne and finished it, but he saw no empty bottles and felt too much pain to be drunk.

He was on the fortieth floor.

And probably sound asleep.

He opened the window. The woman grasped the ledge and hauled herself inside. She dripped mist on the cranberry carpet. Water droplets dotted her blond hair and her pale eyelashes, shrouding her clothes in a spiderweb of dew. "I'm sorry," she said. "I thought your window was open."

"I just closed it."

She wiped her forehead with the back of her hand, making some of the drops roll down her cheeks like tears. "It got cold out there."

"I bet."

She blinked then and looked at him, apparently seeing his confusion. "Where am I?"

"The fortieth floor."

"Oh." She sank into one of the chairs and patted her pocket, pulling out an entry card. "I'm on the forty-third, but apparently the maid closed the window. I've been trying to get in for almost a half an hour now. I didn't know if I could land."

Justin nodded, his confusion growing. He didn't expect her to be staying in the hotel. He thought that, if he looked outside, he would see a girder or window-washing equipment. He half-expected to see a rope attached to her waist or rock-climbing equipment hanging from her hips. Perhaps she was a cat burglar gone awry. Or perhaps she had jumped.

"How did you get here?" he asked.

Her smile was small, almost sheepish. "I flew."

"Flew?"

"Flew."

Justin shook his head. He didn't want to know how she got to New York. "No, I mean here, in my room."

"I just told you." Her gaze was clear. Her face, even without makeup, had an old-fashioned prettiness. He had a dizzying moment when he thought he was seeing a ghost, then the digital watch on her wrist beeped. She reached over and shut it off.

"People don't fly," he said.

Her smile grew, just a little. "I did."

He frowned, thinking there had to be another explanation. There was equipment outside the window, or Elise was playing a trick on him, or he was asleep and dreaming. He went to the window and looked out, and saw nothing but mist and lights and cars far below. He wondered what it would be like to catch a breeze, sail on it, and see the city from above with no glass between him and the lights.

Justin turned around. She was already grabbing the door, letting herself out. She reached up a hand, the hand holding her entry card. "Thanks," she said.

"Wait. Can we talk for a minute?"

She shook her head. "I'm really bushed. But catch me tomorrow. I'm in room forty-three twenty-five. My name is . . . Wendy."

He heard the pause, frowned again, checked her hands. She wasn't holding anything but her entry card. His fingers brushed his back pocket. His wallet was still there. "My name is Justin."

She shrugged. "Oh, well," she said. "I was sort of hoping it was Peter."

He waited about an hour, and at that point, he couldn't take it anymore. He thought of trying to get into the UN, seeing where the parties were, imposing himself on Elise. But he couldn't embarrass himself on an international scale. So he paced the room, and finally, when he couldn't stand himself any longer, he decided to go to the bar.

Justin had forgotten about the mirrors. From the moment he stepped into the elevator, his company quintupled. He felt as if he were in a party with people he despised. When the elevator reached the ground floor, he thankfully turned right, away from the mirrors. The crowd lessened to a single look-alike pacing him. As he went down the stairs into the bar attached to the five-star restaurant, the look-alike disappeared altogether. He was finally alone.

The bar was almost empty, although the restaurant sounded full. Two men in business suits sat on opposite sides of the bar. Behind the glass racks and bottles of booze, another mirror waited for him. Justin decided to take a table. He turned and found himself face to face with Wendy.

She looked out of place here. Her clothes were a little bit shabby and her haircut was two seasons out of style. She had applied makeup inexpertly, as if she were a teenage girl trying for the first time. She held an unlit cigarette in one hand, waving it like Bette Davis in a 1940s movie.

"I thought you were tired," he said.

"I thought so, too." Her voice seemed harsher here, with the trace of an accent. Brooklyn? Queens? He didn't know. He could never tell the variations of Eastern accents apart. "But to have something special happen—it may tire you out, but God, I'm still so wired, there's no way I could sleep."

"What happened?" he asked.

Her smile quirked half her mouth. "I told you."

He glanced around the bar. "Mind if I join you?"

"Please." She waved the chair back with her cigarette hand.

He sat. The chair was soft and plush, too comfortable for a bar chair. He leaned back and ordered a gin-and-tonic from the cocktail waitress. "So tell me again," he said.

The light was dim, but it looked as if Wendy flushed. "You didn't believe me the first time, and you saw it."

"I might believe you now." The waitress set his glass on the table. He moved the glass a half-inch. "I kind of need a miracle."

"Yeah." Wendy sipped her wine. "You look a little lost."

"Not lost," Justin said. "Left."

"Girlfriend?"

"Wife."

"How long?"

"It's been happening for over a year now, but today . . ."

His voice cracked and he covered it by tasting his drink. "Today was the end."

"I'm sorry," Wendy said. She sounded sincere.

"Don't be." Justin took another drink. The alcohol felt good. "It was my fault."

Wendy shook her head. "Two people make a relationship. Two people end it. Surely you had dreams for this once—"

"Computer programmers don't have dreams," Justin said, repeating one of Elise's bitter statements. "They have goals."

"Everyone has dreams," Wendy said. She held her wine with both hands. The soft lighting reflected off a solid gold band on her left hand. She glanced at him over the rim of her glass. "I'm going to be thirty tomorrow."

Her softly spoken sentence surprised him. He didn't understand its connection to their discussion. "Happy birthday," he said.

She ignored him. "My husband wanted to be a millionaire by the time he was thirty. He worked really hard at it, trying some get-rich-quick schemes, opening his own business. He's thirty-five. We live in a one-bedroom apartment near Brooklyn College and he goes to night school. But he's given up. And he's getting bitter. If he couldn't do it by thirty, I guess he figures it wasn't worth doing. Me, I did it. I made my goal."

He looked at the elegant surroundings, her shabby clothes. "You're a millionaire?"

She shook her head. "I wanted to see if there was a little bit of magic left in the world."

"And you found some."

"I found some." She set her glass down, ran her finger along the stem. "And tomorrow I'll charge much too much money on our VISA card for one glamorous evening where I could pretend to be Ginger Rogers and Katharine Hepburn rolled into one."

"Insurance."

She shrugged. "I didn't want to be bitter."

He set his half-empty glass aside and watched her. The light had shifted, surrounding her. She looked ethereal, as she had when she climbed into his hotel room, touched with mist and magic. "Teach me to fly," he said.

"You look heavy."

"I'm not," he said. "I need a miracle tonight. Teach me to fly."

She put the unlit cigarette in her mouth, pretended to take a puff, and frowned. "All right," she said.

They went to his room—perhaps, he thought, because she did not want to taint her earlier experience. She opened his window, leaned out, and breathed the cool air. He loved the way the mist collected on her hair. He stepped beside her, hearing the horns, the bustle, smelling the thickness of city in the breeze.

"It's real easy," she said, her face half-turned away from him. "You think about all of your dreams, and you reach for them, and you'll get lighter and lighter until you can almost hold them. Your bones will get hollow and wings will sprout along your back, and the wind will carry you as far as you want to go."

His heart thudded against his chest. He felt the metal sill dig into his palms.

She hoisted herself on the ledge. "All you have to do is believe," she said, and pushed off.

He reached for her, thinking she was going to fall, thinking she was going to die and he wasn't going to be able to grab her in time. Then she soared away from him. "Just believe," she called.

Believe. He pulled himself on the ledge, his feet dangling over forty stories of mist-filled air. His heart had moved to his throat. He had always been nervous around heights, not quite afraid of falling but not willing to chance it either. She had said he had to believe, and believe he would.

He pushed away. The air felt heavy and for a moment, he was buoyant, then he fell through like a man standing on a child's toy. Dreams, he thought, he had to grab for his dreams and he thought of them—the computers, Elise, his apartment in San Francisco, the walk through the UN—and realized none of those dreams were his. They had all belonged to someone else, someone he never was, someone he hadn't even wanted to be. In those few seconds, windows rushing past him, he searched for his own dreams and could think of nothing.

He wanted to believe, but he had nothing to believe in. The ground came closer, the mist zooming past him like water, drenching him. The cars grew in size, the buildings grew shorter, and finally he screamed, feeling sorry, strangely, for Elise, realizing she would never be able to live this down, never be able to fight the publicity from this one moment of his stupidity.

His scream stretched out and he looked up, feeling a flap of wings. Something soft brushed his face, then arms grabbed him and a body wrapped him tight. Wendy held him, her wings snapping like sheets in the wind. Gently, ever so gently, she eased his fall, letting him drop until his feet kissed the concrete sidewalk.

"I'm sorry," he said, "for ruining your dream."

She shook her head, not even allowing him a moment of self-pity. "You added to it." She smiled, and in the glow of the streetlamps she was beautiful. Her feet weren't touching the ground. He could hear, but not see, her wings. "I always wanted to be a hero. I just thought that was too much to ask for one night." And then she rose away from him, higher and higher, until he couldn't see her anymore.

People passed him like water around a stone. If they had seen anything, they didn't acknowledge it. He took a deep breath, forcing himself to calm down. His hands were shaking, his body was shaking, and his heart threatened to pound a hole in his chest.

He took another deep breath and waited until the shaking eased. Then the hair on the back of his neck prickled. He looked up and wished he could see as Wendy's shadow crossed the moon.

The next morning he got up at six, dressed, and went to the lobby. He paid for Wendy's room and had the concierge leave her a single rose with a message thanking her for all the help she had given him. Then he went back up the elevator, staring at his own reflection in the mirror.

He had been thinking of changing hotels, but he decided that this one wasn't bad. He needed the mirrors, needed the constant reminder that he didn't know the man who stared back at him through the silvered glass. He would spend the next few days walking through Manhattan, looking at Central Park, seeing a show on Broadway, staring at the down-and-outs on Times Square.

The city was filled with examples of dreams, successful and broken. And maybe, just maybe, by the time he left, he would know what he longed for.

It wasn't magic, and it wasn't millions. It was something his, uniquely his.

He would find it. He knew he would.

That much he believed.

Kris Rusch's life has been a continual westward movement. Born in New York State, she grew up in the Midwest, and since 1986 has lived in Oregon. In 1987, she and Dean Wesley Smith started Pulphouse Publishing, and in 1989 won a World Fantasy Award for their work on Pulphouse: The Hardback Magazine. In addition to her dozens of short stories, she has two novels coming from NAL in 1991: The White Mists of Power, a fantasy, and Afterimage, a horror novel written in collaboration with Kevin J. Anderson.

In 1989, she spent three days in Manhattan at someone else's expense, but had no major New York adventures. (Except for the one involving most of the New York police force, the UN, and President George Bush—one of those things too strange for fiction.) She managed to write "Shadows on the Moon" anyway.

The Baby Track

by Howard Mittelmark

"Pressured by their peers to raise an accomplished child and propelled by a competitive life style, parents are trying to get the edge by enrolling their infants and toddlers in classes that promise to teach everything from reading to babies to French conversation to two-year-olds."

The New York Times, 1/8/1989

You want to know what drives me? The simple need to excel, to be the best. No mystery, right? It's just that I've got this case of it like you wouldn't believe.

It's this gnawing thing I've always had. I remember at birth, to pick just one example, Dad's face hovering over me, just this blur, you know what I mean, the way things look when they've just barely cleaned all that icky stuff off of you, and there's still this sort of rocking motion to everything, like after you've spent the day out sailing? Well, there I was, looking up at this monstrous—and remember, at the time, his face was as big as the world—this monstrous thing, kind of pale and fuzzy, with this dark slash across the middle, and I remember thinking to myself, What's that? Looking back, of course, I can kick myself, I should've reached right up and touched it, you know, sort of explored the textures, but I didn't have any control of my limbs at the time. (In fact, if I remember correctly—and I should, the work I put into that memory course—I wasn't really aware that they were mine, they were just these sort of pinkish things that kept on waving right up next to me, and you know how disconcerting that can be.) So what it came down to is that I made a mental note to myself to find out what this thing was, and

163

why the one had the dark thing in its middle and the other one didn't.

So what is it, less than four years later? Well, now I can tell you, that was my Dad, and the dark thing was a mustache. The mustache is gone now—and I'm being real up front with you here, I don't like to talk about this—it's been gone for a while, and nobody ever said anything, and I still get the shakes when I think about it, I just can't figure what happened to the mustache, but the point is that this is the kind of child I am. I grab on to something, I don't let go. I've got this need, this force in me, that makes me reach out and explore my environment. First it was my fingers and toes; then I was onto shapes and, before you knew it, colors.

Is this the kind of stuff you want? I mean, I hate to go on about myself. You know, enough about me. What do you think of my jammies? A lot of my peer group are like that, you know, "me, me, me," and it really puts me off. I mean, I learned sharing last year, no big deal. Why can't they?

So, anyway, if you want the real me, the deep-down core me, it's this success thing. But if you want to know how I got on top of it, how come I can sort of channel it, make it work for me when New York's full of so many other children who can't, children who—can I be honest here?—children who are losers, I think it mostly has to do with a decision I made last year.

There I was—I want you to experience this just the way I did, it's a pivotal period for me, so bear with me, hear me out—there I was, I think it was in my French class, and I'm thinking to myself, I'm a two, and this is it? I mean, I was first in the group in French, I'd done the cooking thing, and Gymboree, hell—I'm allowed to say that—hell, you know I breezed through Gymboree like nobody's business, just flew across those mats, and already my play groups were starting to look to me for leadership. I'll tell you, I didn't want that kind of responsibility. This is a tough town, it puts a lot of pressure on a kid, and despite everything, I'm essentially a live-and-let-live sort of child. But that's the way it happened. I mean, I don't want to brag here, but someone's got to be the first to make a move toward the blocks. Even now, if we're all going to take off our diapers and run around laughing with our arms in the air, somebody's got to get the ball rolling. It doesn't just happen by itself, you know.

So, anyway, there I was thinking, What's it all mean? I mean, with my course load and the way the others were starting to lean on me—should I put *this* in my mouth? should I put *that* in my mouth?—I was having trouble sleeping. Sometimes I'd wake up crying in the night. Then I realized what was wrong. I was taking care of the outside me, the public me, and ignoring, you know, the real me. I had this hollow feeling all the time, like something was missing, and it all seemed pretty pointless. And I thought to myself, This isn't right. So I got Mom and Dad together for a meeting—you know how it is, you push all your food on the floor, they pay attention—and to make a long story short, we canceled the art appreciation and I enrolled in assertiveness training. The way I figure it, who needs art appreciation? I got a nice central location here, I can zip out to the Modern, the Met, the Guggenheim, take it all in any time, if I can just get someone to lift me up.

Anyway, I have to tell you, that course turned my life around. You know, I'd been paying attention to everyone else's needs, not chewing on books, smiling at Mom and Dad, that sort of thing. I finally started paying attention to my own needs. I said, Enough for everyone else, this is *my* time. And I got to know me. I learned to like me. I learned to accommodate the child in me.

And you know, now I feel I'm really at peace with myself. Here I am: I'm a three, I'm heading into preschool, and for some this is a real tense time, there's a lot of pressure, and not every kid can take it. But, well, that's their lookout. I've got a handle on it. With all due respect, whether I get into this preschool or another almost doesn't matter. Because being at peace with myself like this, it gives me the edge.

The above was written a few months before my daughter, Emily Darwin, had her coming out—no party, I can assure you—and I don't know what I could've been thinking. She's pushing eight months as we move into 1990 and she's cutting her teeth on the classics—my copy of Moby Dick *is a sodden mess—but mostly she just crawls around the apartment leaving trails of drool and making these sounds. Loud, high-pitched sounds. The cats are getting real jumpy, and their fur's coming out in handfuls (tiny handfuls, but handfuls nonetheless). You ask me, there's no percentage in it. Next time, I'm renting.*

                                        —Howard Mittelmark

Clash of Titans (A New York Romance)

by Kurt Busiek

Kurt Busiek has been writing and editing comics for some time, but this is his first prose fiction sale. His comics background may show; what we have here suggests what a Marvel Comics story written by the Marquis de Sade might look like. It's about love, death, superheroes, rampant destruction, and apartment-hunting.

He's gone now. They're both gone. But if you've lived in New York for over five years, you remember when the commercials began, and you remember the effect they had. If you moved to New York during that time—and there are a lot of you, too many—the commercials probably had something to do with it. They were my idea, my brainchild.

It all started in a bar. Or, no, it was a few days before that: a hot, humid afternoon, and the air-conditioning was out. We were supposed to be spitballing ideas, but we were just lounging around the big conference table, watching TV, trying not to move around much, and generally complaining. I work for the Mayor's Commission on Tourism; we do TV spots, print ads, and assorted other stuff, all aimed at getting out-of-staters to come spend their vacation cash here. This was around the time the "I ♥ New York" campaign (Fred's idea) was running out of steam, and we were supposed to have an enhancement or a replacement at least in proposal stage by Monday. We were pretty dry. Sarah suggested getting

Ling-Ling and Hsing-Hsing on loan for the Bronx Zoo
and featuring them, but that was it for the last half-hour,
and nobody even bothered to point out it was a lame
idea. It wasn't like anyone didn't know it.

The mayor was on TV, smiling his impenetrable smile
and talking about this thing at Lincoln Center and how
important it was. You might not remember Lincoln Center; it was one of her first major targets. Anyway, the
mayor was going on and on and on, and the crowd was
visibly wilting; I don't know how anybody can ever listen
to that stuff, let alone when the air is warmer and moister
than blood; and Fred suggested, "Okay, here we go: We
trade Hizzoner for Ling-Ling and Hsing-Hsing and make
them mayor. An image change. And a better class of
employer."

"Nah," Jeremy said. "You know pandas. They're so
cute they'd end up mayor for life, and eight years down
the road we'd have the same damn problem."

Then the mayor drowned in a *frzhatsssh* of static, and
when the screen cleared, he wasn't there anymore. Instead, it was Demonica. Electric eyebrows, purple bee-
hive, the works. She glared out into the room.

"O-*kay*," said Fred. "Leona Helmsley's evil twin!" He
settled back in his chair and grinned, raising his Orangina
to her.

"You stupid fucking pigs!" Her voice was like a buzz
saw. I always assumed it was electronically enhanced,
until I met her in person. "You worthless sacks of shit!
You're just wasting space on this planet. I could reduce
you all to dust—to protoplasm!—and it wouldn't make
an ort of difference to the world." She paused, sneered,
and adjusted her goggles. Maybe they were blocking her
view of the cue cards.

"And you know, I just might. It'd be fun. It'd be fresh.
It'd be what you deserve. I've got a sweet little protobomb
stashed under your miserable island, and when it goes
off, it'll trigger the earthquake fault that runs down the
East Coast." She laughed, like the gear chain coming off
a bicycle. "Does that spell it out in simple-enough terms
for you uncomprehending sheep? Can you say earthquake? Can you say disaster? Can you say death and
mayhem beyond human comprehension? I knew you could.

"But you can save yourselves," she continued, hitching

at her leather jumpsuit. She clearly didn't shave her armpits, and by God, that was purple too. "You have that opportunity. You can save your worthless, repugnant lives, and I'll tell you how. You know who I want. You know where that gob of phlegm, that no-good limpdick mediocrity who calls himself Mr. Right is cowering. Deliver him to me. Deliver him to me by midnight tomorrow, or I promise you, New York, you won't live to see . . ."

She was working herself up into an astonishingly kinetic state, but before she could finish her threat, there was a double flash of static: *frzhatsssh, frzhatsssh*. Between them we caught a glimpse of the mayor blowing on his microphone and looking aggrieved, and then the image of Mr. Right filled the screen. Even as early as that, his charisma hit like a physical blow. He sat ramrodstraight. His jaw was firm, his eyes were piercing blue, and his blond hair cascaded over his crimson helm.

Sarah pounded the table and whistled. "Hoo hoo, big guy, take it off! Take it all off!"

You have to understand, this was years before Demonica melted the UN. This was before she created those werewolf things that ate Donald Trump. We didn't know how smart—and how deadly—she was; we just thought she was a nut. She hadn't even done much preempting of broadcast TV at that point—this was one of the first times. Up till now, she'd mostly just broken in on cable, Channel J and like that. It was just this goofy thing, like Al Sharpton. It was fun to watch.

Mr. Right leaned forward on the screen, and his stern, forceful voice filled the air. "The people of New York have nothing to fear from you, Demonica. Truth, justice, and decency will always triumph over your kind of perverted sideshow. Name the place. Name the time. I'll be there—and you'll get taken away in a body bag." His smile was grim, a man who meant business.

Frzhatsssh. Mayor. *Frzhatsssh*. Demonica. "Four o'clock tomorrow, asshole. Tompkins Square Park. Bring your . . . atomic rod."

Frzhatsssh. Mayor. "As I was saying . . ."

Frzhatsssh. Mr. Right. "I'll be there, you frigid bitch. Count on it. You're going down—and you're going down *hard*!"

There was an extended *frzhatsssh*, but instead of the mayor, what we got when it faded was Yogi Bear extolling the virtues of children's vitamins in Spanish.

"I got it," I said. "It'd be perfect. We get them to do an I ♥ New York spot. Mr. Right and Demonica. The new fun couple. Better than Garner and Hartley for Polaroid. Better than David and Maddie, may they rest in peace."

"Better than Ling-Ling and Hsing-Hsing?" Sarah asked.

"Oh, c'mon. What says New York better for you? Two panda bears eating eucalyptus leaves and whatever the hell, or two constipated psychotics with heavy weaponry trying to kill each other?"

"The man has a point," said Jeremy.

Fred turned the TV off. "Yeah, Marty, when they check in at Bellevue to pick up their mail, you can take 'em to the Russian Tea Room for blinis and sign 'em up. Any other brilliant ideas? Monday's coming fast."

And that was it. At five o'clock we split up, headed for home (I caught an early train, for once), and we forgot the whole thing. Tompkins Square Park didn't survive the next afternoon, of course. But even then, people were getting used to that sort of thing.

That Thursday night I was in the city late. I had to go to that Lincoln Center thing, and it lasted for hours; by the time I could get home and to sleep it'd be time to get up and head in again. So the city was putting me up at the Hyatt. Actually, the time that matters, I was around the corner from the Hyatt, at a bar on Lexington Avenue, griping to anyone who'd listen. That meant mostly the bartender.

I mean, what would you expect? Here I'd been working for the city—the city itself, mind you—for almost two years, and I couldn't find an apartment. I spent my days sucking people in to New York by whatever means possible, and I had an hour commute. I lived in Connecticut.

There had to be a very special mathematics governing my job and a team of accountants to supervise it. They monitored my performance carefully, and once I got X number of out-of-staters moved to the city permanently, they'd give me a raise so I could look in a new price range. Of course, that was the price range that had just been completely closed off by the new people snapping up the available apartments. So I kept looking, kept commuting, and my next raise would come just when all the places it made affordable were taken. It had to be a plot.

Anyway, I was explaining this to the bartender (who lived on St. Mark's Place: rent-controlled) when I saw him in a back booth. I wasn't sure it was him, mind you; I'd only ever seen him on TV and I never thought he was that short. But I got a good look when I went by to get to the men's room, and it was him all right. No mistaking that jawline.

He was drinking boilermakers. I got one and another Scotch for me and carried them over. "Mr. Right?"

He looked up, a little bleary-eyed. He'd clearly been drinking for a while. With an effort, he focused on the fresh drink. "Did I . . . ?"

"It's on me." I put the drinks down, spilling a little (it was my fourth Scotch; those things at Lincoln Center take it out of you) and slid into the booth. "I wanted to tell you, you were impressive yesterday. You took care of Demonica and kept fatalities and property damage to a minimum. Nice work."

"Huh. She'll be back." His voice was bitter, and he didn't have the commanding presence he'd had before. Of course, he wasn't in his outfit: he was wearing jeans and an ordinary dress shirt—that might have had something to do with it. Or maybe it was the slurred speech and the defensive slump to his shoulders. "Goddamn castrating bitch. Teleported away, but set it up so it looked like she died. That way she can pop up alive and laugh and make me look like a dork again."

"Demonica's still alive?"

"Always." He knocked back the shot and reached for the beer. "She runs rings around me. I look like King Shit Goombah with the force field and the atomic cannon and all, but it's her show from top to bottom. She knows the equipment inside out. Me, I'm still doping out basic functions."

"What do you mean, basic functions?" I had a little trouble with the words "basic functions," but I forced them out. The whole conversation was starting to seem a little surreal. It must have been the Scotch.

"Well, whaddya think? She built it all, you know."

"You're kidding." I'd assumed Mr. Right built the gadgets that let him fly and stuff himself, but no. He told me the whole story. He and Demonica met in college—he was a computer-science geek; she was the shining star of the physics department—and dated for a while. He ran out of money about the time she vaporized several teaching assistants and they asked her to leave, so she hired him as a lab assistant (she was filthy rich) and started doing her own research over in Brooklyn. The area wasn't zoned for atomic research, but she didn't care. He told me she said laws were there to keep stupid people from having any fun. Anyway, he hated working for her. She was demanding, a real top-decibel perfectionist, and the boss/employee thing screwed up the relationship. They stopped sleeping together and the job was hell, but she never paid him much so he couldn't get a stake together to quit and go for something else.

Eventually he got fed up. He stole a truck, filled it up with stuff from the lab, and left. The plan was to sell the stuff back to her for enough to get out to Silicon Valley and see if he could get a job, but it didn't work out right. She came after him in this stealth chopper she'd whipped up, and started shooting at him. He was lucky enough to figure out the controls on the Rebound Ray, and he bounced her through one of the World Trade Towers. You remember it from the movie, I'm sure. They got the facts wrong, of course—they used what I told them—but it sure made a nice explosion, didn't it?

Anyway, that's how it all started, and it had been building up ever since. They got into the good/evil thing as a sex game back in college, and eventually—I guess "evolved" is the right word—this whole elaborate fantasy. He never did know why he kept playing along after they split up; I think there's something about that kind of couple-specific ritual that makes it hard to stop. Either you both stop at the same time, or you never stop at all. The best part about the whole thing, or at least the part I always liked best, was the poor schmuck didn't even have a secret identity. His name was Wright. Benjamin Wright. We just heard it on TV and assumed it was a code name. Her name was Monica, of course. Demonica was what he called her when they got out the whips and the jelly, and the name made a comeback in the early cable days.

He finished up his story and belched plaintively. "And now I'm almost out of plutonium," he said. "I don't have any money to buy more. I don't even know where to find it. A week, ten days max, and all my stuff won't work anymore. Then I'm dead meat." He started drawing circles in the beer on the table.

"Um," I said, not really sure where I was heading, but unwilling to let the moment pass. "What would you say if I said I might be able to get you some plutonium?"

He looked up at me and wiped a little drool away from his mouth. He straightened up and squared his shoulders, going from pathetic drunk to commanding presence in about a second flat. His eyes were blue and bottomless and deadly, but when he spoke, he killed the whole image. "Who—who are you, anyway?"

We shot the first commercial a week later. That was when he got the earpieces, the ones with the antennae on them. It didn't do anything, but it helped make him look high tech.

We didn't have any kind of budget, so it wasn't like the commercials everyone remembers today. No special effects, no John Williams theme, no action. Just Ben and the American flag. It was a nice piece. He launched into his speech and the camera just loved him. Inside of five words, he owned anyone watching. Just owned them.

What he said didn't matter. It was something about justice and safety and freedom, and his guarantee New York would never fall victim to the kind of encroaching evil Demonica represented, or some such garbage. I've got a copy of it around here, but it just wasn't important. All that was important was that sincerity. It radiated out from him, like he was the sun or something. A nice piece.

It wasn't long after that the sidewalk vendors started selling the T-shirts. We had to close 'em down, of course; we had exclusive licensing rights. But we were never able to keep up with the demand, not from the start. It seemed like everyone had a Mr. Right T-shirt—if not a shirt, a button, a baseball cap, puffy stickers. About a month after the campaign started, I saw a man on Park

Avenue, maybe seventy years old. He had a tweed cap, wool trousers with suspenders, Oxfords, and a walking stick. And a Mr. Right T-shirt—the hot-pink one where he's flipping Demonica the bird. That's when I knew it had gone way beyond a fad.

Demonica got really pissy once the commercials started. They had to list her on a separate scale to see what the murder rate would look like under normal circumstances, and it wasn't long before she outdid all other crime in the metropolitan area combined. Still, the ads worked. They worked like crazy. The day her side of the murder stats officially doubled everyone else put together, the mayor called me into his office.

"Tourism's at an all-time high, Martin, and it's still accelerating." He beamed at me, and I wondered if I should recommend a good orthodontist. "Better than V-J Day. Better than the World's Fair. It's wonderful."

"Even with the JAL plane blowing up yesterday? That was a pretty ugly mess."

"Pfah!" He waved it away. "They were on their way home, and they'd had a great vacation. Besides, isn't that what the big guy's for? To keep us safe from things like that?"

"He didn't stop that one."

"So? So how much worse would it be if he wasn't here at all?" I didn't have an answer; I'd wondered. "Don't be such a Gloomy Gus, Martin. Mr. Right souvenirs are selling like there's no tomorrow, and they tell me some knock-off just showed up in LA, calling himself Joe Orange. Atlanta's got something in the works, too, and God knows who's next. Magazines and newspapers are sending reporters to cover the story full-time. Even *Pravda*'s got a guy on the way. And I just got invited to the White House—to the White House!—to talk about special agent status for the big guy. You've done a great thing, Martin. Have a cigar."

A raise came along with the cigar, and I started apartment-hunting again.

I couldn't figure it. New Yorkers were being turned to stone, mutated into big things with tentacles, hurled into orbit and burned up in re-entry, evaporated—all this by the dozen, by the busload. You'll figure there'd be a vacant apartment somewhere nice. But no. The whole world was flooding in to gawk around and maybe get a snapshot of the Big Apple's Sterling Defender of Liberty—and a lot of them must have liked it here, because they moved in in droves. It was harder even to find places to look at than it was before. It was harder to get on waiting lists.

What can you do?

On the other hand, I did find a way around the cosmic accountants who were keeping my salary in the no-available-apartments range. When we cut the deal, I arranged to be listed on the contracts as Ben's agent, and that gave me a cut of everything he made out of it. He did the commercials for free, of course—it was a public service—but all those shirts, dolls, posters, and junk really added up. Most weeks my check from the licensing people was bigger than my paycheck.

That put me in a new class for apartment-hunting, and once we got the merchandise moving good, I managed to find the first place in years that was affordable and didn't outright suck. It was a two-bedroom on the Upper West Side with high ceilings, wood floors, good light, six closets, and plenty of electrical outlets. And there was more: the building had a doorman. There was a washer/dryer room in the basement. And the apartment had a balcony. A balcony!

It was a pretty stiff deposit (two and a half months), but it was worth it. I was the first guy to see it, and there were three couples scheduled that evening. So I wrote the check and I signed the form and shook hands with the guy. It was mine, all mine.

I was leaving, heading home to make moving arrangements, a smile on my face and a spring in my step, when it happened. I heard a high-pitched whistling and smelled ionized air. There was a dull thump behind me. I turned around and there was a hole in the second and third floors of the building. As I watched, the awning stretched out tight and taut, then started to tear. The doorman bolted.

The base of the building slowly separated from the sidewalk and shrank backward, like a kid stepping into a cold pool. There was a groaning sound. The part of the building above the hole swayed.

People started to boil out of the lobby, but most of them didn't make it. The groan became a roar, the sway became a shiver, and like a cross between a deflating balloon and an avalanche, *kwadathaddathaboom*, the building collapsed, spilling bricks, glass, plaster, furniture, and bodies all over West Eighty-eighth Street.

I didn't know what had happened, not right away. All I knew was that my new river-view apartment, my new balcony, both bedrooms, everything, was all down here instead of up there where it belonged.

I stood there, looking at the wreckage, willing it not to have happened, until, *shkvmp*, a shattered bathtub and an overturned bookcase shifted, and he climbed out.

"Ben. Aw, Ben, you stupid shit," I said.

He saw me. "Marty! What a surprise!" Then he got a good look at my face and looked around. "This—this wasn't the place, was it, Marty? The apartment?"

I nodded.

"Well, gee, Marty, I'm sorry. If I'd known I'd have, I don't know, tried to land somewhere else or something." He brushed some plaster dust off his cape. "Uh, Marty, I've got to go. She's up there at the George Washington Bridge, and it's rush hour. You know how it is."

I watched him gather himself for launch. "Ben?"

He stopped.

"You—you wouldn't need a sidekick, would you?"

"Well, I don't know. You're a little old, but we could maybe swing something. Why?"

"Where do you live?"

"Oh," he said, realizing. "Rumson, New Jersey. It's an hour commute, even in the Fusion-Copter. Sorry."

"Well, it was an idea, anyway." I turned to go.

"Hey, Marty, cheer up. Maybe you can get your deposit back." He sprang, and a split second later was airborne and gone.

Yeah, right. The only way you get your deposit back in New York is to skip out on the last month's rent. I headed back toward Grand Central and Connecticut, walking slow. At least I didn't have to drive out of the city. One bridge or tunnel gets tied up, and the others all turn into sheer hell.

*   *   *

One thing you should understand: there was only Demonica, only ever her. The others were all made up, all actors we hired, their powers cobbled together out of Ben's extra stuff or whipped up by the guys at ILM. The Battery Boys, ShBoom, the Sewer Alligator, Mr. Wrong, GEN-11 (Sarah's idea, and kind of tasteless, actually: a techno-genii—hence the name—supposedly created from the reanimated corpse of a rape victim and seeking vengeance on preppies), the Culture Vultures. All fakes. By the end, we'd even created some for other cities. The Hunchback of UCLA, the Tar Heel, Longhorn— those were ours.

The thing was, Demonica kept winning. Oh, it looked like Ben won a lot, but that was just her being perverse. She faked her own death—publicly, mind you—sixty-seven times, and never repeated a gag once. And every time she did, she was letting Ben know he couldn't do shit to her. Like the time she turned Columbus Circle into a crater and got "electrocuted" by a falling power cable. Ben got a medal for saving the city, but he knew the truth: she said she was going to wreck Columbus Circle, she did it, and she got away. She was every bit as smart as she thought, I'll give her that. But at the same time, you know, she never did her best to kill him, either, never caught him in a death trap she didn't know he could get out of.

Still, to keep people from catching on, we had to cook up our own bad guys. That way, Ben had someone he could beat, and beat every time. By that time, our budget was huge and we could really go to town with the special effects. We made sure we got enough footage to use in the ads—that was still the only reason for the whole project—and tried to make sure nobody important got hurt. It worked out well, for the most part. Occasionally one of them went bad for real, but Ben handled those as well as he did the staged battles. And the time ShBoom wanted to "reform" and be Mr. Right's partner, and we had to arrange for him to sacrifice himself to save the city. But that's another story.

Looking back on it, I think putting Ben on steroids was a mistake. It made him bigger, and it did wonders for his upper-body development, but he'd been in pretty good shape from the start; he probably could have gotten by on his natural brawn. I don't know for sure it was the drugs, though. It might have been the constant adulation, the groupies, the TV coverage, the money—whatever, he was losing touch with reality.

This was around the time he was hanging with Diane Brill and Tama Janowitz. All that's in the Ultra Violet diaries, so I won't rehash it here. But one night, when I was in the office late, he came in through the door—I mean, literally through the door.

There were chunks of wood and splinters everywhere, and what was left fell all over Jeremy's desk, burying all the work he'd been doing on the Rainbow Coalition thing for Ben to do at the Koch Memorial the next week. A couple of cinderblocks came out of the wall, too. (We found the doorknob out on the fire escape the next day.) Anyway, I waited for it all to settle, and he waited too, breathing kind of snarly and staring at me.

"What's up, Ben?"

"How could you do it, Marty? I thought you were part of the cause, the crusade. I thought you were fighting for the same principles. I thought we were a team."

I motioned for him to lower his voice; he was in stentorian mode and could be heard for blocks. "What are you talking about?"

"You. You and Demonica!"

"Oh, that."

" 'Oh, that?' Is that all you have to say? How could you betray me like that?" He picked up my desk and threw it through the window. I hoped nobody was walking by below. "My best friend and my worst enemy!"

"Easy, Ben. It's not what you think."

"And what is it? Do you deny that you've consorted with the Mistress of Evil? That you—my closest confidant, the keeper of all my secrets—have actually been sleeping with Demonica?" He was starting to breathe heavy again and I didn't like the way his mood was headed.

"Ben, sit down." He glowered at me and clenched his fists, but he sat. "If you promise not to destroy any more city property, I'll tell you what happened. Do we have a deal?"

He made a face, but he nodded.

"Okay. First off, I only slept with her once, and it was months ago. And it was nothing, really." He clutched the arms of the chair, and they started to bend. "Look, I could tell you she took control of my brain, right? And I had no choice, right? But I'm not; I'm being honest with you. So settle down.

"You know I've been in touch with her. She demanded a cut from the Demonica action figures in return for promising hands-off on Gracie Mansion. So every six weeks or so we arrange to courier her a cashier's check." He was relaxing now, bored; the details of the business always put him to sleep. "So one time I carried the check myself, because there was something I wanted to talk to her about.

"You remember that time it looked like she got run over by the six train, only it turned out she had a whole lab-headquarters deal set up in an unfinished subway tunnel, and she just ducked into it? I always thought it was kind of lucky it was so close when you threw the train at her, and I finally asked her; it turns out she has a bunch of them, scattered around the city.

"So I wanted to see if she'd be willing to sublet. She must hardly ever use them, so they're standing empty all the time. Some of 'em are in really prime locations, and you know, with the right kind of decor . . ."

He nodded. He still felt bad about that building.

"But she didn't go for it. She was nice about it, but she said she never knew when she might need to activate one of them, and I'd get evicted with no notice to speak of. She didn't want to have to do that. Besides, I have a cat.

"And that was it; I gave her the check and we were done. But it was dinnertime and we were both hungry, so we grabbed a pizza and a bottle of wine, and, well, you know how it is. She was wearing that black Spandex outfit with the garters—you know, the one with the skull on the crotch—and we were all alone in this tunnel, and there was all this funky machinery, and the wine—"

"Yeah, Marty, I know." His voice was normal again. "She always got real horny after a couple of drinks. And she's pretty aggressive."

"You're telling me!"

"But, Marty, it can't happen again. It's a lonely crusade I'm on, this war against the evils that would destroy us. I've got to be able to trust the men around me. And you know how devious she is. She'll stop at nothing, and if she ever learned the secrets I've confided in you . . ." His eyes were glittering, his jaw tight and locked.

"Uh, look, Ben, maybe you need a break. You've been pretty busy lately, haven't had much time out of the suit. It couldn't hurt to go back to being just Ben Wright for a few days." I thought for a second. "How about coming out to Greenwich this weekend? We could catch a movie, maybe go sailing. I can fix us up with a couple of nice girls, you'll like them." A little harmless detox. A reality check.

He stood up and flexed. I always hated that. Looked down at me. "Evil never takes a vacation, Marty. You know that." And he flipped me a salute—a salute, for Christ's sake—as he shot off through the broken window.

I don't know. I think he was starting to believe he really was Mr. Right.

The next time Demonica called to arrange for her check, I asked her how he found out. She said she told him. I ask you. The most brilliant woman in the world, sure, but fucked up beyond belief, right?

I found this luxury condo near Central Park. I couldn't afford it, and I knew it. But I could almost afford it, and it had been so long since I'd seen anything I was even close to, it was hard to walk away. So I was up late going over figures. I had projections from the licensing guys (weighted to reflect three new bad guys I didn't know if we could get on line in time), I had papers from the bank estimating what kind of mortgage I could swing, I had my returns for the past five years. And no matter how I punched it in, it added up to no condo.

The phone rang. It was him.

"I did it, Marty." His voice was hollow; I almost didn't recognize it. I hadn't heard him sound like that since the bar, way back at the beginning. "I did it."

"Ben, what do you mean? Did what?"

"She's dead, Marty. She's really dead this time. I've got the body with me."

I had a horrifying mental picture. "You're not at a public phone, are you?"

"No, no. I'm at home. And she's here. She's dead."

"Yeah, dead. I got it. How did it happen?"

"She called me out again. You know how she does that—whenever she's finished some new gizmo she'll break into the TV channels and challenge me. I have to have the TV monitored all the time, I never know when she's going to break into *Nightline* or *Robin Byrd* or what. One time I missed *Wake Up America*, and—"

"Uh-huh. She called you out. Then what?"

"Well, it was Central Park this time. And as soon as I get there, she shorts out all my stuff. I land, she steps out from behind a tree with this doohickey, and *zap*, none of my stuff works. And it's heavy. It weighs over 250 pounds and there's no power to keep it up, it's just dragging me down, you—"

"Then, what?"

"She starts undressing."

"What?"

"She undresses. She's pulling off her clothes, and I'm almost falling over, the damn stuff is so heavy, and she's coming toward me, and she's got this weird grin on her face, and I don't know what she's going to do, I don't know what she's going to do! So I shot her."

"You shot her?"

"I didn't know what she was going to do. Ever since the first time, when I didn't know if the hardware was going to work for five minutes straight, I carried a .45 automatic, just in case. Security, you know."

"So you shot her."

There was a long silence on the other end of the line. For some crazy reason I thought of that sequence in *2001: A Space Odyssey* where the astronaut's tumbling over and over and all of the colors are coming at you. It was that kind of silence.

"She told me she loved me, Marty." Silence again. "Marty?"

"I'm here."

"She was naked, and there was blood all over the place, and I was holding her, and she said she loved me, and—and—and . . . What am I going to do now, Marty? What am I going to do?"

I couldn't see any way around it. "I don't know, Ben. I don't know how exactly to put this, but I think we're going to have to find a new campaign."

"No more Mr. Right?"

"Well, there's no more Demonica, Ben. And I don't see how we can justify sending out professional criminals to terrorize New York just so you can fight them. There isn't any more threat."

"You did it before." His voice was low, terrified.

"That was different. That was just to juice things up in between Demonica's attacks. This would be fabricating the whole thing from scratch." I didn't tell him the truth; I'd be happy to send the Vultures after him, or the Battery Boys, but we wouldn't be able to keep it going. His equipment had been breaking down recently, and we didn't know how to fix it. I never told him Demonica had been coming in to work on the stuff, to patch it together, that she'd been the one that had kept it going as long as it had. Better to stop now than to let it deteriorate and have to tell him why we couldn't fix it any more.

"But—but . . . What am I going to do? You've got to tell me, Marty. You've got to!"

"Oh come on, Ben. You've had a good run. You made plenty of money and you had your time in the spotlight. It's not like you're out on the street. You own your own home and you've got plenty of capital. Buy a restaurant. Take a trip. Go back to school. The world is your oyster, pal, and you're on vacation. Savor it."

"But—"

"Oh, for Christ's sake! Wake up and smell the coffee, Ben. It's over. Real life is back. Cope, already." I hung up, then took the receiver off the hook in case he called back.

I reached for my Rolodex; this was important. Once the news broke—and it would break; no use hiding it— it'd be the biggest nine-day wonder this town ever saw. But the story would fade. King faded. Lennon faded. Everything fades but Chappaquiddick.

So I had to move fast. The first guy I wanted to talk to worked for *Newsweek*, the second for the *Times*, and after that there were a few other good possibilities. Once this story faded, there'd be a lot of reporters leaving town. If I acted now, while I was the only guy who knew, maybe I could get the inside line on a decent place to live.

*   *   *

I ended up in a roomy walk-through near Gramercy Park, and I've been there almost a year. We came up with a new campaign—you know, the one with the fish— and we pretty much forgot about both of them. I hadn't realized how much everything changed until I heard about him committing suicide in Miami or somewhere, and it got me thinking about it again. It was pretty wild, I guess, looking at it in retrospect.

But, damn, this used to be a fun town, didn't it?

Kurt Busiek has had a hate-hate relationship with New York City almost since birth. Since he lived in the Boston area as a child, the Red Sox were the local heroes, which made the Yankees the hereditary enemy, and everything about New York tainted with their evil. When he graduated from college and moved to Manhattan for several hellish months, he discovered that it was all true—except for the curious fact that all the New Yorkers he met hated the Yankees too. He now lives in Connecticut, but his job at Marvel Comics, where he edits OPEN SPACE, a shared-universe SF anthology series in comics form, keeps him commuting in through Grand Central Station five days a week and keeps his feelings about New York close to the surface.

What Lives After

by Robert Frazier

This is a gruesome little story that considers the question of just where the borderline between life and death actually is. I'm told that the author hadn't intended to submit it for this anthology, but got talked into it. I'm glad he did—but some of the more nightmare-prone readers may not be.

One blast, two blasts:
(The endless feeling of free-fall, though you're sprawled on the pavement. Your skull snaps back against the solid world. Stars merge into light. For a moment there is reversal—you're the woman floating, rising above the skyscrapers, above the Twin Towers and the glittering circuit board of the city. Then: snapback. Pain. Wildly pumping adrenaline.)
—That's it, babe. *Hasta la vista.*
(The sound of mocking laughter above you.)
—Maybe I'll come back before yer dead. Or tear another piece after. Huh? Wouldn't ya just love it?
(Another laugh.)
—Maybe.
The attacker leaves, and you hear:
(Footsteps approaching. A hoarse cough followed by a voice.)
—Goddamn. There's a bitch in here. Oh, Jesus! Frag gun. What a mess.
(A trash can scraping the cement.)
—Just leave her, man.
—No. She's fragged. I'm phonin' it in.
—Geez, man. Forget it.
(A scuffle, then running steps. The lid to a can crashes

like a cymbal close by. Rolls for a moment. Spins around and down and diminishes, it seems forever, into silence. A long silence. Finally, sirens cut through it, grow louder, then stabilize.)

—Down here, I think. The call said behind the dumpster.

—See her?

—Not yet. Yeah. I've got her. Looks bad. We'll need to hustle.

(A squeak of shoes. A sense of movement to your left.)

—No pulse. Wait, I've got one. Get the wheels closer. Easy.

(You're detached. Hovering.)

—Okay. One quick lift.

Maybe five minutes after the attack, an eternity of traffic noise. And you hear yourself say to them:

"Oh, Jesus. Oh, God."

(You echo inside the ambulance.)

—Calm down, lady.

(Fingers brush the hair from your face. They wander. Settle on your shoulder. You get the shivers for a moment.)

—Just talk to us. Okay? Can you talk?

"Why me? I'm not even pretty."

(The siren is wailing. There's a click, a static and hiss.)

—Manhattan Emergency. Do you copy? MEH unit three, on call. Do you copy? Yes. We need an OR and a compdoc. Code Twelve trauma. Full surgical hardware. No. ETA of three to four minutes. Okay, description. About twenty-five. Female Caucasian, with two fragmentary shots taken from six or eight feet. Lucky it was a good model. The spread is tight. One right anterior chest, entrance and exit equal. Hematoma both sides. Is this Drumm talking? Yes, do I copy clear?

"Oh, my God. Oh, no."

—Relax. Just a little longer.

(Click. More static on the radio.)

—MEH, unit three here. Do you copy? Copy, dammit! Come in. All right. It's a Code Twelve. Looks like rape involved, as well. Must've started it off. No. No signs of hemorrhage in the organs. Pressure's about one-oh-oh palp. We've got biosigns on. Rate's about the same, right, Bob? Yes, rate about one-ten. Shit. Okay, I'll wait. Yes. The other? The other's really an arm wound, partial on face. Not a life threat, just looks real bad.

"Ahhhhh . . . Ahhhhh."

—Hold on now, lady. This'll help you breathe.

—Talk to her, Bob.

"Agghh . . ."

—Hold on. Life needs a boost, you know. We get worn out on the beat and can't give it the strength we should. Our asses are on the line. You wouldn't believe some of the jackoffs we're dealin' with. They call up desperate, you know. COME NOW. NOW! Then later, when somethin' doesn't go right, they threaten to sue. I've been through plenty. Not from major saves. No. They're grateful enough. It's the little shit. The bone sliver that didn't scan. Or some exotic infection that starts up in post-op. Or somethin' else. Somethin' goddamn loopy.

—Hey, Bob. Remember the guy from down near the UN Building?

—Yeah. That's a good story. Loopy as hell.

—Tell her. Keep our passenger occupied.

—Well, this man . . . He took a couple punches from a razor glove while comin' home from a banquet. A lot of blood. But he had a history of cardiac, too. That, as usual, became the serious problem. Signs of PVCs after we jumped him once, but the lido didn't raise his threshold. He V-fibbed and stayed back in despite the lidocaine. Had to do CPR fast near the end, then increase the wattage. I could hardly get a capture on biosigns, though. He was breathin', but it was agonal, you know. On the way out. Same with the heart beat. We lost him. The compdoc zapped him once more. Hard. Called it finally. Shut down the monitors. Well, the wife was furious. Bellowed her way into OR. Slugged the woman who was assisting the compdoc on site. You've given up, she said. There's still goddamn brain function. For a long time there's brain function. Ignore biosigns! He lives after. How would you like to be trapped in there knowin' the doctors have given up? Chrissakes! Do somethin'. He's imprisoned in there. In the brain.

—Jesus, what a bitch. I remember her.

—Right, so we find out later this lady is into cerebral research at Columbia. A secret project, like the Manhattan Project, only on extended brain life. Very sophisticated work, you know. She takes us to court, based on the findin' of her studies. But it's not acceptable as science yet—that is, what the government allows to see light. Interestin' case, says the judge. But it's a toss. The judges know what we go through. Got no friends, is what. Not down in the blood factory. Hatty General is not a hospital where real medics want to be. It's the worst in the country. Where else can you get such a bunch of crazies off the street? Paste junkies. Wire addicts. Sickos. Ghetto bums who rip off expensive toys like . . . yeah, frag guns. We're lepers in our profession just for workin' in this city. Tainted.

—You ran into her after, didn't you?

—Yeah. She was better. I saw her in the rush outside the courthouse, and I said, "It could have been worse. He could have died while someone was messin' with him. Right there impaled on the asshole's hands." She called me callous. I guess that's a fair call. We lose our tact out here, you know. Tact and polite, that stuff isn't expedient. Then she said, "I know what you're sayin'. But you're wrong." She looked me straight in the eye. Cool as a Bud hidden between the ice packs in the ER. "There's nothin' worse than bein' abandoned with no place to go. Nothin' worse," she said. Whew! I was glad when that one was over.

(More static. A garble of radio voices and unintelligible syllables.)

—Hey, Bob. They want to know if we have a line in.

—Tell them I'm workin' on *número dos*. Breathin's gettin' raspy, you know. Take it easy, lady. Hold on.

—Yeah, we have a line. And have used a fifty. Breath sounds raspy on her right side. No, everything's mostly closed. Cauterized. Getting a second line in.

(The siren dies away. A couple of sharp turns. Brakes squeal. For a moment, the sensation of rocking in your mother's arms.)

—The eagle has landed.

(Doors creak open. Movement. Air over your face. Rushing sensations.)

—Good work, boys. Easy getting her down. Finish those cutdowns, dammit. We need the blood pumping. She's in shock.

(Pain. They're making more pain.)

—Get moving. Her heart looks bad on biosigns.
(And again.)

Sometime later, you hear:
—Hey . . .
(The overhead light is bright enough to penetrate your eyelids. But the lids won't lift for you to see. You haven't seen anything since the flash of the gunshots.)
—Hey. She's comin' back.
—I'm concerned with cardiac functions. Feed me the data.
—Fed, Mister compdoc. The rate's fifty-five. My age as of today.
—Happy Birthday, dipstick. Just keep feeding.
—Clara on visual. I'm on site with the patient in OR. Blood lines open. Hook up for biosigns. Looks set.
—Visual signs, please!
—She's working to breathe.
(You feel a burning drain in your throat. Weight on your chest.)
—Keep me cued with visual impressions, okay?
(You must tell the woman, help. Please help!)
—Maybe she's trying to say something.
—Opening the T-dopamine. Logging twenty percentile.
—Visual again. She's got to have blood pressure, but I can't see it on the miniscreen here. Am I patched into biosigns?
(The thread slips away.)
—I'm havin' trouble patchin' you and the doc. Anyhow, the pulse is fadin'. We better work without the patch.
—Clara. I want the Nusoprel gun.
—It's double-loaded. In place above the heart.
—Fire one.
(Flare of pain.)
—Gettin' some signs on my monitors, Doc. I'm on amplified, though. They're just barely readin'.
—Fire two.
—Almost a capture there. But she's slippin' away.
—I need your readouts. What's the pulse now?
—None. Must have imagined it.
—
—Okay. CRP authorization. Zap at two hundred fifty.

—Done.

—Again, Clara.

—Done.

(You're attached again. You contract and hover inside your head. Like a hum. A mantra.)

—Jesus, Doc, we're flat on readouts.

—Ready the CPR, Clara. Use three hundred.

—Done.

(The mantra increases to a chorus.)

—Nothin' here.

—Use another.

(The shock rides through you. Passes on.)

—

—Another, Clara?

—I don't think there's much point . . .

—Call it, Doc.

—Logging off biosigns. Give me a time, dipstick.

—Bob. It's Bob.

—You're also a paramedic, right?

—Yeah.

—Sorry. You've got a good rep. I didn't mean to badmouth you.

—Is this mutual admiration time or a wrap-up?

—Leave it to a goddamn woman. Okay. I call it.

—Twenty-two hundred, five minutes. Get that, Doc?

—Yes, time logged. Is there a phone number for the family?

(They left you behind long ago. Just like everyone else.)

—No kin on record. Just done scannin' the data from City Banks.

—A name, guys? She must have a name.

(Do you need a name?)

—Sally Rose.

—Sure.

Still later:

—So sorry, Number Thirteen. This is awkward. But I'm the only one on morgue tonight. And you're heavy.

(He's rough on you. Hands all over you.)

—People know the work's bad. They think I talk to myself to handle the stress.

(Who else would he talk to?)

—But that's not it. I know you're still in there. There was this scientist who brought a suit against Manhattan General. Then Columbia University and her bosses, the U.S. government. I looked up her work on the persistence of brain function. An astounding read. Really. I know you can still hear me.

(His hand scrabbles across your breast. He strokes the nipple.)

—I know you can get some sensory stuff. And you're great. As fine and as flawed as any female this city ever saw. My quintessential babe.

(He touches your face. His hand wanders. Then probes you.)

—You still feel it. You know what I'm doing.

(He withdraws. There's the scrape of rollers as the drawer begins to ease shut. A solid click. His voice is muffled.)

—I'll be back for more. I really like girls with wounds. Bad wounds. We'll have a fun send-off. Won't you just love that? Yes. Maybe you will?

(You can almost hear the darkness close you in . . .)

—Maybe.

(like a pair of hands around . . .)

—Just maybe.

(your throat . . .)

—

"The evil that men do lives after them."
Julius Caesar, Act III, Scene 2

Born in Ayer, Massachusetts: 1951. First hitch-hiked through New York City, by way of a garage band practice: 1969. First read The Stars My Destination, *San Francisco to New York by Greyhound: 1972. First long delay circling Kennedy Airport: 1980. First heard a pitbull speak, Nebula Banquet, New York: 1987. First published story in* In the Field of Fire, *Tor Books, Jack and Jeanne Dann, editors: 1987. Last time even vaguely near New York: early August, 1989, when under the mind-altering effects of sleep deprivation, in flight from Raleigh to Boston (there is a hidden synergy here; no more than a* few—perhaps one—of you will find it), this story came full twist into my head. Thank God, it's exorcised: September 21, 1989.

"You can get anything in New York," states the verbal tourist brochure of the city's streetwise. They're talking endangered species as entrées in a certain restaurant. Talking the crack mobile that drives through the neighborhood like an ice-cream truck. Cambodian porn. Scarification. Anything. The city, then, has always struck me as the model landscape for science fiction, for, taken literally, all things are possible for those living within its boundaries. And for those dead.

—Robert Frazier

Slow Burn in Alphabettown

by S. N. Lewitt

Here's a slice of life in the near future, a look at the ferocious contrasts between rich and poor in New York, by way of Bloomingdale's and Avenue D.

They were burning New Jersey again. Even from Eighth Avenue the yellow-flame light danced over the hydrant-drenched street and made it like an August take on hell, even if summer had come and gone. The roar wasn't muffled by the mix of salsa and hip-hop that blared from competing windows. Even with the music turned way up, the fire sounds fought the beat-box.

"Maybe this time the tanks in Elizabeth'll go," I said to Luis as I watched the water gush from the hydrant and turn red like the flames. The tanks did blow once, when I was seven. We were living over on a Hundred and Sixth then, all the way over on the East Side, and the shock hit the building so hard that the ceiling ruptured and plaster fell all over my bed. Later I heard that the flare was so high it raked incoming at Newark Airport, and school was canceled all over the city the next day.

"Dream on," Luis said. "You got anything cold?"

Right. Cold. And Luis tells *me* to dream on. Well, he can keep on hoping, but it don't make ice. Signs all over the subway keep telling us to conserve power since New Jersey isn't selling anymore and the Island is garrisoned. No juice for the city from them. Politics. Besides, the generator in the basement is on the fritz again, cheapest junk the landlord could install to comply with code. I shook my head and handed over the half-carafe of generic red. Luis sort of smiled and took a slug, spat it out over the tear in his jeans, and set the rest down on the stoop.

"Bad out," he said.

"Worse in," I told him, and that was the truth. Maybe the rot stank worse than the fires across the Hudson, but sometimes there was a breeze like now. Oxygen rushing to feed New Jersey. Maybe it'd all go if the Elizabeth tanks blew, but it'd be worth it for the show. And the breeze might not actually cool down the street any, but it shifted the stench a little and that was enough.

Luis half-sat and half-leaned on the ornate cement ball at the edge of the stoop. One boot heel dug flat into the grunge and the other rested up on the ledge, his hands clasped around the torn-out knee. He looked like some poet trying to catch the shadows strained through the lattice of the West Side Highway.

I gave him decent time to tell me himself before I asked. Luis Vélez never shows at my door unless he wants something. Money, a place to sleep, an alibi, what the hell, he's Luis and he needs me and that's all that counts in the end. He was silent. And then Mr. Marrero, two doors down, came out and started setting up his card table next to the only hydrant that still had all its fixtures. He glared at us and spat on the street, discreetly as if it were just some phlegm and not disapproval.

"Come on," I said; I took the carafe by the neck and led the way. My apartment, third floor, enter through the kitchen and bolt the police lock behind. By the time I turned around, Luis was seated on the long counter tearing the rip in his jeans wider. That was when I saw that the faded white fringe was crusted red.

I sighed and shook my head. "Take them off," I said.

Luis smiled. "I didn't want to offend your modesty," he said, which was a courtesy and a crock all in one so I couldn't reject it. Because he knew damn well that we both meant business, and that maybe we didn't entirely want to. And once he eased the faded denim off the wounded leg it was obvious why he didn't hesitate. He was wearing dark-blue gym shorts with a Mets logo on the right leg. Joe had been a Mets fan forever.

Someday, I swore, he was going to look at me and see me, not Joe's baby sister. Maybe because it was Joe's apartment he thought he could come and ask for things Joe never would have begrudged, and maybe that's why I kept giving them to him. Or maybe he just had too much traditional respect for the sister of a friend.

So I got out the rubbing alcohol and poured it straight into the open wound on his knee without mercy. The little hiss as he tried not to wince with the pain was enough reward. "I'll have to scrub this out," I told him. "You might have got some foreign particle ground in. You weren't down by Needle Park, right?"

"Nothing foreign here, only pure made in New York," he joked. "No, I wasn't anywhere near the park." Well, at least that meant that he hadn't fallen in any of the nazMat they're dumping there. Biologicals. Engineered viruses. All the stuff that closed off the Island and Dutchess County trade last year.

I ignored Luis putting on a brave show but was a little more gentle with my ministrations. After all, I'd made my point. Then I sprayed it with skinseal and Luis turned white.

"Hey, that stuff is regulated, isn't it?" he demanded hotly.

I smiled. "Abrams up at the drugstore used Mrs. Rothman's ID. We're cool."

He looked like he didn't believe me, or didn't want to. It seems to bother Luis when I'm competent and in charge. When I know that Mrs. Rothman had been some kind of radical when she was my age and she would help us out. That was one tough old lady, still selling the *Socialist Worker* down on Houston Street on Saturday and Sunday afternoons. Besides which, Luis didn't really have much choice. At least he wasn't wearing gauze the way they had during the first days of the strike. That was a dead giveaway.

"Who was it?" I asked only when I was all done. He didn't put on his pants, which I didn't expect, but he didn't leave the counter that covered the tub, either, to move to the more comfortable daybed in the main room. "Scabs?"

"Who else?"

I drank some of the wine and ignored his practiced leer. "This is total bullshit," I told him. "So you go and pick fights with them. Big deal. What does it get you? Besides into my apartment, I mean. So they get a little banged up and there's more where they came from. Which is probably Buffalo or something. If you're going to get messed up, you might as well make a serious point."

"Look at New Jersey," Luis said softly. "They're burning. And they're organizing up on the East Side."

"Yeah, so they're burning Jersey. Great. And now we're going to organize Alphabettown. They only blow on themselves anyway, and who cares if you torch Avenue D?" We sat on my daybed and ate potato chips. "So, you want to tell me what happened?" I demanded.

He didn't need to tell me, not really. It was the same every time. Like the time he had come back with Joe's body.

That had been one of the earliest fights of the strike. Joe, Luis, the rest of their squad, had built a barricade down on East Broadway, where it would wreak hell with the Wall Street traffic. Being garbagemen—or ecological engineers, as the city calls them now that it won't pay— they had all the best stuff to build a good barricade, lots of rusty fenders and left front doors, chipped cement, ancient sofa beds with springs and cushions still attached.

I went down to see that barricade in the first days, when the guys would bring their boom-boxes and sit on the top and the rest of us would run up and down with water and peanut-butter sandwiches. I thought it was beautiful, and it was fun. So many people came out. Mrs. Rothman brought half the radical retirement home, all these people who must have been about eighty trying to teach us to sing the Internationale and something called "Blowin' in the Wind." It was just like a block party, with the local hot-dog vendors doing sell-out business. The biggest fight I saw was when the news van from Channel 5 pulled in front of the one from Chanel 11 and the crews had a shouting match over the generator plugs. The police only busted one guy, and that was for selling beer without a license.

Luis and Joe were dancing on the top of the rubble, dancing with the boom-box turned up loud. And they were laughing, all those guys, and I was laughing too. It was a good time, a good day. We felt strong enough to take on the whole police force, strong enough to topple Manhattan, full of pride and dignity because it was our city, too, and not just a place for the gray-suits and the club-goers and the ladies who lunch at Bloomingdales.

I mean, I felt so good that right at that moment I felt like I could walk into Bloomie's and sit down in the lunchroom and order like the Queen of England. I wouldn't worry about trying to sell overpriced perfume to the thin rich ladies of fashion who had nothing better to do than follow every trend in the known universe.

I've never been to a party that good, and that's what it was: a party, not a strike. God, were we all babies then. We didn't know anything at all about what a strike really was. We only knew about barricades and music and too many hot dogs and not enough Rolaids. A couple of the guys got sick, I think from the sauerkraut. Joe gave me the key to his apartment and asked me to go and get him a clean pair of jeans. I never saw him alive again.

Later they said they had information that there was a terrorist from the Revolutionary Council and they were sorry Joe got caught in the confusion, but saying sorry didn't make Joe any more alive. Besides, I don't think it was an accident. I mean, maybe they didn't really mean to kill anyone, not just yet, but there was no accident about when the Tactical Police charged their big brown horses just like the Rough Riders going up San Juan Hill. I saw it all on Joe's TV.

The barricade was too strong to plow down, and so the horses just went straight up, the pigs swinging their clubs and holding their riot gear in front of them. Swinging and smashing heads, blood all over the rusted inner springs and moldy chair seats. Luis was hurt bad, and Rey and Petey and old man Franklin. But Joe got hit on the head and he fell off the barricade and the coroner never did say if he died from the fight or the fall. Then the TPF torched the thing so that it turned the night as red as New Jersey.

They're burning there again, no matter that the city council is about ready to declare war. And why should they care, really? They've got a whole state, reactor sites and refineries and ports and enough state troopers with ammunition to take us on for weeks. The city council can't be stupid enough to think that the gangs would go out for Jersey, too far from their turf.

At Joe's funeral all the pallbearers wore white gloves and gauze bandages. We buried his ashes out on Long Island, visas rushed courtesy of *Newsday*, who wanted the exclusive. The money for the plot coming from the union strike fund. While I sat through Mass, I thought about his ashes in the urn, a human body that is dead, that is garbage, too. All the endings patiently collected for the ground, the dump, the cemetery. A dump all full of sad and broken things like my big brother Joe, who always brought me sky-blue ices after school. When I was seventeen and got caught stuffing a spandex dress in my purse, it was Joe who came down to the station and got me out and swore that it would never happen again. I knew I was in for a beating, Popi was always strict about things like that, but Joe never told. And I never lifted anything again, either.

Father Morales made me cry when he talked about my brother. In front of the church with all the flowers and bells, the urn was almost lost. Such a little bit when Joe had been so big. The priest didn't talk about the garbageman or the striker. He reminded us of when Joe had tried to save the kittens he found bundled in a hefty bag near Park and Eighty-first. How Joe had bought the extra-heavy cream and had dunked the kittens' faces in it to make them drink because they were so skinny, and Joe always felt sorry for skinny helpless things. Even Luis and Petey had wet eyes before we had to drive out to the cemetery.

After the funeral everyone came back to Mama's apartment and ate cold sliced ham. I served the large platters around. Something to do was better than sitting, better than talking to the silent strikers with layers of gauze wrapped around an arm, a head.

Some of the guys were muttering about the police report and about the Revolutionary Council and ignoring me. Joe had always told me that it was just a kid's story, to pretend that there was someone stronger and braver who could rescue them in the night. He never believed in any council, not one that had access to IDs and explosives and had soldiers who were trained and ready to take action. Real action.

Sometimes I dreamed about taking action the way a girl never did, of getting up on the barricades myself and waving a torch, Of having all my brother's friends recognize that I was someone, too, someone with hopes and needs like their own. Joe and Luis and Petey never saw it.

"Are you going to keep the apartment, Noemí?" Luis asked me, bringing me out of my fantasy.

I shook my head. I hadn't thought about it at all, had never thought about leaving home. Mama needed me and I saved money. Besides, I hardly knew Luis Vélez then, even if he had been Joe's best friend.

"Well, think about it," Luis said. "You could help us a lot. Have a place where we could go if there was trouble. And it's rent-controlled. You have a good head for a kid."

"I'm not a kid," I told him angrily, just the way I always told Joe when he treated me like a baby. "I'm almost nineteen and I have a job, a good job, and Mama needs me."

Well, maybe it wasn't such a good job. I hated that place, like going into a big white tomb every day, like the place where we had buried Joe. Another garbage dump, Bloomie's, but it's the people, not the things. Ladies, all of them ladies who chattered about colors and style and size and being thin, who knew that Misako was in and Tomo was out and thought that was important. Acted like it was the whole world when outside in reality people ate pizza and bled and passed around the screwcap and died.

Maybe that was the reason I thought the guys, with all their attitude, were hopeless. They didn't know the enemy, didn't have any idea that we were fighting aliens. That the universe at Bloomie's belonged somewhere on another planet where people ate and thought and lived lives that were incomprehensible to each other. Joe and Petey and Luis too, they were all innocent, shining in their conviction. They had never had a customer wearing a blouse that cost more than my rent look at them as if they were not there, a ghost, completely invisible. Because to them, we are.

"We need you, too," Luis said, and then he turned away and talked to Petey.

Those words, I couldn't get them out of my head. "We need you, too." He needed me. And I couldn't get him out of my head either.

For days I avoided the strike. I didn't turn on the TV, slammed the door to my room whenever Popi and Uncle Carlos talked about it. I even turned my head away and tried not to read the extra-large letters of the *Daily News* headlines. I tried to live the way the other girls at work did, where newspapers mean *Women's Wear Daily*.

But Luis haunted me. On every street I saw Luis and didn't see him. Walking down Seventh Avenue to get a couple of slices of pizza, I saw the men who pushed the clothes racks across the streets, and every one of them didn't look as good as Luis. This one was too short and that one didn't have such black, long hair, and the one across the street didn't have the fine Castillian nose of Luis Vélez. And so I avoided the strike, but I needed to know more, to see him again. Just to catch a glimpse of him on the barricade the way it was with Joe, laughing and turning up the music and eating pork rinds out of the bag.

I avoided the news, but I could not avoid the smell. All of Manhattan smelled bad and it was only May. The streets, which had always been full of litter, were white and pink and pale fax green with paper. Layers of paper covered the sidewalks, and if it weren't for the smell, the whole city would look like a Saturday-morning cartoon, with orange and yellow burger wrappers plastered over a black advertisement over a mile of green-and-white-striped computer trash.

The smell was worse than the dying rats and damp in the subway, worse than the concrete saturated with piss and the dirty water in the buckets the bums used to wipe car windows. The smell was worse than everything, mounting, growing, a thing all its own. It ate the city. It became part of us, embedded in the bread at the gyros stand, the gentle smell of clean cotton T-shirts like laundry soap smelled in a softer time. The smell sizzled in the neon, in the boom-boxes, in the clubs down in the Village and the discos uptown.

The stench was democratic. It didn't care if you lived with closed windows on the top of a building on East Seventy-third and used up three of my monthly allotments of electric, or if you were down in Alphabettown like Luis, with an ID screen on the side of the fridge and the top of the TV, pay as you go, and no microwave allotment at all. It stank the same. Every day when I got out of the subway and entered the whole white block of Bloomingdale's, I enjoyed the evil smell, knowing that the ladies who paid for Chanel and Milano Sotto perfumes were wasting their bucks. The sacred name "Bloomingdale's" couldn't keep the stench out, and it perme-

ated the YSLs and Lagerfields and Ferrantes, the trendy
little rag-rage sweaters and the furs. Evening gowns,
wedding dresses, and housewares all smelled like the
discount shops downtown, and even the elegant displays
for the special focus on Japanese fashion that month
could not escape the smell. Wealth and a Long Island or
Connecticut passport didn't stop the air full of summer-
rotting stink.

Two weeks after Joe died I moved into his apartment,
still under old man Franklin's lease and rent control.
Mama never stopped crying and Popi didn't talk to me,
as if he was mad that Joe had died and I was alive. I
couldn't help that, and I tried to argue with them, and we
had bad fights. Finally it was just easier to go.

Luis came over the second night. He would have helped
me move, he said, but he'd been on barricade duty and
was off now. I looked at him, at his proud and narrow
face with a bruised eye and scarred hands, and I didn't
care what he said. Just so long as he stayed.

"You could be a strong sister," he told me. "You
could be out there, helping us, running things. Getting
medical supplies. Our IDs have been censored, you know
that? No medical supplies, not even aspirin'll pass. My
ID won't work on a phone, either, or a newsmachine or a
TV. It's worse than Workfare allowances."

Buy aspirin? Sure. I'd do anything to keep him around.
Skinseal spray, newspapers, telephone calls, a microwave
on a three-hour-a-month meter for hot meals. Luis once
mentioned trying to pay me back by hot-wiring the microwave meter for a couple more hours, but that carries a
two-thousand-dollar fine if you're caught and it's not
worth it. I found that out trying to walk out with that
dress two years ago.

And then Luis disappeared for a month. I didn't see
him, didn't see his name in the Metro court-proceedings
listings shown every night of the strike, and the strike
was getting worse. They were bringing in scabs from
Buffalo, from New Hampshire, from West Virginia, from
all the places where people were a whole lot worse off
than we were. At least New York is still rich. It always
was and it always will be, with the docks unloading
Italian furniture and English fabrics, with the stock market and the CitiCorp Building and Time-Life at Rocke-

feller Center. And Chemical Bank and half the banks in the known universe, the Saudis and the Israelis and the Brazilians and the Japanese all have headquarters here. And we make clothes for the whole Northern Faction, coats to underwear. There are jobs here, if you're willing to shape up on Canal Street at five and pay an hour's wage to get a day's labor at ABC agency, or Foreman's down the hall.

I heard all kinds of rumors about something going on with the union and the park and I prayed that it wasn't true and, if it was, that Luis wasn't involved. And they were organizing down in Alphabettown and it was his neighborhood, besides. Which I didn't like. I don't go down there anymore, not since the park became the hospital dump and the kids started being born with pieces like fingers or jawbones or whole legs missing. All that HazMat piled up in one place, stinking and rotting in the middle of the Lower East Side.

At work the girls said how it was making the city rotten and how no one from Long Island was going to spend any hard currency. And then we turned to the important things. Marina insisted that she had discovered a product that really kept nails from breaking, and Sonia and Laurie were having a bitter argument over whether plum or mauve eyeshadow was going to be popular for fall. I wanted to kill all of them.

I started going to strike headquarters, mostly to see if Luis would come in, but also to talk to people who thought about something other than the latest fashion. The union's bookkeeping was all a mess, you'd think no one had ever invented a spreadsheet program, so I sort of took over naturally. It wasn't any different than doing inventory, and Mrs. Perry wasn't supervising, sniping as if she were one of the wealthy matrons she served. As for the union guys, as long as a woman sits in front of a keyboard, the men feel comfortable. It's her place, to them, not challenging, not really involved in their world. But at the same time it was a good place, a place of power. I did all the strike fund books, found out where the retirement money was and what interest we had and how much we owned of what companies. Big companies, ones where the gray-suits earn enough to keep the ac turned on to October. Which is next week and they say the heat should break. I'm not betting on it myself.

I sat in front of the computer and smiled and did the books. The guys in the local were very grateful. Chemical Bank and Morgan Stanley down on Wall Street, chunks of Time, Inc., and IBM and Oregon Generators and the Long Island Railroad, although that had been losing money since the commutation laws had been passed. Shares and shares in all of them.

I didn't talk about it much, and no one asked what I was doing. The guys all thought that I was doing whatever it was women did with keyboards, so they joked around and brought me coffee and generally left me alone. What did they care? Power was on the streets, on the barricades, that were in the news every night. The banner headlines alternated between the *Post* and the *Daily News*: how many days out, how many tons accumulated on the city streets. It was late August.

A month later Luis returned. Just showed up on the stoop the Sunday afternoon I took off to do my laundry and scrub the floor and sort the green fuzz out of the fridge. He sat out on the steps and talked to Mr. Marrero about if the heat would break in October and if the Mets might have made the pennant if Jorge Castros hadn't broken his leg on that double play in the second game. Mr. Marrero claimed that Castros was related to him somehow through his wife, maybe it's even true.

"When you guys going back to work?" he asked Luis right under my window, which was open more to let the smell of ammonia out than to pretend that there was a cool breeze.

"It don't work like that," Luis said cheerfully. " 'Cause it ain't just pay this time, you know? Not just the green stuff. It's that we can't burn, like they do in Jersey. We can't do nothing at all, just dump in the designated areas, like off Staten Island."

"They don't burn on Long Island. I got a cousin lives out on Long Beach. They don't burn there. They send it out to sea and sink it," Mr. Marrero said. He's got relatives everywhere, and anything you say he says isn't true and he's always got some cousin or uncle or niece's ex-husband to back him up.

Luis kept smiling. "And take a look what it's done to

Jones Beach, and Long Beach too. It all comes up in the tide. Went up there a couple of weeks ago. They're letting strikers in without visas now, and there's all these dead things piled up in the sand. Fish, garbage, I wouldn't be surprised if Jimmy Hoffa's skeleton washed up in that mess. We have to do something. And we're going to burn in New York or we're going to sink Manhattan under plastic milk cartons and microwave trays and paper. Sink us all down so that it covers up the World Trade Center and someday people come back and dig down and find us again. And it'll be power, too, since Jersey stopped selling. We need it bad. You got decent ac here? We don't burn we'll all be dead. No way, man."

Mr. Marrero started to mutter something under his breath, but I poked my head out and invited Luis in. Mr. Marrero gave me a foul look and said something about decent girls with strange men. Don't I wish.

That time Luis wanted me to hide some papers. I thought we ought to burn them, only that was illegal. Maybe ash them out in the microwave.

"No, there's stuff I might need. My passport, you know?" he said.

Well, it was only one little envelope. I wrapped it in foil and stuck it in the freezer. Luis was impressed with that. Sometimes I open the freezer and look at that package and cry and think about opening it up. Because it belongs to him and maybe there's something personal in there, a note to me maybe, or a picture. I liked to hold it and pretend that there was something that showed he really cared for me. But I never dared open it up, not because I was afraid of Luis but because there might not be anything at all personal to me and I didn't want to know that. I didn't want to think that maybe he just wasn't interested, or had another girl.

So we sat on the daybed eating potato chips because I was saving my allotment to bake a big ham for Columbus Day, and maybe turkey, too, to bring over to my mother's. No lights or TV, I was saving the juice and there was enough light from the fires on the Jersey side to see, at least a little. And I was glad it was mostly dark.

"You remember, remember how me and Joe and Petey used to walk down to Chinatown, to the big theater there, and catch those kung-fu movies," he said. His

voice was soft with forgotten pleasures. "Joe always wanted
to see the ones with the girls fighting and I always wanted
to go to whatever was at the Palace because it was a
double feature for the price of one. And then we'd go eat
and hit Ferrara's for cannoli on the way home?"

Yeah, sure I remembered. Every Saturday night I would
hope, crazy, that this time they would invite me along.
And every Saturday night I would end up with Aleida
and Debbie going to sit on car hoods down by the play-
ground and watch the guys cruise by. But none of them
ever looked as good as Luis and none of them talked as
fine. Debbie and Aleida used to call me shy and scared
and skinny, and other things¹ besides. And all the time I
was searching the street for Joe and Luis and Petey
coming back, wondering if they'd thought to bring me a
cannoli or an ice.

But Luis was already talking again. "I wish I could be
that person again. He was a better person, you know. I
didn't hate anyone then, I didn't imagine hating anyone.
I sat in those movies and watched people beat each other
to death and vomit fake blood made with Karo syrup and
I thought it was all a joke. But it isn't a joke, you
know?"

"Did you do something?" I asked, framing each word
carefully, not sure I wanted to ask and certain I didn't
want to know.

"What I do isn't important," he said quickly. "I mean,
it's what we do, all together. Right? And I promised Joe
that I'd treat you just like he always did, just like you
was my own sister. So I want to tell you, do the books
and stuff, but don't go messing around where you could
get hurt."

Don't treat me like Joe. I almost said it then, but the
words just didn't make it through my mouth. Instead,
other words spilled out, other ideas. "I got it all figured,"
I told him. "The books and the retirement fund, it's all in
there. You wouldn't believe what the union owns. Big
companies, the guys always running us down. You know,
Luis, we should be running this city. I gave the data to
Mr. Millikan down at the retirement home. Mrs. Rothman
said he was some hot radical lawyer once."

I giggled. That wasn't all Mrs. Rothman had said about
him. She had blushed like a girl and lowered her voice

and said that at some prehistoric demonstration in Washington they had camped out together in a church basement, that getting arrested was more than worth the experience. For a little old lady, she sure had some history.

"Well, I don't think a whole lot of lawyers," Luis said awkwardly. "We're better off on our own. Burn the whole thing down, you know? Because we don't matter, no matter who wins. So the union owns some shares in big companies, you think that'll make any difference? It never makes a difference. Only blood and fire, that's the only way to matter. Just wait. I'm going to do something important. Just once in my life I'm going to make a difference, get some respect."

"But you do make a difference," I argued. "You make a difference with the union, with me."

"Right," he said, his face twisted in a nasty smile. "Tell me that this time tomorrow."

Heat rippled through the apartment carrying the smell of ash. The embers in New Jersey were dying. And I was all charged up, crazy. I wanted to beat his head in and I wanted him to touch me, and my fantasies matched the searing night. I wanted, wanted, and I was all bound, wrapped up in layers of tradition and shyness and respect for my brother, all the things that didn't matter alone in the dark.

It was after two when I got off the daybed and went into the kitchen, to the freezer, and retrieved the foil packet. Almost like being a sleepwalker, I got the stuff and opened it without letting the importance sink in. Luis had trusted me, and that should count as good as love.

It didn't. I held the cold foil against the back of my burning neck and let the icy condensation drip down my back. Having it in my hands was like having a little of him. There was no betrayal. We were only closer because I was going to read his papers.

I turned on the light to read and it hurt my eyes. Turned it on in the kitchen, where there wasn't a window so no one could see me up and wonder about a light wasted in the middle of the night. I sat on the counter where Luis had bled, unwrapped the foil, and slid my nail under the flap. The glue wasn't very expensive and I was careful.

As Luis had promised, there was his passport. But there was more than one. Each had a picture of Luis, although one was made out in the name of William deFillipo and another for Michael Ross. The two fakes also had matching ID cards neatly slipped in the passport flap. I looked at them, turned them over in my hands, but there was nothing I was going to get from the encoded data without a reader.

So, I told myself, he was just ready to run. That was it. And the union had provided cover just in case.

There was money, too, wads of cash in Jersey dollars and Connecticut fivers and LA yen. Pink and blue and dark-red ones along with the old-style greenbacks that still pretended to be legal tender, whatever that is. Last time I saw any of those they were wadded up in a ladies' room, about the same cost as toilet paper but not nearly as soft.

I dumped out the bills, and coins rolled all over the counter and floor. There was still one folded sheet left. I pulled it out slowly and smoothed the cold paper over my thighs. It was thick and heavy, more like plastic dough than paper. And I read the archaic handwritten introduction and it was all very clear.

"Give the bearer all aid and support," the thing read in its silly old-fashioned manner. "The Revolutionary Council has approved and sponsors this comrade as a soldier in service to the cause of justice." It went on and I read it all twice over, but I understood only too well without the rest. A soldier. That was the way the gangs talked about the frontmen, the fighters.

No way, I thought. No way. He was just my brother's friend, a guy from the old neighborhood who lived in a railroad-car apartment down in Alphabettown. And the council business was all a crock anyway, made up so that guys like Joe and Luis could pretend they were going to win it on their own, without the gray-suits and the lawyers. Without the corporate shares in the retirement portfolio, without the diligent work of a bookkeeper and an old old man. They needed to believe more than they needed to win.

Bitterness was in my tears, and anger at Joe and Uncle Carlos and the union, too. Because if Luis believed all this craziness, then he was totally gone. And if he didn't, if he had created this whole file just to make himself important, then he was stupid as well as sick.

I couldn't sleep. I lay awake on the daybed watching the car lights paint venetian-blind shadows on my wall. If I hadn't been awake, I wouldn't have heard the footsteps in the street, the light sound of sneakers, and the heavier tread of boots. I pulled the sheet around my body and stood over the window and looked down.

Mr. Marrero was shouting, waving, and there were police all over. Three stories up everything below was clear and cold and distant as the moon. All the colors had faded, and New Jersey's embers had died. There was only silver-white and black and blacker.

I knew, but I held my breath and watched anyway, as if it was a bad episode on TV. I looked straight down and I didn't see anything. The police were focused on my building and Mr. Marrero was pointing and jabbering excitedly to the lieutenant. I always thought he was the type to narc.

Slowly in the black-and-white budget night I saw Luis come forward from the door of my building. His hands were up, but his motion was all fluid, arrogant, daring them with all their gunpower and all their men to touch his lone self.

Maybe he was crazy, I don't know. They kicked him on the pavement and cuffed him and led him away to one of the cars. A long dark streak ran down his neck and over his shoulder. I thought it was just a lock of hair until it dripped on his jeans and then I knew it was blood. Still, he held himself tall and light. All he had left was attitude, style, but that was perfect.

A policeman threatened him with a heavy snub-nose pistol and he pretended not to notice, or rather that it was beneath his dignity to notice. Instead, he looked at my window, looked me straight in the eye. And for just an instant I thought I saw him smile at me before they took him away.

I sat in Mrs. Rothman's and cried. She had the passports, the note, and the money in a heap. I had a cup of tea and a slice of cherry strudel in front of me, but I wasn't hungry.

"You're gonna be late for work," the old lady observed, smoothing the paper on the table one more time, stroking it like it was a living thing.

I didn't care about work. I hated work. More than any other day since Joe died, I couldn't face work. I couldn't face the customers who expect to be treated like movie stars and royalty all at once and pay for the privilege, I couldn't face the supervisors who tried to be like the customers but were meaner and thinner in their desperate grasping. I couldn't face the softness of that world that had nothing at all to do with my own, a place where the music is softly programmed and the carpets too thick to show blood. I couldn't face another minute of Sonia's constant chatter about hairstyles and makeup and Laurie's rabbit terror that she'd be fired for gaining weight.

Bloomingdale's was the antithesis of everything that mattered in life. It was a fake world full of pretend pain, when outside there was Luis arrested and Joe dead and a trash heap of medical waste in Alphabettown.

"You know," Mrs. Rothman said in that faraway, dreamy voice she sometimes used when she was remembering her own days on the barricades, "you know, this paper stuff isn't paper at all. You know that? You know what it is? I haven't seen this stuff in maybe sixty, seventy years, not since I was as young as you are now, and me and Charlie—Charlie Millikan, that is—were still part of the radical student group at Columbia. When we became the SDS. I was a chemistry major, did I tell you that? I was, you know. Charlie wasn't really a student, actually; he was already a lawyer with a reputation, he had defended the Oswego Eight and got tossed in jail twice for contempt. We thought he was wonderful. The way he talked . . . And I hadn't met Mr. Rothman yet. That came later, when we all became anarchists. Anyway, that year I worked in the lab and I did a little research for our group. Plastic explosives. Primitive now, you know. Much better stuff around, but now this is easy enough to get and easier to disguise. Oh, in its day it was state of the art, no mistake there. Just like everything else, it's been outmoded."

She was talking briskly, cutting me another slice of the strudel. That was one thing I liked about Mrs. Rothman. There was no nonsense about her, no self-pitying old-lady stuff to get around like my grandmother. No, when

I'm pushing ninety-two, I want to be just like her, tough and ornery and downright mean when she needs to be.

I wondered what Luis had planned for the explosive. I wondered if he even knew what it was. I touched it lightly while Mrs. Rothman watched me and pushed her glasses back up her nose.

"Finish your strudel. You're going to be late to work," she scolded.

But I had an idea, and for the first time since Joe was dead, I felt real again. Real, and like I knew that there was a special closeness with Luis. Even in prison he would know what I did. And he wouldn't think of me as Joe's baby sister anymore. I would be the strong revolutionary goddess he wanted. And even if he never saw me, even if I never did get him for the night and run my hands through his long black hair and feel his scarred hands on my skin, even then I knew I'd have him. Mine forever, with an act of imagination, of daring that he would have to respect and remember.

I shoveled the last three forkfuls of strudel into my mouth, took the letter, and went to work. The secret grew during the subway ride, as I checked in to the perfume counter and locked my drawer into place. The hushed tones of wealth couldn't suffocate the knowledge in me. The women who passed my counter, eyed the glass art perfume bottles and elegant boxes, they might have thought that my smile was for their chic ensembles or maybe for the chance to sell perfume. Maybe they thought it was because I was happy to be at Bloomie's.

And I was. When I left work at closing, carefully totaling my receipts for the day and checking my drawer, I somehow managed to leave a strange note from some nonexistent Revolutionary Council behind.

I didn't even stop home to change. I took the subway down the East side to Fourteenth, the closest it came to the park. I knew there had been a rally planned, like there was nearly every day of the strike. Tonight was the usual crowd, angry and hot, ready to burn. Old Franklin was on the box, telling everyone about Luis' arrest. It was late enough that he couldn't be the first one to tell them.

Behind him was the mess that had once been Needle Park—Tompkins Square park, that is. Now it was a dump, a heap of evil-looking discarded blood and bandages. Glass chipped from Petri dishes glittered in the cold light. I could almost smell the viral death that lived here, waiting to emerge in the dark. It was a thing of the sewers, like the old stories of alligators and poison snakes that roam under the city, waiting for a chance to strike from the drain gutters. Shrouded in the refuse, it was taking form, creating itself, a monster on the verge of waking.

Mama would say it was only my imagination, but I knew I was right. I waited for Old Franklin to finish and relinquish the speaker's box, which wasn't a box at all but an aluminum stepladder set up on the sidewalk. There were maybe about fifty people gathered. A good turnout. I didn't expect that most of them were here for the harangue. They were here because it was too hot to stay in, and maybe there'd be some action. The strike had been good for that so far.

I stepped up the ladder unsteadily in the high heels I had worn to work. My tasteful autumn plum skirt and matching sweater with their gold and pink trim were out of place down in Alphabettown.

"You know," I said, "we let them dump this garbage here. They don't want to burn it, but we don't need this in our community. Maybe some of you don't care, but we women, the mothers of children here, and the grandmothers, we don't have any choice but to care. We watch our children die every day because of this heap, and no one gives a damn. You know why? You go to Bloomingdale's and you look at the women there, and you know those women don't have to worry about how to feed their children or if they're going to be born deformed. They don't have to consider the reality of burning, that we need the energy and we need to destroy this hazard before it destroys us. Maybe we should just bring it all uptown and then they would listen to us. If the mayor and the city council and the ladies who shop at Bloomingdale's, if they had to live with this evil, then we would get action."

"How we gonna get it up there, girl?" a woman in the crowd asked.

I shrugged. "Well, the dumpster trucks aren't being used for anything else right now. They're in the garage."

I don't know exactly how it all happened. I was there, but Old Franklin got the strikers organized to requisition the trucks, and others to start shoveling the refuse. The women all started knocking on neighbors' doors, and by the time the first truck had rolled up, there were at least four hundred people in the street. We filled the trucks and they rolled out slowly, and people jumped on the back ledge and hung all over them like floats in the Macy's Thanksgiving Day Parade. Others, mostly women, walked alongside. Some carried flashlights and some carried brooms and irons.

The crowd had swelled yet again. I couldn't begin to think of how many people there were. I saw Mrs. Rothman and a group of old ladies from the home marching in cadence, shaking their liver-spotted fists in the air.

We walked up Third Avenue. No one led, but everyone knew where we were going. We were going to burn down Bloomingdale's.

Eat your hearts out, New Jersey.

A third-generation Manhattanite, S. N. Lewitt lived in Alphabettown (between Avenues C and D) for several years before doing the unthinkable and leaving the city to go to graduate school at Yale. There she met Esther Friesner, learned to pass for at least middle class, and incidentally got a degree that her family considered pretentious snobbery. (Actually, they knew she was just too lazy to do any real work, like her brother the garbageman or her cousin the waitress.) She is the author of Cyberstealth *and* Dancing Vac, *both hard science fiction. Lewitt now lives with her husband in Washington, D.C., where she is writing a new book, experimenting with growing things outdoors instead of in the back of the refrigerator, and receiving food packages from her family, who don't believe there are bagels south of the New Jersey border.*

Let Me Call You Sweetheart

by Michael A. Stackpole

New York is a major port, and as such, it has always been a major battleground in the perpetual war against contraband of every sort. Here, Mike Stackpole gives a cyberpunkish slant and a humorous twist to that fight.

The languid drizzle steamed off the alley's brick wall, slowly drifting up through the dead air toward the dirty clouds. The mist unraveled the streetlight's glare into a thousand rainbow threads. Hidden deep in the shadows—safely lurking just out of sight of the traffic on Chambers Street—I reached up and adjusted the microphone by my mouth. My gloved fingers traced the line back to the jack behind my left ear. I snapped it out and back in—the check signal said the full radio system functioned—then ground my teeth with impatience.

I flexed my right hand and tightened my grip on the Smith & Wesson M-19 multi-cart pistol. My thumb caressed the selector lever, but I resisted the impulse to flick it from Tefjac to Blender shells. The M-107 T-plas attachment slung under the barrel, with its two fanglike electrode tangs flaring out on each side, glowed green in the charging coils. I smiled: no hardware problem here.

I looked over at the dark door built into the alley wall opposite me. The streetlight left it untouched, but glowed brightly from the wet, debris-free path cleared by the shuffling feet of lost souls bound for the midnight portal. I glanced at the menu bar on the base of my shooting glasses' right lens; the IR vision program I activated painted the door with shades of gold and red, making it stand out against the darker maroon of the bricks themselves. It even outlined, in yellow, the handprint of the last man granted entry through the metal-core door.

Before I could lose myself in ruminations about the evils enjoyed beyond that door, the call crackled into the speaker sunk in my left mastoid bone. "Sewer detail in position. Sorry, hadda kill two 'gators. Ready."

"Gimme a three-count," I growled into the mike, "then shut everything down."

I stalked boldly from the shadows, my left hand stripping my gray trench coat open. The long coat flapped back around my legs, and the star it revealed on the chest of my shirt clearly identified me as a government agent, one of the elite of the elite. The people huddled in the smoke-easy would never forget their first meeting with an agent of Alcohol, Tobacco, and Confections.

The M-19's muzzle flame blackened the door as the first burst splashed through the lock. Patrons reeled away from the spray of metal fragments as I stepped through the doorway and glanced at "seek" on my glasses' menu bar. My shooting glasses instantly cycled through different modes and settled on Starlight-targeting as appropriate for the smoky, low-light environment I scanned. Red lines blazed to life over my right eye in a cross-hair pattern, and a red dot flared up whenever my pistol pointed at a viable target.

I wheeled to the left where a mutant giant, the stub of a Cuban Corona hanging from his thick lower lip, rose up to loom over me like a tidal wave. He reached for me with hands the size of shovel blades and the half-light glinted from the razor talons capping both fingers on each hand. I triggered a three-shot burst but only realized I'd unconsciously downshifted to Blender shells when his chest flew back and his legs fell in the doorway.

The clonekin at the bar—an Einstein model—raised its four hands in surrender. Not nearly as bright, the vat-thug guarding the back door sprang off the stool it'd occupied and raised a prewar model shotgun. The patrons between us dove for cover, upsetting ash-laden tables and boosting cigarettes into the air like missiles. I almost laughed at the nico-freaks—whose "recreational" addiction was killing them anyway—as they clawed for the smoke-easy's scant cover. I was tempted, for a moment, to let the genegineered hoodlum blast away blindly, but the idea of it getting a shot off before I put it down was as repulsive as pushers selling candy canes to unsuspecting schoolchildren.

The red dot ignited over my right eye and my thumb clicked the pistol back to Tefjacs as I tightened up on the trigger. The friction-resistant bullets blew through the bouncer's body armor. The thug flattened back against the wall, then slid down and settled in a rumpled, bloody heap over his toppled stool.

I raised my gun toward the ceiling and the targeting light shut off. That, and the smile creeping across my features, drained some of the anxiety from the room and lowered stress to lawful levels. "You're all under arrest for violations of the self-protection statutes." Ignoring their complaints and pleas, I nodded purposefully in the direction of one overturned table. "That includes you, too, Councilman Foster."

I laughed at his groan, then smiled even more broadly as the radio crackled and reported the warehouse annex to the smoke-easy had been sealed off. The city's tactical unit, dressed in their smoke-gray and chocolate-brown urban camouflage, streamed in through the open door and started to round up prisoners as I looked over at the biotank-baby at the bar. "Buzz me into the back."

It did, and I stepped over the councilman on my way through the doorway. The scent hit me immediately and my nostrils shut down in protest. Crates of various sizes and shapes filled the long, low, dark warehouse to bursting. Lists of contents boldly stenciled in black stood out on the crates' sides, but I knew instantly they lied. This place reeked of chocolate.

I holstered the M-19 and shut the T-plas off as my newest partner brought a man to me. The suspect struggled fruitlessly, as if his corpulent bulk could possibly prevail against a healthy, young, dedicated patriot. The suspect disgusted me, and not just because he peddled confections to children. Greed I could understand, but stupidity revolted me. One look at his darkened fingers and the stains smeared along his gray suit and I knew he'd not been smart enough to resist the lure of his product.

He sniffed the red-and-white-carnation boutonniere on

his lapel and sneered at me over it. "Well, if it isn't Elliot Nestlé!"

I slapped him once, hard, before I regained my composure. "Insults won't help you now, Cadbury." I looked beyond him at my deputy, Raul Danton, and saw, in his electric, hawk-eyed stare, that he'd deny I'd ever struck the suspect.

I fished the worn card from inside my coat pocket. "You have the right to remain silent for as long as you can. Anything you say or think can and will be used against you in a court of law. You have the right to have an attorney cyberlinked during mindscan. If you so desire but cannot afford one, the court will give you a Rom-based legal expert system for immediate interface." I stared into his blank, chocolate-brown eyes. "Do you understand these rights as I have explained them?"

Cadbury smiled, revealing yellowed teeth. "It'll take more than your interrogators to work through the cognitive jungle they've mesmered into my brain."

I shrugged. "So we can't break you, big deal." I pointed at the crates surrounding us. "You're going away for a long time, Victor. This is serious dealer weight."

Victor Cadbury laughed and his thick jowls bounced to echo his derision. "This?" Ha!" His dark eyes flickered from crate to crate. "As your men will soon tell you, this is just milk chocolate. You've got nothing!"

"Take him away," I snorted furiously. Once again the Coryza, the smugglers' underworld, had anticipated a raid it took three months to plan. All that work and all I got was milk chocolate. Without getting the harder stuff, like Brazilian stinger or, better yet, Swiss white, even I began to doubt my ability to protect Americans from themselves.

My boss, Inspector Harris Martin, set aside the bureau's affairs in the Manhattan South sector just to listen to me rant and rave. "I don't know, Harry," I heard myself whining, "Nothing works. We have men everywhere working to smash the smugglers bringing the stuff into the country, but the more we do, the stronger the damned Coryza gets. It spreads like an infection."

Harry nodded his white-maned head and a serious expression slipped over his face like a mask. "Insidious, that's the word for it. All we can do is try our best to keep things under control."

I shook my head. "How can we do our best when everyone winks at the first flirtations with confection addiction? Think about it, Harry." I turned toward the office's darkened window and stared at the lights blinking atop all three Trade Towers. "When it gets really cold up here, mothers from Montreal to the Boston hub and down into Trumptown make 'hot chocolate' for their children to ward off the cold. No kid will take candy from a stranger, but how can anyone think of chocolate as evil when their mothers give it to them?"

Harry's voice became gravelly as the gravity of the situation once again battered him. "You're right, Mark, we've got a double standard. I can remember an uncle shaving strips of dark, bittersweet chocolate—Brazilian stinger, I think—into the first cup of coffee I ever had. It didn't seem bad then."

I snorted. "Tell me about it. I grew up in Hershey, Pennsylvania Military District. I lived in the shadow of the old factory and I can still remember days when the vile, sweet smoke from the factory would fill the valley. Oh, I saw the evils of chocolate early on." I gritted my teeth and pounded my right fist into my left hand. "I saw the disease get my older brother and have its way with him."

Harry leaned forward. "Acne?"

I nodded solemnly. "The worst, Harry, all over his face and back. His friends told him it wasn't the chocolate, and he believed them. He kept drowning his sorrow and shame in it, and he ballooned. For a while he dealt—selling kisses and bars to kids at school—and could afford the good stuff: Swiss white. But his empire melted like chocolate held too long in the hand." My voice broke. "It killed him."

Harry shook his head sympathetically, giving me time to recover myself. "You couldn't get him into a carob treatment program?"

I sighed heavily, then pounded my fist against the wall. "He was too far gone for that. I remember the last time I saw him, Harry. The boys in Helmsleyville Vice called me in when they found him. There he lay, deep in an alley, ready-to-spread frosting smeared over his face and on his index finger. I don't know where he got it, but the double Dutch chocolate was too much for him."

Harry shivered. "An overdose is never pretty." He picked up one of the gold-foil-wrapped bunnies we'd liberated from the warehouse and examined it closely. "It's hard to believe, sometimes, that something so innocent looking could be so dangerous."

I watched the sugary lagomorph slowly spin in his grasp. The foil clung to it like a negligee and revealed, in a flash of golden highlights, only the benign physical characteristics of an animal lauded in stories and folk tales. It did look innocent, but that made it fouler, to my mind, because it snared the unwary and propelled them into a life of crime and degradation that few successfully escaped.

I stood. "Innocent it looks, Inspector, but I know better. I look at the flag, those thirteen stripes and sixty-seven stars, and I feel proud. Then I look at that rabbit, and I know it and those who bring it to these shores just want to undermine the last bastion of true freedom on the earth."

I leaned forward over his desk and smiled. "And I'll tell you something else, Harry, she's behind this."

The rabbit stopped spinning and Harry's brown eyes locked onto my gaze. "Andrea Tobler! How do you know that?"

I shrugged. "Heard a rumor she'd gobbled up the Cadbury family holdings last year. Besides"—I nodded at the rabbit—"you must have noticed, Inspector, the rabbits are light. They're hollow. How better to bleed more money out of those who crave her foul wares?"

Harry's dark eyes narrowed cautiously and he regarded the rabbit anew. "Perhaps, Mark, you've stumbled onto something." He looked up at me. "I'll follow up on it, and let you know what's happening. Given your history with her, though, I think you should take a few days off. Don't want anyone thinking you've gone 'round the bend over this."

"Gotcha, sir." I smiled easily. "I wanted to spend some time out on my ichthyoculture plantation anyway. Good hunting."

*　　*　　*

Raul looked as disheveled as his Ozone Park apartment when I woke him at midnight. He raked fingers
back through his thick black hair and stared at me. One
of his contacts had slipped, making his right eye look like
a brown moon being eclipsed by a blue shadow, but he
did not notice. "Gosh, Lieutenant Glace, what are you
doing here? I thought you were on your fish farm in
Hoboken."

I shook my head sharply. "That's just what I wanted
people to think. You and I are heading back to Manhattan tonight. She's there, and I mean to get her."

"What, how?" Danton asked as he sprang from bed
and pulled his combat jumpsuit on.

As he strapped his H & K MP-47's belt around his
waist and tied the holster down on his right leg, I explained. "You remember that flower Cadbury had on his
jacket? It was a peppermint carnation, and it's only grown
in Surrey. Coryza buy them in Holland at the flower
market, then smuggle them into the Big Apple. A report
said a shipment of them ended up at Renny's on East
Sixty-second by mistake, and was taken back. There's
obviously a big stash somewhere in the city."

"So they gave us Cadbury to take the heat off?"

"*They* didn't give us anyone." My eyes narrowed. "*She*
gave us Cadbury because he was eating up the profits."

Muscles twitched at the corners of Danton's lantern
jaw. "Andrea Tobler. I never thought I'd get the chance."
His right hand caressed the butt of his gun.

I shook my head. "Anyone else, including even Fred
Whitman, you can have, but Andrea, she's mine."

Images frozen by the train engine's backlight strobed
past the rain-streaked window as the train slashed through
a night darker than Baker's chocolate. I stared at my
reflection until Danton set a hot cup of chicken soup
from the autovend in front of me and the steam erased
my features.

"Earth to Lieutenant Glace, are you O.K., sir?"

I lightened the dour expression on my face and turned
toward him. "Yeah, sure, Raul, I'm fine. Call me Mark,
O.K.?"

"Sure, Mark. I guess I'm still not clear on why you

took the train up from Jersey and we're taking it back into town. Either one of our cars would have been faster."

Muscles clenched at my jaw. "True, but both of our cars are tied into the satellite surveillance system." I shrugged. "All the Coryza needs is a halfwit wirehead to torch the ice on the fed databank and they'll know we're coming."

"I hadn't thought of that." He shivered and sipped gingerly at his soup. "Do you mind if I ask you a personal question?"

I shook my head. "No, go ahead." I expected what was coming; all my new partners eventually asked. None of them could let the rumors die until they learned the real story.

"You were over there, weren't you, sir, um, Mark?" I saw a light flash in his eyes—a light I'd seen in my own reflection long ago. "What's it like in Europe anyway?"

I sipped my soup and got a moment's taste of salt before the liquid scalded my taste buds. "Well, it's not as bad as some would make out, Raul, because it can be very pretty. I mean, yes, it's a decadent place, a hedonistic heaven for those who have a fortune built on mounds of chocolate, but culture is not restricted to their yogurt."

I smiled at a recollection. "I almost blew my cover the first night in Switzerland. The maid had turned my bed down and left a chocolate on my pillow. That threw me off for a moment, but I managed to give it as a gift to a friend. Needless to say, it was close."

Raul nodded solemnly. "Working undercover for the CEA must have been a challenge."

I sighed heavily. "It was that, and so much more. When you spend so much time in the company of confectioners, you begin to lose your perspective. They accepted me quickly because I pretended to be an expatriate avoiding the draft in the latest round of Sino-American martial games in the People's Republic of Columbia, and then they discovered I grew up in Hershey. Within a month I was thick with them, and they sent me to Switzerland because they thought I could do great things there."

Raul swallowed hard and timidly approached the question he'd wanted to ask all along. "You knew her, didn't you?"

I nodded silently, unable to speak past the lump in my

throat. I raised my cup of soup and drank just enough in to force the lump back down. "Yeah, I knew Andrea. A couple of the Cadburys recommended me to her father, Herr Helmut Tobler, and he saw something in me he liked. He brought me to his home in Zurich and started to teach me the business. He appointed Andrea to help refine my German."

My voice dropped off as I pictured her in my mind on that first day. She'd been riding, so a helmet capped her head, but when she removed it, black cascades of hair swept down to frame her angelic face. Blue eyes—naturally blue—regarded me carefully as she strode across the white-marble expanse of her father's ballroom. Halfway to us she graced me with a smile and I felt a blush rise to my cheeks. Slender and petite, she had a strength of character that burned like a fusion generator and suffused her entirely.

Raul cleared his throat. "They say you even loved her . . ."

I nodded. "I'm sure they do, and they think of it as a great conquest for me to have slept with the Queen of Confections. But," I said, staring at him harshly, "I don't think of it that way." My voice lost its edge. "I actually did love her."

Raul watched me with sympathy in his eyes and an unspoken plea for an explanation on his lips. He knew he couldn't ask and he recognized he'd never heard this part of the story from any of his locker-room buddies.

I forced a smile. "I know it sounds like treason, Raul, and that's why I didn't even put that kind of thing in my report. I spent weeks and months helping her. My mission had been to work myself into the Tobler empire, and her father smiled upon our romance. At first I thought I could control things, but I soon fell for her as hard as she fell for me."

Raul shook his head ruefully. "I'm sorry, Mark."

"You shouldn't be, really. I was happy then and I savored every moment we had together. Life is to be lived, within the law, and we really did love each other." I chuckled lightly. "In fact, if not for one word, you might be riding this train with Inspector Martin, coming after me."

"One word?" Raul's surprise at my admission succumbed to his probing sense of curiosity. "What could she say that would drive you two apart?"

I gulped some soup and let the burning sensation fortify me. "Sweetheart."

"What?"

I nodded sagely and stared past the cup's rim at him. "You heard me. Sweetheart. You know I don't often use profanity, but she called me her sweetheart. In that instant I realized I'd almost been seduced by a society and life-style so perverted that they could consider an utterly obscene word a term of endearment."

Raul rode the rest of the way to Manhattan in stunned and horrified silence.

The hoodlum screamed as the azure T-plas ball expanded and engulfed him. The blue lightning skittered over him like a fishnet on acid, firing muscles and singeing hair as it tightened about him. Energy tendrils drifted down his legs and finally reached the earth. They flared argent, then drained down and dropped him like a marionette with cut strings.

I crouched and nodded unconsciously as Raul's voice burst into my head and asked if I was all right. "Roger, Raul, I'm fine. One is down, but I can't find his partner. That sniveling candyman better not have lied to us about the Coryza's security precautions."

"The sentries are right where he told me they'd be." Static crackled through Raul's reply, but I couldn't hear the sounds of gunfire or the hissing of a plasma bolt. "I'm going in, Mark. See you at the rear of the flower warehouse."

Afraid that his transmission might have hidden any sounds in the alley, I turned my head and scanned for Coryza up and down the alley between Peck Slip and Dover Street, but no targeting dot appeared. I glanced at the menu bar on my right lens and switched the glasses over to IR, but the downed thug's smoldering body and the dissipating golden signature of his footsteps were all I could see. I looked up, to cover the roof edges and the rusty fire escape, and nearly made as bad a mistake as the man above me.

I saw his red-purple form and the growing white fire in his hand. I screwed my eyes shut against the brilliant, platinum burst of light on my glasses, and blindly clawed them from my face. I turned and ducked, twisting away from the first burst of tungsten needles from his Colt, but even the hand over my eyes could not keep out the magnesium flare's harsh nova-glare.

Had I been a second or two slower, the flare would have burned my eyes out with its intensity or his initial burst would have torn through my body. I slitted my eyes open but could see almost nothing in the flare's unwavering blaze beyond the gunman's bloated shadow. The flare, held high in the gunman's left fist, drenched the alley with pure light and carved him into a silhouette with a mohawk and the ragtag body armor favored by the Bowery gangs. The Colt looked like it had grown at the end of his arm and, from his position on the fire escape, he triggered another burst that sprayed metal slivers— half of which ricocheted from the fire escape's railing— that drove me back behind the burned-out hulk of an Iacocca wagon.

The gunman laughed and taunted me with accented English. "I play with you like a dog plays with a blind squirrel, eh, el porko?"

"You stupid Goober," I swore at him. "Even a blind squirrel finds an acorn now and then." I pointed my pistol at the fire escape and triggered the M-107.

His scream filled the brick canyon as the first ball of energy sizzled to life on the electrodes. It greedily launched itself at the black iron parasite clinging to the old brick building. A tornado of blue fire whirled around the metal structure and sparks exploded where paint combusted or clothesline remnants burned away. The cyan cyclone dragged in the second and third plasma bursts, then raced skyward like a rocket on a jet of azure thrust.

High above me the gunman danced a jerky, spasmodic tarantella. The energy wrapping him like a cloak detonated his pistol's propellant in a ball of red and green flames and consumed the flare like a nico-freak sucking up his first cigarette of the day. Then blue fingers of electricity reached up and tickled a response from the low clouds above.

The lethal bolt of silver lightning crashed down and fired the entire metal lattice to a cherry red an eternity before its thundered report blasted me to the gritty alley floor. Energy rippled out from fire escape and flowed across the rain-slicked alley like fire over a sea of gasoline. It swept up over the wagon's blackened skeleton and flooded its bones with a crimson glow.

I rolled to my feet, making the best of the protection my insulated combat boots offered. Deafened by the thunder and night-blind without my glasses, I turned toward the warehouse and froze. I saw the scarlet cross-hairs on a third gunman—one I'd not been warned about—and tried to dodge, but the street detritus gave way beneath my feet. I saw the cross-hairs flash for a second, then felt the narc-dart's sting in my throat.

A black storm stole my sight, and the ground rose up to club me into unconsciousness.

Awakening, I heard a laugh I hoped was the last trace of a nightmare evaporating. I identified it instantly and bitter fear rose in my throat. If I was not waking from a nightmare, I was surely drifting into one.

I opened my eyes and swallowed hard past the pain in my throat. Seated, securely bound to a metal chair by rope and leather straps, I found myself center stage in a small enclosure with walls built from packing crates. The wooden boxes, marked similarly to those I'd seen earlier in the evening, rose to a height of twelve feet and nearly touched the fluorescent lights hanging down from the ceiling on long chains. In their backlight I could see a second, crate-laden level and a narrow catwalk passing through the darkness.

Danton sat in a chair beside me. His bruised and battered head lolled to the side, as if they'd broken his neck, but his chest rose and fell with a strength and regularity that told me he still lived. Crumbs of chocolate dappled the thick cords of rope binding him to his chair, and I smiled. He'd resisted eating chocolate despite their torture. With a couple more like him . . .

Fred Whitman's cackled laugh sliced through my private thoughts and sank jagged talons into my brain. I flicked my eyes over at him and stared hard at his face. I lowered my gaze to his cheek, then snickered, "Never did fix that, did they?"

Fred, fear flooding his eyes, recoiled. He reached unconsciously up and touched the broad, twisted scar that scored his right cheek the way cow paths mar hillsides. Then the fingers gently probing the wound hooked into claws and balled into a fist, which he shook in my face. "This time, Glace, you will pay!"

The small cortege at his back nodded, but I could read the pity for him on their faces. Fred Whitman had decided, back when I worked in Europe, that he should be Andrea Tobler's consort. Known then as Handsome Fred, he was very popular with the ladies and assumed he had only to eliminate me and Andrea would fall into his bed. While his campaign against me did result in my cover collapsing, our final battle left him broken and, because his flesh did not readily culture, scarred for life.

Fred turned back toward a table behind him and picked up a clear, fluid-filled bottle with a thick glass stopper. He gingerly teased the stopper loose and a very light vapor rose from the colorless liquid. Holding the bottle in his right hand, he sank a glass pipette into the liquid and capped the cylinder with his left thumb. He pulled the pipette up enough to let liquid drain from its exterior, then held it up so I could see a single drop glistening at its tip.

"Hydrochloric acid, Glace." Fred smiled cruelly and flicked the droplet down onto my knee. The uniform smoked and the acid ate the fabric away. "The surgeons will never be able to reconstruct your face . . ."

I saw the flicker of motion and the glow from above as Fred raised the pipette toward me. The blue energy globe smashed him on his left shoulder and blasted him against the crates to his right. The pipette clattered to the ground and fragmented into a dozen pieces as the full bottle of acid exploded against one of the crates. The blue plasma spun a cocoon around Whitman and lifted him into the air, then dissipated like fog and dropped his limp body to the warehouse floor.

I looked up toward the catwalk and, in the backglow of her T-plas projector, I caught the hint of a smile on her face. The greenish glow lit her face softly and reminded me of many dawns when I'd risen early and just stared at her beautiful face while she slept. Our gazes met for half a second and my heart burned with an emotional fire I'd hoped I'd long since utterly smothered.

She turned from me and stared down at her henchmen.

"Haul Fred out to the gyrojet, then stay well clear of this warehouse." Amid a chorus of affirmations they jumped into action and quickly left Danton and me alone with Andrea Tobler.

I looked over at the crate the acid had eaten through. Floating in the acid lake bubbling with the last remnants of packing material, I saw a dozen golden bunnies. I smiled and nodded to her. "I congratulate you on discovering a way to gouge more profits from your clients. Hollow instead of solid, brilliant."

She returned my praise with a salute. "And I congratulate you on discovering this warehouse. I instructed Victor to remove the flower before he traveled down to your sector, but Fred taunted him, hoping you'd backtrack and fall into his clutches." She pointed up toward the street-level flower warehouse. "The flowers help hide the scent of our product and keep the CEA's silicurs from sniffing us out. In fact, the only mistake you made was in leaving your informant alive. He sold us to you, then sold you to us, and we picked you up as soon as the two of you started conversing on your radios."

I acknowledged my mistake with a grimace, then I smiled and decided to gamble. "This place is blown, Andrea. I left a program running on the department's computer that will inform Inspector Martin of my location by dawn." I slowly scanned the warehouse. "You can't move all of this by then. I win."

She shook her head and fixed me with a reproving stare—the one she reserved for when she felt I was spinning a story. "I doubt that, Mark. You could not lie to me then, and you cannot lie to me now. Besides," she added, raising her T-plas gun, "it does not matter, really."

She triggered a burst of energy that arced off across the warehouse and hit something that promptly exploded and flickered firelight up to the ceiling. The gold and red flames illuminated Andrea and slithered highlights onto her raven hair. "You, Mark Glace, and your aide will die heroically in a fire that consumes the largest stash of illegal chocolate ever discovered in North America."

I stared at her, speechless. Smoke already brought the scent of wood and burning chocolate to me. I swallowed and looked up one last time. "Isn't this a bit much just for two ATC agents?"

"Expensive, perhaps," she mused, "but even the Swiss-white bunnies and the bittersweet chickens are hollow . . . No great loss." Then she smiled at me. "I think 'spectacular' is a better word. But, then, I couldn't do less for the man I love, could I, sweetheart?"

A burning undercurrent of pain coursed up and down my acid-gnawed left arm—despite the dressings, unguents, salves, anesthetics, and doctors' assurances—and held my fatigue at bay. The wooden chair creaked beneath the weight of my tired body as I shifted impatiently in the seat. The scent of fire and hospitals rose up in a cloud so thick that Inspector Martin found himself forced to lean back as he read the transcript of the report I'd dictated in the police van.

He laid the last page down on the pile centered on his blotter, then removed his glasses and used them as a paperweight. He stared at me with red-rimmed eyes. "My God, Mark, that's an amazing piece of work. Playing a hunch you uncover a massive storehouse of chocolate. You escape a flaming death trap and carry your uncon-scious partner to a nearby hospital." Jerking a thumb at the picture of the woman on the wall behind him, he smiled wryly. "When the news broke, I had a call from the mayor. She wants you to report to Gracie Mansion. She's going to hold a press conference and give you a medal."

Harry shook his head, but not a single lock of his white hair fell out of place. "You played it close to the vest. I wish you'd told me your plan so I could have helped."

"That's O.K., Harry, because Andrea didn't need your help this time." The stunned look on his face and the pain coursing through his eyes gave birth to the begin-ning of a stuttered denial, but I cut it off with a snarl. "I wondered how the hell Andrea always knew where we were going to hit, then I realized she had someone inside our bureau. Her money could buy anyone, but you're the only one who could be of real value to her."

Indignation flushed Harry's skin and chased off his deathly gray pallor. "What do you mean, accusing me of taking bribes? How dare you!"

I snorted derisively. "Save it, Harry." I stared at him and he dared not move. "I told her I'd left a message for you detailing my location, and that didn't concern her in the least. The big trick, though, was figuring how she managed to pay you. You're too smart to trust money held in an account abroad for you, but you also know you can't hide money in your bank account here."

I smiled and licked my lips. "I should have seen it sooner, but I didn't until the warehouse was burning down around me." I leaned forward and gestured carefully with my bandaged arm. "You see, the only way I could get out of my ropes was to tip my chair over and inch my way to the acid pool draining from one of the contraband crates. The acid took its time, eating into my flesh while it consumed the ropes. I had plenty of time to stare at the golden forms of chocolate bunnies, and I finally figured out how she got money to you."

I nodded solemnly. "It was a good plan, Harry."

I reached up and pointed my left hand at the golden bunny still sitting on Harry's desk. "As Andrea noted, the loss of hollow rabbits was insignificant in terms of chocolate weight, hence there had to be something of greater value connected to them. Because we use a chemical bath to destroy all the chocolate we confiscate, the foil must be stripped off each rabbit before it's tossed into the vat."

I pulled my pistol and pointed it at Harry's chest. "The acid didn't eat through the foil, Harry. It burned the ropes and burned me, but not the pure gold foil. I'm sure the trashmen who collect the foil for you will betray you when they learn how much it was really worth."

I rose and Harry opened his hands in supplication. "Come on, Mark, be reasonable. There's plenty to split. I can make you a honey of a deal."

The backhanded blow with my pistol snapped Harry's head around. I watched blood dribble down his cheek from where a tang had cut him, then I holstered my pistol and picked up the bunny. "You played me for a sucker, Harry, but it's over now."

Two federal marshals opened the office door and came to take Harry away.

As he passed by me, I crushed the rabbit's hollow head and tossed the candy carelessly into his hands. "Hey, Harry," I called after him.

Tomb w/ View

by P. D. Cacek

*Smog is one of those urban phenomena that
people don't like to think about much. One reason
that environmental hazards are so serious is that
they tend to creep up on us a little at a time, and by
the time we even notice them, they're huge and
unmanageable.*

Maybe we need a new approach?

From his office/living quarters sixty-two stories up, Murray Feinstein watched the noxious brown-gray cloud as it
ebbed and flowed its way down West Sixty-seventh, lapping against the crumbling facades of what used to be
trendy galleries and Indo-Texan eateries, curling into the
narrow gullies between the high-rises, sneaking like a
cat-burglar through broken windows, rolling undisturbed
toward the great emptiness that once was Central Park.

Sighing, he leaned forward until he could see the top
of the deserted office building across the street, then
counted down.

. . . fifty-four . . . fifty-three . . . fifty-two and a half . . .

It was up another half-story since yesterday.

(Good-bye, Casa de Ngo, Sullivan's Ol' Time Boozeria.
Don't forget to write, Steve and Edie's All-night Escort
Service. *Ciao.*)

His breath fogged the glass around his face and he
quickly wiped it away. At this rate, he'd have to start
thinking about moving again soon.

"Moving up in the world." He chuckled softly. "Maybe
even see what the penthouse is like. So who would know?"

Even as he contemplated it, he dismissed the possibility. At least for now. Moving into the penthouse would

have to come later, when the growing smog bank finally swallowed the city. Then he could either try strapping on portable oxygen tanks and walking down all ninety-five stories, or he could light up a stogie and do a belly flop into eternity.

"Probably be dead before I hit, anyway," he muttered, just to hear something besides the steady hum of the Maxi-Plus air-purification unit next to him, guaranteed or your money back. "No breathable air past the twenty-seventh floor."

Murray shrugged. The thought of death really didn't bother him anymore. After all, he was a seventh-generation New Yorker. Death loomed at every street corner, so why let it worry you? The only thing that overshadowed his contemplation was the obvious lack of an audience.

Once, a dive from the penthouse of the Koch Memorial Towers would have made headlines throughout the five boroughs. Now he'd be lucky if the computerized National Guard Surveillance street-sweepers could manage to slurp up all the pieces.

And no one would even see that. He'd be unceremoniously ejected into the East River Land Fill with the rest of the day's garbage. No tears, no muss, no fuss. They probably thought he was dead already.

Murray caught his reflection looking back at him, and shook his head.

"So what are *you* looking at, Mr. This-Is-My-Home-and-I'm-Staying-Right-Here?" he asked the rotund little man with glasses. "That's right, you! You stand there looking like maybe all your friends had the right idea."

His reflection stared back silently.

"Go live in Kansas, you asked them, the Kansas with the tornadoes and pollen so bad each spring you can't breathe there either? So what do the experts know anyway, you told the Hammners. So what if the city's grown so much there's no more natural ventilation? You think the president's gonna let the greatest city in the world die for a little ventilation? No! No, any day now they'll send enough money to fix things, just you watch."

The little man in the reflection pulled nervously at the synthetic nylon body suit.

"So what happens? So the president calls a news conference from his summer home in Cuba and tells every-

body to leave New York. Get out, he tells them, and
don't come back for a hundred years, maybe longer. And
everybody starts packing. So what do you do, Mr. I-Know-
Better-Than-the-President? Do you take the fortune your
family made by supplying kosher meals to the lunar bases
and follow them? No! No, you call in your own experts
and spend a fortune building air-purifiers. And what
happens? Everyone leaves town faster.

"So now what? Now you got your purifiers in half the
buildings in Manhattan, running from a generator you
bought because Con Ed went bankrupt, talking to yourself because everyone's in Kansas, waiting for the next
tornado or dust storm."

His reflection fidgeted with the low-grade magnetic
fasteners on his suit.

"So tell me, how's it feel to be the world's biggest slum
lord?"

His reflection couldn't answer that one.

Nodding, Murray directed his attention downward to
the almost-obscured mauve-and-gold GRAND RE-OPENING
banner across the street. Wong's Old-fashioned Vietnamese
Hot Dog Emporium was gone—devoured sometime in
the night along with its artificially sweetened sauerkraut
and dog-meat chili.

Old Man Wong . . . When the smog closed his ground-
floor eatery, he'd moved up to the third floor. A week
later, his hand-painted banner had drooped listlessly from
a window on the sixteenth. By the time he reached the
twentieth, the old man had somehow acquired a sizable
piece of canvas and eye-numbing paint and had produced
the now-familiar masterpiece of defiance.

He'd made it to the forty-fifth floor when the rats
finally caught up with him.

Murray had been two stories farther up, just getting
settled into his own new surroundings, when he heard the
first screams. He'd left the exterior audio on as he usually did—"Force of habit," he told himself. At first he
thought a police car or some other public-service siren
had mistakenly entered the concrete canyons and was, at
the moment, choking to death.

By the time Murray set down the plastic box he'd
carried up since the third floor and walked to the window, he was just in time to see the old man, rats the size

of poodles hanging on to his arms and legs, crash through the double-strength floor-to-ceiling picture window.

Despite the lunge outward, Wong's right hand had somehow managed to catch hold of the banner and hang on. He hung there for fifteen minutes while one of the larger rats worked on his wrist, and Murray watched all of it. There wasn't anything else to watch since the BBC station in Jersey had stopped transmitting.

Wong fell without another sound and Murray had watched his red-tinted fall until he hit the main smog bank and disappeared from view.

It took another four days before the hand released its grip and followed, and by then the smog was only ten stories down.

Murray felt another sigh building at the back of his throat and quickly swallowed it.

"No," he snorted angrily. "Murray Feinstein ain't finished either."

He patted the air-purifier confidently just as something thudded against the walled-over and reinforced central-heating duct.

"What, you think I want your company? I got enough troubles already, thank you."

Sure, as if the rats weren't enough, now he had cockroaches to contend with. Ah, what the hell, he thought, waving at the kevlar-reinforced covering on the air ducts, New York's always had bugs and rats. So what else is new?

Just like smog, right, Murray?

At first the smog wasn't so bad. After all, hadn't it finally cleared the streets of drug-runners, muggers, street gangs, and political canvassers? So what if the rats and roaches proved smarter than their human counterparts? So what if the only living things interested in your cocka-mamy air-conditioning are looking at you as a blue-plate special? So what's so different?

His neighbor scratched again, thumped twice, and was silent, obviously taking the hint that there'd be no free lunch today. Smiling, he threw his reflection a wink and headed for the room's self-contained food processor. One other benefit of living in a post-1990s Sky-riser—the best syntho-soy products going.

Patting his convex waistline, Murray dialed up the picture of chicken soup and flipped the switch.

The whole process took fifty seconds; Murray timed it on the old-fashioned pocket watch he carried on a chain around his neck, pockets having gone the way of neckties and environmental initiatives. Twenty-two seconds longer than breakfast.

When it arrived it was cold, but only had a half-dozen rat hairs and roach antennae floating in it, so that was something, at least.

Murray set a place for himself on the Real Wood (copyright 1997) desk and skimmed his soup with the plastic spoon the syntho had included.

"Immigrants," he shouted to his reflection as he wiped the spoon off on one of the sheets of rice paper that lay scattered in front of him. "That's what we need. Give this town a real shot in the arm."

He nodded, took a slurp, grimaced, and put the spoon down.

"Just like before. Thousands of immigrants pouring in every day, bringing their energy, their yearnings to be free"—Murray glanced past his reflection to the giant marvels of concrete and steel beyond the glass—"their money."

So who would tell them that he, Murray Feinstein, didn't own every building in the city? Who would complain? Not the real owners. If they'd cared enough for their property and city, they would never have left it for Kansas, may they all sit on haystacks and get needles in their hemorrhoids.

Slapping the table and ignoring the fact that he'd showered the expensive desk with coagulating chicken soup, Murray stood up and held his arms out to the silent city.

"We're gonna make it, kids. Just let your old Uncle Murray handle it. Somewhere on this dirty little planet there are people who are willing to put up with a little inconvenience for the sake of living in New York, and I'm going to find them."

His reflection seemed to fade the more he spoke, blending into the background of silver and gray until it was no longer perceptible.

"Yes, sir, yes, sir—that's just what I'm gonna do."

*   *   *

Murray started his Urban Replenishment Campaign the next morning at sunrise, when he hooked up the portable CB he had picked up on nineteen to the building's antiquated public-address system. Back at the turn of the century, he'd heard, building managers used to talk back and forth across the city on these things.

It would have been like listening to giants, he thought and felt a shiver course its way down his spine.

"Will be again," he promised, wheezing toward the normal gray-green skyline. The smog level ninety-five stories up was still tolerable, thank God! "We're going to have people again—talking, laughing . . . spending money."

Murray keyed the automatic cassette loop on the transmitter and leaned back against the naked metal tower, resting while his recorded voice echoed across the city.

"Bring me your strong, your healthy, your rugged individuals longing for the joy of conquest! Come join the adventure. New York has never been a better investment for the self-starter. Sky-risers awaiting occupancy. Unlimited space. Live high and free above the clouds. Contact: Murray Feinstein, concierge, Koch Memorial Towers. Be one of the few. The proud. The brave!"

Murray listened to it for an hour while he got his strength back, smiling each time it ran. He would let it play throughout the four full hours of daylight, he decided as he set the automatic timer. Better exposure that way. Besides, he didn't know anyone anymore who didn't have to take a whole handful of things to help them through the twenty hours of darkness. Advertising at night would be a waste of good generator power.

Satisfied at last that his message would be heard, and with dreams of a nifty little sideline marketing "I ♥ NOx" novelties dancing 'round his head, Murray pushed himself to his feet and walked toward the top of the covered stairwell.

He was halfway across the asphalt roofing when the small amber light over the elevator door blinked on, indicating a car coming up.

Coming up? Couldn't be! The elevators went out fifteen months ago, when the caustic smog that filled the basement finally ate its way through to the control panel. Murray could only guess what had happened to the building's super—a skinny kid with pimples who slept on a cot next to the panel board.

Murray stared at the light and rubbed his eyes. Keeping his hand over his face, he took as deep a breath as he could without choking, and counted to ten. Must be seeing things, boychik, he chided himself. Been living alone so long you came down with mental diarrhea. One more minute and your brains'll come pouring out your ears.

He took another breath, coughed, and opened his eyes.

The light was still on and now he could feel the all-but-forgotten vibration through the padded soles of his shoes.

Maybe the pimple-faced kid had gotten away, finally got the damn elevator running. Murray smiled at the thought of being able to ride back down to his cubbyhole in mechanical comfort—watching the softly tinted floor indicators wink on and off seductively, listening to the rats squeal as the plastic and steel box slipped downward . . .

. . . listening to the rats . . .

A new image etched itself on the insides of his eyeballs.

Maybe the car was filled with rats. And him, like the rest of the poor schmucks who hadn't had enough sense to get out of the smog when the getting was good, just standing there like the world's biggest kosher dinner. Yessiree, ladies and rodents, right this way for Chez Murray's Rooftop Dining, kosher cuisine at its finest.

He'd be lucky if he made it to the stairs before they ate his legs off.

Murray held his breath and slowly began walking backward away from the double-wide door, convinced that if he took his eyes away for one moment it would open and spew out a lethal, wriggling cargo.

"So why are we tippy-toeing, Mr. I'm-Going-to-Make-Millions?" he asked himself, still backing away. "Think your newfound wealth's going to make any difference now? Fat lot of good money's going to make when you're racing man-killing rodents down thirty-three flights of stairs. You think maybe you can offer them a bribe not to eat you?"

He was less than a yard from the stairwell when the emergency phone next to the elevator door buzzed to life.

"Now that's something I never heard rats do before," he shouted.

Behind him, the transmitter went into its prerecorded spiel. "Bring me your strong, your healthy, your rugged individuals . . ."

Sure, why not? Maybe his message was getting through already.

Smiling, smoothing down what little hair remained on his head, Murray walked back to the elevator and lifted the clear plastic phone to his lips.

"Murray Feinstein here. May I help you?"

The voice on the other end was hollow-sounding, the words echoing slightly, as if the caller were at the bottom of an abandoned well. Naturally.

"You have . . . rooms for . . . rent?"

Murray felt the blood surge through his veins. It was an odd sensation, as if he'd been dead all these long months and never known it. He shook the thought out of his head and tried to suck in his stomach, without much success.

"Have I got rooms? Rooms of every size and shape. You name it, Murray Feinstein's got it."

There was a momentary silence on the line while, Murray presumed, the voice thought it over; then . . .

"Good. We'll be . . . right up . . ."

Murray tossed the phone back into its molded cradle and did one of the only two dance steps he knew. "We," the voice had said. "WE."

"Hear that, New York?" he shouted to the columns of rock and steel. "We got customers! Gonna be great again, just you wait. Won't be any time before we can snap our fingers at them Kansas Cowboys."

To emphasize his words, Murray snapped his fingers just as the elevator doors slid open.

There must have been two dozen of them crammed into a space designed to hold no more than ten. Each wore a crude breathing apparatus over the head, attached to a bulbous air sack that expanded and contracted with each breath, like some kind of external lung. The image turned Murray's stomach slightly, but he managed to keep his smile in place.

Their ragged clothing, which appeared to be made from torn upholstery and curtain material, was so bulky and ill-fitting that Murray couldn't tell which were male or female—or even whether there were mixed genders in the group. Not wishing to offend and thereby blow the whole deal, Murray bowed majestically from the waist, his right hand sweeping backward in a large arc.

There was a muffled twitter from one of the smaller bundles in the crowd.

"Welcome, my friends," he began, as if he'd been saying it all his life. "Welcome to Ko—to Feinstein's Golden Towers. I am Murray Feinstein, your amiable host." He bowed again, less dramatically.

They filed out of the car en masse, as if they were afraid to move independently, and Murray backed up accordingly. As weak as the timid midday sun was, they seemed to shy away from it, preferring to stay in the shadows.

Murray forced another inch of smile to his lips. "Air's fine up here," he said, tapping his chest and pretending to take a deep breath. "Only about a sixty percent pollution rate today. Go ahead, take off your . . . equipment, it's as fresh as a day in spring."

The group shifted uneasily for a moment, but not one made a move toward their heavy face masks. Finally a taller member walked to the front of the group and extended a gloved hand. Murray took it without reservation and pumped enthusiastically.

The hand under the glove felt thin and bony.

"How many . . . rooms do you have, Mr. Feinstein?" asked the same voice he had spoken to earlier.

"How many you need?" Murray countered, letting go of the man's hand and pirouetting in place. Another twitter from the crowd. "I got rights to all the property west of the landfill."

The man nodded and Murray could almost make out the features behind the thick glass. Almost. But not quite. And if the eyes that stared out at him were any indication of the face, Murray was just as glad the man had decided to keep his gear on.

They reminded him of rat's eyes—but not as pleasant.

"We have over . . . a thousand . . . in our . . . group."

"A th-thousand?" Not much for a city that once hosted nine million, but a decent start. Pulling himself up to his full size, another quarter of an inch, Murray leveled what he liked to think of as his "snake charmer's" eye at the man's faceplate and raised one eyebrow. "You got money?" he asked. "New York's mine, but I ain't giving it away."

The group shifted again and the man standing in front of Murray turned to receive a stained gunnysack, then upended it at Murray's feet.

Thick rolls of multicolored New York currency bounced amid tangled lines of gold and gems.

Swallowing the drool that suddenly filled his mouth, Murray nodded as casually as he could.

"Nice, nice. I assume it's all yours?"

The man cocked his head behind the thick mask. "It is . . . now," came the muffled reply.

Bending quickly, Murray swept the fortune back into its sack and stood up. "That's fine. Now, how about we start with this building and work our way out? That sound okay?" He hugged the heavy bag to his chest like a precious child. "I have some wonderful suites down on sixty-two—that's my floor, but anything up to the penthouse will be perfectly all right."

The group seemed to draw back into itself, and Murray sank his fingers deeper into the filthy material.

"I—I mean, of course any building would be all right. Any one at all . . ."

The group inched back toward the elevator. The bitter taste of a deal falling through filled Murray's mouth.

"And—and you can have, you can have your choice of floors. Any floors at all!"

The group stopped.

"*Any* floor . . . Mr. Feinstein?" their spokesman asked.

The smile, forced as it was, bloomed again. "Of course. Should I tell you where to live? Not me, not Murray Feinstein. You live on any floor you want."

Muffled sounds of contentment filtered through the heavy breathing bags. Murray felt his fingers release their death grip on the booty sack.

"Thank you . . . Mr. Feinstein," the spokesman said. "We will start with the bottom floors . . . and work our way . . . up."

Murray felt his jaw unhinge. "Bu—but . . ." Careful, he reminded himself, you almost blew the deal once already. "Won't it be a little . . . well, hard to breathe down there?"

Another mutter passed through the crowd, but this time it sounded like laughter.

"We're . . . used to it . . . Mr. Feinstein." The man took a step forward and Murray felt a shiver go up his spine. "We've been . . . living with . . . pollution for . . . generations now."

"I—I don't understand," Murray said.

The man took another step and gently caressed his face mask.

"Carbon monoxide is . . . *our* life's breath. Because our . . . forefathers chose to . . . dwell . . . below your streets, Mr. Feinstein, we survived this . . . catastrophe."

This time Murray was sure he heard laughter coming from the group.

"When your . . . kind fled the city . . . they left . . . most of their valuables behind." Murray could see the faintest hint of a smile behind the glass. "We have . . . claimed them as . . . you've claimed . . . this city."

Murray hadn't even realized he had continued to back up until his spine struck the side of the covered stairwell. The gunnysack fell almost noiselessly from his hands.

"We're not going . . . to harm you . . . Mr. Feinstein. We have our honor," the man said, bending down to retrieve the bag and then thrusting it into Murray's slack grasp. "We simply . . . want a more . . . comfortable life. And since . . . you are the local . . . real-estate agent . . ."

The man let his voice drop into silence. So, Murray heard himself ask, what are you going to do now, Mr. Smarty-Pockets? Rent rooms to mutant smog-suckers who steal from the dead? Turn New York into a walking graveyard? Strap on your own air tanks for a weekly game of pinochle with a bunch of exhaust zombies? Are you that greedy, Murray Feinstein?

"Of course," he said, slinging the bag over his shoulder. "Now, how about a nice two-bed-and-bath, overlooking Central Park?"

Born in Los Angeles in 1951, P. D. Cacek holds one of the few degrees in creative writing ever awarded by California State University at Long Beach. Spe-

cializing in tales of modern horror and "twisted reality," the author's works have appeared in a number of small-press magazines.

"Tomb w/ View" was inspired by the author's immigrant grandfather (a storyteller in his own right), who had never lost his love of the great city he considered his home.

P. D. Cacek currently lives in Fremont, California, sharing hearth and home with mate and sons—and an objectionable computer named Philo.

A Walk Through Beirut

by John Shirley

A few years back, the science-fiction community got caught up in debates over cyberpunk—what was it, who wrote it, was it the wave of the future or a passing fad, was it the best thing SF ever produced or self-indulgent junk?

John Shirley was one of the more vociferous debaters on the pro-cyberpunk side—and his stories some of the best arguments that there was a lot more to cyberpunk than flash and fad.

He says that he's giving up writing science fiction, at least for a while, and that this is his last story in the genre. Let's hope he changes his mind.

Blackout.

All through Lower Manhattan, blackout.

The street wasn't completely dark; stretching between buildings was a diffuse web of light from the lit part of the city, north of Fourteenth Street, where the affluent had a backup power system. Rusty light fluttered from the fires someone had set in the stores, two blocks up, at Delancey, and a yellower flame guttered in the broken windows of the graffiti-tattooed elementary school across the street. The Children's Christian Militia were bivouacked in the school gymnasium. Dexy could see the desultory beaming of flashlights through the gym's open doors.

The summer of 2022 had been a hot one, was oozing like molten wax into fall. It was still a warm evening, but Dexy knew it'd get colder, maybe about one A.M., so he'd worn his wild-dog jacket. He ran his hand down the stiff, short-furred pit-bull hide and cocked his head, like a dog himself, listening to the whoops and feverish shouts from Delancey, the perverse ringing of breaking glass. A gunshot. Another.

"Oh, totally THRASHIN'," Marilyn yelled, clattering clumsily down the chipped stone steps of the tenement on her high heels. "A *black*-oouuuuuut!" Skateboard under her arm. She was going to skateboard with her heels on? No, she took the shoes off, stuck their spike heels in the waistband of her skin-tight neoprene skirt, so the pumps hung like gunfighter holsters. She jumped on the skateboard, pumped it, its gear system translating the kinetic energy of her leg pump into forward motion, and she shot down the sidewalk. "Come on, Dexyyyyyyyyy!" She had all her animatoos going, the animated images on her skin looping through their horror-story comic-book sequences; her short, translucent jacket was TV-receptive, randomly displaying whatever transmission was passing through her: just now, across her back, it was collaging a CNN image of an astronautics construction worker riding a maneuverer through the unfinished skeleton of the L5 colony, with a PBS shot of a medieval painting of Christ Ascending to Heaven. Weird synchronicity in that, Dexy thought.

As Marilyn receded down the street, her animated tattoos and the luminous blond of her Monroe wig and the shifting pictures on the TV jacket all ran together, blurred into one figure, a Pierrot made of restless media.

She's a McLuhan cut-out, Dexy thought, all reflective surface and no fucking character.

Marilyn did a wheelie, a pivot, pumped back up the street to him. "Come onnnnnn, Dexy!" Using her soft, husky Monroe voice. He was glad Zizz had run off; when Marilyn and Zizz got together, best buddies in giggling affection, it could ill you out.

Coming at him now, her image-squirming outline resolved once more into tattoos and jacket TV reception. On one side of her open jacket a frontal shot of the Boy Ayatollah preaching gravely into the camera; on the other, beyond the DMZ of her bare skin and her upturned, unnaturally perfect breasts, an animated political cartoon from the anarchist pirate radio transmissions showing two cartoonish infants—the Boy Ayatollah and the Reverend

Baer, the Christian Fun general, reduced to sadistic infants, the two of them pulling the wings off of a screaming pigeon whose body was stenciled: NYC.

As she spun out to stop, Marilyn squeezed a tab on her belt, switching on the speakers miniaturized into the bikini under her skirt. The music was another kind of collage, a shaped-static band house-mixed with an old world-beat disco tune. The music boomed from the form-fitting speakers at her crotch. She made rhythmic thrusts with her hips into the crotch box's sonic vibrations. The way she did it, that kind of penetrating thrust, seemed male, to Dexy; that, and a wideness in her shoulders, the knobbiness of her knees, made Dexy wonder again if Marilyn used to be a boy. She was always a little exaggeratedly girlish in her poutiness, heavily adorned with media imagery that might be a kind of stage magic distraction technique—all things Dexy associated with queens. But if she was a transsexual, she was a damn good one. Must've had her Adam's apple reduced, face expertly reconstructed. Lots of hormone pills, too, for softness. He was never quite sure.

If he really wanted to know, he should bop her once. Having sex with her ought to clear up the issue. Not because she wouldn't have a vagina—she might, by now—but because she'd have to use artificial lube, and her clitoris wouldn't look quite right. Unless maybe she could afford a clitoral transplant, like his Uncle Ernie had: the old fag had a clit transplanted into his throat.

"You want to scope the riot or what?" she asked him, tilting her head just to make her glowing hair droop over an eye.

"You don't know there's a riot," Dexy said.

"There's always a riot when there's a blackout. Especially over in Little Beirut."

"That's another thing, Marilyn. They don't call it Little Beirut because they've got maybe some Lebanese living there. You know? It's because of the fighting."

"I don' wanna go alone."

"I'm waiting for the Surprise to come on. I don't want to be in the middle of that kinda mess and have it hit me. I wanna get used to it."

"You took Surprise? Can I have some? I'll give you some speed."

"I only had one hit."

"Buhshit."

"It's true."

"Where'd you get it?"

"Fu."

"Fu? I'll bet he'll be at the riot. I'm stoked. Let's cruise. It'll hit you before we get there."

He looked at her. Wondering if he should tell her why he'd taken the stuff. What he was doing.

But even a brainjammer like Marilyn would probably take time out to lecture him. Give him the same shit his video therapist had come out with. How a decision about self-euthanasia is maybe not something that should be made under the influence of a drug. Suicide is serious; take your time before applying for that SSEU (his therapist stupidly not realizing Dexy would never use a State Self-euthanasia unit, he'd do it himself someway that, at least, had some *statement* about it). And how suicide's usually inadvisable anyway. Blah blah blah. Stating the obvious. Ignoring the fact that he couldn't find another way to make the decision. He'd tried for months. Surprise was all that remained. The only thing that could make up his mind. Or so Fu said. And Fu was the neighborhood shaman.

Surprise. The drug was supposed to talk to you. Tell you things about yourself. Something like ibogaine or ketamine but more . . . cinematic. Less psychedelic. And the hallucinations didn't have a preceding buzz to warn you they were coming. They just slid themselves in with your ordinary perceptions. Hence the name.

"Who did the blackout this time?" he asked absently.

She shrugged, jumping the board up onto the curb and off again. "I heard on my battery box a buncha different claims. The Holy Islam seps took credit—"

"Fucking separatists are lunatics if they think they're going to have an independent Islamic state in the middle of New York—"

"—and the A-Team took credit—"

"Fucking anarchists—"

"—and the skinhead seps took credit."

"Fucking skinhead racist morons."

"I think it probably was the skinheads, they ain't scared of nothing. Too stupid to be."

He said, "Fuck it." And set off beside Marilyn, who was pumping the decal-patchy skateboard just enough to skate a few yards ahead of him, coasting to a stop, striking a pose, waiting till he passed her, pumping again, her movements synced to the world beat emanating from her crotch . . .

He wondered vaguely if she were here at all. Maybe the Surprise had set in, he was hallucinating her and didn't know it. It could be like that, they said.

He'd heard stories about people taking Surprise and having no spectacular hallucinations at all. They hallucinate an old lady pushing a shopping cart in the supermall. A bit of trash in the gutter that wasn't really there: just an ordinary scrap of paper. Irrelevant, boring hallucinations. It depended on who you were, and what was significant in your subconscious, and how perceptive and imaginative you were. That's what Fu said.

So maybe she was a hallucination, he thought gloomily. I'm probably vapid enough to hallucinate my damn neighbor down the hall.

As she went by on the skateboard, he reached out and poked her—poked a cop firing a laser gun, in distorted TV image on her shoulder—and she weaved a bit on the board. "Hey!"

"Just wanted to see if I was hallucinating you."

She grinned, pleased. Misunderstanding. "Really? Jenny was saying my look was unreal today, too."

Dexy stopped, staring up the darkened street, listening, as sirens howled a few blocks west, then more sirens from the east and north.

Sounded like they were converging on something. Maybe on the riot in Little Beirut, maybe on some other blackout action. There'd be trigger-happy police and snipers, up ahead . . .

What do I care about cops and snipers? he asked himself. I'm gonna be dead soon. Aren't I?

He looked around, expecting the Surprise to answer him with a vision. Nothing. Not yet, anyway.

Marilyn used her long, luminous yellow nails to pluck a drug patch from her skirt pocket, peeled the stickum paper off with her teeth, spat it out; the round, slick white paper curled on the street like something curling up to die. She stuck the drug patch up under her skirt, onto a thigh, and shivered as the DMSO carried amphetamine into her. Started chattering. "You feel stoned on that Surprise stuff?"

"Nope."

"Thas whus eerie about it, I heard, that you don't feel stoned an' you don't hallucinate for, like, twenty minutes at a time and then all of a sudden something hits you like a spiked dildo . . . and then it's just gone and for a while there's nothin'; and then . . . and then . . ." Her voice trailed off into a staccato chant that went with the crotch box's rhythm. "And then and then and *then*. And then and then and *then*. And then and then and *then*. And then and—" So forth.

The box was grinding out a groove, the singer was Johnny Paranoid, the lyrics were:

> *There's a truth you can't avoid*
> *Listen to Johnny Paranoid*
> *Life will end in the burning void*
> *Shakin' shakin' shakin' like a*
> *rock-'n'-roll' chord . . .*

Maybe that's a sign, Dexy thought. Maybe it's an aural hallucination. Life will end in the burning void. Go ahead and kill yourself.

Maybe the drug was making him more sensitive to synchronicity messages, too. Either way it was the same message: *"Do it."*

But he was a long way from being sure. He looked around at the street and murmured to the drug, "Show me."

Still nothing out of the ordinary. There were other people out now, talking in clusters, some with flashlights, some with rifles. Or heading in small groups toward the riot, the looting, the action they could all feel, somehow, calling to them from over there . . .

Now the crotch box was playing another tune, "Six Kinds of Darkness," and Dexy thought he could feel the kinds of darkness draped around them, could feel the penumbral layers parting like spiderwebs across him as he strode down the sidewalk in his imitation-snakeskin cowboy boots. Six kinds of darkness and more. Darkness diffused by starlight and the squared-off galaxy of skyline glowing from uptown; the inky darkness in the empty doorways; the striated darkness of the sewer grate; the pooling gray-black darkness as the street narrowed ahead; the raggedy darkness where the school burned with intermittent fires back down the street. The darkness of uncertainty.

Another gunshot from Delancey. And then two more.

He thought, Is this the kind of suicide I want? Hit by a stray bullet? He'd had something like a comfortable overdose in mind, or maybe blow himself up on the stage of some cheap club. Make it a performance-art piece. He'd fantasized about ripping off a car, hiring some of the Palestinian guys he knew over on Houston Street to rig it for him, so he could drive a car bomb into some mob fascist's limo. Like the Yakuza/mafia scumbag who'd taken over Hard Disk CDs and dumped half the label's bands. Including Dexy's band. Blow that sucker up. Take him along to hell.

Just a fantasy. He knew that. Knew it was adolescent too. That's what happens when you're a thirty-nine-year-old rocker, you're an emotional adolescent in a middle-aged body. Embarrassing. No way he was ever going to get past it, either.

They reached a corner, turned left. Marilyn circling him now, looking him up and down. "You got a nice butt," she said.

"Shut up."

"Those Astaire pants are too loose, you should show your butt off with some tighter pants, Dexy. Did you kill that jacket yourself?"

"Oh, right, you bet. Like I'm going to go and hang out in Central Park with a rifle waiting to be eaten alive by a pack of wild dogs. I ain't that fucking desperate."

"You desperate about something, though, huh?"

"That's just an expression. Stop circling me like that, it's making me nervous."

"I'm not circling you . . . *Uh*-oh."

He looked at her, saw her smirk. "Very funny. Don't

play with my head, pretend I'm hallucinating when I'm not. It's fucking dangerous."

She said something he couldn't make out under the boom of the crotch box. "What?"

"I said I'm sorry. Are you mad at me?"

"No." Like he even knew her well enough to get mad at her. They were just run-into-each-other-at-clubs acquaintances. See-each-other-in-the-hall-and-bitch-about-the-landlord acquaintances.

"You going to give up getting your band back together? I noticed you grew your hair out natural color. You should get a scalp-up, a dude like you, in his thirties . . ."

He winced. She went on, obliviously.

". . . a guy like you looks younger with a scalp-up."

"I don't care if I look younger or not." He didn't sound convincing, even to himself.

"No?" Marilyn looked away. Her luminous wig swinging a little off-center as she looked around. "Let's go this way." She picked up her board and added, "I think I can get us past the police blockade." She led him through a brick-strewn vacant lot. They risked an alley, walked up north a half block, turned left—the noise of the blackout riot growing like excitement in a boy watching his first porn video—and then they had to sidle through a trash-gummy space between two old tenements. And then . . .

Then they were in a party. Or a riot.

It was both. First the shouting, crashing sounds. Voices distorted by the cavelike echo of smashed-open storefronts. They stepped out onto the sidewalk, saw the shadows that filled the shop-lined street boiling with action. The street was crowded and the crowd was street. Dexy made out the scene in flashbulb flashes from light-sources that came and went. An erratic comet, zigzagging, was someone with a chem lantern running by, carrying a ripped-off virtual-reality set under his arm, running past a bunch of teenagers tug-of-warring back and forth, fighting over something he couldn't see.

A storefront window disgorged something rectangular and bulky: a sofa being pushed out a window. Flamelight from other storefronts. Fistfights, over there—and there. A chunky Hispanic mother scrambled after her three grade-school kids, shouting at them in Spanish, her eyes bright with fear, but no fear on the wide-open faces of the kids, only unfettered delight as they ran helter-skelter through the riot.

The air was scratchy with smells of smoke, cigarettes, spilled beer, an acrid smell that might have been some kind of gunpowder. There was a stuttering series of detonations: strings of firecrackers going off, whoops and laughter from the people who'd set them; a small sky-rocket arced up, trailing a confetti of fire. A group of people in a smashed-open adult-video store passed a hashpipe; someone threw a bottle at a window, *bonk*; it bounced off, but they tried again with a brick, *crash*, tinkle of shattered glass hitting the sidewalk; an angry shout, more firecracker bangs, louder than the first, in a storefront to the right . . .

. . . as Marilyn squealed happily, "This is so *THRASHIN*'! Let's STEAL something!"

. . . and Dexy realized that the detonations in the storefront weren't firecrackers, they were gunshots, maybe some underinsured shop proprietor was trying to protect his goods, and someone screamed and there was a string of muzzle flashes. Dexy backed away from the curb, feeling suddenly agoraphobic. Snipers turned up at these things, all manner of lunatics, and at some point the cops would get it together and move in, shooting first and not necessarily rubber bullets.

Dexy backed till he stopped against a brick wall. Looked around, trying to get a handle on this thing. Was it a faction riot? Christians rioting through Islamic holdings? Muslims looting the Christians? Maybe the Sikhs looting the Hindus . . .

But the crowd was mixed and so were the storefronts. Pizzerias, discount dives, a shop that dealt in luminous tattoos and bone-implant radios. The DEA's licensed recreational drugs kiosk—untouched because everyone knew there was no stock in it at night. A hairdresser's, a manicurist, and a scalp-up place offering: *New Scalp-Ups— Scalps painlessly remolded! The new Shaps [sic] are Hear [sic]!* A group of angst-rockers stood with a black hooker in a doorway, passing a stem around, getting some serious Bic-thumb from smoking synthetic rock, arguing about whether or not they really got a hit that time. One of them, a short girl in Harley boots and a stained wild-dog skirt, her knees bruised and scarred from skateboard fighting, reached up into her scalp-up, fingered out a "bottle" with a couple more rocks of synthetic crack. Her scalp-up was molded on her hairless scalp—of transplanted cartilage and collagen and skin—into a three-dee sculpture of a really nasty car accident.

Just the usual neighborhood stuff.

The street was barricaded off at the corners, way down by the smashed Citibank ATM station on one side, and by the uptown R subway station on the other. Cars turned sideways, trash cans piled up, old oil barrels, heaped furniture, burning boxes. Police lights whirled beyond the barricade. Some sort of ominously brisk activity there. But not much. They were waiting for backup, Dexy guessed—there was too much going on, all over downtown. This was probably just one of half a dozen outbreaks. Maybe some shelling, too: He thought he heard the distant *CRUMP* of mortar fire.

In the middle of the street, in front of him, the crowd was thickening like a bee swarm, and most of them were dancing, a kind of rollicky, improvised carnival dance to a beat box . . .

Marilyn's beat box. She was pumping in the thick of the riot, slamming to the beat box's thud. She's gonna get hurt out there.

A Hispanic guy with a sweat-sheened face, wearing a ripped spangled-paper jumpsuit, ran by on bare and bleeding feet, giggling, "Awright awright awright *noche partida*." His testicles waggling like a dog's tongue out a rip in his jumpsuit. Guy looked happy as a fag priest french-kissing Jesus, Dexy thought.

Was the guy even there? Dexy wondered. Maybe there was only five people in the street and the rest was the Surprise.

No. This was real. So far.

He spotted Marilyn again. The crowd was clumping around her. Around the music booming from her crotch. Marilyn dancing, shaking libido in their faces, wallowing in the attention. Someone bringing out a steel drum, someone else a conga, adding salsa to the beat box's drumming, Hispanics and blacks salsa-dancing and skanking, sharing bottles and dust joints; someone rolling an oil barrel up, setting it on end, cramming it with crushed boxes and wood, squirting charcoal-lighter fluid, tossing in a match—WHUF! of flames blossoming over the rusty old can . . . And Marilyn was pressed by the crowd in toward the burning can—the dancers began to circle her— Marilyn dancing giddily on, a creature made of TV and moving tattoos overlapping indistinguishably in jittering firelight . . .

Stupid bitch is going to get hurt, Dexy thought.

And for some reason she was his responsibility. Or maybe she was his point of orientation. Whatever, he was getting scared for her. It was as if she were some crystallization of his crisis, and it didn't matter at all that she was really no one to him.

He took a deep breath and started toward her, preparing to plunge into the crowd. And saw Bunny García, Dexy's old guitar player. That fuck-head. Bunny popping up out of the crowd, in his open guerrilla jacket and black rubber pants, Brazilian-made high-top skates, grinning, going, "Hey, *qué pasa*, Ugly?" Doing some kind of new complicated handshake on Dexy's palm so fast he couldn't even feel it. Bunny with his Marshall-Amp-with-a-screaming-skull-for-a-speaker scalp-up, expensive animated tattoo on his chest showing an eighteenth-century pirate crew looting and raping on a twenty-first-century yacht. He'd had it for a year, though, and it was getting old fast; the animations beginning to flicker and fade. Couldn't afford to change it now. Must've been cut off by his parents—his dad was the biggest bookie in Spanish Harlem, owned this huge kitschy house with gold wallpaper in Brooklyn Heights. Bunny used to brag about his mob connections, which turned out to be bullshit when the band needed them: when they were hassled for payoff money so they could go onstage at a mob-owned place called the Cat Club, and suddenly Bunny was whining, "Hey, I got to use those mob favors for something important sometime, you know?"

So here was Bunny, now Bunny, the prima donna who burned through solos faster than everyone else and bragged about the pickups on his fingertips that were installed

at the guitar-surgery clinic like no one had ever done that
before; Bunny, who'd ditched him to join some dweeb
hip-hop rockoreography band. Here was Bunny, all of a
sudden acting like a deep comrade. "I don't have any
money and I don't have any drugs, Bunny," Dexy said.

"I don't want shit from you, man, except to say it's
good to see you, we oughta get a jam on sometime." Still
grinning, doing that junkie rub with the back of his hand
on his nose, the other hand in the pocket of his green
Brazilian-guerrilla-fighter jacket—an affectation if ever
there was one, since Bunny'd shoot a hole in his foot if
he ever picked up a gun.

"Yeah, right," Dexy said, twitching as somebody
smashed a bottle on the street not far behind him. Someone else shot out an unlit streetlamp. He looked around.
"This shit's getting out of hand."

"Don't worry about it," Bunny said as the tumult went
into third gear, the crowd noises beginning to really roar.
Flames licking out from a third-story window across the
street; red light rippling across a very short Asian guy
humping a tall black woman in a doorway; she was squatting some so he could thrust up under her African skirt.
Her bare breasts glittering with bead insets. The man's
face straining with concentration, not wanting to miss out
on this opportunity; the woman laughing hysterically. A
group of children dragging a mattress, while another
child, following them, tossed matches on it. The matches
went out, but he kept trying. An old Italian woman in
widow black with a looted fake-Tiffany lamp under one
arm and a holo-set under the other, hurrying bent-backed
through the thickening smoke. A couple of Iranian-looking
dudes, submachine guns under their arms, on the other
side of the crowd, just looking around. Marilyn still bob-
bing in the party midst, by the fire. People still crowding
her, but she was keeping her head up, like she was
treading water.

Sirens warbling from three or four directions, but no
direct action from the cops here yet. How long could it
last?

"Those Iranian guys, or Arabs or whatever they are,
you see 'em, Bunny? Maybe that means they're gonna
use this opp, do a push. They start by shelling, mortars

and RPGs and shit. I'm gonna get Marilyn, get the fuck out of here."

"Hey, I'm telling you, don't worry about it, man. You was always getting worried about shit—"

"That's the only reason we ever had a rehearsal or got a gig together, because I worried," Dexy snapped. "I hadn't, we'd never have done shit. You and Lunk'd sit around and play TV themes and smoke dope all day if I didn't worry and hassle you. We got two gold records, the only reason is because I worried. Those sessions were all worry, Bunny, and I was the only one who ever did any."

"That's mostly right, man, but that was because you was the one who loved the worrying, loved chewing your nails and pushing and nagging like a daddy. You fell into that role, see."

Dexy stared at him. It was amazing how well he could hear Bunny with all this noise going on. It was as if they were in a bell of glass, with the riot raging on around them but not touching them. The noise and bustle of it was there, but muted, distant.

"Hey, Bunny, you like playing in that rockoreo shit? doing those disco moves in that bourgeoise uptown club? Those implants makin' you jump like that? I couldn't stand to be puppeted around by some fucking dance computer fucking with my nervous system. The music's already robot shit—"

"Of course I don' like it, man, what you think?" He scratched his crotch. "But Hemo wasn't happenin'. The band just wasn't happenin'."

"And you had a habit to support."

"Oh, yeah. Everybody's got something to support, Dexy. Or what? Everybody. You too. You got to pump up that big lead-singer ego of yours with lotta clothes you can't really afford. Parties. Where's your royalties money? You got into some drugs too. Blue Mesc. You and Rickenharp used to get together, do Blue Mesc for two days and nights straight, then whine about it when you had to crash. Where's your money from those gold records, Dexy? Where's the money from that endorsement you did for that Soviet Microphone Company? What happened to that slick loft you used to have in Chelsea? You living in a dump down the hall from that hustler Marilyn, with roaches for roommates now." Smiling with an uncharacteristic gentleness all the time, as he said this. "Truth is, Dexy, we all stumbling around trying to get by the best we can. I was hurting and someone offered me a way out of the pain, that's all. To you it was disloyalty, or some shit. To me it was survival. For a while. My parents cut me off, wouldn't give me any more money after I got busted for dope. I got kicked out of that apartment I had in the old World Trade Center—did you see that place, after they made it into apartments? Huge honkin' old skyscrapers turned into apartments, I thought it was gonna be great, but I moved in and it was just another big shitty tenement, kept up as bad as any place in the Bronx. A slum in the sky. And pretty soon, I didn't even have that. I was just trying to get by, man."

Dexy shook his head in amazement. "You must be getting some good dope. I never heard this kinda speech from you."

"I talked to you, my way, but you never listened. You were too busy bitching. You got to stop blaming people for stuff. Your old man, for instance, how he never understood what an *artiste* you are; your girlfriend, who was supposed to stick with you even when you brought home a drippy dick from half the groupies in United Europe. She was supposed to just understand. And you get into diddly little fights with Kevin Keys about the band's musical direction . . . Shit, Dex, you could've compromised, the man only wanted two tunes out of each set. Now you're getting some gray hair, you're slow coming out with lyric ideas, the record company drops you when sales nosedown, and you want to blame everybody else and take it out on us. Going to kill yourself to punish us. Get yourself on the cover of a magazine one last time. Shit."

"You killing yourself for years with dope, you should talk." Wondering, How did Bunny know about the suicide thing? Maybe Bunny had come over when he wasn't home, maybe he still had the key. Maybe he'd gotten nosy, played back Dexy's video therapy program. But, no, Dexy'd deliberately scrambled up the shrink program because he'd gotten pissed off about its advice; got drunk and programmed a rat's head onto the animated shrink and made everything it said come out in rodent squeaks.

"I *did* kill myself with dope, in fact," Bunny said offhandedly. "About two A.M., this morning. They haven't found my body yet. It was an accidental OD—I'm not a wimp like you."

Dexy's mouth dropped open. "You're—"

"Surprise!" Bunny said.

"—a hallucination. Or a ghost."

"A hallucination. But I did die. Or anyway, Bunny died."

Dexy felt a chill that seemed to shiver even in his hair and teeth and the tip of his tongue. "You're talking to me from the Other Side? I mean, there is life after death?"

"Oh, no. Well, I don't know. Bunny's talking to you from inside your own head. Bunny's a hallucination. But you're on the frequency where you can pick up on some things, is how you know that Bunny is dead." The hallucination talking about Bunny in the third person now.

The Bunny thing turned and looked at the place the Muslim guys had stood. They were gone. "They've decided to do a push through here, use the riot crowd for cover. They going to expand territory."

"Oh, shit."

"Works out good. You stay here, Dex, you get killed. Go down in a riot: shot dead by militia, or by cops, pretty good rock-'n'-roll death, wouldn't you say?" The Bunny thing's face was changing. Sucking into itself. Skull pushing out through the skin, eyes becoming little glints in sunken sockets. Gums shriveling back, teeth exposed. The scalp-up sinking into itself, rotting off, ragged sections of yellow cranium showing through in patches. But he kept talking. More or less in the tone of voice Dexy's video-shrink used. "Remember that time, before the city was Balkanized, you lived in Chelsea? And you walked down to Houston one night and blundered right into the first Islamic Fun uprising. You couldn't believe it, your little downtown art and rock scene just irrelevant, silly-looking because these guys in cheap paramilitary outfits come running down the sidewalk like kids playing army, busting caps with those Kuwaiti carbines. They take part of the East Village and the whole of Soho hostage, all those pink-boy Soho art galleries and, like, neo-neoexpressionists an' shit, all of 'em suddenly under the gun? I remember an anarchist friend of mine laughing about it saying, Yeah, now *that* is art! It was kind of cool, the Soho artists and the deputy mayor, all of 'em held hostage by the Islamic Funs—"

Dexy nodded. At the time, not so long ago, it had seemed outlandish, outrageous, bizarre, and scary as hell. They'd thought it would blow over any day. It just couldn't go on. But then the Islamic Funs started making demands, the Boy Ayatollah took over that little TV station, the choppers come in from the artificial islands where the Libyans were building up all that arsenal—it had just started unfolding like something totally out of control and it wasn't so funny anymore.

Thinking about this, Dexy watched the Bunny thing becoming shorter, as if his legs were melting. His eyes had vanished completely now. His neck shrink-wrapped his upper spine; his clothes hung on him like his bones were a hanger. Dexy watched in horrified fascination. It was as if his metamorphosis was some anthropomorphic parody of the city's own transformation into Little Beirut.

The Christian Funs had come out of Queens, down from Upstate and Maine, with their private red-neck militia; the mayor looked the other way, even told the National Guard to let the ChrisFuns through the blockade. And then the sniping started, the mortar shelling. It was weird how fast you got used to seeing people killed. How some mindless social inertia could keep you in the cross fire while Christian Fundamentalists shoot at Islamic Fundamentalists and the MosFuns shoot back at the ChrisFuns. Photos on the front page of the *Post* showing a Black Muslim grade-school classroom after it was hit by a mortar shell . . .

"Yeah, that was a key moment, that picture on the *Post*," the hallucination was saying, reading his mind because it was his mind. "Remember that one? Those burst-open kids? Art my fucking ass. That's what turned people against the ChrisFuns, so they had to dig in, in their own part of town. Just when you think it can't get worse, *bang*. That's when there was all that serious shelling back and forth and the hostage thing gets worse and both sides block evacuation moves and backers airdrop supplies and ammo and nobody can get up the nerve to take responsibility for the political risk of sending in the National Guard or the marines or whoever . . ." Now his flesh was puffing out again, blowing up into a different person, a smaller person with a different face entirely. Fast-forward animation.

And the riot went on in the background, someone dumping a garbage can off a roof so it tumbled end over end, fell onto a group of people who screamed as it struck them; a bottle arced and smashed nearby. Flying bricks. Marilyn struggling now, trying to get out of the crowd, panicking. The music warping as some punk in the crowd ripped her crotch box from her. All of this some distant backdrop as the metamorphosing thing jabbered on, ". . . because if they did that, sent the army in here, there'd be a huge bloodbath, all this innocent bloodshed, so they spend months in negotiations, and the JDL gets involved in the fighting and the kid militias spring up and it gets worse, shooting on the street every day, everybody starts to get used to it, the black marketing spreads out, gangs like the Crips make deals with the factions and use the faction territories for hideouts. And here's Dexy, now, stuck in the middle of all this, because you can't afford to move. Partly because about the same time you lost your record deal. That's when it happens, right? So your cash flow dries up and here you are on the edge of the fighting. But, hell, that fits your rock-'n'-roll feelings about things, right, Dex, you *like* that action, right? Oh, sure. You're ready to rock till you're dead anyway because you're an *artiste*, you're *chosen* to incarnate That Energy, that's what you always believed—" There's nothing worse than a sarcastic hallucination.

The Bunny García thing was gone; the hallucination had become a boy. A fourteen-year-old brown-skinned boy in a turban. The Boy Ayatollah, the child Imam, looking both stern and cherubic. Both a familiar media figure and something exotic, in his black-and-red robe. "So, then, my friend," the Boy Ayatollah said. "What are you scared of? My people are coming here tonight, and many will die, and you can go down among them, in some kind of glory—what kind of glory is uncertain. But some kind. What are you, then, afraid of?"

Dexy's mouth was dry. He had trouble talking. But the kid was so earnest, he was talking right to the heart of him. Dexy had to answer him. You couldn't lie to this kid. Finally, he said thickly, "I'm afraid of dying. But I'm afraid to go on the way I have been and just sort of shrivel up into just another shuffling old geezer, too. I feel like . . . like I'm not alive anymore because I can't do the thing, you know, the thing that . . . I don't know how to say it . . . The thing that made me feel like being alive meant something."

"Have a look around with me, won't you?"

The boy put his hand through the crook of Dexy's arm, strolled with him down the street along the edges of the crowd. It had thinned out some.

Dexy could no longer hear Marilyn's crotch box booming. They'd taken it. Maybe hurt her.

Then, *crunch, squeal*. As a police armored car with an earthmover-blade for a battering ram smashed through the barricade by the Citibank, whirling the watery-neon shine of its cherrytop beacon over the lizard-skin asphalt, cops in armor and heavy riot gear running behind it, booming out unintelligible warnings with bullhorns, firing tear gas, the rioters scattering . . .

The Islamic Funs choosing the same moment to come pouring out of the subway station and the old burned-out Tad's Steakhouse from the other direction, probably not seeing the cops' push till too late, firing at anyone handy. Going for an expansion of territory in the Holy Name of Allah and in the glory of the Sacred Martyrdom of the Boy Ayatollah's precocious New Fundamentalism . . .

Triggering the Christian Funs, who were financed and armed by the Birchers and the KKK, to open fire from the rooftops, chickenshit snipers, as usual, so that a few of the onrushing Fathers of the New Islamic American State went down, writhing . . .

(Dexy wondering at his own fearlessness, here. It wasn't suicidal fearlessness—it was a sense that he was protected, surfing the Luck Plane . . .)

"Now see them again," the Boy Ayatollah said, his voice, through the screaming and gun-shooting and sirening, coming with eerie lucidity. He waved his hand, and Dexy saw the gunmen and the rioters were not men and women any longer.

They were small children.

All of them: the Skinheads, Brownshirts for the ChrisFuns, dropping into the fray, now, from the fire escapes; the Islamic Funs darting down the street; the rioters and looters; the police coming from another direction. All of them were transformed—or revealed: they were children. The cops' battering vehicle was a toy thing of cheap plastic in bright primary colors, and there was a jolly clown's face painted on its earthmover-blade. The children who had been Christian and Islamic Funs militia weren't playing army; they were frightened kids in costumes, running through a maze that wasn't quite there. Their play with guns was hysteria, crying and laughing at the same time, seven-year-olds with toy guns that impossibly killed like real guns. Children, all of them, children with a searching in their faces—all of them weeping, mouthing Mama, Daddy, all of them running someplace . . . You could see they were running to some hypothetical shelter, trying to get past the other kids, driven through them as if they were running from something—yes, Dexy saw them clearly now: The children ran from flying apparitions of translucent violet plasma, etheric fiends screaming at them in hot pursuit; creatures that were all mouth and no eyes . . . the children trying to get away from the apparitions, firing at one another as they went . . . as the scene got darker, and darker and darker . . . the apparitions flowing down into the shadows . . . until the children alone remained, their guns vanished, just children blinded by darkness, flailing about, colliding sightlessly, stumbling at random this way and that.

The apparitions had melted down into long, attenuated cables of ectoplasm that interlinked the various groups; a network of the stuff, linking the children who were Christian Funs; other skeins linking children who were Islamic Funs; other nets linking the cops . . . The nets tangling, the tangles violence . . . The children mouthing something else now . . .

All of them saying the same thing, though they made no sound at all. Saying, Where are they? When will they come?

The Boy Ayatollah remarked, "They're waiting for the adults to find them, Dexy, to bring them out of the dark-

ness, the permanent blackout of uncertainty." The Boy
Ayatollah looked at him earnestly. "But, Dexy, the adults
never come. The adults never will come, my friend. The
children are on their own forever."

"Oh, man. Don't say that." Dexy near tears.

"It's nothing to you, though. You're a rock star. A
performer. A rock-'n'-roll hero. 'You're all just fucking
peasants as far as I can see,' John Lennon said, long ago.
You want to live fast, and die young, no? What is all this
suffering to you?"

"Shut up. That's pure crap. Just shut up."

"You prefer one voice to two? It happens mine is
fading . . . anyway . . ."

Surprise: the hallucination passed. The Boy Ayatollah
was gone; the darkness eased, the full noise of the
street roared down on Dexy like a runaway bus. And the
children were transformed, magically matured, once
more adult rioters, cops wrestling with them; other cops
firing suppressive rounds at adult gunmen. Looters flattened on the street, crawling to avoid the gunfire. A
couple dozen were fallen and wounded. Some of them
dead.

But some were still quite active. Dexy saw two pasty-
white skinheads dragging Marilyn into a looted storefront.

Dexy told himself, You should run and help her.

A bullet spat asphalt near his foot, and he jumped
back, the back of his head feeling soft. He ducked into
the shelter of a darkened concrete doorway. The fear
finally hitting him, now that the hallucination had passed,
adrenaline whiplashing through him. Run. Cops hunkered behind the armored vehicle, moving past him,
shouting warnings at the Islamic Funs who were backing
off; the bullets still flying; the crack of another sniper
rifle on the roof. Run. Get out of here. Back the way you
came.

But the two guys were out of sight, now, in that storefront, hidden in there with Marilyn, doing something to
her . . .

Shit.

Run, man, nothing you can do to help her.

But . . .

Forget it. Maybe you wouldn't get killed—maybe just

suffer. Maybe a bullet to the spine, quadroplegia or something . . .

But, shit. Marilyn.

He grabbed a ten-inch piece of broken pipe from the sidewalk, ran across the street, behind the cops, sprinting toward the storefront. A bullet whined past, close enough he nearly wet his pants.

The storefront. A Korean grocery-import store. In the shifting red light from the cop car and the fires, the buttress sections of old grime-gray brick walls to either side of the storefront looked like squared-off pillars at the entrance to some ancient temple. The graffiti spray-painted over the buttresses seemed cryptic as the pagan glyphs of the temple's forgotten race . . .

The drug hadn't completely worn off. He was just reaching the curb in front of the Korean storefront, hearing Marilyn screaming something, when the second-story window above the storefront erupted outward, showering broken glass past the rusty fire escape. Dexy looked up and saw a cloud of spinning glass fragments falling toward him, glittering red in the hellish light. Surprise: the cloud of glass slowing, stopping in midair, floating there, was now a cloud of moths whose softly beating wings were of broken glass and whose faces belonged to demented angels. Showers of glass shards: silicon grace. He gaped at the hallucination . . . and the broken glass fell on his face.

He shrieked, "*Fuu*-ucccck," and dropped the pipe, clawed at his eyes. Felt splinters of glass like pin feathers on his cheeks. He thought, My eyes!

But he blinked . . . looked around. The glass had missed his eyes. He let out a long breath and, stomach quaking, plucked shards from his face. Too freaked to feel any pain yet. And again remembered Marilyn. (As behind him were screams, cracks and rattles of weapons, more sirens, laughter, someone pleading.)

He reached down to the pipe lying in the broken glass. Saw fragmented reflections of himself in the glass, jigsaw mirrors, lying around the pipe. Picked up the pipe. Saw the glass move by itself, the jigsaw parts coming together, fusing the pieces of his reflection. A kid. A lost kid. But someone was standing behind the kid. Himself:

as an adult. Who put his hand on the kid's shoulder. The
kid was Dexy at seven. The adult had come, after all.

Dexy was running into the Korean store then, fla-
grantly proud of himself for coming to Marilyn's rescue.
Looking for the men who would be raping her.

There—in the light from a chem lantern, over in the
corner, beyond overturned shelves tumbled with Korean
ideogrammed packaged foods. There they were.

Dexy stopped, staring.

Marilyn was bending over the two men who'd dragged
her in. Both guys were out cold, bleeding from head
wounds. She still had the spike heels she'd used on them
in her hands. She dropped the shoes, squatted beside
them, legs awkwardly apart, barefoot still, like a little girl
toying with a mud pie, singing something tunelessly as
she poked through their pockets. All she came up with
was a half-empty pack of THC syntharettes. She stuck
them into the band of her skirt. Dexy noticed a half-
dozen synthetic-crack drug patches, the street-made kind
shaped like iron crosses, on her arms. "You shouldn't
mix coke with meth," he heard himself say. "You shouldn't
be taking any of that shit, anyway."

He stared at her as she turned, smiled loopily up at
him. He felt foolishly disappointed when he realized he
didn't need the pipe bludgeon. Odd, because he didn't
really like fights. He tossed the pipe aside. Turned and
looked out the broken storefront.

Looking at the fighting. Rioters running from cops,
yelling they were ready to surrender but getting their
heads busted in anyway. Skinheads and Christian militia
fighting with Islamic Funs. He thought about what had
nudged the Islamic Funs into taking over their sector:
persecution from city administration and landlords who
wanted the immigrants moved out for real-estate development—jingoistic legislation, too, restrictions on Muslim
rights to build mosques that had come from an increas-
ingly conservative government controlled by Christian
Fun bigots. The Christians feeling pressured by a growing
Islamic community; the Muslims threatened by the Christian reaction. This wasn't Little Beirut—this was the whole
planet. This was Jews and Arabs, Sikhs and Hindus,
Communists and Capitalists. This was the way they all
were.

In the face of that suffering, the pain of that societal autism, his petty priorities, the primacy of his career, seemed irrelevant. Pathetic, insignificant. So much self-indulgence. Particularly, suicide.

Dexy seeing again, for a flash moment, the confused children—children caught up, he saw now, in a desperate effort to find their way home by superimposing a purely arbitrary order on the chaos of an overwhelming uncertainty. Arbitrary ideological nets tangling, children strangled in the mesh.

Any mesh. Anything you artificially attached importance to. Some mesh of meaningless priorities that tangled you, choked you. Some arbitrary identity . . .

Like being a rock star. Just for example.

He went to Marilyn, reached out, grabbed her hand, pulled her to her feet. Squeezed her hand. She was real. Probably not a real girl, not originally, but he didn't care.

"You checkin' to see am I a hallucination again?"

He nodded. Realizing that a bubble had burst, somehow, a membrane had split: the drug had worn off. But it had spoken to him. Something, anyway, had spoken to him.

The gunshots were diminishing outside. People coughing from tear gas. Lights wheeling in his peripheral vision. Curls of smoke.

"I feel like I'm gonna be real, real sick," Marilyn said, slumping, clutching herself.

"I know where there's an anarchist clinic, they'll give you a shot to take you down. After that, you better stay away from drugs. They fuck up your priorities."

She bent over and threw up. He waited. Finally, she straightened up, spat a few times, and croaked, "Can we get outta here through the back?"

"I think so. Come on." He picked up the chem lantern, helped her clamber past the overturned shelves and Korean produce. She was shaky, now. There was blood trickling from under her wig. They paused, and he peeled the wig off her and looked. It wasn't bad, just a scalp cut.

As they went out the back way, into the narrow walk space that led to the quiet of the next street over, she said, "This was a hot date. What you doing tomorrow night?"

"Resting up. So I can apply for a job with my head

screwed on right. I was offered an A-and-R gig at Roadkill CDs . . ."

"You giving up partying? Going to go real serious?"

He hesitated, then said, "Not really. I'm gonna have spare time. There's something we could do, just for fun, if you want. You know how to play an instrument?"

"No. But I can sing. Real good."

"Can you?" He smiled. "I can play bass. Good enough. Fuck it, then. Let's start a band. And *you* be the lead singer."

As they stepped out onto the sidewalk of an empty street he peeled the drug patches off her and tossed them away. The drug patches fell into the gutter and curled up like dead things.

Though John Shirley currently lives in California, he lived in New York City's East Village for ten years. While there he was lead singer of the rock band Obsession, and he authored Cellars, *a horror novel about the underside of New York. He's published numerous SF novels, including* Eclipse, Eclipse Penumbra, *and* A Splendid Chaos. Heatseeker, *his first collection of short stories, has been published by Scream/Press.*

The Last Real New Yorker in the World

by James D. Macdonald and Debra Doyle

*New York is a tourist mecca—the Empire State
Building, the Statue of Liberty, the Broadway the-
aters, the colorful inhabitants and history. It's like a
regular theme park.*

Maybe someday it'll be a theme park.

The supercharged Duesenberg landed in front of the
house just as Jimmy Moskovitz was on his way to work.
Dutch Schultz and Mad Dog Coll stepped out.

"Get in the car, Jimmy," the Dutchman said. "You're
going for a ride."

Coll held open the Doozie's front door. Jimmy Moskovitz
slid inside and glanced to his left. The man behind the
wheel was Killer Burke.

Coll and Schultz got into the back seat and Burke put
the car in motion.

"I've been expecting something like this for quite a
while," said Moskovitz. "But aren't you guys mixing up
your periods a little? Fred Burke came before Vincent
Coll and George Schultz had their feud."

"This is the way the boss likes it, and I like what the
boss likes, so shut up," Dutch explained.

"Come on, Schultz," Jimmy said. "The real Dutchman
never had a boss. He's turning over in his grave to hear
you talk like that."

Silence was the only reply from the back of the car.
The driver turned south onto the Detroit/Indianapolis
flyway and picked up speed to join the pattern.

The flyway bent east to circle the Chicago Crater.
"This has something to do with New York, doesn't it?"
Moskovitz said.

"That's NewYorkLand® to you, scum," Killer said. "You'd better talk right."

" 'Land,' maybe. But not 'New York.' I still say it."

"That's what the boss wants to talk to you about," Coll said. "You've been responsible for a dip in attendance all by yourself."

"So they send the clowns to get me," Moskovitz said. He looked up to heaven and raised his hands in a why-me gesture. "Sometimes I think I lived too long."

"I can fix that," said Burke.

"Shut up," Schultz said.

They dropped out of the main flight path at the Ossining interchange and took local control from the NewYorkLand grid from there on in. They flew down the broad expanse of the Hudson at low altitude and slow speed: all the traffic in this branch was coming to and from the tourist landing areas. As they turned, the NewYorkLand skyline was visible to the right of the river. The Empire State Building and the Chrysler Building rose above all the other skyscrapers.

The Doozie landed in the Battery Area Parking Zone, and the three hoods escorted Jimmy Moskovitz onto the private people mover that led to the parts of NewYorkLand that tourists never got to see. The underground slidewalk carried them through a waiting room where three Fiorello La Guardias were eating hot dogs, and on past side tunnels marked by white-on-green signs: APOLLO THE-ATER, GRAND CENTRAL, EAST VILLAGE.

A young woman in burn makeup was coming out of the tunnel marked TRIANGLE SHIRTWAIST.

"Hey, what are you doing here?" Mad Dog shouted at her. "Don't you have somewhere to be?"

"The first show just finished," she said. "I'm not on again until twelve o'clock.

"Goddamn enforcers," she added under her breath as the slidewalk carried Moskovitz and the others away.

Burke laughed. "You're still on Central Time, Vinnie," he told Coll. "I used to make the same mistake all the time when I was riding the Century Limited, coming back from doing a job for Scarface."

"You guys can drop the act," Jimmy said. "I know who you aren't."

"You don't understand," the Dutchman said. "We

stay in character all the time. It's what makes NewYork-Land℠ so authentic."

Jimmy snorted. "If it's so authentic, why is the Empire State Building only a third the size?"

"It's made of the original stone," the Dutchman told him. "So what's your problem? And the Empire State Buildings in NewYorkLand Europe℠ and NewYorkLand Asia℠ are just as real. All built from the original stone." The slidewalk stopped at a heavy wooden door. "We're almost at the boss's office. Be respectful."

The hoods escorted Jimmy down a long hallway past more wooden doors. At the last door, a nice young man in a bellhop's uniform sat behind a desk.

"The boss will be with you in a minute," he said. "Working on a complaint."

"Anything I should know about?" Schultz asked.

"Some guy and his wife come here from Des Moines," said the bellhop. "They spend the whole day and don't get mugged. Now he wants his money back."

Mad Dog Coll scowled. "If those jerks in the Mugging Division are screwing up, this whole place is out of control."

"Budget cuts," the Dutchman said. "Based on loss of trade. And Jimmy, here, is the guy responsible."

"Ought to put him in charge of muggings," said Coll. "See how he likes it when NewYorkLand℠ can't deliver one of its specialties, and it's all his fault."

The buzzer on the desk sounded. "Ready for you," the bellhop said.

The door opened and Moskovitz stepped through into the huge office on the other side. Mad Dog Coll walked beside him on his right and Killer Burke walked beside him on his left. Dutch Schultz followed close behind. The door swung shut after them.

Jimmy looked around. The windows on the four walls showed the view from the top of the World Trade Center. Far below, in the harbor, the Staten Island ferry was a spot of gaudy orange among the drab merchant ships and the tiny white pleasure boats.

"Holovid, taken before we demolished the original," said a voice from the high-backed vinyl chair. The chair swiveled around. The woman in the chair was wearing a

T-shirt that said "My Parents Visited NewYorkLand™, and All I Got Was This Lousy Shirt."

"The show only runs three days, then it loops," she continued. "If I had it to do over again, I'd get a week."

Jimmy stared for a minute. "You're running New York?"

"You were expecting Boss Tweed?"

"I was expecting something different. A guy with a cigar, maybe."

"Clichés," said the woman. "I'm doing clichés all the time. Tourists love 'em. Then along comes this guy, calls himself 'the last real New Yorker in the world,' and what's he's expecting? Another cliché." She leaned back in the vinyl chair. "So the reason I asked you to come here was to ask you to just shut up."

Jimmy nodded approvingly. "You said that very well. You almost got the accent."

"I got a good language school here," she told him. "Nobody gets to meet the guests until they learn to speak like New Yorkers. It's more than just talking too fast and being rude, believe me."

"Is this where I'm supposed to be impressed?" asked Jimmy. "When you've got Vinnie Coll and the Dutchman acting like best buddies, and the Triangle Shirtwaist Factory burning down on the same afternoon you're celebrating V-E Day in Times Square, and a souvenir shop where the Port Authority Bus Terminal ought to be? I'm supposed to smile and tell you that this is good?"

The woman gave a faint, exasperated sigh. "You don't have to say that it's good. Just stop telling everyone how bad NewYorkLand™ is, and quit driving away business."

"I can't change the facts," said Jimmy. "And the fact is, this isn't New York. It isn't even where New York was. This is Passaic, New Jersey. And nobody lives here. What's New York with nobody living there?"

"A lot better than some cities. Take Chicago."

Jimmy shook his head obstinately. "At least Chicago isn't a bunch of actors running around pretending."

"Look," said the woman. "We're getting nowhere. This is your last chance. No more books, no more interviews, no more holovid documentaries running down our operation. Just a fat check every month, and your name on our letterhead as a Special Historical Consultant. Either take the deal, or don't."

*　　*　　*

"Gee, that was exciting!" Billy exclaimed. "A guy getting rubbed out in a barber chair!"

His mother frowned slightly. "I didn't read anything about that in the guidebook."

"One of the 'Special Shows, Scheduled from Time to Time,'" Billy's father said in a knowing tone. "Let's ask the hot-dog vendor what it was all about."

The hot-dog vendor was glad to oblige. "You've just witnessed a recreation of the killing of Albert Anastasio by Murder, Inc."

"Did you have to use so much blood?" Billy's mother asked.

"We pride ourselves on authenticity, here at NewYork-Land™," the vendor replied. "You guys want kraut on your Coney Island® dogs?"

James D. Macdonald was born and raised about forty miles from New York City, in the heart of upscale Westchester County. (He also spent six months at the incredibly downscale Brooklyn Navy Yard, but that's another story.) Visiting the city was always a treat for him while he was growing up, and even now, after having seen London, Paris, Rome, Buenos Aires, Istanbul, and Rio de Janeiro, the word "city" calls up for him a mental image of Manhattan. The way it should be.

Debra Doyle was born in Florida (not in the part that's New York South, either) and raised in a small town in Texas. She first encountered New York during grad school, and is still amazed that anyone lives there at all. "Visiting New York," she says, "is like chatting with a witty, charming homicidal maniac."

The idea of NewYorkLand™ was Doyle's; she first proposed it after passing through a toll booth at the Holland Tunnel.

Doyle and Macdonald have collaborated on eight novels, several short stories, and four kids. They live in New Hampshire, because New York taxes can kill you.

Tunnel Vision

by Esther Friesner

One of the inspirations for this volume was Esther Friesner's fantasy novel, New York by Knight, *so I always knew I had to include a story by her—and I'd have wanted to anyway. As well as writing superb fantasy, some of it hysterically funny, Esther is one of the founders of the cyberprep movement—a satirical response to the brouhaha about cyberpunk.*

The following story isn't cyberprep. It may be cyberpunk, but I'm not sure. If it is, it certainly takes a new direction for the subgenre. Whatever it is, it's got Esther's usual wit and manic invention, and is a lot of fun to read.

The cop lit a joint and dragged the smoke deep into his lungs while his partner fiddled with the infrared controls on her helmet. It was dark in the abandoned railway station, but not that dark; Koolfuse torches ought to be enough to help them as they ferreted out the last of the derelicts. What was Brenda fooling with all that technocrap for?

Unless it was true what the guys said about Brenda's sister being a far-gone chiphead. Maybe this was Bren's way of touching base with her near-and-dear.

The chip and the dip—how fitting.

Dave took another hit—short this time—and pinched out the smoking end. Frugally, he tucked the roach inside his paddy vest. Good shit was hard to come by on a patrolman's salary, even when you bought your Flatbush Gold from the boys in Evidence.

He wanted to get this job done. Something in his belly told him cops weren't supposed to be playing glorified exterminators, even if the roaches were human.

"Damn." Brenda took off her helmet, her fresh service cut making her head look like a hedgehog that had lost an argument with a weed-whacker. She ran a palm over the bristly blond stubble. "Musta took Ralpho's hardshell instead of mine. This muffuh's too big on me."

Dave sighed with all the immemorial weariness of the patriarchally put-upon. Without a word he took Brenda's helmet, made a few minor adjustments, and handed it back. It fit perfectly, and the shiny visor with its infrared scan system fell across Brenda's brown eyes with the discreetest of clicks.

He made no comment about women and mechanical devices, even though Brenda's incompetence with the whole spectrum of *res robotica* was a transprecinct legend. Her former partner had been less reticent. He was expected to recover eventually, though children were out of the question.

Brenda didn't bother to thank Dave. Thanks would come later, in a firefight if necessary, should their quarry turn out to be more formidable than the nest of winos and bag ladies mentioned in the tourist complaint that had brought them into this ancient shell to bat clean-up. That had been known to happen.

A pretty gold star and a lot of ugly black crepe were cluttering up a holo of their whilom mate, Gary Turtletraub. Officer T had responded to a hysterical call from the visiting CEO of Shimizucorp—something about a giant, fire-breathing lizard attacking the Plaza Hotel. Gary had played it for too much *sake* laced with *chasm*—the synthoceutical that made crack look like cream puffs—coupled with a really unfortunate viewing choice from the hotel's video archives. He went into the Palm Court prepared to confiscate a tape of *Godzilla Rapes Mars*.

He had had no way of knowing that the Plaza was then hosting a convention of Junior Achievement sprats whose field of choice was genetic manipulation. Eleven-year-old Tommy Benson of the Montgomery, Alabama, chapter of DNAces had to pay reparations to Officer T's widow after his enhanced (and escaped) gecko got through with the poor man.

Like Bren always said, there was a word for cops who made too many assumptions in New York City: dumbass slab-fodder for the buzzardmen down at the morgue.

This was more than *a* word, but no one ever pointed this out to Brenda. That would be real dumbass.

"So where'd the doof say he saw the raggie?" Brenda demanded.

The broken shell of the information booth was at their backs, the indifferent eyes of the painted constellations on the cracked ceiling looking down on them.

Dave jerked his thumb in the direction of the big staircase at the western end of the building. The upper flights were impassable, choked with the rusting bodies of scrapped autos. A little sunlight filtered in through the grimy windowpanes, striking one last sparkle from senescent chrome. The visual irony was thick enough for inclusion in the best of the new *anime* chips.

Dave was no chiphead, filling his brain with big-eyed, small-assed Japanimated *bimbo-sans* in his off-hours. He liked his Heavy Moral Lessons drawn from life, like this indoor scrapheap.

He knew the story by heart: once upon a time, the Vanderbilt Street entrance to Grand Central had been the best pickup and drop-off point for taxis. It predeceased the rest of the station by about fifteen years, when a gang of militant thuggeelis from the Yale Club down the block had used it to jellify their seventy-five Harvard Business School captives during the great Alumni Fund Drive Wars of '27. Not even semi-intelligent enzymes had been able to eradicate the smell fully, though they had been bright enough to learn that taxi drivers made mighty good eating. By the time the Department of Environmental Retaliation defeated the ACLU's microlife rights specialists and took back the Vanderbilt Street entrance, no one wanted to use it anymore, except folks who were tired of looking for a parking space in midtown.

However, there was still another, unblocked staircase leading *down*.

"What'n Hackensack was that civvo muffuh doing, sticking his snout into the lower level for?" Brenda growled. "Shit, coulda got his ass drilled good, little barbecue sauce, and no one ever hears from him again, spare us this creakin' mole gig. But nooooo! He hasta make it out alive to tell the tale. Asshole."

Dave decided not to tinker with Brenda's character analysis of the civvy complainant. If he disagreed, Bren would play tiddledywinks with his kneecaps. If he voiced agreement, the trailer embedded in his larynx would broadcast it right back to Maggie in Supervision. His demerits for bad-mouthing a taxpayer would be hard copy on his record by the time he returned to the stationhouse. *If* he returned. Bren had a similar implant, but she never seemed to give a rat's trust fund about black marks; something to do with those long Personnel Attitude Adjustment interviews she had with the captain three times weekly.

Dave opted for a grunt and the practical, "We'd better get going."

They negotiated the stairwell with caution. The first flight down split into two sections, cutting a hard left and right respectively, but both options ending up in the same place: the lower level. Taught by Turtletraub's misfortune, Bren and Dave had done their homework. The Museum of the City of New York still housed floor plans of Grand Central Station even though the postwar demise of American rail travel had made such items historical curiosities.

"Sorta like teevee," Bren had remarked a little wistfully. She didn't care for the *anime* chips at all, which rather left her noncarnal leisuretime options at nil.

"It's clean," Dave said as they chose to take the right-hand stairway together rather than separating.

"Too clean," Bren grumbled. "So's the left one. I seen it. I don't like it. It ain't natcherl." She paused halfway down the second flight of stairs. From there, by cool fusion-generated torchlight or built-in infras, the cops had a clear view of a large, open area. Brenda's nose twitched like a bunny's. "Smell that?"

Dave sifted the air for himself. "I don't smell a thing."

Bren punched him lightly in the chest. " 'Swat I mean, dickhead. I don't smell nothing neither. No sweat, no puke, no pee—"

"No shit," Dave deadpanned. He checked his vest pocket. "You busted my joint, Bren."

"I'll bust your for real joint, muffuh. Think! Where you got raggies, you don't got showers. Always stinks worse than a month-old mackerel where those buggers den."

"So maybe the civ got it wrong. Maybe the only bag lady he saw was inside his head."

"Him?" Bren spat on the immaculate steps. "I seen him and he wasn't no chippy."

"I don't mean *anime*. No bag ladies in that stuff anyhow."

"Well, what else is there?"

"He did say he was an amateur artist, an *anime* wannabe."

"Oh. Yeah. Did he say he dropped his pad and ran when the raggie snooked up on him?" She mimicked the complainant's nasal whine perfectly to say, "Oooh, offissas, it was *tewwible*. That nasty, nasty woman just *broke* my ahtistic constipation!" The old Bren came back to punctuate her performance with an eloquent spit. "Civs. Why do they go looking to high-dive into pigshit?"

"Could be he came down here to, you know, get away from it all, get some inspiration, and he got to daydreaming." Dave spoke for the benefit of Maggie and the Internal Affairs fans back home, but for Bren's eyes alone he made the sign of a chasm-smacker taking a plummet. She snickered and nodded.

Dave took the rest of the steps two at a time until he hit bottom. He scanned as much of the area as he could with his torch.

Nothing; not the merest suggestion of life, even in the distant shadows. There were deserted storefronts, gutted of everything vaguely valuable years ago, when the station first closed down. A couple of pay phones still hung cockeyed from a cement support pillar, useless relics of a gone age, too busted up even to be of interest to antique fanciers. All their unvandalized brethren had been carted off, leaving raw spots on several other pillars the torch beam touched. The light swept back and forth, back and forth over emptiness and silence unbroken by even the dusty scuffle of crawlies fleeing the light.

Not even a roach. Now *that* was unnatural, and frightening.

Dave flashed his light across the ceiling, desperate to turn up some small and revolting denizen of the dark. No *cucarachas*, no winged Hawaiian cockaroaches, no South African poor-man's-sushis, *nada*. Dave's stomach clenched tight as a taxpayer's asshole.

Behind him, he heard Bren snicker again. "Still think we're playing a candy game?" She grabbed the Koolfuse torch and used its beam as a pointer. It picked up a small, rectangular pad of paper and a scattering of charcoal sticks on the otherwise spotless floor. "There it is, right where the civvo said he dropped 'em. Wonder if he ever got the stains out of his undies?"

Dave clicked down his own visor and activated the IRs. Suddenly he wanted both hands free. Taking back the torch, he approached the abandoned sketchpad carefully. The light picked out a clumsy, amateurish rendering of a fantasy scene: a handsome man in arcane, uncomfortable-looking clothes deep in conversation with a gloriously beautiful woman. Dave recognized the background. It was one of the derelict pay phones, restored by the would-be artist's hand to working order. Beneath the woman's bizarrely cantilevered shoes was the scribbled title, *Ghosts*.

"What do you make of this, Bren?" he asked, holding up the pad.

A long whistle escaped Brenda's lips. "Mmm-*mmh*! Daddy, buy me *that*. Now that's the way I wish we could tilt back and unhinge: watching people who aren't penciled in first." She sighed. "In my dreams, maybe, and last night all I could come up with was reruns of *The Hijinks of Yoko, Geisha of Rigel IV*, from when I was a kid. Sure would like to know the name of that civ's supplier. You don't see stuff like that on generic shit. Whaddaya think he was doing, Dave? El gulpo, el jabbo, or el snorto?" She pantomimed all three major methods for kissing reality bye-byes.

She did a very good, very contagious snort. Almost by reflex, Dave mimicked it. Then he froze. He sniffed the air again, and this time what he did smell scared him worse than what he didn't: lilacs.

Immediately he knew that Bren had smelled them too. She was at his side so silently that he almost gave her the Elbow of Death in the paddy vest. He saved his own life by pulling the blow at the last minute. Brenda did not take kindly to being touched, let alone punched, without proper remuneration. It made a man quietly proud to have such a seasoned pro for his buddy.

"Where do you think it's coming from?" Dave's whisper sounded rougher than sliding down a sandpaper banister.

"Where do you think, bobo?" Bren shot back. Her

eyes were unreadable behind the visor, but he could guess at the contempt they held for him. "The tunnels." She nodded toward the row of ancient adits.

They followed their noses, literally. The smell of lilacs lured them down the row of gates, all darkly agape, like a line of slaw-jawed chipheads taking in the latest animated adventure of *Pirate Sumiko and the Golden Lion.*

It was hard to imagine the vanished times this place had seen, times when these same halls had reverberated with the sound of a multitude's hurrying footsteps—and when no decent woman was safe on the streets, no child secure from the hands of kidnappers, perverts, and black-market infantrepreneurs.

They reached the far end of the row of platform entrances. Dave peered through the gate, then doused his torch and took another look. He thumbed back his IR visor and gave it a third try. There was no doubt. "I see lights down there."

"You know it, twerm," Bren said, shouldering him out of the way. She flipped back her own visor for an unenhanced gander of her own. "Them raggies, they don't got cats' eyes, ya know." She snorted springtime. "O.K., this mus' be the place. We go in, we go down, and we leave a lotta pretty packages for the clean-up crew." She checked the charge on her paralyprod.

"I hope we don't have to freeze too many," Dave muttered. "It's a Saturday night, lotsa heavy dating. Bellevue can only defrost so many p'rallies at a time, and half the smooth movers in New York end up popsicled when their ladies pull a purse-size wand on 'em. They always leave the raggies for last, and if someone's frozen too long, sometimes they can't—"

"Then I guess it's a good thing I'm not planning on frozen raggies, huh?" Bren gave Dave her most ferally charming smile and the tease of a glance at her prod control. It was not set for *immobilize.*

"Bren . . ."

"Got a problem, Dave?" she inquired sweetly. "True what they say about your mama?"

Dave's face burned. When a man joined New York's Finest, part of the sugar on the deal was the promise that his entire past got swallowed up by a bureaucracy so awesome in its bulk and appetite that not a pip of info ever leaked its way back into the world. Supposedly—but even bureaucratic brontosauri barfed a bit, on occasion.

Hence the rumor about how Dave's mama had been one of the victims of Surro-Gate, the big in-vitro-veritas mislabeling scandal. Her clients were enraged to learn that the baby bumper crop they'd paid for so dearly to harvest from her womb were not the seed of Julliard graduates.

Julliard, no; Joliet, yes.

Disgraced, she became a raggie who left her last contracted-for-but-unpaid job in the care of the Little Flowers of St. Koch to be raised for city service. So the rumor ran, explaining why Dave was soft on raggies.

Dave bit down on any reply. Instead, he made a big business of setting his prod to the gentlest of freeze-frame settings and said, "We're in, we're out, and we move fast. Watch your back." They passed the gate.

There were more stairs, a lone flight angling steeply downward. Below, a strand of Koolfuse lamps cast a soft white glow over a train platform so immaculate that you could convince a politico to eat off it in a nonelection year. As the two cops walked warily down the platform, taking shelter behind every pillar that afforded cover, they became aware of the fact that they were acting like a pair of paranoid assholes. No one else was in sight, not for the length of the platform or the train tracks paralleling it.

That still left the tunnel.

At the end of the platform, Bren hunkered down and turned the controls on her IRs up to maximum sensitivity. Dave did the same. An obscenity of astonishing ugliness and creativity escaped her lips when, even thus aided, she could see nothing down the tunnel. She vaulted down onto the tracks, signaling Dave to follow. Gravel crunched beneath their boots. Catwalks and dead graffiti were all they could pick out as they crept deeper into the darkness.

Dave paused only once in his inching progress. He cast a look back the way they'd come, and saw that the well-lit platform was no more than a thumbnail-sized blot of brightness behind them. A hundred misgivings fought for dominance in his gut. Why did they have to bag the raggies at all?

Oh, sure, raggies were no good for business, especially with so many minimalist tidyfreaks coming over from Dai Nippon. Mustn't upset the big *boburas'* ideal of street-sterile while they were over here to sheepdog their holdings. Anything didn't please the pursestring poohbahs, out it went: like movies, like TV, like any live-actor video that wasn't so choked with all that SF F/X shit there was maybe the chance you could relate it to reality. You want reality? Live it. You want fantasy? Turn chiphead and do *anime*.

The raggies wouldn't categorize. They were walking monkey-puzzles made of bits of this world and their own secret kingdoms. You saw one of them and you couldn't help but . . . wonder. And wonder was the messiest mind-trick of them all. It took people's minds off business. So the raggies had to go: out to the other boroughs, away to the friendly offshore pharmaceutical testing labs, off to Connecticut in exchange for a per-capita commuter-tax break. But the raggies didn't want to go sometimes and they could be mighty clever about staying put.

Maybe we've taken the wrong tack down here, Dave thought. Maybe that lilac scent's a red herring, though it sure smells better. Maybe these raggies got someone who's read up on pheromones, using what he knows to snag cops same as Ja—same as Iranian beetles. One last thought knifed through his brain: Maybe we should turn back.

Then it happened. The darkness of the tunnel ahead just . . . dropped. A tsunami of light flooded Dave's skull with searing pain made all the sharper by the IRs' enhancement. He heard an animal screaming and knew it was himself. No, on second thought, it was Brenda. He was still sucking in enough air to back his own lung-busting bellow of agony. Black stars flowered over his eyes.

Just before the final darkness, he thought he saw a heavenly vision: the same long-limbed, gorgeous woman from the civvo's castoff sketch of ghosts. She was rising half-naked from the tumbled linens of a large bed that appeared to float a meter above the ground. She looked right at him, and with the acute, slo-mo sight that takes over in times of disaster, he saw her reach out to him. She couldn't do that and hold her topsheet in place at the same time.

So there is a God, he thought, and fainted.

"Oh, dear, did I wake you? I'm sorry."

Dave came to gazing up at the underside of a wash-cloth. He tore it away and tried to sit up, but the assault of light was too much, even the muted glow of the single pink globe near his head. He groaned and sank back onto what he thought was a very comfy pillow.

"That's right, take it easy," said a whiskeyed female voice in his ear.

He twisted around, squinting, and saw that he was cradled on a most delectable human futon. It was the woman of his dying vision, the woman of the sketchbook.

"Where am I?" Dave asked.

His personal angel giggled as she readjusted the wash-cloth on his brow. "Darling, don't tell me that's the best you can improvise. 'Where am I?' Honestly. You're just perfect to play Nicholas, my long-lost husband—*if* I can get George to write him back in, the superficial swine—but we are going to have to work on getting you some more original lines than that."

"Hah?"

"Or that." The lady shifted, forcing Dave to sit up. His eyes felt better and his head had stopped swimming. Now he saw that the two of them were quite alone in what looked like the coziest of nummy-nests. Out of her embrace, he perceived that there was an actual bed supporting both of them and that it was firmly in touch with the ground. Like the rest of the furnishings, it was as lushly padded as its mistress. A similarly sympathetic color scheme of rosy pinks and deep mahoganies prevailed throughout the room. There was also a thick curtain of gauze obscuring one whole wall for some reason.

Dave didn't have time to ponder the mysterious curtain long. Without warning, his hostess had her arms around him and there was no debating whence the lilac-scented breeze now. Her breath was hot and spiced with cinnamon, a counterpoint to her major olfactory theme. The high gloss of her scarlet lips stirred up a residual throbbing in his temples, but damned if he was going to say he had a headache at this juncture. He closed his eyes and prepared himself for paradise.

He got not passion, but persiflage: "Oh, Nicholas, I'm

so glad you've come back to me. After you left Rainbow Valley with Janine, I thought I'd never see you or little Tiffany again, and her with that mysterious disease. But now you're back, even if my father did try to have you murdered at the country club. It was all Stella's doing, you know. That witch has had such an evil influence over him ever since Prince Fabrizio did her out of the controlling interest in Mellofone Industries. Dearest Nicholas, I—"

Abruptly the tirade and all physical contact ceased. Dave jerked, eyes wide, at the unheralded absence suddenly surrounding him. The lady was a paean to nimbleness. She had managed to whisk herself to the far end of the bed and was now glaring at the gauze curtain.

"Well?" she shrilled. "Good enough, George, or are you still going to keep Rachel as just a spear-carrier?"

A small, weary voice riffled the curtain. "For the billionth time, Lani, I don't get to decide anything about the characters. I'm only the writer."

"Bullshit, George," the lady replied. "Try telling me it wasn't you who cobbled up a fat part for that new slut. And I know whose fat part!"

"She showed a great deal of promise, Lani." The voice crumpled in on itself abjectly. "I never saw anyone take to Rainbow Valley so quickly. You know what a strain it is for me, shouldering the plot on my own, let alone lines for all of you. When someone can improvise to the plot line like that, well . . ." The voice was more chipper now. "She's a natural."

"And what is this?" Lani's hand shot out to collar Dave and give him a good shaking. "Chopped liver? They came down together, they must've worked together topside. Maybe mimes, God knows, but if you use one, you've got to use the other, and I say we use him as my Rachel's long-lost husband—"

"You're under arrest," Dave said.

Lani pursed her lips. "Now you ad-lib?"

"I do what I said: I arrest you in the name of the law of the City of New York and the Internal Revenue Service. You have the right to remain silent. You have the right to commit *seppuku*. You—"

"Oh, Lord, the IRS Police!" The gauze curtain whipped itself into a frenzy and a lanky, horse-faced man emerged.

"I knew it, I just knew I should never have let Katryn give her class those street-theater lessons."

"Now, George"—Lani tried to soothe him—"you know we've got to do our improv exercises. There's nothing worse than a stiff character. You didn't object when Vince and I did our little nostalgia vignettes on the lower level. There was a silly little bug of man squatting there with a sketchpad, but he never so much as flinched when he saw us."

"Of course not! He probably thought you were a flashback. But if you play a part that's too close to reality . . ." He groaned. "When Carissa came back and claimed she'd done such a convincing bag lady that she frightened a tourist, we all thought she was egobooming, but if the authorities have been called in!"

Dave got out of Lani's grasp and walked over to the distraught fellow. What he'd heard, what he'd seen, combined to make him especially careful with his words. "You people—you're not raggies?"

"Your mama," Lani sneered.

Dave winced, but persevered. "You're actors? Real, live actors? Like in the Olden Days?"

"Not that olden, Officer," George answered with a twinkle. "Rainbow Valley is one of the younger sets down here."

"There are some utter fossils producing Sands of Destiny off of platform one-twenty-three," Lani put in.

"Producing?"

"They still work live, strictly for the New York market, but Rainbow Valley's taped for export." George smiled. "So, you see, your unscheduled appearance on the set won't be at all difficult to edit out. Unless you would like to be written in?"

"I, uh—"

"You'd have to do some improvisation. Can you act at all?"

"Buh—gah—urh—"

George frowned and shook his head. "Oh, dear. Not good at all. Not even worth trying a trade with those nice Stanislavsky Methodists in tunnel one-nineteen." He patted Dave's shoulder. "Don't call us, we'll call you."

All Dave's confusion burst out in a shrill "What in hell are you lunatics *doing* down here?"

Beautiful even when peeved, Lani answered, "Somebody's got to keep the soaps going."

Dave lost full motor control of his jaw. Trained reflexes made him grab his own throat and gasp, "Maggie, send backup to lower level, Grand Central Station, to home on my sig—" Something crunched under his fingers. He felt a host of tiny particles floating between his larynx and the overlying skin.

"I'm afraid you've ruined your equipment, Officer," George said. "That scream of yours when Bill and Gloria accidentally fumbled our backdrop—all the lights right in your eyes. When our sound man checked out your partner's implant, he said the decibel level overloaded the system."

Dave tensed. IRS Police implants were cheap clones of cheaper knockoffs; it saved the taxpayers' money. Maggie wouldn't even have picked up that megascream as anything more than a clutter of static before the system outed entirely. Implant cockups were an old story at HQ. No one in the precinct could suspect he was in trouble. There would be no automatic dispatch of backup units. He and Bren were on their own. Bren . . .

"My partner, Bren . . . she's all right?"

"Just ducky," Lani snarled. "Why not take her home?"

"Lani," George chided. "You know the rules."

"But she's a badger, Georgie-Porgie," Lani replied in a syrupy voice. "Like her partner. He doesn't want to stay—do you, you no-talent bore?" Dave regarded her with stony eyes. She shrugged. "You see, George? You know the rules, too. No prisoners. If he leaves without her, he'll be back with troops. It'll be the end of Rainbow Valley and the rest. He'll have to take her."

"You bet I'm taking her," Dave snapped. "You better not try stopping us, either."

"*Nous?*" George looked offended. "You heard Lani. We have our principles. And, Lani, darling, don't muddy the well. You know we don't have to make this a both-or-none deal." To Dave he added, "You can leave whenever you like. We do ask that you pay an eentsy visit to Dr. Woolcott on the set of City Hospital before you go. He used to be a real physicker before he took to the stage, a specialist in drug-enhanced hypnosis. You won't even feel the needle going in, and you won't remember a thing about us. Much more civil all around, that way."

Dave lunged for the writer and seized him by the throat. "I want to see Bren now!"

"Dave, you asshole!"

Dave dropped George and stared. The words and voice were familiar; what he saw was not.

She twirled before him, her white satin skirts billowing, faceted earrings and necklace shattering the light. Silvery slippers glinted on her feet, and the aroma of roses spiraled up from her bristly hair.

"Like it?" she asked.

Dave blinked. It couldn't be. Brenda had *simpered* at him. "Bren, is that . . . you?"

"No, it's not. Isn't it wonderful?" She swished her tiered skirts with enthusiasm. "I'm going to be Arianna, Prince Fabrizio's suppressed half-sister. I just discovered that my real mother, Vetiver, was wrongfully imprisoned in the Rainbow Valley mental hospital through the machinations of the prince's scheming mother, Ludovica. That makes my illegitimate son, Rory, fathered by international jewel thief Percival O'Hara, the true heir to the throne. But if Wilhelmina ever finds out Rory's alive in the convent . . ."

She took a deep breath and flung herself into Dave's arms. "Oh Dave, don't you see? This is better than *anime*! This is real life! This is what I was born to do! Go back to the surface, tell them I fell down a hole—there are lots of holes underground, aren't there? Tell them I took the raggie with me. Tell them anything, only don't tell them what's really down here."

George came up softly behind her and said, "A visit to Dr. Woolcott would guarantee his silence."

Bren laughed lightly. "You don't know our debriefing boys. One needle mark that wasn't on an officer when he left HQ and they're in with the brain-probes. There's not a secret made that they can't ferret out. Sometimes with real ferrets. You forget we work—*he* works—for the IRS." She gave Dave a fond look. "Our best bet is to let him go back on his own and lie like hell. Won't you, Dave? For me?" Her lower lip trembled.

He had never seen her so happy. She was a woman

transformed, elevated, fulfilled. There was only one reply he could give her: "What's in it for me?"

Her eyes were moist with emotion. "I'll let you live," she breathed.

"Package for you, Dave," said the mailbot. It deposited the bubble-wrapped oblong on his doorstep and zipped off to safety, in case of high explosives or Junk Mail Reaction Syndrome.

Dave grinned as he picked up the package and took it into his apartment. He could hardly wait to see this one. In a corner of the room the revamped TV and its attendant VCR stood among other antiques Dave had bought as a blind. Only he knew the effort he'd invested in making them functional again. He tore off the bubble-wrap, turned on the set, and slipped in the cassette. The familiar theme of Rainbow Valley swelled as the camera zoomed in for a close-up of Arianna standing over Wilhelmina's body with a dripping scimitar.

"It went off by accident," she told Rachel, who screamed.

Underground theater was alive and well in New York.

You can't get any more New York than Brooklyn, nor more Brooklyn than Flatbush, which is where Esther M. Friesner was born and raised. Post-elementary school she attended Manhattan's Hunter College High School, with the additional education of a subway commute daily, for six years, from age eleven. Still in love with the rails, Ms. Friesner much prefers Grand Central to Penn Station, and visits frequently on her way from her Madison, Connecticut, home. Her favorite soap opera is politics. She has used her New York background in the fantasy New York by Knight (NAL/Signet), and will do so again in an upcoming trilogy from Ace: Gnome Man's Land, Harpy High, and Ragnarok and Roll. Other recent titles include Demon Blues, Hooray for Hellywood (both Ace), The Water King's Laughter (Avon), and Elf Defense and Sphynxes Wild (both NAL/Signet).

A Nice Place to Visit

by Warren Murphy and Molly Cochran

Here we have a tale of a rather unpleasant future world where New York is a vacation paradise, but you really wouldn't want to stay there.

At exactly 5 P.M., a buzzer sounded and twenty-five hundred computers clicked off simultaneously, their green screens flashing *1700 Hours* just three times before turning dark.

Greg Heany stood up behind his gray plastic desk but waited in his small cubicle until the stampede toward the elevators had thinned out. He left only when a uniformed guard came onto the balcony overlooking the honeycombed maze of cubicles and motioned for him to leave.

Outside, it was sleeting. Heany pulled his coat closer around him and tried to keep his balance on the slick pavement as he passed the thousand-long line of persons waiting at the bus stop.

He decided to walk home, something he had been doing more frequently lately. It was a dismal, bone-chilling walk, the sky, as always, dead and gray, the air humid, the smell noxious. But at least he was not shoulder-to-shoulder with an endless swarm of people.

Heany kept his head down as he passed block after block of concrete buildings. He remembered when he was a child and the buildings of Buttzville had not been so high. Some people had kept gardens on their rooftops, and his grandfather, before he died, had told him about roadways that used to run between towns like Buttzville and Alpha with green fields on either side. And Gramps had actually seen photographs of houses surrounded by grass and flowers with blue skies in the background.

But of course that had been a long time ago, way back

before the population had exploded, and now Heany walked home in the cold icy sleet because it was the only time the sidewalks were clear of people and he could move as fast as he liked without bumping into anyone else . . . the only time he could pretend he was more than a bee—a drone at that—in a crowded hive.

He rubbed water out of his eyes with his knuckles and wondered what he was so depressed about. It was Friday. The work week was over, and tonight and tomorrow night the baseball games would be on television.

They came from the big stadiums in Venezuela and Zimbabwe and Australia, and he always watched with longing as the players flew around the bases out in the clean, free fresh air, the sun beating down on them from a bright clear sky.

He could almost feel the precious wood in his hands, taking a practice swing, planting his feet just right in the batter's box.

"Batter up!"

The silence from the crowd. The flinty eyes of the pitcher glancing over to third, then riveted on him. A nod, the pitcher's lips tight with concentration, and then the ball shooting out of his hand, coming, coming . . .

"Crack!"

The good warm feel of the bat making solid contact. The ball soaring out far over the outfielders' heads.

Home run! Ladies and gentlemen, a home run for Greg Heany! And the crowd is going wild!

The sleet melted under his collar; he felt the cold grit of it against his skin and thought sadly that baseball was just a game that other men played.

He had missed his chance. In his teens, he had had his tryout, but he had failed. He had been a whiz at gymnastics and had good speed on the treadmill, and he and his best friend, Fly Werner, had gone for the annual baseball tryout. But they had not been good enough to win a training spot in the baseball leagues. Baseball required space and only the very best were entitled to the use of space.

Sorry, Heany . . .

Greg had taken his disappointment stolidly, but Fly Werner had tried to drown his sorrow in a case of beer. Later that night, he had wound up in a fistfight with a

squad of policemen and quickly been sent off to a training camp for reeducation and relocation, which was the
government's newest way of dealing with crime and
criminals.

Heany had never seen his friend again. Nor had Fly
Werner's family, although a year later they received a
government letter that said their son had been retrained,
given a new identity, and was living now in a new city, "a
happy, prospering member of society."

Heany climbed the gray concrete steps to his apartment. Down the hall, someone's kid was crying. Maybe
someday he and Lynn would be able to afford a kid.
Maybe the kid would grow up to be the baseball player
his father never was.

He hung his sopping coat on the rack inside the door
and waited for Lynn to start yelling at him for not taking
the bus. But when he walked into the rug-sized living
area, she was standing at the small table where they ate.
Two candles were lit on the table; her short blond hair
shone in their light; her face was wreathed in a broad
smile.

For a moment, Greg thought he had forgotten something
—an anniversary or a birthday—but suddenly his wife
squealed and ran over, hugging him. Before he could
speak, she handed him a crumpled envelope. "I'm sorry
it's such a mess," she said. "I just got so excited when I
read it."

It was an official government envelope with "Government Clearing House" printed in red for the return
address.

"Our vacation," he whispered.

"Read it. Read what's inside!" Lynn was nearly
shrieking.

He could hardly believe it. They had applied for a
vacation nearly five years before, filling out dozens of
forms in triplicate, going for interviews, mailing in semi-
annual application updates. But because of the nation's
overcrowding, there were far more people who wanted
vacations than there were spots to handle them, and it
seemed as if their turn would never come.

But it had and in bold type in the middle of the page,
Heany read:

NEW YORK.

"Oh, my God," he said.

"New York. The best of all the vacation cities, Greg. And for a whole month." Lynn buried her face in his chest and began to sob.

The silent helicopter soared through the grit-laden gray sky and over the mountainous New Jersey skyline and Lynn could not resist pointing out the most famous skyscrapers.

"There's the RCJ Building. And the Sony Pentacle. And look! The Mitsubishi Towers."

"Tallest buildings in the world," Heany said, and put his arm around her. Even though he had nothing to do with arranging the vacation, he felt a sense of pride at bringing his wife to the greatest paradise on earth. And, hell, who said he had nothing to do with it? He was a good worker. His attendance record was excellent. He rarely made mistakes. And he had never complained about the apartment, despite the leaky plumbing and the bad television reception. Administrators noticed things like loyalty to the government.

And why shouldn't everyone be loyal? He knew from his work at the computer center that the birthrate continued soaring, and yet the government was still able to feed and clothe and house its burgeoning population, although he had not a clue on how they were able to do it.

And the government had also made crime just a memory. When his old baseball friend, Fly Werner, had been sent away, that had been just the start of an experimental program. But now it was an accepted part of the national agenda. And it had worked. Another feather in the cap of the government, Heany thought.

The helicopter passed over the river separating the giant industrial and commercial complex of New Jersey from the domed splendor of Manhattan. Lynn sipped in her breath as they descended toward the clear crystalline dome that covered Manhattan. "A whole city's underneath that," she said reverently. "But what's around it?" She pointed to a thick gray rim around the base of the dome. From their altitude, it looked like a giant bird's nest sheltering a great shiny plastic egg.

"I don't know."

The helicopter dropped lower and gradually the bird's nest grew clearer. It was not made up of wood at all but big slabs of broken concrete and flaps of cloth and rusted metal, and for a moment Heany thought he saw a face down there amid the garbage, its skin gray, its eyes staring up at the black dragonfly of the helicopter.

"What is that, mister?" Heany asked the pilot.

But the pilot did not answer because in the next moment, the dome's window, a giant square carved into the curved surface, slid open with a whoosh and the helicopter swooped inside.

"We're here, baby," Heany said.

Their apartment was in a long, low building designed around a central fountain, where tropical plants lined the walkways. No building was taller than one story here. The sky above, inside the dome, shone so clear and blue that it almost made Heany's eyes tear.

He took a deep breath. The air was fragrant with flowers. He closed his eyes and pictured the trim lawns in the photographs he had heard about from his grandfather.

"Come on," Lynn said, waving the plastic key card in front of his face. "Don't you want to see where we're going to live?"

He took a last look back at the fountain and sauntered toward his wife, who was so excited she could barely get the key in the door. When it swung open, she pressed her hands to her mouth.

The living room—itself larger by half than the Heanys' entire apartment back in Buttzville—sported a thick carpet on which sat two large couches covered in silk and a number of smaller upholstered chairs with real wood arms. A piece of furniture that might have been a bar stood under a massive wall TV, which was turned on and tuned to a breathtaking aerial photograph of Manhattan. Superimposed on it were the words: *Visitors' Guide to New York*.

Lynn and Greg walked past it in awestruck silence into the chandeliered dining room and, beyond that, the ceramic tiled kitchen, where a basket of fresh fruit had been set on a counter.

"A banana," he said, touching the yellow crescent lightly to see if it was real.

"Fresh bread in the breadbox," Lynn sang.

He opened the refrigerator. There was a platter of cold cuts, a drawer filled with green vegetables, and an eye round of beef wrapped in brown paper. Greg blinked. The last time he had tasted beef was at the company's Christmas banquet, and that time it had only been a sliver no larger than a coin. He had saved half of it to bring home to Lynn.

"I'll have to ask someone how to cook it," Lynn said from behind his shoulder.

The doorbell rang. Lynn's face was suddenly pained. "Oh, Greg, maybe it's all been a mistake and they're coming to take us home."

Greg laughed. "Leave it to you to find the ant in the picnic basket," he said as he opened the door.

Two people stood there, a couple. The man was swarthy and muscular, the woman taller than he was, with very long, very red hair above a ridiculously high forehead.

"Hi, we're the Frezzas," the woman said amiably.

"Dan and Brenda," the man added, offering his hand. Greg shook it and introduced Lynn.

"We live next door. Hey, I know you two just moved in, so we won't bother you. Just wanted you to know that if there's anything you need, don't hesitate to ask, okay?"

"Well, honestly, I was wondering about the meat in the refrigerator," Lynn said.

"How to cook it? No problem," Brenda said. "Hey, nice apartment, Lynn. Can I take a look?" The two women were off.

With a shrug, Heany invited Dan Frezza inside. "I'd offer you a drink, except I don't know where the liquor store is yet."

Frezza laughed. "You don't need one here." He went behind the bar in the living room and slid open a cabinet. Dozens of bottles lined the shelves. In a separate refrigerated compartment were cans of beer and soda, and a freezer with an ice maker. "When you run low, just leave a list of what you'd like on Channel One of the TV. Same with groceries, pizza, sandwiches . . . anything you want will be delivered. It's all explained on Channel One." He gestured toward the big TV screen.

"Yeah," Heany said. "I haven't tuned in yet."

Frezza tossed a beer over to Heany. "Anyhow," he said, "you won't be eating in much. Great restaurants in this town. The best. And the shows, the clubs . . . all free, of course. Everything here's free." He took a deep drink from the chilled can. "All I can tell you is, you're going to love it here. I wish we never had to leave."

"How long have you been here?"

"Five months."

Heany whistled. "That's some vacation. You an executive?"

"Naw. Programmer. P-Eight, St. Louis. How about you?"

"P-Nine," Heany said. "Buttzville, Ohio. How'd you get a five-month vacation?"

Frezza beamed with pride. "Won it in the lottery."

"What?"

"The lottery. Every night they got this lottery with about a hundred different prizes . . . Here, Channel One explains it better than I can."

He touched a button on the TV, and music poured into the room from six hidden speakers.

"Welcome to New York," an echoing baritone voice said as the picture dissolved into a dizzying montage of city sights. "This is Manhattan, the Big Apple, the town with everything . . ."

Frezza shot the tape into fast forward. "You can see the whole thing later. I'll just show you the part about the lottery."

". . . eligible as soon as you arrive," the baritone voice picked up. The screen showed a couple jumping for joy and embracing each other. As the announcer spoke, the picture showed other couples in similar states of ecstasy. "You can win a one-month, two-month, three-month (the couple was now popping the cork on a bottle of champagne), four-month, five-month (older couple with tears in their eyes), or six-month extension on your vacation in glorious Manhattan."

Then suddenly, it was Dan and Brenda Frezza on the screen, the muscular Dan holding his wife over his head like a barbell.

Frezza swelled with pride at seeing his own image. "That was for real," he said. "They come right to your apartment with this TV camera—"

"Shhh." Heany leaned closer to the screen.

The picture shifted to a shot of a woman fainting in her smiling husband's arms. "Or the Grand Prize . . . A Lifetime Extension," the announcer boomed.

The picture showed the couple being escorted into a shiny black helicopter, waving to the camera.

"Say good-bye to your cares forever. Live in splendor in Millionaire's Row, in palatial mansions like these . . ." The camera focused on a row of distinguished three-story gray stone residences. "With your own household staff, private air travel service, and a yacht in the Atlantic for those times you simply have to get away," the announcer said jocularly. "Plus lifetime passes for you and your family to travel anywhere in the world—"

Frezza shut it off. "Anyway, that's about it," he said. "The extensions are paid, naturally. My job's still waiting for me back home, and I got a pile of uncashed checks sitting in the bank."

Heany sat staring at the blank screen.

"Sounds good, huh?" Frezza slapped him on the back.

"Huh? Yeah. Lifetime Extension . . ."

"That's the biggie." He sighed and raised his beer can in salute. "Here's hoping, right?"

"Greg! Greg," Lynn shouted excitedly from down the hall. She came running down the corridor clutching a red evening gown. "Look at this, Greg. The closets are filled with them. All kinds of clothes, gorgeous things, all in my size, in my favorite colors. There's tons of clothes for you, too. And Brenda says the stores are free, Greg. You just go in and pick up whatever you want. Free!"

"Great, honey." Heany shook his head and Dan Frezza laughed.

"Guess you'll be a shopping widower for a while," he said. "Happens to all of us at first. But you won't have to sit around twiddling your thumbs. Say, while the ladies are busy trying on clothes, I could take you around a little. How about it?"

"Sure," Heany said.

Down the block a friendly jogger waved as he passed the two men. There was actually room to *run* here, Heany thought in wonderment.

"Play tennis?" Frezza asked, gesturing to a large fenced court.

"No," Heany said. "We don't even have a court in Buttzville. Everything's paved over."

"I know. Wall-to-wall people and concrete. The whole country's like that," Frezza said. "*Except* for New York. This is the place for everything, all right." He breathed deeply, as if he had spent his entire life in Manhattan and was proud of it.

On Fifth Avenue, the taxis sped soundlessly down the broad, uncrowded boulevard. There were no private cars, no buses, no trucks. A woman wearing diamonds smiled as she walked past them, going in the opposite direction.

"Where else you going to see real diamonds on the street?"

"Boy, that's one thing you can give the government credit for. Getting rid of crime. That reeducation really works," Heany said.

"Yeah," Frezza said. "But who knows about people? I mean, here you are in New York and everything's free, so why even think about stealing something, right?"

He looked to Heany as if inviting an answer, and Greg nodded.

"So I hear about this guy who tried to swipe some jewelry. Stuck a diamond ring up his butt and tried to escape with it." Frezza laughed uproariously at the image.

"What happened to him?" Heany asked.

"He tried to go over the wall with it," Frezza said, "and they got him."

"They? The police?"

"*They.*" Frezza pitched his voice low and jerked his thumbs in opposite directions. "The ones who live outside the dome."

"Who are they?" Heany asked, but Frezza shrugged the shrug of someone who doesn't know the answer but is not willing to admit it.

Heany looked around. He remembered the sprawling bird's nest of debris surrounding the beautiful, enclosed egg of the city. He remembered the gray, haunting face he had seen peering out of the concrete-and-steel wreckage.

"Relax, kid." Frezza laughed. "Whoever they are, they can't get in here. We got an electrified wall three feet thick all around Manhattan." He clapped his hands. "Like to play ball?"

"Huh?"

"Wait'll you get a load of this." They turned a corner, and Heany saw the most beautiful sight he had ever seen in his life. It was a baseball diamond, right on the corner of Sixth Avenue and Fifty-fourth Street. It seemed to stretch for miles, the brown earth and green grass. A dozen men—not enough for two full teams—were playing in the warm sun.

"Want to cut in for a couple of innings?"

Heany grinned. "Wouldn't mind," he said.

"Batter UP!"

Oh, God, it was just like his daydreams. The wood in his hand, the clean breeze in his hair, his legs twitching with anticipation.

"Go, Heany," Frezza shouted from along the foul line where he was standing.

"Out of the park, Heany," came another voice.

A practice swing, dig in the heels, there's the pitcher nodding to the sign . . . He's not too bad, the pitcher, maybe a baseball tryout reject like me, pretty fast, got a curveball, I know that . . .

Crack!

"All *right*," Frezza screamed behind him as Heany dropped the bat and ran for all he was worth. First . . . Where's the ball? Second . . . third . . . He entertained the notion that someone might have caught the ball on the fly, and the lot of them were standing around laughing their heads off as he ran gamely around the bases, but he didn't care. He could run, dammit, and he was running, running in this spacious, beautiful, clean place, running toward home plate . . .

Someone was there, motioning for him to slide, and he tossed his body at the ground, sliding past home plate. At the last possible moment he reached out a hand and touched the plate just before the catcher lunged at him with the throw from the outfield.

"Safe!"

And the men cheered and slapped him on the back and someone put a beer in his hand.

"Good going, Heany!"

"Grand slam!"

"Attaboy!"

He held his knees, out of breath, gasping the sweet air, and one thought echoed like a song through his mind: Lifetime Extension.

"Do you like it?"

Lynn paraded in front of him wearing a short dress of dazzling blue sequins. Diamond earrings hung like little twin waterfalls from her ears, and her hair was halfway down her back.

"Is that a wig?"

"No, silly. I had my hair lengthened. I was going to have the top plucked, too, like Brenda's, but there wasn't enough time."

"Good," Heany said.

"Don't you like the high-forehead look?"

"No." He slipped on a white dinner jacket. The fit was perfect. Now he understood why the vacation application updates had always asked for accurate body measurements.

"But she's gorgeous," Lynn whined.

"She looks like Benjamin Franklin," Heany said, whisking her into his arms. "You're gorgeous." He kissed her. She was wearing perfume. No one could afford perfume back home.

"You, too," she said shyly. "Greg, it's all so wonderful, isn't it? It's going to be hard to go home."

He thought of her back in Buttzville, leaving at five in the morning to take three buses to her job as a supermarket checkout clerk because his salary alone couldn't pay for the dingy one-room apartment they'd waited a year to get. He thought of Buttzville itself, gray and stinking, and of how he and Lynn were doomed to stay there forever, because low-level programmers were not permitted to move. And even if they were, where would they go? He was practically unskilled, and Lynn was no genius, either.

Then he thought of his grandfather, who had seen green fields and photographs of a time when people had grass in front of their homes, when kids played baseball, when women wore perfume, when most of the country was like New York City, and it didn't all end in a month.

"Yeah," he said. "It's going to be hard."

*   *   *

They went with the Frezzas to a Broadway show featuring some of the most famous entertainers in the world, supper at the Palace, which specialized in full-course, late-night dinners, and dancing at the Chalet Club, where a full orchestra of synthetic instruments shook the Harlem dance hall until it rocked. Then they came back by subway, riding in a bright, leather-upholstered car while a distinguished-looking waiter with white hair served them drinks.

"This is the guy I'd like to trade places with," Frezza said, clapping the waiter on the arm. "You get a Lifetime Extension without even winning the lottery."

The older man smiled good-naturedly. "Somebody has to serve the drinks, sir," he said.

Brenda leaned over, a little tipsy. "Say, how'd you get this job, anyway?"

"Federal appointment," the waiter said.

Frezza slapped the table. "Don't it figure?"

The subway let them off at the west entrance to Central Park, just a few blocks from their building.

The moonlight was bright above the fragile shadows of the cherry blossom trees. It was artificial, of course; the dome blocked out moonlight just as it blocked the sun. But the illusion was beautiful. The four of them walked in companionable silence through the gardens and past the swan lake, where the beautiful rare birds slept on the glassy surface of the water.

"It's hard to believe that at one time people were actually afraid to come into the park at night," Brenda Frezza said. "There were muggers."

"Muggers?" Lynn tried out the word and Heany realized that his wife, younger than he, had grown up in a world that had never even heard of crime.

"Yes, muggers," Brenda said. "People who robbed people and beat them, or just killed them for fun."

"Fun?"

Brenda laughed. "My great-grandmother came from New York. She lived to be a hundred and five. Oh, the stories she used to tell! They scared me half to death."

"Like what?"

"Oh, you don't want to know."

"But I do!" Lynn was bug-eyed and breathless, a little girl begging for a ghost story at bedtime.

Brenda settled her taffeta skirt on the bench. "Well, she told me about how these people used to rape and stab old ladies and cut off their fingers just to get their wedding rings. Or if they wanted a pair of sunglasses somebody was wearing, they'd just kill whoever had them."

"No!"

Brenda smiled, enjoying the spotlight. "There were gangs on motorcycles, dope addicts, devil worshipers who took little babies and murdered them . . ."

Lynn's hands flew to her mouth.

Heany laughed and tickled her, only partly to ease her fear. The truth was, he was feeling pretty uncomfortable himself. Even the thought of killing was somehow tasteless in this paradise.

"Where were the police during all this?" he asked.

Brenda shrugged. "I guess there were just so many of them that the police couldn't keep up."

"So what'd they do with them?"

"I don't know. Granny never got to that part."

They all dissolved in laughter. "Fairy story," Lynn taunted. She looked at Heany for support, but he said, "Some of it sounds true anyway. That's why the government started the reeducation and relocation program. That's what got rid of the criminals once and for all."

"Well, thank heavens for that," Lynn said starchily.

Just then they heard a *swoosh* overhead, and all four of them glanced upward. A pall of fetid air descended on them like a cloud. Heany coughed. Then they heard a noise like the wild "hahh" the fans in a baseball stadium made on TV when a ballplayer hit a homer.

"What's that?" Heany asked.

"Damn." Frezza pointed overhead. "See the lights?"

Above them, the twinkling lights of a helicopter moved slowly through the opening in the dome. When it had passed through, the square window slid closed again.

"We missed the lottery. That's the helicopter carrying the grand-prize winners. Maybe it would have been us."

"If you're not home when your name's announced, they give it to somebody else," Brenda said ruefully.

"Oh, no," Lynn said.

"Yeah. Those folks are on their way right now to the feds in Washington, to arrange their papers for life."

"A life here."

"You got it, sweetie. Lifetime Extension."

Heany still stared up at the domed sky. The side of it came down very near where they were standing. Only a few hundred feet away was a brick wall less than fifteen feet high, the upper edge of which met the dome's base.

"Is that the wall you were talking about?" he asked.

"That's it," Frezza said. He laughed. "Only it's not brick on the other side. No one can go within ten feet of it over there without being fried."

Heany looked back up at the dome. He remembered the smell and sound that issued through the small opening when the helicopter passed through. It was the sound of death, the smell of death.

"What are you guys talking about?" Lynn asked, rubbing the goose bumps off her arms. "What's on the other side?"

"Them," Heany said.

The unnamable, the unspeakable. *They* were somewhere out there, starving and screaming in the night. *They* were wandering through the rubbish, looking at a ten-foot-high fence that separated them from paradise. *They* were what lay outside New York City.

And Heany knew that he had to win the grand prize in the lottery.

He had to.

Heany didn't win at the next drawing, or the next, or during the week after that, or the following week. He began to experience a sensation of pure, bile-in-the-mouth anger each time a name was drawn. Dorothy Lund, one-month extension. Fineas Alexandrov, two-month extension. Tyrone Washington, six-month extension. And the grand prize . . . Hold your breath, folks, here it comes . . .

(Greg Heany? Please say Heany, Greg or Lynn, it doesn't matter, just say the name, okay? I won't abuse the privilege, I'll stay a humble guy. I won't even say I won, ever, not ever . . .)

Allison Gow, LIFETIME EXTENSION!

Heany kicked off the set with his foot.

"Honey, don't be like that. Let's just enjoy our vacation here, as long as it lasts—"

"Go to bed, Lynn."

"Come with me."

Heany turned the set back on, but switched channels to "Library."

"Please, Greg."

He waved her away. He keyed in the index for The New York (High) Times. The newsread, which was published in New Jersey, was little more than an entertainment guide, but it published all the winning lottery numbers.

He couldn't find a pencil and paper, even in New York, so he raided his wife's makeup bag and, with an eyebrow pencil, wrote down the winners for the past week on the sleeve of his shirt. Then he went back another week, and another, searching for a pattern.

There had to be one, he reasoned. There had to be a system that would help him win.

By daylight, he had covered both sleeves, the entire back, and most of the button side of the shirt with handwriting. Heany was disheveled and frustrated to near tears. There was no pattern, except for the obvious fact that most of the Grand Prize winners had previously won extensions on their original vacations. You didn't just have to play to win, he thought bitterly. You had to stay to win. Only winners need apply.

God knew that excluded Greg Heany, loser extraordinaire.

"Honey, what are you doing?" Lynn stood blinking in the doorway at the red-eyed, bare-chested mess that was her husband. "Why are you writing on your shirt?"

Heany looked down at the inch-long nub of brown eyebrow pencil in his hand. "Testing your makeup?" he ventured.

He stood up, feeling the protest in his legs, and put his arms around her. She felt so good in her pink satin pajamas. Back home she'd be wearing his old T-shirts again, and at about this time of morning they'd both be sitting down to a breakfast of stale bread and tea from used bags.

"You're filling out," he said, nuzzling her neck.

"Getting fat."

"Keep it up."

"I'll do my best. A strict diet of caviar and hot fudge sundaes for the next five days, I promise."

His desire drained away. "Is that all we've got left?"

She nodded, biting her lips. "That's it."

He looked away.

"It's been great," she said, and he could hear the quaver in her voice.

"I wish I could fix it," he said hoarsely. "For you. For the kid we could have if we lived here . . ." Slowly he picked up the notebook-shirt. "None of the winners has children," he said, feeling his heart skip. It meant nothing yet, but at last there was a common denominator.

"Nobody in New York has children," Lynn said.

Heany's head swiveled over to her. "What?"

"There aren't any children here. Haven't you noticed?"

The skip slowed down. So that was it. A couples-only vacation. That was why they were accepted.

"And nobody has parents, either. At least no one I've met."

"Oh," he said dully.

"Brenda and I got to talking with some friends of hers at the beauty shop. We'd all had a bunch of Mai Tais, and I guess things got kind of maudlin, and Brenda told how she and Dan had had a baby once, a boy, but he died before he was six months old, and then I said my parents were killed last year in a car accident, and this other woman Joanne said her parents were dead, too . . ."

Heany tuned her out. He was exhausted. He had stayed awake all night for nothing.

". . . funny how it turned out we were all orphans, and our husbands were, too. Anyway, it may all be a coincidence."

"Uh," Heany said.

"Get some sleep."

"Okay." He lumbered past her.

"I'll wash your shirt."

"Uh."

"Oh, you know another thing?"

Please make it fast, Heany said silently, then turned around and propped himself up in the doorway with what he hoped was an attentive look on his face.

"That woman Joanne—the one at the beauty shop—"

"Yes, Lynn," he said patiently.

"She used to live in the same building as one of the Grand Prize winners. Flora Delgatto, her name was. They arrived here on the same day, and they were really close, I mean *really*, you know, like the Frezzas and us, and they both kept winning extensions . . . Greg, you wouldn't believe how lucky Joanne is, six times she's hit, I'm not kidding—"

"Lynn," he said, looking pained.

"Okay, okay. The point is, after this Flora Delgatto hit the big one, Joanne never saw her again. Not even a phone call. Can you believe it? I guess living in Millionaire's Row went straight to her head. Honestly, if we ever hit, I wouldn't forget my friends. And if they told me I had to, I wouldn't accept the prize. So there."

Heany felt himself coming awake.

Dan Frezza had mentioned the mansions, too. "Just where is Millionaire's Row?" Heany asked.

Lynn raised her eyebrows. "How would I—"

He snatched the phone cradled on the side of the TV.

"Operator," a voice said.

"Number of Flora Delgatto, please."

"We do not give out telephone numbers, sir," the voice said politely. "With the constant turnover of vacation guests, it would create a nuisance. We hope you understand."

"Could you connect me, then?"

"Surely."

"What do you want to reach Flora Delgatto for?" Lynn whispered.

"I want to talk to her. Maybe she knows something now that she's won. It can't hurt to try."

"It's five-thirty in the morning."

Heany glanced at the time on the TV screen. He'd forgotten the time. That would be a great way to start a friendship. Excuse me, Mrs. Delgatto, you don't know me, but I'm waking you up at this ungodly hour just so you can do me a favor.

He was on the brink of hanging up when the operator came back on the line. "That number is busy, sir. Will you try again?"

A feeling of relief swept through him. "Yes. Yes, I will. Thank you." He turned to Lynn. "Line's busy."

"She must be an insomniac." She giggled.

"Don't wash my shirt," Heany said. He picked her up and carried her into the bedroom. "Let's find something else to do."

At ten o'clock he tried Mrs. Delgatto again. The line was still busy.

"That lady does nothing but talk," he said irritably. He flipped on Channel One and scrolled to the section on the lottery.

". . . eligible as soon . . ."

". . . one-month, two-month . . ."

He pressed the scroll button deftly, searching for the picture.

"Live in splendor in Millionaire's Row, in palatial mansions like these. . . ."

He froze the screen. "That's where she lives," Heany said. "Have you seen it? On any of your shopping tours around the city?"

"No," Lynn said, exasperated. "Look, I don't think you should bother this woman. The lottery's just a matter of luck. You can't . . . Oh, what's the use?" She padded into the kitchen and sank her teeth into a peach. "Sometimes you're just the most stubborn man in the world."

The picture on the screen vanished. Heany keyed in a map of Manhattan. He pinpointed where he was, on Fifty-first and Seventh, then systematically worked his way north, south, east, and west, looking for Millionaire's Row.

There was no such place.

But of course not, he thought, feeling stupid. It wouldn't be called Millionaire's Row on the map. It was probably a place like Nob Hill in Buttztown, where the P-21's and the genetic engineers lived. There was no Nob Hill on the Buttztown maps, either, just Addison Avenue or 115th Street or Noriaki Place. You had to live there to know.

He put on a lambsuede jacket, stuffed the shirt with the names of the lottery winners written on it inside the pocket, and walked out. If he could find Nob Hill, he could find Millionaire's Row.

And if he could find Millionaire's Row he could find Flora Delgatto.

And if he could find Flora Delgatto, he might have a chance.

He walked all afternoon, starting at Riverside Drive and working his way east. Up and down the impossibly beautiful thoroughfares, searching for a grotto, a fenced-in area, a RESTRICTED sign, a sentry. What would he do if there was a sentry? he thought with a sudden ache of panic. Kill him in order to have a chat with Flora Delgatto? Of course there would be a sentry on Millionaire's Row. They wouldn't want hoi polloi just wandering in there, would they, tourists with cameras, midnight partygoers? The whole idea was probably just a waste of . . .

He blinked, looked around. He was standing in an alley. He'd walked so long that he'd become oblivious to his surroundings.

Great, he thought, that's just great. He might have passed it ten times over, for all he knew. He didn't even have any idea where he was.

His feet were throbbing murderously. That's right, Heany. Come to paradise and spend it slogging through the streets. You could have been playing baseball, you chump. You could have spent the afternoon making love to Lynn, instead of . . .

He gasped audibly.

There, standing at the mouth of the alley, were the mansions.

The same ones on the tape. Millionaire's Row.

A young woman in a maid's uniform was walking down the street. Heany flattened himself against the wall of the alley until she passed, then peered out again.

No sentries. No walls, no signs, no gates.

There are times even I can get lucky, he thought.

He walked straight to the door of the nearest three-story building. It probably wouldn't be the Delgattos', but they might know where she was. Hell, who said he had to talk with Flora Delgatto? He had all their names. Any of them would do.

Heany combed his hair back with his fingers as he approached the large wooden door. It swung open before he could knock. The man on the other side of it was old and aristocratic-looking. His expression was one of faint surprise.

"I'm sorry," Heany began in a rush. "I know you don't know me . . ."

His eyes narrowed. The man was wearing a blue uniform with stripes on the sleeves. "Yes?"

"You're . . . you're the waiter on the subway."

"That's right." The man offered a polite smile. "May I help you with something?"

Heany's mouth formed an O. He slapped his forehead. "I got it. You work here. Second job, right?" He laughed. "For a moment I thought—"

"I don't work here. I live here. As a matter of fact, I'm on my way to work now, and I'm running a little late, so I hope you'll excuse me."

As he made his way past, Heany glanced inside the door. It was a small entryway, filled with buzzers and mailboxes. Beyond it was another door.

"Hey!" Heany ran after the man.

"I really do have to rush." He smiled apologetically. "Don't want to lose my job, you know."

"You mean this isn't Millionaire's Row?"

The man laughed. "Hardly. This street is the municipal workers quarters. The apartments aren't nearly as nice as yours, believe me."

He remembered the woman in uniform walking down the street. "Municipal workers? Like maids?"

"Maids, cabdrivers, shop clerks, maintenance people, telephone operators . . . everyone who keeps New York running."

"But the tape. On Channel One. It shows these buildings. These particular buildings."

"Ah, yes. The tape was made before Manhattan was complete. Creating it was a colossal job, you know. It took decades. I suppose they had to use something, and these buildings are the tallest in the city. There are so many of us, and even one-room apartments take space. On the outside, they look impressive. Perhaps that's why the planners chose to photograph it."

"But where's the real Millionaire's Row?"

The old man shook his head. His eyes were smiling and kind. "I'm sure I don't know," he said. "Workers aren't permitted to wander around as if we were guests here."

They arrived at the subway station.

"Sorry I wasn't able to be of more help," he said as he rushed down the steps.

"Thanks anyway," Heany called.

He looked around. It was nearing sunset. His feet were throbbing. The East River was a block away. He had nowhere else to look.

Heany sat down with a beer at the bar of an outdoor café facing the river. The diffused pink sunset reflected off the water onto the interior of the dome, making an awesome sight. Outside, a helicopter sailed soundlessly across the sky, towing a huge bundle dangling beneath it.

He turned to the bartender. "What's that?"

A woman's voice spoke into his ear. "Food drop," she said.

He whirled around on the stool. She was saggy, mid-forties, Heany guessed, and rendered grotesque by the bald pate that women seemed to think was attractive. She was also deeply inebriated.

"For them." Her eyes wavered, searching for a focus. "Feds drop the food from the air, so nobody has to get close to 'em. Like feeding Christians to the lions in old Rome." She laughed at her own joke. "My name's Julie. You got a name?" She placed her hand on his thigh.

He shifted his leg away. "No."

"Okay, no-name. How long you here for?"

Heany wondered which made him feel more uncomfortable, the drunken woman or the burning soles of his feet.

The feet won. "Four more days. I'm Greg."

She walked her fingers up his arm. "Where you from?"

"Buttzville, Ohio."

"That sounds exciting. Almost as big-time as Nome."

"Alaska?"

"That's the one. The pleasure capital of the Northwest." She raised her glass in salute. "Oh, we don't go around in animal skins or anything. Bob—thass my husband, Bob Neumeyer—you know him?"

Heany shook his head.

"Lucky you. He's out chasing women now. He's always chasing women, it's like his hobby." She threw down her drink and signaled for another. "Anyway, Bob's an S-Nineteen. Food Engineering. He makes some bucks, but we've got to live near land. That's sort of his laboratory.''

Heany put down his beer and stared at her. "Land?" he said quietly.

"As in dirt. Or in Nome, snow most of the time. You want a thrill a minute watching snow fall, move to Nome."

He looked down. "I would if I could," he said.

"What are you, some kind of P-person?"

"Yeah. P-Nine." He laughed bitterly. "A P-person, that's me."

She shrugged. "Well, Greg, if you're unhappy, run away. Join the Noahs." She laughed with a cruel edge in her voice.

"The Noahs?"

"That's what they call themselves. Nome's the last bastion of bona-fide crazies."

"What do they do?"

"Plant trees. Breed sled dogs. Live in igloos." She crossed her heart. "It's true, I mean it," she said, beside herself with mirth.

Heany sat back in stunned silence.

"They're runaways from Nome, mostly. People who freaked out from one thing or another. They live in the tundra, on the edge of the National Food Engineering lands."

"Are . . . are they allowed?"

" 'Course not," Julie Neumeyer said with disdain. "Think people can go around grubbing on the earth like cockroaches? But it's hard to catch them. They keep to themselves, up in the high country. Anyway, the cops have better things to do than chase crazies through the snow, and as long as they don't bother anybody and don't ask for any of our food . . ."

He stared out at the sunset. How wonderful, he thought, to plant trees and run with a sled . . .

The vision burst almost as quickly as it appeared. Running away to the Alaskan tundra from Nome was one thing. From Buttzville, Ohio, it might as well be Mars.

Julie sighed. "So that's what I'll be going home to. The snow'll be up to my ass by next month."

"You must have won an extension."

"Nope." She slogged down the rest of her drink and called for another. "No extensions. Bob's not eligible."

"I thought everyone was eligible."

She shook her head. "Food Engineers are necessary, according to the feds. Can't leave the job for the rest of their lives." She shrugged. "So we get six weeks straight here every year. What can you do? At least until we lick the food problem. Bob hears we're getting close. Some new kind of animal protein or something. But until then, no extensions."

She nearly emptied her glass as soon as it arrived. "I knew a winner once. From Nome. Thought I'd look him up when we got here."

"Did you?"

"Tried. Called him." The ice cubes in her glass clattered against her teeth. "The line was always busy."

Heany felt as if a jolt of electric current were coursing through his body. "Excuse me," he said.

At the café's public phone he asked for Flora Delgatto again.

"I'm sorry, sir," the operator said. "That line is busy. Will you try again?"

"Hold it," he said, pulling the eyebrow-pencil-covered shirt from his jacket pocket. "Try Elmer Jarell."

"That line is also busy, sir."

"Dorothy Crassner." He ran his finger down the names.

"Busy."

"Arthur Anderson."

"Busy, sir."

"Elizabeth . . ."

The phone went dead.

He dropped the shirt by the phone and walked back, his legs feeling leaden. Outside the plexiglass dome, the helicopter moved lazily back in the direction it had come, its burden gone.

"Food drops . . ."

"Christians to the lions . . ."

"So nobody has to touch 'em . . ."

"Food Engineers are necessary . . ."

"New kind of animal protein . . ."

"What are you, some kind of P-person?"

"We're all orphans here."

"Christians to the lions . . ."

"Christians to the lions . . . ."

"What's the matter, Greg?"

"Who are *they*?" he asked numbly.

"What?"

"Outside the dome. Them."

She made a face. "They're New Yorkers," she said in a whisper. "All the ones that were here before the city was rebuilt. The muggers, the drug addicts, the criminals the jails didn't have room for. New York—the real New York—belongs to them now, except for here under the dome." She examined her fingernails, clearly bored by the turn of the conversation.

"You'd think they would have died off by now," Greg said.

"I guess they're good breeders. Lowlifes always are," she answered. She signaled to the waiter for yet another drink.

"Why didn't they reeducate them, relocate them, like they do with other criminal types?"

"Who knows?" the woman said. "Who cares? Maybe they're hard cases and it wasn't worth the effort?"

"If they're such hard cases, why the hell do they stay there? Why don't they escape? What's in it for them? What the hell does the government keep feeding them for?"

"Hey, are we going to talk about them all night? I could think of something better for the two of us to do with our night. C'mon, have a drink with me."

The bartender turned up the volume on the TV. An announcer with beautiful women on either side of him waved a card in the air. "And tonight's Grand Prize winner, the recipient of a Lifetime Extension for herself and her spouse, is . . . Brenda Frezza!"

There was a barrage of canned applause as a door onscreen opened up. Brenda stood in front of the camera wearing a red dress, her makeup running in black streaks down her face. Dan was at her side. They were holding hands.

"Thank you," she mouthed through the illusory cheers. "Thank you, thank you."

"Oh, my Christ," Heany said. He left at a run.

Greg sprinted the distance from the café to the park, watching the lights of the black helicopter twinkle as they passed through the opening in the dome and swooped toward the building where the Frezzas and the Heanys lived.

Got to stop it, got to stop it . . . The words set up a rhythm for his legs as he ran, his heart feeling as if it were bursting from his chest.

There was no Millionaire's Row. There was no Lifetime Extension. If he could get there in time, if he could shout it in front of the TV cameras, maybe Dan and Brenda would have a chance, maybe it wouldn't happen . . .

Then the lights twinkled overhead again, going away this time, out of the city.

"No," Heany screamed. He ran with the helicopter, below it, as it floated out of the dome's open window and the stench of the air outside wafted in along with the sound, the "Hahh" of expectation and triumph, the blood cry.

"No!"

He crashed, running, into the brick wall. He reeled back, senseless, tears and blood on his face.

Running wildly, he found a park bench. He carried it over to the wall and propped it up on its end. Then he scrambled onto it, holding on to the branch of a maple tree for support as he climbed high enough to press his face against the plastic of the dome.

He screamed at what he saw.

The helicopter was hovering some thirty feet above the ground. Dangling from its open belly were two ropes. At the end of them were Dan and Brenda Frezza, their faces contorted in panic. The wake from the helicopter blew Brenda's red dress in all directions as the ropes grew longer, longer, closer to the mob of gray-faced human creatures below, their arms outstretched toward the quarry, their hungry eyes glistening, their mouths slack and waiting while the ropes descended.

Them.

Dan Frezza reached over to his wife in the eerie, horrifying silent movie on the other side of the dome. He held her hand as the two of them were engulfed by the writhing, blood-starved sea of humanity around them.

As the helicopter rose again, a fistfight broke out, obscuring Heany's view. One man threw a chunk of broken concrete at another. Silently, his victim's head cracked open and a stream of red blood gushed out. Fires broke out in several different locations. Two gangs of young men dressed in rags came at each other with knives in a dreadful, silent dance.

The festivities were underway.

"Christians to the lions . . ."

On the ground, Heany could see a scrap of red from Brenda Frezza's dress.

He slid down the wall and wept there.

"Greg, where have you been?" Lynn's voice was shrill with excitement. "The Frezzas won! The Lifetime Extension! Oh, you should have seen it, the TV cameras were here and everything . . ."

Heany took her in his arms and held her, held her as if he would never let her go.

"You've been in the park, haven't you?" She smiled and pulled something from his hair. "Look, a maple seed."

She put it into his hand. "This could grow into a tree, if it had some land," she said quietly.

He looked at her face, so beautiful, so filled with hope.

"I love you," he said.

"This is the first time anyone has requested an early termination of vacation, Mr. Neumeyer," the attendant at the heliport said with a smile as she escorted the couple into a small waiting room. "But it's all been arranged. You'll be back in Nome by midnight."

"Thank you," Heany said.

The attendant nodded and left.

"I'm scared to death," Lynn whispered, huddled in her threadbare coat.

"I am, too. We could still go back to Buttzville."

She took his hand. "No. No, we can't. I'm not going to look back anymore. You're sure of this, aren't you, Greg?"

He nodded. "There is no Lifetime Extension. Whoever gets picked gets tossed . . . tossed to them. It's what keeps them in their cages back behind the walls. And I don't think it's just New York. I bet it's every vacation city. Los Angeles, Chicago, all of them. That's why they only pick orphans, people without parents or children." He closed his eyes for a moment and continued speaking. "And I don't think there's any reeducation or relocation program either for criminals. I think they collect them and drop them here and let them live or die, whatever happens."

"But why, Greg? Why doesn't the government just dispose of the criminals? Once and for all?"

"I think these are experimental livestock farms. And someday, all of them are going into the food chain."

Lynn shuddered. A tear appeared in the corner of her eye. She squeezed his hand and kissed his cheek. "Is there someone we could tell?"

"Who'd believe us?" he said.

"We can try," she said. "You and me, slugger."

The TV in the room came on, suddenly and without prompting. "And now for this evening's New York Lottery," the announcer said.

Heany jumped up angrily to turn it off, but there was no switch.

"I think they have to watch it in the heliport," Lynn said. "This is where the helicopters come from to get the . . . winners." The last word seemed to stick in her throat.

Heany sat down and turned away from the set as the announcer listed all the people who had won extensions.

"And now, ladies and gentlemen, the name of the Grand Prize winner, recipient of a Lifetime Extension in fabulous New York City . . ."

Heany shivered. He felt sick. Somebody else was going to end up on the other side of the dome, and there wasn't a damn thing he could do.

"Tonight's winners are . . . Greg Heany and his lovely wife, Lynn!"

Lynn gasped.

"Take it easy," Greg whispered, feeling his heart hammer.

"We'll take you right to the Heanys' beautiful West Side apartment for a firsthand look at the winners with Jo Jo Gaines, who's standing by on Remote One. Take it, Jo Jo!"

"Greg?" Jo Jo called outside the Heanys' door. There was a bouquet of red roses in her hand. "Open up in there, Greg!" The announcer-on-the-spot was a smiling young Asian woman, the bearer of great gifts in front of a closed door.

"Not home? One, two, THREE." Canned moans of disappointment. "Guess you missed your chance, Greg. We'll switch to remote number two. Is the name of the alternate winner ready?"

"Ready, Jo Jo," an equally enthusiastic announcer said. Lynn stifled a sob.

"We'll stop it, baby," Heany said softly. "Somehow we'll stop it. We'll have to stay on the run, but we'll get the word out. Someday, somehow . . ."

She nodded as the attendant entered the small room. "Your flight's ready, Mr. and Mrs. Neumeyer," she said cheerfully.

"Thank you."

"All ready to go back to the cold weather?"

"Sure are," Greg said with a heartiness he did not feel.

"What are you going to do back in Nome?"

He took a deep breath and brushed the tears from his eyes. "I'm going to build a baseball diamond," he said.

"Is that all?" she said, in a tone that would have been sarcastic if it had not been canceled out by her perfectly genuine smile.

"No," Greg said. "That's not all. But it's a start."

Husband-and-wife team Warren Murphy and Molly Cochran have written more than one hundred books, sharing a dozen national awards, including three Edgars from the Mystery Writers of America and a Shamus from the Private Eye Writers of America. Murphy is also the creator of the long-running satirical superhero series, The Destroyer—thirty million sales and source for comic books, films, and TV.

Their first collaboration, the Edgar-winning Grandmaster, was an international best-seller. Their latest, The Temple Dogs, a suspense novel set in Japan (where Cochran was born), is published both in hardcover and paper by New American Library. Cochran and Murphy live in an historic manor house in Bethlehem, Pennsylvania, with their young son, Devin.

Long Growing Season

by Robert J. Howe

*In a rural future Brooklyn, a woman encounters an
unusual sort of haunting.*

Molly was pulling weeds when she saw the first one. He
was dressed in old-fashioned business clothes, and he was
carrying a briefcase. Molly blinked and stood up. He was
facing away from her, looking down along the line of the
old street. She couldn't imagine what he was looking at
so intently—the "street" was nothing more than a weed
patch, a little straighter than most, but otherwise unre-
markable.

"Hello," she called out, walking slowly toward the
man. She didn't want to sneak up behind him, but she
was more than slightly vexed that he was on her land, as
well-marked as it was.

The man continued to peer along the track and paid no
attention to her. "I *said*, hello!"

She took another step toward him, her irritation building, and suddenly he wasn't there anymore. Molly stared
dumbly at the spot where he'd been standing. There were
no footprints in the soft ground, not even the least distur-
bance. She poked the ground gently with a forefinger,
making a small dimple in the soil.

She felt her forehead, wondering if she had heatstroke.
She wasn't sure, if she did have heatstroke, that she'd
feel warm to herself. She took the rest of the afternoon
off from her chores.

Nothing else seemed out of sync that afternoon. She
lay in bed reading and trying not to think about her
apparition. He was like a dream. When Molly was a little
girl she'd had a bad case of conjunctivitis, caught from

swimming in the dirty water in a bomb crater, and had fever dreams for a week. Her mother told her afterward that she'd been talking to her father the whole time. Of course, he was dead by then; he'd been in the air force in Australia.

Molly remembered him holding her hand while she had the infection. The man she saw in the field seemed just that real. She shook her head. It had better not be anything that serious; you took too many afternoons off in the farming business and you starved all winter.

Molly looked up from her book at the calendar painted on the wall. Only nine more weeks until the first frost. "I'll turn in early," she said to herself, "so maybe I'll get most of the heavy work done before it gets hot tomorrow."

A few days later, she was eating lunch in the shade of the barn when she heard the low beating of helicopter blades coming from the ocean. A blue-and-white Mitsubishi passed over a few seconds later and made a wide sweep over her land. The pilot then set it down on the northern edge of the old park, about a hundred yards from the house.

The cat hid from the strange man. Molly wished she could hide, too. She imagined how wild she must look to the land-reclamation agent; she'd stopped shaving her legs and underarms, and she was dressed in a pair of baggy shorts and a soiled T-shirt with the arms hacked off. In contrast, the agent was wearing neatly pressed khaki trousers with a forest-green shirt and shiny oval badge. His shoes looked like he'd just walked them out of the department store, and he smelled faintly of cologne.

The agent smiled from behind his silvered flying glasses and held out a clean (but *surprise*, calloused) hand.

"Hi, I'm Ed Wong."

She shook hands, proud of her own calluses, and smiled back. "Molly Tanaka."

"Molly?" the agent said, not letting go of her hand. "Are you nisei?"

Molly took her hand back, none too gently. This was one of the reasons she'd come East; she resented having to explain that her family had lived in California since the First War with Japan in the forties. And she hated the Japanese for making her a stranger in her own country.

Wong took off his sunglasses. "I'm sorry. I, ah, it's become fashionable lately for some of the military governor's wives to pose as rural gentry. I . . ."

"Do I *look* like gentry?" she asked, not at all mollified.

"No," he said, a bit too emphatically. "I mean, people think I'm one of them, if you can believe it."

Molly could—not that Wong looked anything but ethnic Chinese to her, but most Americans still thought all Asian people looked the same.

Wong looked uncomfortable. "I really am sorry," he said. "Are your folks—"

"My mother was repatriated," Molly said coldly. "My older brother as well. My father died in the Philippines campaign. I was born in '34, so I just made the cutoff."

"I don't know what to say."

Molly softened a little at that. "It's okay. They actually wanted to go back, if you can believe it." It was something Molly couldn't forgive her mother for, though she didn't say that. "What do you think of my spread?" she asked instead.

He gestured around. "You've made quite a bit of progress here. It looks good." He sounded relieved to be on a safer topic. "I just came down to see if you needed anything, and to introduce myself."

Molly smiled. "And to make sure that I didn't stake out any more land than I was entitled to."

The agent's expression didn't change, which brought him up a notch in her estimation.

"That too. I didn't measure exactly, but you seem to be close enough."

"To the foot, I think. Would you like something to drink? I'm afraid I have only water."

"Water's fine. I always get parched when I fly with the doors off."

Molly gave him the grand tour after he'd drunk two huge glasses of water. She faintly resented his intrusion from the outside world, but he seemed pleased with all the work she'd gotten done on the farm, and aside from his initial faux pas, he hadn't done anything to put her off.

His stock rose a few more points when they looked at the stable. Satan, the stallion, actually let Wong rub his nose.

"Are they a breeding pair?" he wanted to know.

Molly nodded. "I hope so. They used up most of my credit. I'd have been able to bring along a whole lot more tools and equipment if I'd just paid somebody to fly me in here."

Wong shook his head. "They're worth everything you paid for them. For one thing, you're going to need them when you start cultivating bigger fields. And for another, they'll pay back the investment a dozen times once she foals. This land is too good to be deserted forever; once you have neighbors, colts will be worth their weight in Q-chips."

Molly looked at the agent curiously. "You seem like a city boy. How do you know about horses and crops?"

The agent shrugged. "You come from the coast, what do you know about it? I might have been a city boy, but there weren't any left in Ohio when I grew up. I went to school on the coast, but the government sent me to land-reclamation training right here. I was the first one in my class to graduate from here. I never thought I'd like the Phoenix City project—I wanted them to send me someplace really wild—but, you know, now that I'm here, I wouldn't want to go anyplace else."

"Do you know much about New York?"

"About as much as anyone. They teach us a lot about it in rec-school."

"It's tough to imagine this place as all skyscrapers," Molly said.

"That's because it wasn't. This part was Brooklyn. It was more like a suburb. They had some big buildings, I guess, but they also had a lot of parks and trees. Makes it easier to cultivate. Plus the bombing pretty much dusted everything above ground level anyway."

"Is there anyone else in your area?"

"A few, mostly across the river in Jersey. I guess they used to raise cows there. It was probably even more rural than this."

"Do you miss Ohio?"

"Do you miss the coast?"

"Not really."

"Me neither. I just wish I could settle down and get a farm going. A few more years, I guess."

"Will you settle around here?"

"If there's still claims open. Otherwise, Jersey is nice, too. Better than Ohio."

Molly walked with him back to the helicopter and they shook hands again. But instead of climbing into the aircraft, he stood with one foot on the skids, making small talk. It took her a while to realize that he was attracted to her. He was very polite and circumspect about it, but there it was. Molly thought about taking him back to the house, but she realized, a little sadly, that she didn't want him. He was nice enough, but too different in his neat clothes and store-bought haircut. She wasn't even wearing underwear. Besides, people were too damn undependable.

At last he climbed reluctantly into the aircraft. "Is there anything you need when I come back?"

She shook her head, not wanting to give him an excuse to return too soon.

"Okay, then. I should be back in about two months or so."

She nodded and stepped back from the aircraft as he lit off the engine.

He waved once, then pulled the helicopter out of its ungainly squat and skimmed up and across the park. When she got back to the house, the cat was digging in the garbage.

The rest of the month was warm, with just enough rain. Molly picked tomatoes and some early squash and practiced canning. Just before the end of the month there was a terrific thunderstorm.

The cat sat at the window and watched the rain hammer down. Molly stripped down to her skin and took a bar of homemade soap out into the deluge. The cold rain felt good on her skin, and she wasted soap lavishly, enjoying the downpour. She was just beginning to get chilled when she saw the old woman.

She was on her hands and knees in a vacant corner of the herb garden, turning the rich dirt over with a small hand trowel. Molly covered herself with a worn scrap of towel and took a few steps closer. The woman was oblivious to the rain, and indeed, her flowery print dress seemed to be perfectly dry. She looked about sixty, but her thick, knobby hands turned the clayey soil with obvious ease. Molly took a step closer to the woman and reached out to touch her. The woman looked into her eyes just then and smiled. A moment later Molly was staring at two muddy pools where the woman's knees had compressed the soft earth.

"Jesus H. Christ," Molly said, using one of her father's favorite oaths.

Her first thought was that these visions were the first sign of an impending nervous breakdown. Maybe I'm just lonely, she thought, maybe I should have told Ed to come back sooner.

She shrugged that thought off. She didn't feel lonely. Right then she didn't know what she felt. An ugly qualm swept through her; maybe there was lead in the drinking water . . . She might lose everything.

She blinked, trying to clear her eyes of soap and rainwater. She wasn't even sure she really saw knee prints in the dirt. Or the soil that was turned over. Heavy metal poisoning is supposed to cause hallucinations and insanity, she thought. What do I have to check for lead?

She thought there was something in the first-aid box. She ran into the house. Without bothering to dry off or dress, Molly dragged out the first-aid chest. In a compartment in the lid was a yellow plastic case with the legend POTABLE WATER TEST KIT stamped on it. She tore open the case and skimmed the instruction book until she found a section on heavy metals. She read the section twice before she performed the test.

There was no lead in the drinking water, or in any of the utensils and storage containers, which she tested using another kit. It was full dark out when she realized that she was still naked and shivering.

Molly worried about the incident for several weeks afterward, occasionally thinking of a new source of lead poisoning and testing it only to find nothing. Eventually she let her worries go in the press of chores to be done while bringing in her small harvest.

The grinding labor of getting the crops in single-handedly left her with barely enough energy to eat a small, cold meal each night before collapsing from exhaustion. By the time the harvest was done, she'd come down with a heavy cold. She stayed in bed for the better part of a week then, anxious about the chores she should be doing, but more afraid that her cold would become pneumonia unless she took care of herself.

Being sick made her feel her self-imposed isolation for the first time since she had left Los Angeles. She even missed her mother, which made her homesick and angry. Her mother was an elegant, cultured woman who'd hounded a squadron of servants into keeping the house like a museum exhibit, and who'd left Molly to her own devices once she'd demonstrated more interest in books than in fine clothes and other things ladylike.

"Molly Chan, you are big for a girl anyway," her mother would occasionally chide. "Men are intimidated by bookish girls. If you're going to read so much, at least try to be a little more graceful about it."

Molly had ended even that minimal discourse when, at nineteen, she'd told her mother she had no interest in becoming a geisha. That had earned her a week of evenings in her room; her mother was too tightly controlled to do anything else.

Molly spent as much time as she could around her father—he was away a lot on business—especially after the geisha incident. He knew all kinds of things, and they could talk for hours without running out of things to discuss. She often wondered what her father saw in her mother.

And to think she'd been happy to move to Japan; she didn't even speak the language beyond a few words she'd adopted as affectations for her club friends. And her father dead less than a year. He'd looked so small, standing in his olive-drab flight suit next to an F/A-18 loaded with bombs and guns.

Molly shuddered. Every time she thought of the Japanese propaganda broadcasts saying how benevolent they were for not using nuclear weapons, her stomach turned. This, as much as anything else, stiffened her resolve never to return to their strongholds on the West Coast.

It rained a great deal in November, and every morning for two weeks there was fantastic ground fog. Molly walked the borders on those days, the cat trotting behind her. By degrees the weather turned raw, then bitter cold, forcing her to dig out her heavy winter clothes. Except

for a few isolated stands of pines the green faded from
the land, making it seem to her more like a city than it
ever had. With the foliage gone the gray bones of the old
buildings could be seen pushing up here and there through
the brown earth.

The first of December brought an abrupt change in the
weather. The sun came out, and aside from the sharp
wind off the bay, the temperature was almost balmy.
There were few outdoor chores to accomplish by then,
yet she wanted to enjoy the last of the good weather.

She was sitting in front of the house sewing rabbit-
pelt gloves when she saw Rip Van Winkle. At least that
was who she immediately thought of him as. He was
walking across her property, east to west, and he looked
exactly like the illustrations from a book she'd read as a
child, *Washington Irving's Treasure Chest*.

He was dressed in what must have been the style of the
early Dutch settlers of New York, and carried an ancient
muzzle-loaded rifle over his shoulder. His hair was long,
longer than hers, and he was wearing a cumbersome-
looking black frock coat. He sang softly to himself as he
marched across the stubbled fields, seemingly unaware of
Molly and her house.

The vision was so patently and ludicrously yanked from
her imagination that Molly laughed. She picked up a
flake of stone and lobbed it sidearm at the apparition's
back, intending to prove to herself how insubstantial
these ghosts were.

Instead, the stone struck the heavy black coat with a
thud, sending up a small puff of dust.

The man whirled and leveled his gun in Molly's direction. "Hallo! Who's that now?"

Molly froze, unable to move or utter a word.

"Hallo?" Though they were in plain sight of each
other, the man moved his head slightly from side to side,
as if he were trying to peer through obstructing vegetation.

When no answer was forthcoming, he scowled and
cocked the hammer of his rifle, then fired the museum
piece from the hip.

The explosion and black smoke brought Molly to sudden and terrified life. She bolted from her stool and
threw herself through the door of the house. Without
thinking she yanked her own rifle from its rack and

chambered a round. Her breath coming in heaving gasps, she then peered from a corner of the door. The man wasn't in sight, making her think he was creeping up on the house. She dashed out the door, hoping to see him before he could reload his one-shot weapon, but there was no sign of him. She stalked around the house and barn for an hour before she was satisfied that he was gone.

I have gone completely around the bend, she thought as she readied herself for bed that night, or these things are real. The one that shot at her seemed substantial enough; he left boot prints all around the barn. Molly thought grimly that she'd almost found out the hard way how real his bullets were.

She had been just beginning to believe these visions were some kind of benign psychological response to the solitude when this incident had happened. She felt badly shaken, not just by the threat, but by the possibility that she was having a breakdown. She could almost believe today's apparition was just a man dressed up in a costume except that he disappeared into thin air. She'd followed his boot prints away from the house, but they just seemed to stop. The ground was soft enough to take impressions; it was just as if he'd faded into the earth. And the terrain was bare for miles in that direction.

Molly had been closer to death; during the war her area was bombed two, sometimes three times a month, but there were always other people around. *This* she had to face all alone.

The visions reminded her of a haiku by Marguerite Higgins, the resistance poet:

IN DEAD EARTH SPIRITS
IN LIVE CONQUERORS NO LIFE
SPIRITS ALWAYS WIN

If these earth spirits were real and not a sign that she'd had a breakdown, then at least the Japanese haven't subdued them. Just the same, she thought, I'm not going out without the rifle anymore.

The first snow came in late December: a thin, hard grit

that blew horizontally against the windows like a stream of tiny bullets. Molly was indoors, stripping gut for snares, when she heard the helicopter. By the time she'd pulled on her boots and parka, the aircraft was sitting at the edge of the old park with its blades drooping to a stop.

"Hello, Molly."

She looked at the land agent incredulously. "Ed! What brings you out in this miserable weather?"

"Just making the rounds. Weather isn't too bad as long as the instruments do their job."

"You came out here for a routine visit?"

The agent laughed a little self-consciously. "And to see you."

This made her distinctly uncomfortable. Still, she would feel worse turning him away out of hand.

"Well, the least you can have is a cup of hot tea for your troubles."

"You have tea?"

"From herbs. I grow them myself. Come on."

He looked around her tiny house with frank interest while she boiled water, then they sat at the plank table with the two steaming mugs.

"It looks like you're doing real well," Wong said, gesturing around the room with his mug. "As far as I can see, you're ready for a long, hard one."

"I am. I like the feeling that I did this all on my own; it's why I came out here."

"Still, it must be nice to see another human face sometimes, no?"

Molly nodded faintly. "I suppose. But I like being alone. You really didn't have to fly out here in this weather. I wouldn't have minded if you waited until it broke."

"That might not be for a few months."

"I know."

She was slightly embarrassed by the ensuing silence, but she felt her point had been made. He was clearly uneasy, though he didn't seem ready to leave.

"Is there anything else you need?" he finally asked.

"No."

"Do you have a rifle?"

She looked at the agent curiously. "Yes, for hunting."

"How about a pistol?"

"What on earth would I need a pistol for?"

"To protect yourself."

Molly looked at Wong as though he'd taken leave of his senses, but she had an uncomfortable notion of where the conversation was headed.

"From what?" she asked finally.

The agent stared into his cup for a long minute. "Some of the settlers have been seeing strange people on their property."

"What do you mean?"

"There's a small family living a few miles east of the old airport—they packed up and moved back West because strange people kept looking in their windows at night. They were dressed in old-fashioned clothes, and they never said or did anything; they just looked."

Molly hesitated. "Have you ever seen these people?"

"No."

"Then I'd suggest there isn't much to it. People who are cut off from their past lives like that sometimes have odd reactions to the solitude. They should have stuck it out."

"Have you ever seen anything like that?" Wong asked.

She returned the agent's stare coolly. "No, I haven't."

Wong shook his head. "Look, Molly, I'm not the bad guy here. I'm just trying to find out if there's anything to this, and to make sure you're okay."

"Because you have a personal interest?" There, she thought, it's out in the open now.

"Because it's my job," he said a little sadly. "Look, I'm sorry . . ."

"About what?"

"About everything."

When the helicopter lifted off from the edge of the park, she wasn't sorry to see it go. She didn't wish the agent ill; he really did try to do his job, and it wasn't his fault if he was attracted to her. At least he was gentlemanly about it. As the aircraft dwindled to a speck against the gray sky, Molly wondered why she'd resisted the impulse to tell Wong everything she knew about her earth spirits. This state of mind worried her more than her encounters with them.

* * *

January and February were hard, cruel months. Even with the fire roaring and wearing all her warmest clothes, Molly felt as if she was never completely warm. She partitioned off the barn so that the horses used only a small part of it, on the theory that it would conserve body heat. She wasn't sure that the animals needed it, but it made her feel better to do something. She spent long hours making plans for the spring, drawing and redrawing planting charts, and figuring out the most efficient way to work her acreage. Having seen her modest holdings increase, even slightly, from one year to the next, gave her a sense of security and accomplishment. When her eyes smarted from too much wood smoke and small print, she would bundle herself in her warmest clothes and walk the perimeter of the old park.

It was easy to tell where the old park had been; a ring of ancient trees enclosed a sea of wild grasses and saplings, bare and silver-barked in the cold winter sun. At the edge of the park proper was Gerritsen Inlet. Looking south, she saw that everything was a sheet of treacherous saltwater ice. She knew the bay itself probably wasn't frozen, but from where she stood it was difficult to tell where the ice ended and the water began.

Because she was bored and had more than a touch of cabin fever, she decided to walk along the inlet toward the ocean. Less than a mile from her house she turned back, numbed by the steady wind from the sea. She was concentrating on the cold when she saw the prints. They weren't like the clearly cut boot prints she'd left in the gritty snow, but they were definitely human, and there were at least a dozen different sets.

Very slowly she scanned the brush in the direction the prints led, but saw nothing moving inside the fence of tall grasses. She was sure the prints hadn't been there when she'd left the house. She was afraid to move, and afraid to stay out in the open. She wished she'd brought the rifle along, and she wished she was back in the security of her house.

This time they saw her first. When she looked up from the tracks, about a dozen people were standing in a semicircle in front of her. They were dressed in furs fashioned into crude parkas, and their boots were merely more furs bound around their feet with thongs. They had high cheekbones and their eyes had a vaguely Asian cast. They carried spears with stone points. They very clearly saw her, and were conferring with one another in a soft, sibilant tongue. The first thing Molly thought was that they were between her and the house.

She couldn't bring herself to say anything, and though every muscle in her body quivered with tension, she stood rooted before them, only her eyes following their movements.

There were several youngsters in the group, and one took a step toward her, only to be promptly yanked back by an elder and admonished.

After discussing her to their apparent satisfaction, they turned away and made off through the heavy grasses, barely stirring the tips of the brush in the process. Molly stood absolutely still as long as she could, then broke and flew back to her house at a dead run. She didn't allow herself to think until she was bolted behind her door.

This was the strangest yet. They certainly knew she was there, and she had been close enough to smell their breath. She no longer had the slightest doubt that these earth spirits were real. She didn't know how they came and went, but they spoke, and they left prints in the snow, and they stank.

They reminded her of the descriptions of the first natives of the continent. She could imagine them migrating across the Bering land bridge from Asia.

Molly thought of how stupid it was to have gone out again without her rifle, though she didn't know what she would have done with it had she had it along. Just thinking about it made the hair on the back of her neck stand up. She sympathized with those people who moved back West: she was beginning to wonder if she should do the same.

Still, they didn't hurt her, and Lord knows they could have; their spears were crude, but they looked very businesslike. She thought again that she should have told Wong about them.

During the following weeks, Molly forced herself to leave the house, going a bit farther afield each time. Gradually her fear faded, and though she took the rifle with her whenever she left the immediate area around

the house, she otherwise settled back into her winter
routine. She hadn't thought about the earth spirits in
days when an explosion rocked her house.

The force of the blast blew the windows out and made
the roof timbers creak ominously. Molly threw herself
under the table, a childhood reflex that left a sour taste
in her mouth. She crouched motionless under the table,
listening, until her ears started to ring and she realized
that the explosion had temporarily deafened her. She
heard the moaning while she was pulling herself erect by
the edge of the table.

Outside the window was a long brown scar where the
explosion had cooked away the snow. A man dressed in
dusty green body armor was lying in the middle of the
bare patch, curled into a fetal ball and clutching his
abdomen.

Molly stood at the window for what seemed a long
time, staring at the wounded man. The metallic taste in
her mouth was intensified by the sight of the familiar
uniform and combat gear. The man moaned again, then
gave a long, liquid cough. She hesitated at the window
for another moment, then turned and grabbed for her
parka and first-aid box. By the time she was out the
door, the soldier was gone.

She stood over the pool of blood, trembling and sick,
waiting for the next thing to happen. The viscous red blot
soaking into the earth reminded her of human sacrifice.
The adrenaline drained slowly from her bloodstream,
leaving her feeling cold and weak. Though every step was
a burden, she drew water from the well to wash away the
blood. When there was nothing more than a deep-brown
stain in the middle of the bare patch, she dropped the
pail and returned to the house.

She deliberately avoided thinking about anything and
stripped off her clothes. Naked, she crawled under the
stale, rough bedclothes and willed herself to sleep.

The cold woke her early the next morning. Frigid gusts
of wind rattled the shards of glass still hanging from the
window frames, and a thin gruel of snow coated much of
the floor. It took Molly several minutes to recall what
had happened to the windows. When she remembered
the explosion and the soldier's moans, it took an effort of
will not to pull the covers over her face and retreat back

into sleep. She forced herself to dress and build a fire in the fireplace.

She was standing next to the fire stamping her feet when she saw the cat. He was lying across the room from the windows and looked almost asleep, except for the snow that had settled on him during the night. He was stiff when Molly picked him up, and had two tiny blood clots at his nostrils from the concussion. The pathetic little corpse broke her self-control. She sat on the floor and cried like a heartbroken child—first for her dead pet, and then for herself.

By the time she'd dug a shallow grave in the frost-hardened soil, she was too exhausted to cry anymore. In a kind of trance she cut a precious blanket into squares to cover the gaping windows. A fair amount of wind blew through the fabric until she greased the squares with animal fat. Come the first warm day, the fat would stink terrifically. It seemed a rather distant and unimportant consequence to her. While she fed lavish amounts of wood into the fireplace, she thought about how much human effort was spent just keeping warm and fed.

The weeks after the explosion passed with very little thought or effort on Molly's part. She performed the bare minimum of chores necessary to keep herself comfortable and spent the rest of the time sleeping. It was only when the warm weather arrived, with its attendant effect on the atmosphere in the small house, that she left her bed.

Besides making the house more livable, the physical labor of spring cleaning proved to be therapeutic for her. With the longer days and cleaner house—she'd burned the greasy strips of blanket that covered the windows—Molly had a feeling that she'd survived the worst. On her first trip away from the house she found that her fear of the earth spirits had been cauterized by the explosion. The sight of tracks near the inlet provoked only a mild curiosity in her.

I have as much right to be here as they do, she thought. She'd had precious little security in her life, and none of it before she took over the land. Back on the coast you could always lose a job, she reasoned. And even if you didn't, the currency could be devalued again, or there could be another food shortage. The Japanese manipulated the markets for the benefit of those back in Nippon, and it would never be otherwise.

Worse, it would mean giving up her life for that of something approaching a concubine, given the property laws they'd instated. Her mother could live like that—before she'd been repatriated, it had been a point of pride for her to be so popular with the Japanese officials—but not Molly.

That night she dreamed about the earth spirits. In her dream they hunted winter rabbit with spears and built huge fires. Afterward the people danced. In her dream Molly tried to dance, too, but for some reason she couldn't get up off the dirt. The harder she tried to get up and join the dance, the more tightly she felt bound to the ground. She was still trying to join the dance when she woke up.

Though she didn't waste much time on it, this lack of fear teased at her intellect whenever she came across footprints or other signs of the earth spirits' passage around her property. On the first really hot day, Molly put aside her chores and went down to the ocean. She stripped off her shorts and shirt at the high-tide line and ran into the icy surf. She swam out far enough to make her arms feel weak and leaden, then floated on her back until the chill began to creep into her bones, then she backstroked lazily to shore and stretched out in the sun.

After a short nap, she took her tattered clothes into the water, dunking and wringing them out until they felt clean. While the clothes dried, she went clamming in the shallow flats, digging up nearly two dozen of the littlenecks in a quarter of an hour. It was as she settled down for an after-lunch siesta that she noticed the building.

It was taller than most of the buildings in downtown Los Angeles, and appeared to be rising out of the sea a few hundred yards from where she was sitting. Crowds of Japanese lounged on balconies that looked out over the ocean, and as she watched in disbelief, a buslike conveyance rolled up to the front of the building and spilled out more brightly clad sons and daughters of Nippon.

Molly stared open-mouthed at the building; it looked like a hotel. Tinny music and bits and snatches of excited

Japanese drifted across the water to her. As she looked on, the scene grew more detailed, as if coming out from under a fog bank. A highway stretched from the hotel to others like it along the coast, and boats with multicolored sails plied the water beyond them.

She realized she was naked when a group of men on the nearest balcony began calling and waving to her. Though she only spoke pidgin Japanese, the meaning of their suggestions was clear enough. Repulsed, Molly turned her back on the beach and gathered up her clothes. As she dressed, she looked over her shoulder to assure herself that no one was coming toward her from the ocean. Once dressed, she wasted no time heading away from the beach. She looked back again before she descended behind the dunes, and noticed that the scene was becoming indistinct again. She stood there, watching, until it had completely disappeared.

Of all the things she'd seen, this was the strangest. It was different from the other earth spirits somehow, and not just because of the buildings or the Japanese. It felt different, as if she were on the outside looking in, rather than the other way around.

Since Wong had asked her about the earth spirits, she hadn't really worried about her sanity, but now she had to wonder if all the settlers weren't suffering from some kind of mass hysteria. She was in relatively good spirits until she saw the hotel filled with conquering Japanese. *What would I do if they really did build a resort here,* she thought.

As the weather warmed, there was more and more to do around the farm. Though the extra acreage she'd planted had given Molly a sense of accomplishment at first, the extra drudge work that came with it was beginning to wear on her nerves. More than one morning she had to resist the temptation to leave her chores waiting and go exploring or clamming. Early summer always awoke the wanderlust in her, but this year it was stronger than she'd ever felt it. More worrying was that she felt not so much the need to see new places, as to escape from the farm.

Two weeks after the incident on the beach she felt justified in taking another holiday. She left the house early in the morning and headed southwest toward a patch of coast about an hour's walk from the house. Rather than the flat, sandy type of beach that was common around the inlet, this area was predominantly rocky and open to the full power of the surf. The swimming was rather treacherous, but the south beach had extensive mussel beds and tidal pools where she could spear blackfish and doormat-sized fluke.

Though it was still early in the season, the underbrush was already thick and difficult to traverse. With every passing year the land not under cultivation grew more wild. Despite the difficulty, Molly enjoyed the walk. She often imagined what the country must have looked like before it was settled. As tenacious as the vegetation was, it would take hundreds of years before the forests returned to their original state.

Less than a mile from the beach—she could smell the ocean—she stepped out from a wall of wild reeds and onto a flat, grassy lawn partially bordered with white stones. Two beefy, middle-aged white men worked from the back of a vehicle, the likes of which Molly had never seen before. The bed of the vehicle hovered noiselessly several feet above the ground, where the two men unloaded rocks from it and placed them along the border of the grass. Every so often, one of the men would nudge the bed forward with his hip, causing it to coast a few feet and stop.

Before the men noticed her, Molly slipped back into the tall grass and crouched on her haunches. She watched for several minutes as the men worked, silent except for an occasional grunt as they lifted or set down a stone. There was a tiny cab on the front of the vehicle, the door of which bore the rising-sun logo. A radio crackled inside the cab, emitting a squeal of static and a burst of Japanese. One of the men wiped his hands on his coveralls, reached into the cab, and took out the radio. He spoke into it in flawless Japanese, which surprised Molly. After a minute he set the radio back into the cab and rejoined the other man, who had not stopped unloading rocks.

The green, parklike belt stretched as far as she could see up and down the coast. Far to her right a huge house stood overlooking the water. When the men had moved a dozen or so yards away, Molly reached out and hefted one of the smaller stones. Its weight felt substantial enough, and when she put it back down, she saw that tiny flecks of white adhered to her hands. She sat in the tall grass for a long time, waiting for the scene to change, but nothing happened. Had she not been along this part of the coast just a month earlier, she would have believed it was real. As it was, the scene sorely tested her sense of reality. When the men started working their way back along her side of the grass, Molly slipped back through the brush and headed for home.

All the way back to the house she thought about what she'd seen. She was beginning to think she'd seen the future; if that was the case, she didn't like it. What was worse, it seemed to be invading her everyday life. The other earth spirits, even the one who shot at her, seemed benign by comparison, though more haunting . . .

Molly stopped in her tracks.

"Holy Christ," she said aloud.

That was exactly what they were doing. And now what Molly was doing, though she hadn't realized it before. The earth spirits were haunting her, whether by chance or not, and now she was haunting the Japanese.

For a long time she sat on a little hill, mulling over the implications of her theory. By the time she was ready to go home, it was getting dark.

If she was right about the haunting business, it was only going to get worse. There might be a Japanese city right in her back yard someday, like Sacramento or Eugene. She supposed she could always pack up whatever she could carry and move along south. Molly'd started with less here than she could carry with her, and could do it again if pressed. Almost anything would be better than living with her mother's people, whether they thought she was a ghost or not.

For the next few days Molly threw herself into her work, staying on the farm because she thought it the least likely place for her to see more Japanese. One afternoon she was grooming the horses outside the barn, her attention focused wholly on removing a bad mat from the mare's tail, when she realized that she was being watched. Two Japanese, a slight woman in her twenties and a much older man, were standing in the middle of her yard area, staring at her.

Molly resisted the temptation to stare back and instead observed the pair unobtrusively from behind the animal. The man put one hand on the woman's waist, an automatic, proprietary gesture. The woman, who was holding a box of some sort, merely stared. Intensely uncomfortable under their scrutiny, Molly considered taking the horse into the barn and staying there until the pair went away. If she did that, however, she would have to pass within inches of them to reach the animal's halter. After more than a minute of squirming under their frank appraisal, she began to get angry.

I have as much right as they do to be here, she thought. More! This is *my* land.

Slowly and with no apparent purpose, she worked her way around the horse with the comb until her back was less than a foot from the pair. She took a deep breath then and turned, returning their stare with a stony, bored glare. The woman averted her eyes immediately, but the man continued to stare at Molly for several seconds. She let her breath out imperceptibly and stared right through the man, her face completely immobile. Finally he broke and with a rough word turned and pulled his companion away.

Molly watched them go, not moving until they were well out of sight. When she looked down, she saw that she'd driven the teeth of the comb into her palm hard enough to draw blood.

She thought they must have been on a picnic; she hoped she'd ruined their appetites.

She went into the house and looked in her mirror, an action she'd become unaccustomed to, given the layer of dust on the glass. Her face was narrower than that of the woman she'd scared off; Molly realized with a small shock that she looked very much like her mother.

That thought recalled the woman's timid reaction to her just a moment ago. She was amazed to think that she and the man she was with were afraid of her. Which was, now that she thought about it, just what her mother's reaction would have been. Her mother had always been a little afraid of her.

"Huh," she said aloud, sitting down with a thump on

her bed. She was more than a little uncomfortable with this sudden insight into her mother's psyche. She ran her fingers through her coarse black hair.

I am not going anywhere, thought Molly. This is my place, and this is where I stay. She thought about that family near the airport that Wong had told her about. They'd gone back to the coast because the earth spirits kept looking in their windows. Judging from the way they ran the war, the Japanese conscience wasn't so tender. But she didn't have to make it easy for them.

After living twenty-odd years in fear of their bombs, she wasn't above looking in a few windows.

Molly looked at herself again in the mirror. Then she went outside to wait for the Japanese.

Robert J. Howe currently works as a public-relations writer for Brooklyn College, and is a BC graduate, with a degree in journalism and history. He attended the 1985 Clarion East writers' workshop, writes a regular column for The Brooklyn Paper, *a local weekly, and has sold short fiction to* Weird Tales, Pandora, *and* Fantasy Macabre. *He's a member of the Space Crafts Science Fiction Workshop in Cambridge, Massachusetts, and won a handful of Brooklyn College writing awards, and the New York Press Association Scholarship for work in community journalism.*

Of his story here, he says, "I grew up in Brooklyn and lived there most of my life. I see a kind of natural beauty there that urban sprawl hasn't completely erased. 'Long Growing Season' is my spring-fever story. It was easy to imagine my character developing an attachment to the land, especially once it had been rendered more or less wild again."

Candelabra and Diamonds

by Don Sakers

This book contains a wide variety of stories, covering many of the subgenres of science fiction and fantasy. It's only fitting to include that classic type of science fiction, space opera.

So here we have a space opera in the grand tradition—set in New York.

Jocelyn's party had been planned for months. Her computers had hired the very best catering firm, a troupe of New Sardinia dancers had recorded a holoshow, and the finest delicacies were ordered from all over the Galaxy. Now, Lady Jocelyn decided to take a hand in the planning herself.

Her child, Jassie, would have to be disposed of during the party. She was a delightful child, but it was not proper to have a six-year-old at an adult dinner party. Jocelyn sent an autoservant to fetch Jassie, and thought furiously.

There had been an unpleasantness associated with Jassie; a malfunction in crèche machinery and suffocation. But the Adelhardt family fortune could counteract anything, be it imperial decree or untimely death. Money was spent, special permissions granted, and the clone was every bit as charming as the original. Lady Jocelyn had wiped the unpleasantness from her mind and sent the new Jassie to the best crèche she could find.

By the time the child arrived, all dimples and damask, Jocelyn had made a quick holophone call to the crèche director.

"Good morning, Mother," Jassie said, bowing deeply.

"Good morning, dear. The crèche cybernet told me that you have been learning about England."

"Yes, ma'am."

"I've told the computer that you may go on a trip to the museums of England. And afterward, you'll sleep with your crèche-mates in Buckingham Palace. Would you like that?"

"I would love it, Mother."

"Good, then. Run along and pack a bag. The flier will be here soon." As Jassie departed, Jocelyn thumbed a switch that put her in contact with the house computer. "See that Jassie packs her bag properly with overnight supplies. I don't want her interrupting the party calling for things she's forgotten."

"Acknowledged, madam."

Next Jocelyn turned to the holophone. She dialed a number, punched a code to get past the autosecretary, and found herself face-to-face with a dark-skinned, amber-eyed man in Imperial Navy uniform. "Karl Loewenger," he answered quickly.

"Hello, Karl," Jocelyn said warmly. No mention of last night's argument . . . it was done and gone, an unpleasant incident best forgotten. "Will you be at my party tonight?"

He glanced offscreen. "I don't know, Jocelyn. Patalanian Union ships are engaged with ours near Tethys. I should stay here in case I'm needed."

Jocelyn concealed a frown. "You've been working hard lately, Karl. I think you'd enjoy a break."

"Aren't you the least bit concerned about this war?"

She shrugged. "You should learn to put things in their proper place. Let the day be for war; night belongs to the moon and to revelers."

Again the glance offscreen. "All right, you've convinced me. It looks as if the Navy will hold at Tethys. What time should I be there?"

Jocelyn looked at the caterer's outline. "The first course will be served at seventeen; maybe you could be here around fifteen-thirty to help me greet guests?"

Karl shook his head. "Jocelyn, I can't figure out why I like you so much."

"My essential untainted innocence?"

Karl smiled. "I doubt it. I'll see you at fifteen-thirty. Brandix be with you."

"And you." That was sweet of Karl. Although irreli-

gious himself, he never forgot that she was a devotee of
Brandix, and never neglected to observe the proper forms.

Whistling, she reflected that Karl would be much hap-
pier if he would just become a Brandixian. He paid too
much attention to the unpleasantness.

War. Absurd.

Iaranori and Humans were cousins; perhaps that was
why Tenedden felt for them. In his nearly undetectable
ship he followed the Patalanian attack force that moved
in tachyon phase toward Terra. It was not the usual
business of a Galactic Rider to participate in military
missions—Tenedden was on assignment from the Museum of Worlds on Nephestal, doing what the sedentary
scholars could not. Humans were important enough in
the Grand Scheme for records of their actions to be made
and stored with the long millions of years of similar
records on Nephestal.

Tenedden knew the story of scores of galactic em-
pires, beginning with the history of his own race. Like all
the others, the Human Empire was now meeting with
disaster, conflict, and dissolution. Sociologists among the
Daamin, the Galaxy's most educated race, had long since
shown the course that the Terran Empire would take in
its fall; this Patalanian attack was a key moment.

Action at Tethys, of course, was just a feint. The real
Patalanian force was the one Tenedden rode with, six
hundred ships strong, to sack Terra.

If he were of the Daamin, Tenedden wondered, would
he feel this sadness at the coming fate of Humans? Over
the aeons the seed vessels of the Pylistroph had dropped
bio packages on many worlds. What if the people of
Earth had sprung from Daamin spores, not Coruman as
his race had? What if they were not kin? Would he feel
different?

No, he decided. The tragedy of the fall of a mighty
race was one that could not fail to touch the heart, no
matter what stock that race had sprung from. Bards
among the Riders would sing for millennia of Earth and
her strange children, long after the fortunes of Humanity
had passed through the many reversals that the Daamin
predicted.

Had he been a Daamin, Tenedden thought, maybe he

would be able to watch the fall of Humankind and ap-
plaud the artistry of it. Kayya Trnas, the leading scholar
of Terra, hung on every word of Tenedden's reports and
expressed approval at the smallest nuances of cause and
effect. But Tenedden was not a Daamin, he had not had
centuries to learn calm contemplation of the Universe's
tragedies. He was an Iaranor, and enough like a Human
that his wide eyes misted when he thought of the Patalanian
attack force finally reaching its objective.

Even on holophone, an Imperial audience was an Imperial audience. As soon as Jocelyn answered the phone,
the regal voice of the Imperial Herald commanded her,
"Compose yourself! Her Majesty Virginia Carroll will
see you." From the Imperial Palace, the view segued to
the throne room, then the Empress in a most impressive
zoom shot.

Jocelyn allowed a tiny frown to cross her face. Her
Majesty looked so old! And she was not quite thirty, a
few years younger than Jocelyn herself.

"Good afternoon, Lady Jocelyn."

"Good afternoon, Highness." Jocelyn didn't want to
comment on Virginia's graying hair and drawn face. Virginia could have transplants made from a clone body and
be good as new. Of course, then she would not then be
permitted to sit on the Whirlpool Throne—the Empire
had learned from the previous century's excesses by Dirk
Fodon. Jocelyn was of the private opinion that giving up
the Throne would be good for Virginia. Most of the
woman's present problems stemmed from wallowing every day in the concerns and unpleasantnesses of others.
Her Majesty would be better off without that.

"My lady, I'm afraid I will not be able to attend your
party tonight. I am sorry to cancel at such a late hour. In
my place I will send Mayor Hua."

"Oh, dear." Hua Chi-fen, as Mayor of New York, was
directly responsible for an entire hemisphere of Terra,
but he was not the Empress. "May I ask why, your
Majesty?"

"Have you read this morning's State of the Empire
Report?"

"Why, no." The State of the Empire Report averaged
three megabits of data a day; although she knew people

who read it religiously, Jocelyn didn't need that kind of anxiety either before or after breakfast.

Her Majesty, of course, didn't just *read* the daily reports: she had them imprinted upon her brain through RNA transplants and cyborg computer connections. The ordeal had to be draining. No wonder Virginia looked ready to perish.

"Well, my lady, if you get a chance you might check out the latest speech to the Patalanian Senate by President Masilek. The Union is talking escalation again, so I must be here in the palace."

Jocelyn fought to keep a smile. "We do as we must, your Highness."

"I knew you would understand, dear."

"Perhaps you will come to my next party . . . ?"

"Of course. Send me an invitation. If you will excuse me, now . . ."

"Naturally. Brandix be with you."

Her Majesty smiled and then her image faded. That was as it should be. It would not be right for the Empress to favor one religion over another, so she officially had none.

Jocelyn reached across her desk to the DO NOT DISTURB button, pressed it. Then she dialed some soothing music and closed her eyes.

The Empress was not coming to her party. That was a discomfort. The teachings of Brandix said that she could not allow discomfort to bother her. If she did, she would be robbed of happiness.

"This hour, call it one. All that has gone before, forget it; wipe it out; it can hurt you no longer. All that will come, prepare to meet it."

Recitation of the sacred litany made Jocelyn feel better. So the Empress was not coming . . . she would have an enjoyable party anyway. Her guests would be happy, she would be happy. If Virginia Carroll chose to turn her back on proffered happiness, well, there was nothing Jocelyn could do about that.

Guests would be arriving in less than two hours, and there was still much to do. Lady Jocelyn turned off her privacy directive and turned to face the last few decisions before the party.

*   *   *

Five hours after she'd awakened, Lady Jocelyn felt ready for her party. As a final check she stood at the main holophone terminal and let her gaze roam through the closed-circuit links of Mansion Adelhardt.

The house soared two-thirds of a kilometer high, nearly scraping the Manhattan Dome. From top to bottom all was in readiness. Each room was cleaned, supplied with food and drink, and attended upon by some member of the army of autoservants. From the flier pad on the roof to the subterranean gardens, all was ready.

And here, in the vast multipurpose room, a table was set to rival any in the Galaxy. Crystal plates and dishes, finest silk cloths and napkins, silver and platinum utensils—the table was a riot of happy colors. Down the center of the long table ran Lady Jocelyn's most prized possession: a single candelabrum with a thousand branches, fashioned from a single piece of coral from the ocean of Promethia. Almost like a living thing it seemed, each of its arms holding a candle.

Jocelyn gave a command and the lights faded. Tiny, careful autoservants floated like fish among the coral branches, lighting candles as they went. Each tallow, lit, added its own light to the table, its own shadows to the dance that took form among the priceless tapestries that hung on the walls.

Her favorite tapestry was in the place of honor, hanging behind the table's head: bright medieval hunters chased a beautiful white beast through a fantasy forest. *The Hunt of the Unicorn* was over thirteen centuries old; yet, thanks to the tireless house autoservants, its colors were as brilliant today as the moment it had been stitched.

Jocelyn had first fallen in love with the three Unicorn Tapestries as a little girl, younger than Jassie. She'd seen them displayed in the ancient Cloisters Museum here in New York, and had badgered her grandfather as unmercifully as only a little girl could. Reproductions wouldn't do—even then Jocelyn had a taste for the finest things—and she would be content with nothing but the originals.

Only now, after much practice, did Jocelyn appreciate the subtle diplomacy that had made it possible for Lord Edward to acquire *The Hunt of the Unicorn*. Terra's museums, nearly destroyed by the bankruptcies of the twenty-first century, were always short of funds—but money was not enough. One must also soothe the egos of museum curators, calm the passions of boards of directors. There were ways . . . and Edward Lord Adelhardt was a master. So little Jocelyn had her beloved tapestries: one in her bedroom, one in the entry hall, and *this* one, the most beautiful of the three, in her dining room, where all her guests could admire it.

Jocelyn held her arms before her, slender and brown. From fingers, wrists, and shoulders came sparkling radiance, her diamonds throwing off gemfire like shooting stars. Ankle and hip, thigh and breast, Lady Jocelyn Adelhardt stood in a luminous corona of beauty.

She smiled. The party could begin now.

If only, Tenedden thought, it were not necessary for the Human Empire to pass in this fashion. If only it did not have to be torn apart from within like a body whose diseased defenses were turned against itself. He knew that the end of the Terran Empire did not mean the end of Human happiness in the Galaxy. He knew that the Terran Empire was ripe and ready to drop and that in the long run its demise would be healthier for all. But it was as painful a thing to watch as the laser-flash that saves a friend's life at the expense of a rotted limb.

Tenedden sighed. The Galaxy was embroiled in a struggle, of which the fall of the Terran Empire was only a footnote. It was characteristic of that struggle that much of beauty and worth must perish.

And, in this case at least, it was the job of Tenedden and his fellow Galactic Riders to diminish that perishing. Humankind had produced much that was artistic, much that was a worthy addition to the harmony of the Universal Song: paintings and sculpture and music that would otherwise end in the flames that would take Earth before too many days were over. Tenedden and the score of other Riders who approached Terra in their small ships would do their best to rescue those things that were greatest of Human achievement. Cultural coffers full, those ships would fly to Nephestal, where the Council of Free Peoples had set up the Museum of Worlds. And there, the treasures of Humanity would be stored and cared for until Humans would once again take them back and keep them from harm.

For every piece of art he saved, though, Tenedden knew that hundreds would burn. For every museum the Riders visited across the blue face of Terra, ten would collapse unmourned. Whatever the reasons, whatever the inevitability, the Sack of Terra would be a brutal thing.

The party was taking a dark turn. Jocelyn sat next to Doctor Khria, the Adelhardt Family's cyborg physician, and fretted. Right now the doctor was holding forth on the possibility of an escalation of the war. His deep voice boomed from audiocircuits and carried to the farthest listener.

"Anyone who examines the economics of the situation will quickly discover that the Patalanian Union cannot realistically increase their war efforts against the Empire. Patala is simply too poor to afford it. In the last fifteen years, the Union has doubled its volume by annexing the Transgeled—surely the poorest section of the Galaxy to begin with. The economy of Patala is now very near the breaking point."

"All the more reason for them to strike out against the Empire." Rog Fontino was a pompous fool who thought himself an adviser to Her Majesty. Jocelyn knew for a fact that Virginia Carroll never listened to the man. "If Patala can annex rich Imperial territories—Geled, for example—then they would be in much better shape."

This had gone far enough, Jocelyn decided. "Please, let's talk about something else."

Doctor Khria waved a waldo at her; she could swear he was shushing her. "My dear Fontino, Patala is finished. The top mathematical sociologists of the Empire agree—"

"Please—"

"Doctor Khria, mathematical sociology is a dead science, and has been since its failure to predict the attack at Karphos twenty years ago. I repeat, if Patala is doomed as you say, then they must be even more desperate to strike at Terra." Rog Fontino looked around hastily. "As a matter of fact, I have some informants who—"

"I think that is quite enough, Rog." In bright candlelight, Karl Loewenger looked both taller and massier than he was. His Imperial Navy dress gown, space-black with stunningly white rear-admiral stripes, combined with his clear, strong voice to shut Rog Fontino's mouth instantly. "Her Majesty's staff is well aware of any danger that Patala poses, and the Imperial Navy stands ready to counter any action. In the meantime, this is too depressing a subject to discuss at my Lady Jocelyn's dinner party; I will thank you to shift your conversation to another topic."

As Karl moved away, Jocelyn stood as if to run after him, then sat down in confusion. Karl had prevented an unpleasantness. Why, then, did she feel the beginning wispy fingers of concern?

Waving for more wine, she concentrated on Doctor Khria's tale of an exciting and tricky operation.

When a holophone call came for Karl, he excused himself from the table and went into another room, followed by a number of curious looks. Rog Fontino, only a handful of seats away from Jocelyn, turned to her and said rather too loudly, "Why has the Admiral left the table, my lady? Is there something we should know about?"

"I'm sure it's nothing," Jocelyn said, aware that her assurance sounded lame. Unvoiced tension ran up one side of her table and down the other. Guests stirred uncomfortably. So far, Jocelyn had done her best to squash all talk of war, sneak attacks, and other such depressing subjects, but she couldn't be everywhere. And now, far from enjoying her own party, she was trying to make sure things did not turn out uncomfortably for her guests.

Time to change the subject again. "Mayor Hua, while we're waiting for the next course, why don't you entertain us?" The Mayor of New York, it was well known, never went anywhere without his flute. He had performed often with the Imperial Symphony on New Sardinia, and Jocelyn knew that his music was captivating enough to make a good distraction—only the worst boor would talk while Hua was playing.

The mayor began playing, and Jocelyn's lapboard signaled a message for her. She leaned back in her chair and saw a tiny image of Karl Loewenger standing atop the board. His voice sounded in her left ear, from a miniature speaker in her earring.

"My lady, I must see you at once. In the entrance foyer."

Jocelyn smiled, nodded, and stood. Hostess's privilege—everyone else was stuck in their seats for the duration of the meal, unless they asked to be excused; Jocelyn could come and go under pretense of tending to the dinner.

She hurried to a dropshaft and bounced down fifteen stories to the entrance foyer. Karl stood on flagstones amid dwarf trees, fastening his dress cape.

"What is it?" she asked.

"I have to go. That call was from Terrad; all Earth-based ships are being scrambled."

"But why?"

He shook his head. "Patalanian ships have engaged our navy outside the orbit of Jupiter. Now, don't worry, Terrad is on it and reinforcements from Hafen have pretty well softened them up. I won't be going into combat; I have special duty at the palace."

Jocelyn felt a strange anger build within her. "On the night of my party—how dare they? I've been looking forward to this for months, and now it's all spoiled by . . . politics!"

Karl reached an arm around her shoulder, firm and supporting and smelling of musk. "Your party will turn out right, Jocelyn. I'll be back in a few hours. By that time I expect this will all be a roaring celebration of Imperial victory."

"No it won't. Everyone is so concerned about this stupid war, they'll all want to go home. Or worse yet, they'll turn on the holonews and we'll all have to watch it. Oh, *damn* the Empire."

He smoothed his hand over her forehead, brushing back her hair. "Hey, where are your Brandixian ideals now? Remember, you're not supposed to pay attention to problems. 'This hour, call it one . . .' "

She forced a smile. "You're right. I'm letting this bother me too much."

"That's the right attitude. Now I have to go; when I get back, I expect to see you happy." A quick kiss and then he was gone.

She bounded up the dropshaft to the mansion's highest level, a glass-walled penthouse that had once been her grandfather's office; now, all the furnishings carefully preserved, it was Lady Jocelyn's private shrine. Whenever she was in too much danger of losing perspective, whenever she failed to summon up the inner peace that every Brandixian should have, she came here.

Soft music and muted lights were a perfect background to the splendor of Manhattan spread out below. Jocelyn stood at the window, gazing uptown, and felt the peace of the city seeping into her soul. Neighboring buildings were great spires of light, reflected in the facets of the dome; more distant structures merged into a sea of close-packed stars that eddied around the massive, glowing edifice of the Imperial State Building. Under its dome, Jocelyn thought, the city resembled the galaxy that it ruled: the bright hub of government surrounded by lesser pinpoints of orbiting stars. Dark lanes—traffic routes, parks, and service areas—were like the dusky paths of dust that threaded through the galaxy's brightness.

New York, Jocelyn thought with pride, was the most magnificent city on Terra . . . the most magnificent in the Empire.

With the Brandixian litany on her lips and tranquillity in her heart, she turned back to her guests.

Half an hour later Karl's prediction seemed well on the way to fulfillment. Good food and splendid company, Jocelyn found, worked wonders to calm tension. From the depths of its tapes the house computer dug out happy songs to play; from the depths of the family wine cellars Jocelyn dug out three-century-old Euphratean port and sparkling champagne.

Again her lapboard signaled. A metallic voice spoke in Jocelyn's ear: "Her Majesty Virginia Carroll requests that all citizens attend to a bulletin to be transmitted in five minutes."

Ah, this would be the announcement of victory that Karl had anticipated; the party would pick up greatly in the euphoria of triumph. Via the lapboard Jocelyn signaled autoservants to prepare for a victory toast, told the computer to ready tapes of the Imperial anthem.

"Attention everyone! Her Majesty will address Terra." Jocelyn touched another switch and one wall of their room faded into a holoscreen.

Neutral gray sparkled and suddenly it was as if Her Majesty were in the room with them. Jocelyn noticed that Virginia was wearing, not the Spiral Crown of the Empire, but the hideously ostentatious Crown of Terra.

"Fellow Terrans," Virginia said, "the attack we have dreaded is come. It is with heavy heart that I must inform you that the Imperial Navy has been engaged with Patalanian battleships for almost half an hour as I speak to you.

"Terrad has fought strongly, and the Navy has acquitted itself well. Many citizens, both of Terra and of other worlds, have gone to the Ancestors today in glory. But their effort is not enough."

Consternation broke out at the table. In the screen, Karl Loewenger suddenly appeared, his back to Jocelyn. "We are ready, your Highness," he whispered.

Virginia Carroll turned to Jocelyn's guests. "Citizens, I must leave you. Patalanian ships will be above Earth in a few minutes; my advisers think it best that the Imperial Household withdraw to a safe location.

"This message has been recorded; when you hear it, I will be gone. Patala will be within striking distance of Earth. We shall leave half the fleet to protect Terra; the other half will withdraw to Laxus, where we will take up residence in the Octagon Palace. Know that our thoughts and prayers are with you and that Terra will not be given up without a fight."

Karl reached out a hand to Virginia, led her offscreen. The view broke up and died.

Pandemonium reigned around Lady Jocelyn's table. In candlelight she glimpsed Mayor Hua, his face pale and his hands quivering. Then the guests rose, flung excuses at her, and began departing.

Dimly, only half-aware, Jocelyn bade good-bye to fleeing guests, still trying to be the perfect hostess in a world gone mad.

"This hour, call it one . . ."

Alone suddenly in the vast dining hall, Jocelyn stared dumbly at her diamonds, spiracles of light dancing to each candle-flame. On the wall, a proud unicorn stumbled, confused, in trackless unfamiliar forest. Lost, she was lost. Where could she be?

Only after a few minutes did she realize that her lapboard was signaling an incoming call. Almost unaware of what she did, she keyed it onto the large holoscreen.

Karl's face, streaked with sweat and dirt, filled half the hall.

"Jocelyn, I'm sorry I couldn't warn you sooner, but Her Majesty put limits on communication until her ships are safely away from Terra. This is a recorded message, taped before I left.

"I know you'll be confused and upset by this. But you must do as I say—and do it at once. Get a ship and get off the planet. The Navy can't hold the Patalanians off forever, and most of our strength must go toward protecting Laxus. So get off-planet as soon as you can.

"I will find you, don't worry. I don't know how long I'll have to stay at Laxus, but no matter how long it is, I will come back to you. My love is with you."

The message started to repeat before Jocelyn came to her senses and switched it off. She had to find a way off-planet.

"Computer, prepare my private yacht for takeoff."

"Madam, your yacht is in for repair. I am informed by the repair shop that the yacht has been stolen. They have agreed to replace it as soon as a new one comes in."

"Then get me another ship."

"The family garage is empty. Maintenance supervisors have signed out all ships."

Jocelyn shook her head. "Let me see the planetary newschannel."

The screen flickered. Before Jocelyn was a scene from the center of Eisenhower Spaceport. The air was alive with starcraft, all swarming upward like so many migrating birds. The unemotional voice of a commentator droned, "Martial law has been declared but seems unenforceable. In panic, people steal anything that can fly and try to get into space with it. In a moment we'll switch to orbital cameras and get a look at the Earthspace picture."

"Turn it off."

Her yacht was stolen. No matter; she knew what to do. She had cousins on Leikeis, only five parsecs away. They would take her away from Earth. She punched the call into her lapboard and seconds later the screen lit up with the slender, dark face of her cousin Darlene.

"Darlene, this is Jocelyn on Earth. Can you please send someone to pick me up? I'm supposed to get away from here as soon as I can."

"Jocelyn, the news is full of Terra. They say you're under attack. Is it terribly exciting? You must tell me all about it."

"You don't understand." Without warning, the screen went blank. Jocelyn punched buttons, but nothing happened. Then the seal of Imperial Centcom appeared in three dimensions and brilliant color, and a voice said, "Imperial Centcom regrets that all service to Terra has been suspended. Service will be resumed as soon as possible. You will not be charged for any interrupted calls. Imperial Centcom regrets that spacegram service to Terra has been suspended for the duration. For information regarding space mail rates, please call the Terran Post Office. Thank you."

Service suspended? Then things were getting really bad. Then . . . the Patalanians might be winning. What would they do? Would they land? Would they loot the city, the world? Would they take prisoners?

What was to become of Jocelyn?

Her first tear was like the first tiny crack in a dam. After it worked its way through, more followed, and Jocelyn bent her head and wept.

Tenedden slipped past both Patalanian attackers and Imperial defenders without much trouble. The concern was for wings and phalanxes of ships, not for single vessels. He anticipated trouble with Terra's ground-based heavy laser cannon, but they could be dodged. Galactic Riders were trained for this sort of thing, and Tenedden was one of the best. That was why he had taken this mission.

His computer-drawn map directed him to the eastern coast of the smaller continent in the northern hemisphere; his ship located the city that was his first goal, and dropped into landing trajectory.

How long? Minutes . . . hours? Lady Jocelyn didn't feel a part of the world as she strolled through Mansion Adelhardt. She felt like some visiting figure in a holoshow, a spirit from across space.

How long until the Patalanian Navy broke through and descended to Terra? How long until flames leapt upward toward the stars, until bombs exploded, until people died by the thousands?

Filled with an intense morbid curiosity, Jocelyn made her way to a compterminal and demanded the last few State of the Empire Reports. She looked at stories concerning meetings of the Patalanian Presidium, and was horrified by the words flowing across the screen.

President Masilek had sworn to destroy Terra if ever he got his hands on the world. And the people had cheered him. Cheered!

The door buzzer pulled Jocelyn away from Masilek's threats. She tidied her hair and sent her holographic image by closed-circuit to the entrance foyer. Rog Fontino and a number of others stood in the lobby, wide-eyed and dirt-streaked.

"Oh, dear, what's wrong?" Although she *knew* what was wrong, knew to the depths of her soul that things were wrong and would never again be right, Lady Jocelyn couldn't help taking up the role of convivial hostess.

"My lady, we are unable to leave the planet. This is to be our last night of life, and we do not wish to spend it among the rabble that fills the streets."

From behind Rog, another of Jocelyn's erstwhile guests pushed forward, a woman in a gown sequined with sapphires, a few strands of hair out of place in her stylish coiffure. "My good Lady Jocelyn, we are civilized people. This may be the death of civilization. We want to spend our last night in celebration. When the Patalanian troops come to destroy us, let us show them that we are true citizens of the Empire: let us perish with a goblet in our hands and a song on our lips."

There was applause; Jocelyn herself was stirred. Before today, she knew, she would have totally agreed, would have run to snatch a few more seconds of the good life before it vanished forever.

If only she weren't so confused. If only she could wipe out this unpleasantness, as she'd wiped out so many others.

Her guests were waiting for her answer, and some inner sense of duty rescued her from uncomfortable thoughts. "Of course, I will be glad to celebrate with you. We will show them of what we are made."

And what *are* we made of? Is it all dance and wine and music?

Her guests scrambled for the dropshaft, and seconds later they swarmed into the dining room in candlelight and jewel-flash.

The planetary news played on the large holoscreen while Jocelyn's guests amused themselves. Try as she might, Jocelyn could not forget her predicament, could not keep her eyes from the screen. If only she could forget . . .

"This hour, call it one. All that has gone before, forget it, cancel it, wipe it out."

But I can't wipe it out. It exists, exists as horribly as those black ships descending from the sky. It can't be wiped away; I can't pretend that it doesn't matter.

The holoscreen collapsed to darkness, Jocelyn's lapboard went dead, the music ground to a halt, and from the candlelit dining room there was suddenly a scream. All over Mansion Adelhardt, mechs and autoservants hit the floor and rolled, lifeless.

"What's happened? What's going on?" Jocelyn felt the claws of panic settle around her neck. If the candles weren't lit, it would be dark . . . dark and dead in the middle of a dying city.

Rog Fontino made his voice heard. "The sunpower stations have been knocked out. Somewhere there should be fusion reactors as backup. They should be activated soon."

Jocelyn pulled her arms tight around her body. The first time in centuries that New York was without power. She hated to think what would be going on out there. All over the city—all over the world—dropshafts would fail and people would fall to mangled deaths. Transport, heating and refrigeration, computers, lights . . . all gone.

And gone with them, the automatic defenses of Mansion Adelhardt. With that realization, Jocelyn felt the last bit of security fly from her.

With a startling flash the holoscreen came back on and muted music started up again where it had stopped. Jocelyn's lapboard lit up with a dozen damage alarms that somehow weren't important now. Her senses were glued to the official-looking man in the holoscreen.

"Those areas of the planet with backup fusion reactors and alternate energy supplies should be going on backup systems right now. Citizens are urged not to use more energy than is necessary, since backup systems are not as reliable as sunpower units."

As if it could matter, Jocelyn thought, now or ever. Just the same, she played her fingers over the lapboard and deactivated two-thirds of the autoservants, cut lights all over the mansion.

The defenses, however, she kept up.

Wailing and screaming had stopped, but still the party was not back on its feet. Suddenly the woman who had spoken in the entrance foyer poured herself a goblet of wine and laughed heartily. The laugh was taken up by the other guests in a desperate fashion.

Rog Fontino made his way to Lady Jocelyn's side. "My lady, I hesitate to mention this in front of the others, but perhaps it would be a good idea to locate any weapons that you might have here. Just in case."

Jocelyn, feeling oddly competent, queried the computer for the location of her brother William's hunting lasers. With Rog's help, she instructed autoservants to bring the guns up to the dining level and stack them in an adjacent room.

What to do? Jocelyn felt like a spider among the fronds of an aquarium. She was imprisoned in a tiny bubble, and outside was an environment that would kill her. In her case, the bubble was an area of light only as large as her dining hall, and outside was the darkness and chaos of a world gone mad.

Planetary newschannel was off the air; there was nothing to see in the holoscreen but gray splashed with flecks of color and the reflections of scores of candle-flames. Her beloved unicorn was only a faltering step ahead of the cruel hunters. Jocelyn watched the lights dance and twist, listened to the drunken laughter around her, and tried to bring things into some sort of balance.

Brandixian philosophy told her that the world was all a minutely-detailed construct of her mind and the minds around her. All this: the Patalanian attack, the despair and confusion, this was all unpleasantness, illusion imposed upon her world-view. If everyone agreed to disbelieve, all unpleasantness would vanish.

But the Patalanians would not agree.

Aware of the clinging, suffocating dark and yet unable to do anything but hold to the last light of burning wicks, Jocelyn did not know how to await death.

And the lapboard signaled her. Why couldn't it leave her alone? Maybe if she could marshal her thoughts, she could yet make the final effort to disbelieve and dispel this chaos. Maybe if she could only have silence and concentration, the sun would rise on a joyful world rather than blackened stumps.

Someone was trying to enter the mansion.

Jocelyn sent a holoimage of herself to the front door, now locked and barred by house security. Outside, the street was darkened. At the door was a tiny, frail woman dressed all in dark blue. Around her neck was the stylized cross bearing a woman's face: the symbol of the worshippers of the goddess Meletia.

"Thank the goddess you're still alive," the woman said. "Many houses on this street are deserted."

"Who are you?"

"Sister Karin Theresa of the Sisters of Mercy. It is not good for you to stay in the towers. They will be demolished soon. We ask people to come with us, to find shelter."

By now two or three of Jocelyn's guests were interested, and they gathered behind her to look at Sister Karin's tiny figure.

"Shelter? Where?"

"Deep in the subway tunnels, the ancient fallout shelters and underground refuges. There is at least a hope of survival."

Jocelyn looked around the dining room. The candles burned warmly, her diamonds sparkled reassuringly. All was familiar, and familiar meant safe.

No more.

Rog Fontino moved forward. "We will come, Sister. There are eighteen of us."

"Come quickly. If you have food, bring as much as you are able. And weapons, if you have them."

Jocelyn allowed Rog Fontino to guide her in summoning autoservants to bring packaged food from the kitchen.

A laser rifle was thrust into her hands; she held it loosely and stepped into the dropshaft, descended twenty stories until she reached ground level. There, she fumbled with a laser-pulse key that opened the doors, and followed Sister Karin and the others out into the street.

Cobblestone, brick, macadam, or concrete, the streets of New York were widely considered anachronisms. Other parts of the East Coast Metropolitan Corridor—Boston, Richmond, Baltimore—had centuries ago torn up and built over their streets, and now made do with pedestrian walkways, subways, and skybuses.

New York had a character all her own. So many of her streets were famous Galaxy-wide for their part in the culture and history of the race: Wall Street, Fifth Avenue, Broadway, Christopher Street, hundreds of others. More than thoroughfares, they were museums and monuments to the past.

Jocelyn wondered why she had never really seen the streets before. Oh, most of her life she had commuted in fliers or, at worst, on the subway—but still, like any New Yorker, she had spent a good deal of time walking in the city. And it was not until tonight, with streetlights out and every shadow a threatening presence, that she had seen the streets.

The ingenious, curious pattern of drainage grids caught her eyes. Had she been designing the city, she would never in a million lifetimes have thought of providing for disposal of the rainwater that was sprinkled from the dome every other Tuesday to clean the city. Where did the water go, she wondered, after it went down those grates? Did it eventually wind up in the river, or was there some central recycling plant? How about the dirt that went along with the water?

Sister Karin led the way to a nearby subway station, and they all walked two abreast down a ramp worn by the passage of millions of feet. And they entered another world.

Here, at least, there was light. Emergency lighting, garish white, had probably not been lit for centuries—and yet it burned.

She'd never liked the tunnels. No matter how mechs polished, there was still grime, grit, and dirt in the subways. No matter how often old tiles were torn off and replaced by new, someone always managed to scrawl graffiti on them.

Still they went down. Long ago, a frightened populace during the first century of interstellar exploration had feared war, and had put their energies to building shelters. Lady Jocelyn remembered reading that there were hundreds of kilometers of shelter tunnels and caverns, some contiguous with the subways and some even lower. Apparently Sister Karin was taking them to one of the lowest shelters.

The ground trembled briefly. Sister Karin looked back, her face streaked with sweat and her eyes hidden by dark shadows. "The Patalanians have arrived. The domes will have been cracked. Soon buildings will start to fall."

Again Jocelyn was suddenly made aware of the nightmare in which she moved, and wished desperately that she could close her eyes and make it all go away. She stood still, shut her eyes, and with all the willpower at her command she believed as hard as she possibly could.

The ground shook again beneath her feet, and the person behind her bumped into her urgently. Sighing, she kept moving, deeper into the earth.

Never before had Jocelyn seen so many people. There were thousands. They must have come from all over the city. She marveled at the organization of the Sisters of Mercy.

Right now, Sister Karin had pressed Jocelyn into service feeding rations to children. Most of the kids didn't want to eat; they were uncomfortable and wanted to go home. Many had lost parents and crèche-keepers. But if they didn't eat now, Sister explained, food would spoil.

Power was gone, only candles and self-powered floodlights remained. Food storage and preservation units were out, mechs and autoservants lifeless hulks. The Patalanians had destroyed fusion plants, and now New York had nothing.

Nothing but the character of her people.

Jocelyn bounced a baby girl on her lap and tricked her into eating a mouthful by pretending the spoon was a diving starship. She thought of Jassie . . . but the thought didn't hurt. She had never really known her daughter well enough to miss her.

The next child in line wanted even less to eat. Jocelyn handed the youngster a diamond torn from her bracelet. The infant cooed with delight and allowed Jocelyn to ram fully ten spoonsful down his throat before spitting the last one back at her.

It was only later, when she rested and listened to the dull rumblings that penetrated the shelter's airtight walls, that Jocelyn felt restless and went to find Sister Karin. The old woman was ministering to the wounded.

She took Jocelyn to a corner between supply boxes. "What can I do for you, Jocelyn?"

"Sister, most of the people in this shelter won't live to see the end of the week. We have food that's spoiling rapidly, it's death to go outside, and everything we know is torn apart above us. And yet . . ." It sounded so silly, so criminal, that Jocelyn hesitated.

"And yet . . . ?"

"Well, I feel that I'm alive for the very first time since I was born. Is that wrong?"

"You were a disciple of Brandix?"

"Yes. But I—I don't think I am any longer."

"I should not criticize other religions. The teachings of the Brandixians have brought happiness to many people. But I wonder about the worth of this happiness. Disciples of Brandix are very good people, but they are not artists, or saints, or even devils."

"I think I see what you mean. For the first time in my life I'm uncomfortable, and I can't make discomfort go away. And suddenly I remember what it's like to be comfortable, and it . . . it means more to me now. I've seen the underside of life, the dirty tunnels and the darkness, and so the sight of a flower or a diamond means more than it ever could before."

"I think you are right, Jocelyn." Sister Karin leaned over Jocelyn, kissed her gently on the forehead. "What will you do with your new-found life?"

Lady Jocelyn Adelhardt looked around herself. "Sister, I can't stay here. You *can*, you've lived life the whole time, you've faced everything that bothered you. I haven't. I've always been running away from things I didn't like."

"Jocelyn, child, the tunnels offer some hope of survival. And after, we can build Earth anew. You know that the Empress has moved the capital to Laxus."

"It hadn't dawned on me. But you're right: she'll never be back."

"You mustn't sound glum. Now Earth is out from under the spotlight. For the first time in history, Earth is no longer the trend-setter for the Galaxy. We can build any type of civilization we want now, without having a thousand planets look over our shoulders."

"With all our cities destroyed, all order wiped out, we can rebuild a civilization?"

Very softly, Sister answered, "You mustn't confuse order with civilization. Often the two are utterly different.

"Jocelyn," Sister Karin continued, "this city is unique on Earth. Diversity, vitality, call it what you will: there are half a billion people on Terra, and ten million of them live under our domes. Old Earth boasted over two hundred languages and a thousand distinct cultures. Now you can travel around the globe and outside the pre-tech enclaves, you'll hear only Anglich, and Imperial is the only culture you'll meet." She patted the dirty concrete floor. "Except in New York. Old Earth's cultures and languages survive here." She shrugged. "If we're to rebuild civilization, we're going to need all that diversity. We're going to need the talents of every person."

From far above, there came another muted roar. Jocelyn nodded. "Thank you, Sister. But I can't stay. I'd like to help build the new world, and maybe I will. But before I'm able to do that, I have to build myself. And there are some things I have to face before I can accomplish that task."

"As you will. You can at least stay the night?"

"The night is almost over. I'd like to see the sunrise . . . for the first time."

Sister Karin pulled herself to her feet, accompanied Jocelyn to an airlock. Then the old sister gave Jocelyn a hug. "This tunnel will take you to the subways. From there you can go up by the ramps and stairs. If—if you are asked for, what shall I say?"

"Tell them that Lady Jocelyn Adelhardt is dead. She is—at least, the one who existed before tonight."

Sister Karin bowed her head, and Jocelyn entered the airlock. The door shut firmly behind her.

Mansion Adelhardt still stood. It was oddly untouched,

the door still open where Jocelyn had forgotten to close it behind herself.

She went in, found the emergency stairs. It was an exhausting climb, alone in the dark, but Jocelyn didn't mind. She was getting to know herself, and even the feeling of tension in her calves was welcome.

There was still food on the dinner table. The candles still burned, most of them. She remembered that they were tiny oil lamps and that they would stay lit for days. Her lapboard was on the table where she'd discarded it, chairs still sat where they'd fallen before china and crystal place settings. Then terror seized Jocelyn by the throat and she reached for the table to steady herself.

The Unicorn Tapestry . . . the Unicorn Tapestry was missing. Bare plaster gleamed starkly where it had hung.

She had thought herself beyond emotion, all feeling burned out of her by the night's fires. Jocelyn was surprised to find herself outraged at this thievery. Anything else, but not the tapestry, not the one thing in this mansion that she'd truly loved.

Angrily she burst through a door to the adjoining kitchens. Autoservants lay awkwardly here and there, indistinct shadowed shapes in the weak light from the dining room. At once Jocelyn knew she was not alone; then from the dimness emerged a squat, dwarflike creature, barely more than a meter tall. It was clothed in what appeared to be a uniform, and its parts—arms, legs, head—were roughly humanoid. Still, there was no danger of believing the thing Human: its misshapen head was too large in proportion to the body, and it sprouted two great ears as well as two large, limpid eyes and a tiny, leathery mouth.

The creature was struggling with a mass of fabric, which Jocelyn recognized as her tapestry.

Jocelyn squared her shoulders despite her desire to run. "W-who are you?" Stupid, why should it recognize Anglich speech?

The creature let the tapestry fall and spread its stumpy arms, its hands held forth with palms up. "I am Tededden of the Karessai Helyarren Teshra." His speech was heavily accented, but Jocelyn could understand him. "Forgive me, I thought this building deserted."

"What are you doing with that?" She gestured to the heavy tapestry.

The creature—Tenedden? What sort of name was that? —cocked his head. "My mission is to preserve. The fine art of your folk. This is the center section of *The Hunt of the Unicorn*, no?"

"Yes." Her long climb in the dark, the undisturbed stillness of the table . . . Jocelyn wondered if she were dreaming, lost in some unreal nightmare while the city fell about her. She put her hands on her hips. "That's *mine*."

"Ah, you are"—he glanced at a wristband—"Lady Jocelyn Adelhardt, the mistress of this house."

"I am. And that tapestry doesn't belong to you. It belongs to *me*."

Tenedden stepped back. "It belongs to you? What will you do with your tapestry, Lady Jocelyn Adelhardt?"

"I . . ." What? Suddenly, Jocelyn saw herself as if from outside her body: a sad, foolish woman clinging to the last empty symbol of a vanished life. Clarity of vision struck her with almost physical force, and she could do nothing but laugh.

"Nothing," she replied. "It's not mine, really. I was just taking care of it."

"I promise you, I shall convey it to those who can care for it far better than any on this world. Your tapestry will be cherished through the ages, Lady Jocelyn Adelhardt."

She nodded. "Take it, then, with my blessing."

For a moment nothing more was said. Woman and creature simply stood, staring at each other, sharing something that neither completely comprehended.

Then Jocelyn whispered, "Are there many of you?"

"Too few," Tenedden replied. Then, kindness evident even through his strange accent, "We cannot take passengers. There is no place for—"

"Refugees? No, I didn't expect there would be." Jocelyn's weariness suddenly caught up with her, and she steadied herself against a table. She forced a smile. "I know what you're doing. You're saving that which is the best of us. Thank you."

Tenedden lowered his eyes. "The best is within you," he said simply. "I must depart before sunrise, and I still have much to do."

"So do I."

"My ship waits outside this portal." He pointed to an access door that led to a long-unused balcony.

"Let me help you." Though her arms ached and her feet were like lead, she lifted an end of the tapestry. Tenedden took the other end and led the way to where his ship floated in the black night. "The other two sections—"

He stopped her. "I have not room. They are yours yet, Lady Jocelyn. Keep them safe. Keep them as a reminder." He touched her hand, his skin cold and dry. Then the ship closed around him, and before she could move, it was gone, lost in distant smoke and cloud. Jocelyn felt her cheeks, and they were wet. No matter, she had reason to cry.

She moved back into the dining room. The table waited, lit by flickering candles; other tapestries stared at her from the walls. The room was like a dream, a dream that waited for her to return to its stifling, comforting security.

No longer. Her diamonds flared in brilliant splendor, arcing through the air to land amid branches of coral. A lust seized her. Delicate branches of the candelabrum broke in her hands, shattered against the wall. Oil, spilling, set tapestries afire, until the whole room blazed like a pyre.

Like the pure flames of dawn.

She left Mansion Adelhardt behind, fire showing through upper windows, and stumbled off down the streets. She wore the two remaining sections of the tapestries like a noblewoman's cape.

Smiling through her tears, Jocelyn stopped at a corner flowerbox, removed a white lily, and sniffed at it, and then headed for the river with the blossom in her hand.

Tenedden left Earth behind with sunfire just bursting over the eastern limb. Again his piloting skill and tunable antigrav got him past the Imperial cordon with no trouble.

Every now and again, as his ship drove on toward Nephestal, he looked back at the tapestry that occupied a place of honor in his cabin. Tenedden was no expert on Terran life-forms, so he didn't know if the animal pictured was reality or legend . . . but he did know it was great art.

And this was why Terra had to perish, why the Human Empire had to fall. He finally understood, and felt no more guilt. Only sadness.

Terra and the Empire had made life too easy for Humans. And no one could have created *The Hunt of the Unicorn*, who had not felt pain as well as pleasure, who had not felt hunger and cold.

At least, Tenedden thought, we have managed to save this . . . this and a myriad other works produced by this great, tragic people before they tamed the galaxy.

And later, when Humans—perhaps even the same sad, tragic Lady Jocelyn Adelhardt whom he'd met in that darkened tower—when they produced more art, wrung from the passion of this time; when they had suffered and passed from the height of Galactic domination—then the Galactic Riders would return *The Hunt of the Unicorn* to Terra, and Humans would possess it once more.

Glad that he could weep, Tenedden activated his ultrawave and requested landing orders from Nephestal.

The fight had been a hard one and the cost was great, but at last Karl Loewenger stood on a Terra once more free of Patalanian domination. His ship waited above him, the last of the Imperial flotilla, which had already withdrawn to Laxus. Sooner or later, when enough survivors came of age, Terra would have her Home Guard back. Until then, Imperial scouts would check her daily and a battleship would make monthly visits. Now it was time for the Fleet to return to the business of defending a crumbling Empire.

But first, Karl had unfinished business of his own.

Life sensors assured him that there was no one alive in the burned-out wreckage of Mansion Adelhardt. But he had to be sure, for corpses did not register. And he'd promised to return to her.

The dining hall was largely intact. Karl found what he wanted among the blackened stumps of Promethian coral: a diamond brooch that bore the emerald-eyed wolf's head of House Adelhardt. Jocelyn had worn it a thousand times—including that last night.

Karl shook his head. It would take too long to search for bones, if they'd be identifiable. He slipped the brooch

in his bag. Thank the Gods she didn't live, he thought.
She could never have managed.

He bowed his head for a second. Brandix, whatever
and wherever you are take care of her. Then he departed.

From the street below, a dirty woman watched the
I-class imperial battleship sail away from Mansion Adelhardt, drifting like smoke in the steady breeze. It would
be going to Dunsinane, she guessed, to inform the next
of kin.

It would have been so easy to stop the ship. A wave, a
shout, and they would have investigated. Karl would do
no less.

Jocelyn, once Lady Adelhardt, shrugged and turned
back to the subway entrance. There was a new city to
build, and no time to waste recalling dream-lives from
the past.

*Don Sakers was launched the same month as
Sputnik 1, so it was inevitable that he should become a science-fiction writer. His work has appeared
in leading genre magazines (Analog, Amazing, Fantasy Book) and twice he has had short stories included in Donald A. Wollheim's Annual World's Best
SF volumes. His novel The Leaves of October was a
nominee for the Baltimore Science Fiction Society's
Compton Crook Award for best first sf novel of 1988.*

*Don lives in a suburban Baltimore apartment, nick-
named "Don's Acres," with his companion of many
years, Thomas Atkinson. His household also contains three computers (Alan Turing, Christopher
Morcom, and The Giant Space Amiga), a pseudo-
fish named Ghoti, over five thousand books and
magazines, and absolutely no cats.*

In The Good Old Summer Time

by B. W. Clough

As has been told in other stories here, New Yorkers take a fierce and stubborn pride in their city, no matter what its flaws. Even a runaway greenhouse effect that destroys civilization as we know it may not be enough to change that.

The titles riffled through his brain whenever the rains slacked off farther inland. Then the shallow sandy waterhole would go brackish and the edge of craziness crept closer. Sultan of Baghdad-on-the-Subway was his favorite. He also liked "proud inheritor of the mantle of Donald Trump."

But when the water grew sweet again, his head steadied wonderfully and he knew his name. On those days he toured his domain, sandals flapping, Broadway-show songs buzzing tunelessly in his throat. It was a combined police patrol and scavenger hunt. Whenever anything edible washed up on the beach, he dined: a crippled sea gull, some gritty clams, dead fish. The rest of the time he kept an eye out for muggers, graffiti artists, and people ripping dashboard tape decks out of cars.

One day he topped a sand dune south of Rockefeller Center and got a nasty jolt. A neat little settlement had sprung up since he last came up Fifth Avenue: air-conditioned bubble tents, two sleek new desert trucks, stacks of supplies. Mylar solar collectors were staked out along the slope, uphill from where the rusty steel beams stuck out of the sand. A crew of archaeologists scraped at a precise square-sided hole beside an ancient cement slab.

"What the hell is this!" Enraged, he half-fell down the sandy slope and put a foot through one of the collectors.

"You don't have no excavation permit! I bet you didn't even pay the toll at the Holland Tunnel!" He kicked the flimsy mylar away and bared his yellow teeth.

The newcomers conferred together in some foreign language before a spokeswoman stepped forward. "Good morning," she fluted. "We are a research expedition from Gobi State University, in Mongolia. I am Dr. Tendal, specializing in archaic western dialect. We have papers from the authorities in Morgantown."

"The devil with that! You don't have papers from me!"

"Ah! I beg your pardon, I do not know your name."

He thumped his chest so hard that a puff of dust rose from his ragged jacket front. "Fiorello La Guardia. Mayor of New York."

The wind shifted, bringing with it a whiff of salty air from the shallow salt flats of the Upper East Side. This time the high-speed clatter of Japanese, or whatever it was, went on for a while. Someone consulted his portable computer terminal, and the junior team members drifted away to their careful digging again. Finally Dr. Tendal turned to him. "Our profound apologies, Mr. Mayor. We will be happy to pay any fines and fees, within reason. What money is current here?"

"In New York it's the subway token," he said, very huffy. "I'll bet you hicks don't have any."

"We have only Appalachian dollars and Panasian yuan," she said. "Perhaps you will accept payment in kind."

"Kind of what?"

Dr. Tendal smiled. "Perhaps some freeze-dried noodles, or candy . . ."

"Trying to grease a municipal official, huh?" he yelled. "Dammit, I'll have you know this is a clean town!" Furious, he shambled away along the slope. The Asians had to consult the computer's archaic slang listing to learn what he was talking about.

He wandered around Tribeca for several days, muttering evilly and slashing at drooping marsh grasses, before he went back. Of course they were still there. This time Dr. Tendal only nodded and smiled at his invective as she unwrapped a rice candy bar. The gluey sweet brown grains stuck to his teeth in a very foreign way. He forgot all about the excavation permits. "A restaurant, right? You're going to build a Chinese restaurant."

"You might say that, Mr. Mayor," Dr. Tendal said politely. She sat in the shade cast by the light awning that kept the sleeping tents cool, but he paced and fidgeted in and out of the shadow.

"You should go to Chinatown, down that way. They only build the tall skyscrapers here and on Wall Street, 'cause that's where the bedrock is."

She raised an eyebrow, surprised. "We know that. But I wonder where you learned it?"

"So maybe Mott Street is better for a restaurant. Lemme pull a few strings at the Chinatown Benevolent Association for ya—maybe there's a vacant storefront."

"You do that, Mr. Mayor." He shambled off into the brassy noon sunshine on the errand. Dr. Tendal gazed after him, speculating.

When he was out of sight Prof. Singh approached, a tall plump figure, and spoke in Asiatic. "You know it may not be a kindness to feed the old kook, Hsu-peh. Remember what is said about wild birds. Once they grow to rely on bird seed, they starve when you stop giving it out."

Dr. Tendal sighed. "I could wish my charity is disinterested, Nolan, but it isn't. Of course he's crazed, living here alone. But the old man knows things about the ancient city."

"Perhaps he's a derelict scholar from some other research expedition," Prof. Singh suggested.

"No, it may be more interesting." Dr. Tendal leaned forward. "Maybe he's found something, an old library or newspaper archive."

"Documents? After a thousand years of immersion?" Prof. Singh's dark eyes glowed with a genuine thirst for knowledge. "Talk to him about it, Hsu-peh! If you can get a sense of the parameters of his knowledge—"

"Let me gain his confidence a little and we'll see." Dr. Tendal gazed out across the dunes, where the heat shimmered like silk in the air. At home, in the lush wheatfields of Central Asia, no one went hungry or homeless, and she felt unsure of what would be best to do. "To feed a hungry man," she said, "cannot be quite wrong."

In a very short time, without being much aware of it, La Guardia was spending most of his day midtown, near the site. Dr. Tendal listened with flattering interest to his complaints about the traffic and the garbage collectors' strike. She even took notes. Since he did not speak Asiatic, she was able to consult Prof. Singh freely.

"What do you think?" she asked him after translating the latest of the mayor's grumbles.

"Ask him whether he reads anything," Prof. Singh suggested.

"Only the tabloids," the mayor said when the question was put to him. "The *Times*'d be a perfect paper, but it doesn't have the funnies. Or you mean maybe magazines?"

"Yes, magazines," Dr. Tendal said. "Where do you read them?"

"Down at the main public library: Forty-second and Fifth. O' course you got to watch it these days. That park behind the library used to be so nice. Now it's so fulla winos and street people, you can't hardly sit on a bench anymore."

"Can you take us there?"

"Sure, it's only six blocks."

"We can take one of the trucks," Prof. Singh said eagerly.

The mayor enjoyed the ride hugely, yelling directions and bouncing up and down on the seat like a child. Dr. Tendal hunched over the glowing screen on the dashboard. The coast here was salt marsh, coarse tufts of rank grass struggling in the briny shallows. No ruins could be seen; the sea had reclaimed everything. But the truck's computers were programmed with the ancient maps, so that the screen could display the sites they were passing.

When the truck lurched to a halt, Dr. Tendal said, "This is indeed the right location—Fifth Avenue and Forty-second Street."

Prof. Singh said, "We can cross-check it with the ultrasound." His hand moved over the controls, and a new display flicked up onto the screen, dimly revealing what lay hidden directly beneath the truck: layers of sand and silt, anonymous blocks of stone, a straggle of pipes and plastic conduits, half a subway car. "There's no library here," he exclaimed, unable to hide his disappointment.

"Sure there is, lookit the stone lions." The mayor pointed at a clump of brush. Dr. Tendal caught her colleague's eye and tapped her forehead. Prof. Singh sighed and said no more.

When they got back to camp, she made a proposal. "Suppose we fix him up, restore his reason. Then we could get a real answer, instead of this moon mist and daydreaming."

"You do have the most original ideas," Prof. Singh said. "But is it possible? Should we not consult a specialist, a mental doctor?"

"This dig is on a budget, Nolan. It wouldn't be anything major, just one of the standard over-the-counter psychotropic drugs. I could have one included in our next supply shipment."

"And, if all went well, we could give him a ride back to civilization when we close the dig for the season," Prof. Singh mused. "It might be the best thing that ever happened to the old man, if he's nothing but a castaway from Appalachia."

"Heaven knows how he survives here in the wet season," Dr. Tendal said. "Since we can see a way to assist him, I think it's our duty to do so."

"We might genuinely do him good," Prof. Singh conceded.

"That's the ticket," Dr. Tendal said. "I'll radio out the order today."

The drug arrived and Dr. Tendal dissolved the doses in cupfuls of sweetened tea. Well accustomed to Oriental foods now, La Guardia never noticed the medicinal flavor. The directions on the pill packet promised some effect in seven days. Dr. Tendal waited with quiet interest.

Like a thousand shining spears the dawn pierced La Guardia's head. He groaned and rolled over to a sitting position. For the first time in memory he had a headache, and he didn't like it.

Something seemed wrong about his little cave between two slabs of eroded concrete. "This isn't Gracie Mansion," he said aloud. He crept out into a land that looked foreign but felt familiar. His feet automatically took him to the shallow water hole. He stared at the silty puddle for a long moment and then went on without drinking.

The awful loneliness of the empty country gave him

the creeps. He shuffled along, faster and faster, his heart pounding. He would have given his right arm to see a cop, or a hooker, or even a mugger. Somewhere among the dunes was something familiar and important that he had lost. But he couldn't remember what it looked like, and so he had to peer across the wasteland and around the stubs of skyscrapers like a lost dog.

After hours of stricken stumbling he chanced upon the dig. The relief was so great he almost sobbed as he tumbled down the slope into the camp. The digging team immediately saw that something was wrong, and sent for Dr. Tendal.

When she hurried up, he was sitting where they had put him, in the shade of an awning. A fine tremor shook him, as if his engine were set too high. Dr. Tendal hid her excitement and spoke quietly. "Would you mind telling me your name?"

"Mayor La Guardia, o' course," he said distractedly.

She clicked her tongue in annoyance. Perhaps his condition really did call for professional attention. "And how do you feel today? Something has distressed you."

"What's happened to the city? Where's New York?"

"This is the site," Dr. Tendal said with exemplary patience. "When the sea level rose during the greenhouse heating phase, the city was drowned, a modern Atlantis. In the dry season, however, it is quite safe to visit now."

He stared blankly, without seeming to understand, and she hastened to speak of more cheerful things. "Life here during the monsoons must be very hard. We thought you might wish to return with us to the mainland. You must have friends or relatives in Appalachia or Canada. You would not be so lonely there."

The mayor said, "Lonely. Was I? Not until recently."

"We brought you back to reality," Dr. Tendal said. "These pills are wonderful. You must keep up with them, and see if you do not feel better every day." She pushed the medicine package into his hand, and smiled. "Now you are set to rights, you will be happy."

"I was happy." His hand shook, but he upturned the packet. The little white pills sifted out onto the sand. Dr. Tendal exclaimed with irritation and crouched to pick them carefully up. When she rose from her knees, he was gone, back to the bright lights.

My daughter is a five-year-old dinosaur fan. Her current imaginary country is called Dino Land, and I undertook to write a story to take us there. It was obvious that all of Dino Land's essential features (hot weather, the Gulf of Mexico extending to Kansas, and so on) could be nicely resurrected with the help of a runaway greenhouse effect, which would raise the sea level and trash the weather patterns. At this point Lawrence Watt-Evans suggested a future New York City as a destination. Luckily all the stegosaurs and triceratops didn't insist on coming along for the ride this time around.

I have written four novels, the latest of which is The Name of the Sun. My numerous extended family lives in New York, and it is my second home.

—B. W. Clough

Afterword

by Eric S. Johansson

My original guidelines for contributors said the stories could be set anywhere from tomorrow to the end of time; well, this one's at the end of time, and that's about all I can tell you. It's the author's first sale.

The universe was dying. Galaxies flickered out, leaving only darkness and dust. Mankind was dying with the universe, and nothing could be done to stop it.

By a fluke (or divine intervention) the last human alive was to be found in New York. The city had died with the universe; its bright lights had finally gone dim.

The echoes of his footsteps followed him to the edge of Central Park. Looking up, he could just see the dull red glow of the last star in the sky.

A gun nudged him in the small of his back. "Gimme your wallet, buddy," said a voice.

Then the last star winked out.

Eric S. Johansson does not live in New York. Now you know why.

The Making of *Newer York*

At first I thought that I'd invented the name *Newer York* myself, but it's been pointed out to me that I almost certainly remembered it instead, from Philip K. Dick's novel *The Man Who Japed*, which I read and adored long ago. More people should read Philip Dick's work. It's good for you.

I want to thank D. Alexander Smith for telling me about the "Future Boston" project, which helped convince me that this anthology might work out.

I was convinced to include fantasy, as well as science fiction, in this book by three novels: *The War for the Oaks,* by Emma Bull, which is set in Minneapolis, rather than New York, but has a wonderful sense of place; *New York by Knight,* by Esther Friesner, which demonstrates that high fantasy can work in our New York; and *Stalking the Unicorn,* by Mike Resnick, which demonstrates that other New Yorks can work, too. I'm very pleased and proud that Esther and Mike were willing to provide stories for this book, and in particular that Mike made his a sequel to *Stalking the Unicorn*. All three of these novels are highly recommended by the management, which is to say, me.

Several contacts were made, and some of the writers recruited, through the GEnie computer network; the Delphi computer network was also useful for communicating with contributors. My thanks to the fine people at GE and at Delphi for their help.

Martha Soukup not only provided a story of her own for the book, but actively sought out others for me, two of which are included. Thank you, Martha!

I've undoubtedly forgotten several other people who deserve mention, and I hope they'll forgive me. An anthology like this is a collaborative effort, not just by those whose names appear on the finished work, but by a good many others. I'd like to thank everyone who submitted stories, even those I couldn't use, and everyone who passed on word that I was doing this, or otherwise helped out, but I can't possibly remember all the names. Consider yourselves appreciated.

—Lawrence Watt-Evans